Tuppence to Tooley Street

Harry Bowling

D1344530

headline

First published in 1989
by HEADLINE BOOK PUBLISHING

This edition published in paperback in 2008
by HEADLINE PUBLISHING GROUP

1

ISBN 978 0 7553 4036 1

Typeset in Times by Avon DataSet Ltd,
Bidford-on-Avon, Warwickshire

Printed and bound in Great Britain by
Clays Ltd, St Ives plc

Headline's policy is to use papers that are natural, renewable and recyclable
products and made from wood grown in sustainable forests. The logging and
manufacturing processes are expected to conform to the environmental
regulations of the country of origin.

HEADLINE PUBLISHING GROUP
An Hachette Livre UK Company
338 Euston Road
London NW1 3BH

www.headline.co.uk
www.hachettelivre.co.uk

To the memory of my parents, Annie and Henry Bowling.

With special thanks to Edie Burgess for her help,
advice and her special knowledge – what a gal!

Harry Bowling was born in Bermondsey, London, and left school at fourteen to supplement the family income as an office boy in a riverside provisions' merchant. He was called up for National Service in the 1950s. Before becoming a writer, he was variously employed as a lorry driver, milkman, meat cutter, carpenter and decorator, and community worker. He lived with his wife and family, dividing his time between Lancashire and Deptford. We at Headline are sorry to say that THE WHISPERING YEARS was Harry Bowling's last novel, as he very sadly died in February 1999. We worked with him for over ten years, ever since the publication of his first novel, CONNER STREET'S WAR, and we miss him enormously, as do his many, many fans around the world.

The Harry Bowling Prize was set up in memory of Harry to encourage new, unpublished fiction and is sponsored by Headline. Click on www.harrybowlingprize.net for more information.

By Harry Bowling and available from Headline

As Time Goes By
The Chinese Lantern
The Glory and the Shame
Down Milldyke Way
One More for Saddler Street
That Summer in Eagle Street
Waggoner's Way
The Farrans of Fellmonger Street
Paragon Place
Ironmonger's Daughter
Tuppence to Tooley Street
Conner Street's War
The Whispering Years

The Tanner Trilogy
Backstreet Child
The Girl from Cotton Lane
Gaslight in Page Street

Chapter One

Dunkirk

A blood red sun was dipping down behind a clump of trees and evening shadows lengthened across the flat French countryside as the two soldiers journeyed towards the coast. Private Danny Sutton felt deathly tired under the weight of his pack. He glanced at Albert Sweetland, the young soldier from the Royal Norfolks, as he trudged along with a cold determination, his thumbs hooked through his pack-straps. Danny gritted his teeth and cursed to himself as he tried to keep up.

The road the two soldiers travelled was busy. Laden trucks drove past carrying battle-weary troops. Civilians rode past on bicycles with large bundles slung across the handlebars, and occasionally a horse-cart went by carrying French women and their young children perched on top of their salvaged belongings. Up ahead, the tar-black pall of smoke from the burning oil installations at Dunkirk was rising high in the already darkening sky. The guns had ceased and it was strangely quiet. A faint bird-song sounded from a hedgerow and Albert held up his head.

'That's a jay. First I've heard this year,' he said.

'Is it? I wouldn't know a jay from a cock robin,' Danny

replied irritably. 'I can reco'nise a sparrer though,' he said as an afterthought. 'Plenty o' sparrers in London. Quite a few chickens as well. They keep 'em in their backyards where I come from.'

Albert grunted and hoisted his pack higher onto his sore shoulders.

The two soldiers lapsed into silence. The mention of chickens had conjured up visions of food which niggled at their empty bellies. Danny tried to forget that he hadn't eaten all day. Christ! What a mess, he thought. Two starving infantrymen without a rifle and a round of ammunition between us. He puffed and hoisted his backpack higher onto his shoulders. They had to reach the coast as quickly as possible. The bloody remnants of the British Expeditionary Force were being squeezed into a pocket around the port of Dunkirk. Danny and Albert had seen their units decimated, and now the German Panzers were closing in behind them.

A breeze had sprung up and Danny shivered. The stocky figure of Albert plodding on steadfastly in front made the young cockney feel a grudging admiration. The country boy was not the most talkative soldier he had met but he seemed able to go on marching for ever. They could smell the stench from rotting carcasses of farm animals and it mingled with the acrid smell of the burning oil dumps as darkness settled over the French fields. It was May 29th, and only a few days away from Danny's twenty-first birthday. He was feeling pessimistic about his chances of being around to celebrate the occasion. If he didn't find a place to rest pretty soon he felt sure he would fall asleep on the march and sink beneath the muddy ditch-water. He tried to focus his mind on home. He attempted to picture his family in Dawson Street, and Kathy from the next turning, but all he saw were the faces of his comrades as they faced the onslaught of the German troops.

An old woman shuffled slowly along the road, her frail body

bent forward in the shafts of the creaking cart which rattled and jumped over the uneven surface, the contents swaying and bobbing around; a shrouded figure sat slumped in the back. When the woman reached the two soldiers she stopped and put down the shafts. She looked at them with baleful, sunken eyes and her lips moved silently. They could see she was very old: her face was skeletal and her hollow cheeks puffed out with her exertions; her dark clothes hung in tatters and her skirt touched the cobbles. Slowly she turned her head as they passed, her eyes narrowed, and she mumbled something, then her body bent as she picked up the shafts and set the cart into motion once more. The shrouded figure on the bundles rocked back and forth and Danny caught sight of the face. His flesh crawled and he gripped Albert's arm. 'Gawd Almighty! Look at it!'

Albert stared at the grey, bloated face of death and he turned his head away. 'It's been dead for at least a week,' he muttered, unable to decide whether the corpse was male or female.

'It's tied on,' Danny whispered.

They could now smell the stench and Danny retched into the hedgerow. He felt Albert's hand on his shoulder and he straightened up. He had looked upon death before, but this was different. 'Let's go,' he said, shuddering.

They trudged on for a few paces then both reluctantly looked back down the lane. The stretch was deserted. There was no sign of the cart.

The light had faded and Albert quickened his pace. Danny tried to keep up with him, and after what seemed an eternity the two young soldiers reached the edge of Dunkirk. For a while they trudged wearily along the bomb-damaged streets, then Danny leaned against a wall. 'It's no good, Albert. I'm done in,' he said breathlessly. 'We gotta find a place ter kip fer the night.'

Albert pointed to a row of shattered shops further along the road. 'What about there? The roof looks solid at least.'

They walked over and entered a small shop. Inside a group

of soldiers from the Middlesex Regiment sat propped against the walls. One of the soldiers nodded at them and then pointed to the back of the shop. 'There's a tap out back,' he said.

The two went outside into a small courtyard and washed the dust from their dry throats before filling their water bottles. Danny raised his pale blue eyes to the dark sky. A few tiny stars twinkled through the smoky clouds, and he thought of his home in Bermondsey. His folk might be looking at those same stars right that minute. He thought of Kathy and vowed to put things right with her if he ever got out alive . . .

He knew he had done wrong by taking her for granted. She had always been there when he needed her. It had always been him and Kathy ever since they were youngsters. She had been content just to be with him and he had to mess everything up. The other girls never meant anything to him; he could hardly picture their faces now. But there was the image of Kathy, strong and clear in his mind, as it had been throughout the long months away, filling him with a sense of calm. Only now it was too late. His sister had told him in her last letter that Kathy was seeing someone else.

Albert had gone back inside and now Danny bathed his feet and used the last of the boracic powder on his raw heels. He rummaged through his pack and found another pair of socks and a field dressing. Once he had bound up his feet and put on the clean socks he felt a little better. The desire for food was giving way to tiredness and he went back into the dusty interior and slumped down beside Albert. The young soldier who had first spoken to them leaned over and nudged Danny. 'Ain't yer 'ad any food terday?' he asked.

Danny shook his head. 'Me stomach finks me froat's bin cut, mate.'

The soldier grinned. 'Don't worry. Oggy Murphy's out on the scrounge. 'E'll find somefink.'

Time passed and Danny felt his head drooping. Albert was

already snoring, his head resting against the crumbling plaster. Suddenly there was a commotion. Danny looked up and saw a huge soldier standing in the shop doorway. He walked in to ragged cheers from his comrades. He was bareheaded and his shaven skull shone in the light of the candle. His features were large and his fleshy lips were parted in a wide grin. 'Oggy's got the goods,' he said in a bellowing voice.

He placed a sack down on the floor and immediately one of the soldiers grabbed at it. Oggy cuffed the young man smartly around the head. 'Wait, me beauty. There's bottles in there!' he growled.

Everyone was now wide awake. Oggy laid down a bundle beside the sack and grinned at the group. 'Wait fer it,' he said as he reached into the sack.

Soon Oggy had spread out the contraband on the dusty floor. There were six bottles of red wine and two sticks of bread. Oggy then opened the bundle and produced three tins of corned beef and a chunk of mouldy-looking cheese. Last of all he felt into his uniform pocket and took out a packet of Craven A cigarettes.

'Cor! Where d'yer get that lot, Oggy?' the young soldier said admiringly, rubbing his head.

The ugly giant of a man touched the side of his nose with the tip of his finger. 'Never you mind, sonny. Oggy could get court-martialled fer nickin' officers' grub an' comforts.'

The food was shared out as fairly as possible and everyone in the room ate in silence. The wine tasted like vinegar but it helped the food down their dry throats. When the meal was finished some of the troops lit cigarettes, and Oggy pulled out a wooden pipe and packed it to the brim with tobacco which he took from a greasy pouch.

The loosely hanging shutters rattled in the wind and gunfire sounded in the distance. After a while the soldiers began to fall asleep. Albert was snoring again, his head tilted forward onto his chest. Danny tried to think about home but tiredness prevented him from focusing clearly. His head drooped and he fell into a fitful sleep.

Danny was awakened by the noise of the Middlesex troops mustering outside the shop. Albert was in a dead sleep and he jerked violently as the young cockney shook him by the shoulder. 'C'mon, Albert. It's time ter go,' he said, yawning widely.

In the grim light the two trudged slowly down towards the harbour. The scene that met them caused the two comrades to look at each other in disbelief. Thousands of troops were milling around, and long ragged lines of exhausted soldiers were wading out into the water in an attempt to board the small craft that were coming inshore. One large transport ship was moored at the jetty, and the long line of troops was four deep as the loading went on. The queue stretched back to the sea road and military police struggled to keep order.

'It looks 'opeless,' Danny said, puffing hard. 'We'll never get aboard that ship.'

Albert pointed to the beach. 'Let's catch a rest in them dunes. The tide's coming in. There'll be more boats soon.'

The two had only just made the dunes when the air attack started. Planes dived out of the sky and bombs fell, exploding in the water around the transport ship. The long line of waiting troops dived for cover as more planes swooped low and machine-gunned the defenceless men. Screams of the wounded and dying rose above the roar of the aircraft and the noise of the gunfire from the ship. Bullets whipped up the sand and soldiers were caught as they tried to clamber aboard the overturning craft. The bodies of the dead floated back to shore.

Danny lay beside Albert in the dunes as the aircraft made repeated runs over the churning water; they pressed their faces into the sand and waited, hardly daring to move a muscle. As the carnage went on, thick, black smoke filled the sky and the lifting sun became red. When at last the planes roared off out to sea, the two young soldiers picked themselves up and dusted the sand from their uniforms. They could see the transport still intact by the jetty. Already the lines were forming up once again and more men began to wade out towards the few boats that were still afloat. Stretcher bearers moved along the beach and soaked, grey-faced men moved into the shelter of the dunes. A small group of bedraggled troops came by and one called out to Danny and Albert. 'We're trying La Panne. It's hopeless here.'

Danny looked at his pal. 'Where's that, Alb?'

Albert pointed along the sea road. 'It's a couple o' miles on. What d'yer reckon?' he asked, looking at Danny.

The young cockney slumped down into the sand. The thought of another two miles walking on his raw and blistered feet made him feel sick. He looked around. At that moment he felt ready to give up. 'Let's wait till the tide comes right in, Alb. There'll be more boats then,' he said unconvincingly.

Albert was feeling too exhausted to argue and he slumped down beside Danny.

The sun rose overhead and the planes came back. The intermittent strafing went on until the sun began to fall towards the west, and then there was a lull. Danny mustered his last reserves of energy and stood up. 'C'mon then, Albert,' he groaned. 'Let's try that uvver place while it's quiet.'

They left the dunes and walked wearily along towards La Panne. The road was busy, and they reached their destination only to see the dunes crowded with exhausted soldiers. As they walked along the sands a voice called out to them, 'No luck at the jetty then?'

The two looked over and saw Oggy's men sheltering in a hollow. They went and sat down beside the shivering Middlesex lads. One of the soldiers nodded towards the sea.

'We all got dumped in the drink, jus' when we reckoned we'd made it. We 'ad ter tow Oggy back. 'E can't swim.'

Oggy looked embarrassed. 'All right, all right. Don't tell everybody. Yer won't get a medal fer it,' he growled.

The soldier grinned and turned to Danny. 'The boat we got on was a small fishin' boat. The feller told us they're sendin' a lot more soon. That's what we're waitin' for.'

'What 'appened ter the bloke?' Danny asked.

The soldier's face suddenly became sad. 'Poor sod didn't make it. 'E got a bullet in 'is back. 'E only come ter 'elp us,' he said, looking down into the sand.

A breeze began to blow, chilling the soldiers as they waited on the sands. The strafing had ceased completely and an eerie quietness settled over the dunes. Danny suddenly turned to Albert. 'What did yer do in civvy street, Alb?' he asked.

'I was a clerk in a firm that sold farm machinery. What about you?'

Danny eased his position in the sand. 'I was a bookie's runner. Me ole man wanted me ter go in the docks wiv 'im, but I wasn't 'avin' none o' that. 'E's bin in the docks all 'is life. All 'e's got ter show fer it is 'ands like dinner plates an' bronchitis frew workin' out in all weavvers.'

'You going back to being a bookie's runner?' Albert asked.

Danny grinned. 'When I get out o' this mess I'm gonna get rich. Don't ask me 'ow, but I'm gonna make a pile. I might even do a bit o' buyin' an' sellin' like those Yiddisher boys over the Mile End Road.'

It was late afternoon when a flotilla of small craft appeared on the horizon. As the boats drew near to the shore the aircraft returned without warning and strafed their attack. Men were stranded in the water and those waiting on the sands ran back into the scant shelter of the dunes. One young soldier from the Middlesex saw an upturned boat floating near the water's edge and he ran towards it. Machine-gun fire cut him down and his body floated face up in the water. Oggy's men jumped up and raced down towards the shore. Danny and Albert were following behind when the country lad fell face down in the sand. Danny could see the growing red patch on the back of his uniform blouse.

'C'mon, Alb! Get up!' he screamed, bending down and dragging his pal into a sitting position.

Albert groaned as Danny tried to lift him.

'Can yer stand, Albert?'

Albert coughed and flecks of blood appeared on his lips. The young cockney looked at the white face of his comrade. 'They've got the boat upright, me ole son,' he said. 'C'mon, you can make it.'

Albert coughed again. 'It's no good. Help me to the dunes. I'll be okay,' he gasped.

Oggy was in the boat and pulling his pals in with him. He shouted for the two to get a move on, but Danny realised that Albert was not going to make it and he waved the boat away.

Planes were still strafing the beach as Danny half carried and half dragged Albert back to the meagre shelter of the dunes. When he had propped his pal up against a sand mound he searched through Albert's discarded pack and found a field dressing which he pushed beneath the country lad's battledress to stem the bleeding. Albert opened his eyes and groaned. Danny gave him a sip of water from his field bottle and Albert leaned his head against the sand.

'You go on. I'll be okay,' he mumbled.

'Shut up, yer silly bleeder,' Danny said gently. 'They ain't takin' stretcher cases on the boats. Soon as one comes in I'll carry yer out. Leave it ter me.'

As he looked along the sands Danny could see stretcher bearers running along to pick up the wounded. He could see Oggy's boat riding out a few yards offshore. The men had oars in the water and the big soldier was standing up in the prow waving frantically. 'C'mon! We're waiting fer yer!' he bellowed out.

The young cockney stood up and tore off his battledress. 'All right, Albert,' he said. 'We're gonna make that boat. Did yer 'ear me?'

Albert's face was grey and he tried to speak. Danny bent over him and held his face in his hands. 'Listen, Alb. Yer'll 'ave ter grit yer teef, me ole mate.'

Albert screamed with pain as Danny hoisted him to his feet and dropped him onto his shoulder. Danny's feet sank in the soft sand as he moved slowly down towards the water's edge. His breath came in short gasps and sweat was running into his eyes. His legs buckled under him and he fell. 'Okay, Albert. One more try. We can do it!' he said panting.

Albert was past caring. His eyes had glazed and his mouth hung open.

'Get up, yer stupid bastard, can't yer?' Danny screamed at him. 'I'm not leavin' yer ter die on a Froggy beach! Wake up! Wake up!' he shouted, shaking the lifeless body roughly.

A firm hand gripped his shoulder. Danny looked up through clouded eyes and saw a medic standing over him. 'Go for the boat, son. We'll take care of your pal.'

Tracer cut across the sky as Danny stumbled into the cold water and swam for the boat. Oggy reached out a huge hand and hoisted the breathless cockney aboard. Danny dropped onto the planking shaking and Oggy patted the young man's back.

'Yer did yer best, son. Yer couldn't 'ave done more,' he said quietly.

Danny pulled himself up and looked back to the shore, to Albert's lifeless body. Oggy's men were pulling on their oars and the boat began to move slowly away, fighting against the tide. The big ships were getting larger against the evening sky and the overcrowded lifeboat was headed for the nearest of them. Low-flying planes were roaring over the shallow waters, raking the helpless boats with machine-gun fire; men screamed as they were hit and went over the side. Danny saw the plane coming towards the boat.

He felt no pain as he fell into the cold sea. He could not move his limbs and he waited for the sea to swallow him. The last thing he remembered was the ugly face of Oggy Murphy beside him in the water.

Chapter Two

On the night of the 30th of May 1940 a military vehicle emblazoned with a large red cross left the quayside at Dover and drove the few miles inland to the red-brick Cavendish Home for the Elderly. The hospital stood in spacious grounds where flower beds were set amid chestnuts and willows. The walls of the buildings were covered with vines and a wide gravel drive led up to the entrance from the gates. Until the German army had swept across Europe, the place had been a serene refuge for the elderly and convalescent. Now it had been converted into a military hospital, filled with feverish activity as the casualties from France were brought in from the boats.

The vehicle pulled up at the entrance and medical orderlies quickly took off the stretchered wounded. A pretty dark-haired nurse helped wheel one of the casualties into the operating theatre, and two hours later she was on hand to take the unconscious soldier into a high-ceilinged ward. Throughout the night the young man lay comatose. Sounds of the night outside and sounds in the ward could not invade his sleep, but as the early morning rays of sunlight stole across the high white ceiling and lit up the white walls, the young soldier opened his eyes.

Danny Sutton's drugged mind stirred and he saw a whiteness everywhere. He began to wonder whether he was dead.

His pain-wracked body sent signals to his befuddled brain and he knew he was still alive. There was no pain in heaven, and he knew he was not in the other place, for it was too white and bright. A wave of sickness overcame him and a soft body pressed against his head as he was attended to. He could smell soap and he felt soft, cool hands on his forehead. Danny breathed out deeply and sank back into a heavy sleep.

For two days and nights the young soldier drifted between sleep and consciousness. He was transported far away in his fitful dreams. He was back on the beach at Dunkirk and his screams were ignored. He was back home, and he searched for his family. He heard iron-rimmed wheels on cobblestones and he saw Kathy, but she walked past him. He could see his family gathered around the kitchen table. His father wiped his large hand across his straggly moustache as he read the letter. His glasses were set on the end of his nose and the sleeves of his collarless shirt were rolled up high. His grey-haired mother dabbed at her eyes with a tiny handkerchief and tears rolled down her thin, lined face. Danny could see his three sisters: Maggie, the eldest, sat beside her husband Joe; Lucy held the hand of Ben, her fiancé; and Connie, the youngest, who was a year older than Danny, sat beside her mother and sobbed loudly. Maggie's two young children were playing in a corner. In his dream Danny was sitting at the table but his family ignored him. He felt himself being drawn away from the room and he struggled, trying to bang on the table. He opened his eyes with a start and the pretty nurse patted his forehead.

'You've been dreaming,' she said in a soft, lilting voice.

As the days passed slowly Danny grew stronger. He began to wait impatiently for the pretty dark-haired nurse to come on duty, and when she changed the soiled dressings around his chest he could smell the fragrance of her hair. He had been told that a shell splinter had pierced his lung and another fragment had been removed from his thigh. The wounds were healing slowly, but after one week he was able to be wheeled into the sweet-smelling gardens of the hospital.

One afternoon Danny was sitting in the warm sunshine. The fresh smell of new-mown grass hung in the air, and early butterflies fluttered amid the spring flowers. The retreat seemed far away from this peaceful scene. Danny saw the nurse walking towards him and noticed how her hips swayed slightly. She wore a cape around her shoulders which flapped as she walked, and when she reached him she stood with her arms folded. Danny saw the pretty flush of her cheeks and noticed how her dark hair was swept up around her tiny ears. He had heard about patients falling for their nurses and he could quite understand it, if all nurses looked like her. She reminded him somehow of the girl back home – the one he had lost – and his eyes fixed on hers.

She smiled at him. 'I'm going back on duty soon, soldier boy. I'm supposed to take you back, or you'll miss your tea,' she said in her sing-song voice.

'Danny's the name,' he grinned. 'What's yours?'

'I know it's Danny, but we're not supposed to get fresh with our patients,' she grinned back.

The young cockney started to propel his wheelchair, but the nurse stopped him, as a sharp pain shot between his ribs.

'And what do you think you're doing, Danny Sutton?'

'I was jus' goin' ter push me chair over ter the seat,' he said. 'You could sit down an' talk ter me fer five minutes.'

'Just five minutes,' she said in mock seriousness as she walked around the wheelchair and pushed her patient over to the wooden bench.

The sun was slipping down in the afternoon sky and already a pink tinge lit up the western horizon. It was cooler now as a very slight evening breeze rose. It rustled a loose strand of the girl's hair and she patted it down as she talked.

'Why do you insist on knowing my name?' she asked.

Danny grimaced. 'I can't keep on callin' yer "nurse". It sounds too . . . I dunno.'

'Let me tell you, Danny. If Sister heard you calling me anything but nurse I'd be in trouble.'

'I wouldn't get yer inter trouble. I'd only use yer name when we was alone – like now,' he persisted.

'Listen, soldier boy, we're not likely to be alone. And anyway, you'll be off in a few more days.'

Danny looked into her dark eyes. His hand went up to his chest and he grinned. 'I'm goin' ter 'ang this out as long as possible. I'd really like ter get ter know yer better, honest I would.'

The nurse flushed slightly and glanced into Danny's pale blue eyes. His vivacity attracted her and she warmed to his serious look. She noticed the way his fair hair tended to curl above his ears, and the way he had of grinning suddenly. She liked the humorous twitch of his mouth and the way his eyes seemed to widen when he spoke. 'They'll be sending you to the other hospital in a few more days,' she said smiling.

'What uvver 'ospital?' he asked.

'Why, the convalescent hospital up in Hertfordshire. It's supposed to be very nice there.'

'Cobblers! I like it 'ere fine,' he said quickly.

The young nurse's eyes opened wide in surprise. 'Danny Sutton! Don't use that word! I don't like it.'

Danny touched her arm and she stiffened noticeably. 'I'm sorry,' he said. 'It's jus' that, well, I'd like you an' me ter get ter know each uvver better. 'Ow the 'ell am I gonna find out more about yer up in bleedin' wherever it is?'

'Okay,' she replied in resignation. 'My name is Alison Jones. I'm twenty-two, and I come from Cardiff. Is that enough to be going on with? Now come on, I've got to get you back for tea. By the way, if you mention my name in front of Sister or the doctors, I'll never speak to you again. Is that understood?'

Danny grinned and raised his hands in mock fear. 'Understood, Alison.'

When he got back to the ward, Danny learned that only the more seriously wounded were to get visitors. The others would have to wait until they reached the convalescent hospital. He was not unduly worried; he did not want his parents to see him until he became more mobile. He thought about the letter he had scribbled, telling his family that he had only a few scratches. He knew that they wouldn't believe him. His mother would cry into her handkerchief, while his father would polish his glasses and read the letter again. He pictured the scene back in Dawson Street, Bermondsey. The neighbours would call round to commiserate, and that would only start his mother crying again. He thought of Kathy, the girl from the next street, and wondered if she would get around to dropping him a line.

Casualties had been crowded into the old vine-covered buildings, and as soon as the less severely wounded were able to travel they were transferred to other hospitals around the country. Danny found himself waiting with a dozen or so soldiers at the hospital gates for the coach to arrive. It was only three days since he had persuaded Alison to tell him her name. He had managed to snatch a few minutes alone with her once or twice and she had told him a little about herself. She came from a mining family; her father had been killed in a pit accident when she was a child, and her mother had been left to bring up a large brood with little help. Alison told him about the hardships during the miners' strike, and how the illnesses often caused by coal-mining affected the families in the Welsh Valleys. She said she would have liked to study medicine but it had been impossible, and nursing had been the only alternative. She told him that nothing else mattered to her. Danny responded by telling her about his home in dockland and how his family had suffered during the strikes for better working conditions. Her wide dark eyes had become sad when he told her the stories he had heard from his mother, of his father coming home bloodied on more than one occasion after clashes with the police at the dock gates. Alison's frank sympathy had surprised him. She said that there had been many dark stories when the army had been called in to threaten the striking miners in the coalfields. Danny had become captivated by her pretty looks and lilting voice as she chatted away to him. He wanted very much to see her again when he got his medical discharge, although Wales seemed a very long way from his home in the grimy, rundown area of London's dockland. He felt that Alison liked him, and he wondered whether she would agree to meet him again. She had seemed happy and relaxed in his company, but when he had attempted to find out about her life outside the hospital she had been quick to change the subject. He wondered whether or not there was someone else in her life, and he became anxious. His feelings for Alison had grown during those all too brief interludes, and he realised that he was now beginning to think of the Welsh nurse rather more than of Kathy back home.

The coach pulled up at the gates and the waiting patients were hustled into their seats. Danny looked around urgently as his name was called and an orderly helped him to climb aboard. There was no sign of Alison. He sat down despondently and stared out of the window as the coach driver climbed aboard and started up the engine. Suddenly he saw Alison. She waved at the driver and he opened the door for her. She came along the aisle, her face flushed, and when she reached Danny she quickly gave him some letters which she had in her hand. 'Good luck, soldier boy,' she said lightly.

Danny looked up into her dark eyes and she bent her head and kissed him lightly on his cheek. He could find nothing to say but he gave her a huge grin as she stepped off the coach.

*

18

The driver pulled into the Three Counties Hospital near Hitchen after a tiring journey and the casualties found themselves billeted in prefabricated wards; the hospital had been built in 1938 to accommodate the possible civilian casualties in the event of war. Danny settled quickly into the routine and he was cheered by the fact that he could now get around with the aid of a stick. After a week at the hospital his parents visited him. Alice Sutton fussed over him and said how thin he was looking on the hospital food; Frank Sutton sat uncomfortably on a small garden seat and tried to have a word with Danny when his wife ran out of things to say. Danny felt uncomfortable with them and was glad when it was time for them to go. He felt guilty for his lack of patience as he watched his parents walk arm in arm through the hospital gates. They seemed to have aged; his father was still robust, but his thinning hair had gone completely grey. His mother was lined and frail, and she looked diminutive beside his father. Danny couldn't understand why it had been so difficult meeting his parents, and he felt sad as he turned and limped back into the ward.

After the weekend visits the hospital settled down to its usual routine. Danny spent most of his time in the hospital grounds. His wounds had largely healed and he could now walk without the aid of a stick. He realised that his twenty-first birthday had passed and he had hardly even remembered it. The days passed slowly until he was finally pronounced fit enough to travel home. The documentation was completed and he had his medical discharge book, a travel warrant, some back pay and a bundle of dressings. As he was piling his belongings into a suitcase Danny saw a figure hobbling towards him. 'Well I'll be blowed. Look who it is,' the soldier said, grinning widely. 'Remember me?'

Danny recognised the soldier as one of Oggy's crowd. ''Course I remember,' Danny said loudly with a huge smile. They shook hands, and the slight young man sat on the edge of

Danny's bed and ran his fingers through his wiry hair. His face became serious. 'I saw yer mate cop it. I didn't fink you was gonna make it ter the boat.'

Danny shook his head. 'I can't remember much after you lot pulled me aboard.'

The soldier eased his plastered leg. 'Me, you an' Oggy was the only ones ter make it.'

Danny gasped. 'I felt sure Oggy drowned. 'E couldn't swim, could 'e?'

The wiry-haired lad laughed aloud. 'If you ever bump inter that ugly gypsy yer'll 'ave ter buy 'im a pint. 'E saved your life. We was 'oldin' on ter that upturned boat fer dear life. Oggy 'ad yer roun' the neck. We was in the water fer ages before we was picked up. Me an' you ended up in different 'ospitals.'

'Where did Oggy go?' Danny asked.

'Back to our depot, I s'pose. 'E never 'ad a scratch on 'im. I tell yer mate, 'e saved both of us that night. I was ready ter give up, but 'e kept on shoutin' fer me ter 'old on. What a great feller, that Oggy Murphy.'

''E sure is,' Danny said quietly with a smile. ''E can get pissed at my expense any time.'

'Me too,' the soldier said, nodding his head. 'They give out medals fer less than what Oggy did.'

Danny finished his packing and clipped the case shut. The two shook hands and the young cockney walked out into the bright sunshine to wait for the coach that would take him to the station. He felt a sudden dismay. The lifeboat had been packed with soldiers and only three of them had survived. The day seemed to have grown cold, and he was glad when the coach finally arrived at the hospital gates.

War-time King's Cross was full of life. There were uniforms everywhere, servicemen moved about the station with kitbags slung over their shoulders, and sandbagged entrances and exits were flanked by large war posters. Military policemen stood in pairs, biting on their chinstraps and eyeing the itinerant servicemen with a cold severity. Danny stared hard at one pair as he walked past them, but they ignored him. He saw placards outside a kiosk tempting the travelling public to read more about the capitulation of France, and he was struck by the serious expression on everyone's face. The news was bad. He had managed to catch some of the radio bulletins while he was at the hospital, although the matron had forbidden the nurses to let the patients listen. Danny had heard about Italy declaring war on Britain, and it made him think of those Italians who lived around the docks. Some had shops, like the Arpinos and the Lucianis. He had played with Tony Arpino as a kid; together the two of them had got into their first scrape with the police. Danny remembered how Tony, who was a year younger than him, had run home crying after a cuff around the ear from the street bobby, and his enraged father had taken the belt to him for bringing disgrace upon the good name of Arpino. Danny himself had scooted off home with two large cooking apples still stuffed down his trousers, his head ringing from the whack. Danny wondered what would happen to the Italian families. The news broadcasts had said that the Italian nationals were being rounded up and interned and he did not expect to see Tony Arpino or Melissa Luciani around dockland. The whole thing seemed ridiculous to him – Tony was as cockney as anyone in Dawson Street.

Danny walked through the station exit lost in thought and the scene that met him at the busy junction brought him to a halt. Everywhere there were signs of war. Neatly stacked sandbags fronted office buildings and public institutions; there was a public shelter near where he stood; outside, a poster demanded retribution, and another implored everyone to 'Dig For Victory'. Trams and buses all wore a canvas-like material on their windows, and every building had the criss-cross pattern of brown paper strips over its larger panes of glass. The traffic noise on that Friday afternoon in June 1940 made Danny feel light-headed. He wanted to get away from the stir and disquiet of King's Cross and back home to his own familiar surroundings. First though, he needed a cup of tea. There was a stall only a few yards away outside the station; he gripped his almost empty suitcase and went up to the counter. The only other customers were two taxi drivers who were talking loudly together. The stall-owner looked at Danny cross-eyed and he ordered a mug of tea. As the tea was being poured into a cracked mug one of the taxi drivers nudged his mate and then looked up at the stall-owner. ''Urry up with that pie, Sid,' he said.

Sid peered over his beaked nose at the leering cabbie. 'Can't yer wait five minutes?' he moaned in a nasal tone. 'Bloody pie ain't warm yet.'

Danny put down a threepenny bit and picked up his mug from the soaking wet counter. As he sipped the hot tea he watched the cabbies. The vociferous one returned his stare. 'Joinin' up, son?' he asked with a smirk on his face, his eyes glancing down to the suitcase at Danny's feet.

The young cockney looked hard at the cabbie. Danny sensed an unpleasant seriousness and aggression in the cabbie and he was not prepared to be insulted. He took the mug away from his lips and his eyes hardened. 'No. I work the 'alls,' he said quietly.

'You on stage then?'

'That's right.'

The cabbie looked down again at Danny's suitcase. 'You a magician or somefink?' he smirked, looking at his silent friend for support.

Danny's eyes glinted. 'Matter o' fact I'm a ventriloquist,' he said. 'Trouble is, I've 'ad me dummy nicked. You wouldn't like ter earn a few bob, would yer?'

The stall-owner turned and roared with laughter as he banged the hot pie down on the counter. 'Got yer there, didn't 'e?' he rasped.

The cabbie's round face flushed and he looked away from Danny's challenging stare. 'Poke yer pie,' he sneered as he turned on his heel and walked away from the stall. Danny exchanged a smile with the other cabbie as he moved off to catch up with his friend.

Sid looked at the young cockney. 'Are yer joinin' up, son?' he asked quietly.

Danny put the mug down on the counter. 'No, I'm goin' back 'ome. I was at Dunkirk.'

Sid's crossed eyes lit up. ''Ere, son, you 'ave this pie on me. Best pies in norf London, straight.'

Danny took the hot pie and fished into his trouser pocket for some change. 'I can pay. I've got money,' he said.

'Nope, I insist yer take it. Me an' my ole Dutch cried when we 'eard about it on the wireless. Must 'ave bin terrible out there.'

Danny nodded and bit into the steaming pie. A few customers came up to the stall and Sid became very busy serving tea and shovelling fresh pies into the metal box on top of the tea urn. Danny thanked him and picked up his suitcase. As he walked away Sid turned to his customers and said knowingly, ''E was at Dunkirk. 'E only looks a kid.'

Danny walked along the busy thoroughfare until he came to King's Cross Road. A few yards down he saw a bus stop where a queue was beginning to form in the early evening coolness. Danny had been waiting about ten minutes when a number 63 bus came into sight. The queue shuffled forward anxiously as the bus squeaked to a halt. The conductor leant out from the platform and counted the passengers on. 'No pushin'. There's anuvver one behind,' he shouted authoritatively. He pressed the bell as Danny stepped on the platform. 'Put yer case under the stairs, son. Full up inside. Yer'll 'ave ter go on top.'

Danny climbed to the upper deck and found the last remaining seat beside a dapper-looking man in his sixties. He had a well-trimmed goatee beard and wore a pair of gold-rimmed spectacles. The bus jerked away from the stop, accelerating quickly as it moved down the King's Cross Road. Danny saw the long queue outside the working men's hostel waiting for their chance of a bed, and the second-hand book market traders packing away for the day. Farringdon Road was heavy with lorries, taxis and horse-drawn carts, and to his left Danny caught a glimpse of the now deserted Smithfield Meat Market. The bus passed under Holborn Viaduct and reached Fleet Street before it stopped. The hustle and bustle of the City had always fascinated Danny, but it now seemed there was a strangeness in the way people hurried by. Everyone seemed to have a serious expression, and nearly everyone was carrying a newspaper under his arm. There were no smiles, and no one was standing still. As the bus got under way again and started over Blackfriars Bridge Danny saw the exodus from the City as crowds flowed along the pavements overlooking the river.

The little gentleman next to Danny chuckled and tapped the window. 'Look how calm that River Thames is down there beneath all those frantic people,' he said.

Danny smiled cautiously. The bus had reached the centre of the bridge, and down below the grey water sparkled in the evening sunlight. Barges were moored up for the night, crane arms were secured against the closed and bolted warehouse loop-holes, and the ebbing tide lapped lazily against the mud-streaked stanchions.

'That is the greatest river in the world, young man,' the man continued. 'There are longer rivers and wider rivers, but where else is there one with such character? It's our heritage,' he said with conviction, his small eyes glaring at Danny through his spectacles.

'You're right there, pop. It wants some beatin',' Danny grinned.

The old man nodded his head. 'I know I'm right. And yet those crowds we just passed, they seem to walk over that river without even noticing it.'

'Well, I s'pose they see it every day. They mus' get fed up wiv the sight of it,' Danny said.

'"When a man is tired of London he's tired of life",' the man said, his eyes twinkling. 'I worked in the Royal Mint for more than twenty-five years, young man. Do you know where that is? Well let me tell you, I walked over Tower Bridge twice each day for all that time. I never once got fed up with the sight of Old Father Thames. It *is* London. Without that river this city would be nothing. London would dry up like a desert. It's your heritage, young chap.'

The bus stopped at the Elephant and Castle junction and the old gentleman bid Danny farewell. Danny eased up against the window and the vacant place was taken by a large lady who puffed noisily as she sat down. He stared out of the window, excitement building up inside him as he recognised the familiar sights of South London. At the Bricklayers Arms he got off the bus and walked towards the river. The evening was cool and clear, and starlings were chattering noisily in the leafy plane trees. The quiet thoroughfare had taken on a cloak of war. Windows were criss-crossed with brown paper strips and sandbags were piled against factory entrances. He saw the shelter signs, the war posters, and the arrow that pointed to the first-aid post. He noticed the splashes of white paint on the kerb stones, and around the boles of the large trees. He glimpsed the iron stretchers strapped to the roof of a passing car, and up ahead the huge imposing mass of Tower Bridge.

He could now smell the Thames and the docks, the spices and fruit, and the pungent smell of vinegar as he walked past a quiet factory. At Tooley Street he turned left and saw the familiar wharves and warehouses to his right. Small streets led off opposite the large buildings and it did not take him long to reach Clink Lane. The next turning was his street.

The slanting hitching post was still leaning towards the wall and the little houses on both sides of Dawson Street still looked as he had remembered them. The railway arch at the end of the turning had been given a coat of paint, and Granny Bell's front step gleamed as white as ever. Danny saw the Brightman children swinging around a lamppost on a piece of fraying rope, and ginger-haired Billy, the Birkitts' youngest, sitting in the gutter slowly counting a pack of cigarette cards. Billy Birkitt stared at Danny with a fixed grin. Danny smiled back, but he did not know that young Billy was only displaying the gap where his two front teeth had been. He spotted Crazy Bella who was standing arms akimbo in her doorway. She gave him a stare and then went in.

Nothing seemed to have altered in the months he had been away. His own front door was closed; it still had the same cracked knocker-pad and the withered weather-board. Number 26 Dawson Street was like every other house in that tumble-down turning: the windows were clean, the front step was whitened, and the street door sorely needed a lick of paint. Danny stood outside his house for a few seconds before he knocked. Apart from Crazy Bella and the children no one had seen him. He raised the knocker and banged it against the plate. His mother opened the door and stood staring at him.

''Ello, Mum,' Danny said. 'Well ain't yer gonna let me in?'

Chapter Three

Alice Sutton looked up at the mantelpiece and noticed that the clock had stopped. She got up and put on her glasses before opening the glass door of the chimer and moving the minute hand around to the half-hour. Still the clock did not start ticking. She fished out a key from beneath the ornate stand and wound up the twin springs. A sharp tilt woke up the pendulum, and the clock started again. Alice could have sworn that she had wound the thing that very morning. It was supposed to be a seven-day timepiece, at least it had been when it was given to her and Frank as a wedding present more than thirty years ago. It's getting old, like the two of us, Alice thought.

'Good job Dad didn't see yer do that, Ma,' Connie laughed. 'Yer know 'ow 'e fusses over that clock.'

Alice grinned and sat down amidst her three daughters. Tonight she felt happy and contented. For the first time since last October, when Danny had gone off to France, the family were all together – all except the two grandchildren, who should be in the land of nod by now, she thought. Tomorrow she would be spoiling the kids. Tonight it was the turn of her grown-up children to be fussed over, and she got up again to gather up the tea things.

'Stay put, Mum. I'll make us a fresh pot,' Maggie volunteered.

Connie got up and followed Maggie out into the scullery. The back door was ajar and voices could be heard coming from the small yard, where the men of the family were gathered for a quiet drink.

Alone in the parlour with Lucy, Alice turned to look at her daughter, eyes filled with concern. Lucy had seemed rather quiet at tea time, she thought. It was a pity, because everything had gone off so well. The large rabbit stew had been ample and the plum duff with treacle was scraped clean from everyone's plate. The little wooden table looked nice with its linen tablecloth and best dinner plates. She had squeezed seven places around the table, and Connie had helped out by eating her dinner sitting in the armchair. Even Frank looked well scrubbed and sober, although he had stopped off on his way home from work for a couple of pints, as was his usual custom on Friday nights. Alice had noticed that Danny struggled to finish his meal, but she would soon get him used to her big meals again and get some meat on his bones.

Lucy was staring down at the empty grate and Alice leaned back in her chair and folded her arms. 'Well, out with it, girl. What's troublin' yer?'

'Oh it's nothing, Mum. Really it's not.'

Alice pulled a face. 'If there is somefink worryin' yer, I wanna know.'

Lucy sighed and looked into her mother's lined face. 'It's Ben. The tribunal is on Monday and I'm worried about the outcome. We've talked about this before, Mum. Ben said it's no good us thinking of getting married until this thing is sorted out. Ben might have to go to prison, or be sent on war-work somewhere. It's so worrying.'

Alice stared at her daughter. Lucy was in many ways different from the rest. She had been very bright at her lessons and had attended the central school. She had even learned to speak in a way that was different from the others. Lucy sounded her aitches, which had, at first, caused problems with the others until Alice put her foot firmly down. 'If she's gettin' a good education it's nat'ral fer 'er ter speak proper. She'll get a good job one day, an' I don't wanna 'ear any more mickey-takin' from any of yer. Is that understood?'

Everyone in the Sutton family paid attention to their mother when she spoke up, and the mickey-taking ceased. Now, as the latest of Lucy's problems emerged, the matriarch was ready with a sympathetic ear and good advice.

'Listen, my girl, you've chosen yer partner. One day, God willin', yer'll 'ave 'is children, but in the meantime yer gotta face up ter fings. There's a war on, people are dyin', an' a lot more will go before there's a peace. Your Ben 'as decided 'e ain't gonna kill anybody, even the bloody Germans. All right, 'e's got 'is point o' view, same as all of us. Trouble is, there's a lot in the papers an' on the wireless about those anti-war people, like Mosley an' 'is crowd o' Blackshirts. Then there's the Communists, an' all those uvver bloody aliens. People tend ter lump 'em all tergevver. It reminds me o' that ole Irish chap me an' yer farver saw up on Tower Hill once. 'E was speakin' to a crowd, an' 'e said. "Those who are not fer us, are agin us". That's what yer up against, me girl. That's what Ben is up against. 'E's gonna find it 'ard an' it's gonna get 'arder. People in the pubs an' on the street are gonna shun 'im. They're gonna call 'im a coward an' all the uvver names they can lay their tongues to. It won't be easy, but yer gotta be prepared fer it. If 'e's really the feller yer want, then stan' by 'im. Oh, an' anuvver fing. Yer gonna get some nasty letters, mark my words. They did it in the last war. People used ter send white fevvers frew the post. Anyway, if yer prepared, it won't be so bad. Just you remember, whatever 'appens round 'ere, Ben's always welcome in this 'ouse. Neighbours can turn funny if they like, but this family stays tergevver. We've always bin a close-knit family, an' that's the way it's gonna stay.'

Lucy's brown eyes filled with tears and she hugged her mother.

Out in the backyard of 26 Dawson Street, four men sat in the darkness. The night was cool, and stars were shining down from a clear sky. The black-out regulations were being enforced rigidly, but the back door was kept ajar, letting just enough light out to illuminate the crumbling stone floor and the crate of ale. Danny sat in a broken-down armchair, his father squatted on an upturned bucket, and Ben and Maggie's husband Joe shared a bench made up of a plank of wood stretched over empty tubs. Ben was the only one who wasn't drinking. Danny sipped his glass of beer and found that he wasn't enjoying it. The meal had seemed huge and the events of the evening had tired him. The greetings from his sisters had been tearful and he had felt embarrassed. Joe and Ben had pumped his hand, and his father had hugged him tightly until his chest hurt. Their questions too had been fast and furious. Danny wanted to forget his recent experiences, but the questions opened new wounds and made him feel shaky. He shivered although the night was warm.

Joe Copeland was talking. 'The ships 'ave bin turnin' round quicker than ever lately. We've bin doin' late shifts fer the past fortnight.'

'Careful, Joe,' Frank piped in. 'Yer can get an 'eavy fine fer careless talk.'

The men laughed and Frank shifted his weight on the pail. 'You can laugh, but I bet that poor ole feller in the paper ain't laughin' after yesterday.'

'What was that, then?' Danny asked.

'Well, 'e was goin' on about all these taxes, an' some ole biddy reported 'im. Next fing yer know 'e's summonsed. The ole beak give 'im six weeks. I tell yer, yer gotta be careful what yer say these days.'

'Yeah, it's what they call emergency powers,' Joe said, pouring himself another drink. 'I 'eard a funny one last week. There's this ole geezer who's got a car. 'E's a manager of a big business. Well 'e just so 'appens ter leave 'is motor car outside the Town 'All while 'e gets some permits renewed. Anyway, up comes a bluebottle an' checks 'is car. 'E finds it ain't immobilised, or so 'e finks, 'an 'e only goes an' lets all the tyres down. Not bein' satisfied wiv that, 'e goes an' sticks a summons on the car. 'Course when the bloke comes an' sees the copper doin' 'is party piece, 'e nearly 'as a fit. What the copper didn't know was that the car *was* immobilised. Instead of takin' the rotor arm out, the driver took the wire off the coil or somefink. Anyway, it was just as good. This geezer's fumin'. 'E runs back in the Town 'All an' phones up the 'ead one at the local police station. Accordin' ter the feller what told me, this bloke an' the 'ead copper were ole drinkin' mates. The outcome was, there's a copper pumpin' up the tyres wiv a foot pump, while the 'ead one an' this geezer are 'avin' a right ole piss up in the boozer next door.'

The laughter made Maggie put her head round the door. 'What's goin' on out 'ere? Filfy jokes, I expect,' she said.

'No, I was jus' tellin' 'em about that car-owner who 'ad 'is tyres let down.'

Maggie grinned. 'Don't laugh at 'is silly tales. Yer only encouragin' 'im. I fink 'e makes them stories up, honest I do.'

The men were still laughing as Maggie took the tea into the parlour.

Dawson Street was dark, with the two lampposts out of service for the duration of the war. The black-out curtains were effective, and the distant stars offered scant relief from the darkness. The two corner shops at the Tooley Street end of the turning, the oil shop and the tatty little sweet shop, were shuttered and deathly quiet, and the only sign of life came from

The Globe public house which stood on the corner of Clink Lane. Inside the pub a piano was knocking out one of the old favourites. The door of the jug-side opened and closed, and a woman came out. She walked quickly, a shawl draped around her hunched shoulders. She turned into Dawson Street and hurried to number 23. The woman was mumbling to herself as she fumbled the key into the lock and pushed open the door. As she let herself in the gas jet in the passage went out. Without taking her shawl off, she reached up and dropped a sixpence into the meter slot and turned the handle. The coin dropped and she chuckled.

Back in The Globe Annie Barnes was worried. Annie lived in Dawson Street, and she knew Crazy Bella very well. Bella never ventured out at night, least of all to change coppers up for a sixpence. If Bella's gas ran out she would sooner light candles. And something else worried Annie Barnes. Two weeks ago Bella had had one of her turns. She had stood in the middle of the street and threatened to blow the whole turning up sooner than let the Germans get it. Fortunately, old Doctor Kelly was on his rounds and he had managed to get Bella indoors and settled very quickly. No one had paid much attention to Bella's threats except Annie. Her husband used to work for the gas board, and he had said how easy it was for a gas leak to prove disastrous. Annie got even more worried when Bill told her about the explosion in Prentis Street some time ago, where a whole row of terraced houses had been demolished by a gas leak.

Annie Barnes quickly finished off her Guinness, buttoned up her coat and hurried out to see her friend Alice Sutton. Alice would know what to do. In any case, she wasn't going to knock on Bella's front door on her own. Bella scared the living daylights out of Annie Barnes. As she passed number 23, Annie shivered and crossed the street. At the Suttons' front door Annie stopped and looked over her shoulder before rat-tatting loudly.

The women of the Sutton family were sitting together in the parlour, drinking tea and talking about the possibility of getting Maggie's two children evacuated. There had been an air-raid warning on the Monday of that week, although it had been a false alarm. The all clear had sounded hours later, and the only effect it had was to make people jumpy the next day from their loss of sleep. It had made Maggie realise however that the children would be much safer away from London. She had talked it over with Joe, but he was unhappy with the idea of sending them away. Already there were bad stories about the reception some of the evacuees had encountered and many families had got their children home after the initial panic at the outbreak of war. Maggie struggled with her conscience and she was listening to what her mother had to say about it.

'It strikes me,' Alice began, 'that no matter what decisions you make, it's in the 'ands o' the Almighty. I always say, what will be, will be. There's nuffink anybody can do about it. I mean yer could send the kids away, an' you an' Joe could get killed, Gawd ferbid. You'd 'ave a couple of orphans on yer 'ands.'

'Don't talk like that, Mum. You're givin' me the creeps,' Maggie said.

'Well it's no good tryin' ter dodge the issue,' Alice went on. 'None of us know what's gonna 'appen. There's those bloody leaflets they put frew the door last week. Did I show yer? Anyway, it's about what ter do if there's an invasion. Cor, it turns yer cold jus' ter fink about it.'

Connie was sitting on the floor, her hands clasped around her knees. She looked up at her sister, her blue eyes open wide. 'I know, why don't you go wiv the kids? You 'aven't got a job or anyfing ter worry about.'

Maggie looked at her disapprovingly. 'Don't be silly. 'Ow could I go an' leave Joe? I mean, there's 'is food, an' yer know 'ow useless 'e is in the 'ome. I bet if I was away the place would go rotten. 'E can't even boil an egg.'

'Well 'e'd bloody well 'ave ter cope. Lots o' men 'ave done it,' Connie retorted. 'The Arrowsmiths 'ave all gone away. Freddy Arrowsmith manages.'

Maggie laughed aloud. ''E's got a fancy woman, everybody knows that. She does 'is washin' an' ironin', an' she cooks fer 'im. Who knows, I might go away, an' 'fore yer know it, Joe's found 'imself a fancy woman?'

It was Connie's turn to laugh. 'Don't be silly, Maggie. Joe's not that sort.'

'Don't yer be so sure,' said Maggie. 'All men are the same. They want their bread buttered on both sides. Mind you, I'm not sayin' Joe would stray. It's jus' that I'm not gonna give 'im the chance.'

The loud rat-tat made the women jump. 'Who the 'ell can that be?' Alice said quickly, getting up and leaving the room.

There was a murmur of voices and then Alice called out, 'Frank! I want yer.'

The family hurried out into the passage. 'It's all right everybody. It's Missus Barnes. She's worried about Bella. You wait 'ere. Me an' yer dad are goin' over there.'

Frank put on his coat and followed Alice out into the street. The turning was deserted and dark. The two of them accompanied Mrs Barnes across the cobbles and knocked loudly on number 23. There was no answer. Frank bent down and peered through the letter box. Suddenly he straightened and pushed Alice aside.

'Stand back!' he shouted as he threw his weight against the front door. It gave easily and Frank stumbled into the dark passage. The smell of gas was strong. He put his hand up to his mouth and ran through into the scullery. Crazy Bella was lying on her back with her head on a pillow inside the open gas oven; she looked up at Frank, her staring eyes glowing cat-like in the darkness. Frank reached for the gas taps and discovered that they were not turned on. He left Bella lying there and staggered back into the passage. The gas jet on the wall was hissing and unlit. He turned it off quickly and ran back into the tiny scullery and opened up the window. Half carrying and half dragging Bella he succeeded in getting her out onto the pavement.

'Keep yer eye on the silly ole cow,' he said. 'I'm goin' ter see if I can get Doctor Kelly.'

The chimer on the Suttons' mantel showed five minutes to midnight. Ben and Lucy were saying goodnight at the front door; Maggie and Joe had already left; and Connie had gone to bed. Danny sat in the parlour with his parents, his eyes heavy with tiredness. His father was noisily sipping his tea.

'What I can't understand is why she didn't turn the gas stove on. Seems a silly way ter do yerself in, if yer ask me,' Danny said.

'Doctor Kelly reckons that ole Bella 'ad no intention of doin' 'erself in,' Alice said, passing a mug of tea to her son. 'I'm inclined to agree wiv 'im. Doctor Kelly reckons she was doin' it all fer somebody ter take notice. An' we did, didn't we?'

Frank put his empty mug down on the table. 'Yer right there, Alice,' he said.

''Ave they took 'er away?' Danny asked.

'No, Doctor Kelly give 'er a sedative. 'E said 'e's comin' ter see 'er termorrer. I was talkin' to 'im afterwards,' Alice went on. 'What 'e reckons 'appened was that she went purposely ter get that sixpence. She was tryin' to attract attention. They all know she don't venture out at night. Somebody in the pub was bound ter take notice, an' sure enough, somebody did.'

'What about the gas?' Danny queried.

'Well, what we fink 'appened,' interrupted Frank, 'was that she put the tanner in the meter after the gas 'ad run out. She was so concerned about settin' it all up, she forgot about the passage gas jet. Jus' fink of it. She sticks 'er 'ead in the gas oven an' nearly gets gassed wiv' the passage jet. Silly ole cow.'

'Don't be like that, Frank luv,' Alice said. 'She's ter be pitied. She ain't got a soul in the world, 'cept us folk in the street. If it wasn't fer you, she'd be laid out on a slab right now.'

Frank got up and stretched. 'It's Annie Barnes she should be grateful to. Anyway, I still fink she's a silly ole cow,' he grinned, winking at Danny. 'Well I'm off ter bed. Nice ter 'ave yer 'ome, son. C'mon, Alice. It's bin a long day. Let's get some shut-eye.'

Danny climbed the stairs to his room and lay down in the darkness. He was exhausted after his first night back home and was grateful his family hadn't pressed him too much when he declined to go to the pub. He smiled as he recalled the look of disappointment on his father's face and how he had brightened up when it was suggested that he fetch a few quarts of ale from the 'off sales'. Danny stared up at the cracked ceiling, which was illuminated by the pale moonlight, and cupped his hands behind his head. His thoughts turned to Kathy Thompson and the night they had parted. Kathy had been moody all evening and when they returned from the Trocette Cinema they had stood in her doorway. He remembered trying to kiss her but she pushed him away.

'You seem ter fink you can grab 'old o' me an' kiss it all better. Well I'm tellin' yer now, Danny. Yer'd better make yer mind up who you are s'posed ter be takin' out. I ain't playin' second fiddle ter that trollop Janie Arnold.'

'What yer talkin' about?' he shouted, his eyes narrowing.

'You know very well,' she replied. 'You was seen in The Crown wiv 'er. You was all over the silly cow, so I was told.'

Danny grabbed Kathy's arms. 'Who told yer that?'

'Never mind who told me. But I'm tellin' yer this – eivver yer stop playin' around, or me an' you are finished. I can't believe yer doin' this ter me again, Danny. All the time I've known yer, yer never change. Yer've always bin the same. I'm sick o' tellin' yer, an' sick of 'earin' what's goin' on be'ind me back.'

'Well if yer believe uvver people before me p'raps it's better if—'

There was a loud clattering at the end of the turning and as Danny looked up Kathy stiffened and stepped into the open doorway. Charlie Thompson had turned the corner blind drunk and he had staggered into a pile of rubbish. He swore loudly and kicked out at some empty tin cans he had knocked over. Danny knew that Kathy was terrified of her father. She had told him how he often threatened to throw her out of the house, and how he knocked her mother about viciously when he came home drunk. Kathy had backed into the passageway. 'I've gotta go,' she said. 'Farver'll kill me if 'e finds me out 'ere while 'e's in that state.'

'Wait a minute, Kathy,' Danny said.

Charlie Thompson did not appear to have seen them. He reeled across the pavement and leant against the wall. Danny watched in disgust as he bent over and was loudly sick.

'Kathy, wait.'

'I can't, Danny,' she sobbed, as she closed the door on him.

The young cockney stood still for a few moments then walked away in confusion. Charlie Thompson was still leaning against the wall with his head hanging down.

It was the last time Danny saw Kathy before he went off to war.

Chapter Four

Danny woke up in panic, his whole body soaked in sweat. He could still hear the Company Sergeant screaming out for everyone to watch their flank. He sat bolt upright in his bed and grasped the iron bedrail with both hands, his breath coming in short pants. Gradually, his pounding heart began to slow down and he was able to recover his breath. He swung his legs over the side of the bed and rested his head in his hands. A beam of morning sunlight lit up the tattered carpet by the side of his bed and felt warm on his bare feet.

Danny wiped the cold sweat from his face and neck with the sheet and looked around the small room. It hadn't altered since he was a lad. The old wardrobe in the corner was the one he used to hide in, and the marble-topped washstand with its cracked china bowl and water jug was the same one he used to hide his secret possessions in. The door was always sticking, and it needed to be tapped in a certain place to free it. Danny leaned forward and pulled on the lift-up handle. The door would not budge. From down below came the grinding noise of the wringer being turned and the sound of the wireless set next door blaring out a popular tune.

Danny looked at the alarm clock which stood on a chair beside the bed – it showed 10.30 a.m. His right leg felt stiff and the puffy scar on his ribs itched. The noise of the wringer ceased and he could hear Connie singing in the yard. Danny got up slowly and peered through the window. His sister was pegging out the washing, her fair hair covered with a headscarf and her feet encased in a pair of carpet slippers; an apron was tied tightly around her trim figure and knotted at the back. Danny stared down into the yard for a few seconds before getting dressed. He felt tired and shaky as he opened the bedroom door and walked out onto the landing between the two flights of stairs.

The kettle was boiling over as Danny entered the scullery. Connie rushed in from the yard and turned off the gas tap. ''Ello, bruv. We wouldn't wake yer. Mum's gone shoppin' an' Dad's gone fer the paper.' Connie poured the boiling water into the teapot. 'Did yer sleep well?'

'Like a log,' Danny lied.

'Want some brekkie? We've got bacon an' eggs, or eggs an' bacon?'

'Go on, finish what yer doin',' Danny answered. 'I'll get meself somefink.'

Connie grinned. 'Get in the front room, bruv. I'll call yer when it's ready. Mum said we've gotta make a fuss o' yer fer a couple o' days, then yer can fend fer yerself, okay?'

Danny smiled as he went to the sink and splashed cold water over his face. Connie handed him the towel and watched closely as he dried his face. 'You look pale. D'yer feel all right?'

Danny threw the towel over the back of the chair. 'Tell yer the trufe, I was fast asleep an' I 'eard this screamin'. I thought yer got yer fingers caught in the mangle. Then I realised it was only you singin'.'

Connie laughed, her white teeth flashing. 'Don't be lippy,' she said, tossing her pretty head in the air. 'Now get in the uvver room out o' me way while I do yer breakfast.'

*

The Globe was full of the usual Saturday morning crowd. The public bar buzzed with conversation as dockers and stevedores from the backstreets piled in for their 'constitutional'. Becky Elliot, the buxom barmaid, and the 'Missus', Harriet Kirkland, busied themselves behind the bar, while in the more sedate saloon Eddie the guv'nor leant on the counter listening to Biff Bowden, the proud owner of Shady Lady. Eddie was a slight man in his mid-fifties, with a clipped moustache and heavily tattoed arms. His sandy hair was well brushed and kept in place with brilliantine. He was a straight-backed character who prided himself on the cleanliness of his pub, a fetish that had stayed with him since his time as a drill sergeant in the Queen's. Biff was a regular to the pub, a robust character in his late forties with a hearty laugh. His moonface remained impassive when he was sober, but when inebriated Biff's features became excessively animated, contorting his face into outlandish expressions.

Biff remained poker-faced as he raved about the exploits of Shady Lady.

'I tell yer, Eddie, that dog clocked the fastest time it's ever done on Monday. It'll walk its next race, you mark my words.'

'Well if I'm gonna stick a few bob on it I'll want it ter run, not walk,' Eddie said pointedly, winking at the group who stood to one side of the counter.

The owner of Shady Lady was not easily put off. Biff was knowledgeable about nearly every money-making scheme that had been devised in the area – he had been the creator of most of them. Biff could spin a good tale and get backing for his ventures – and he was versatile. He had been known to sell patent medicines in the street markets, and he had once peddled a hair restorer which was guaranteed to produce a mop of curly hair. He also marketed a certain 'tonic' that was supposed to have wondrous powers, especially where there was a flagging sexual desire. Biff Bowden always produced evidence to support his claims: in Petticoat Lane he had a hulking by-stander who swore he was once at death's door and the medicine had saved him; in the lesser markets a curly-haired individual testified that he was once bald; another said he had rekindled the burning passions of youth, and that at sixty-plus he was still adding to his brood. At one market in North London, a woman had rushed up to Biff Bowden's fellow conspirator and said that if he was still producing children, they were certainly not hers, and she had chased her startled spouse from the market. Biff had quietened the alarm by saying that the tonic must have made the man over-sexed, and he was sold out in no time at all.

If Biff had a weakness, it was his inability to pick a winner. Most of his hard-earned money was lost at the dog tracks. It had seemed to him that the obvious answer was to get a dog of his own. Unfortunately Shady Lady was lazy – a diet of Guinness and sausages did not appear to be successful – and on two occasions at least the dog didn't even bother to leave the trap. But Biff would not give up, and he engaged the services of a trainer who was finally able to get the greyhound at least to run around the track. Eddie Kirkland told his pals that in his opinion Shady Lady was on a new diet, which probably included Biff's special tonic.

It was around noon when Danny walked sheepishly into the public bar and sidled up to the counter. The Globe was his local and he was prepared for some sort of reception. Becky Elliot took him completely by surprise however by grabbing his face in both hands and planting a kiss on his lips.

'If it ain't me ole Danny boy come ter see me,' she laughed.

Danny wiped the scented lipstick from his mouth as well-wishers slapped him on the back and asked how he was.

Becky called the guv'nor into the public bar. 'C'mon an' see who's just walked in, Eddie.' The guv'nor shook hands warmly and told Becky to give Danny a pint on the house. Harriet Kirkland came over and put her hand on Danny's. 'Nice ter see yer back, luv. Are yer okay?'

Danny nodded, his attention divided by people who wanted to buy him drinks and others firing questions at him.

'Leave the boy alone,' Becky said, prodding one of the customers in the ribs with her finger. 'Let 'im drink 'is beer in peace, can't yer?'

When the excitement died down Danny took his drink and sat down to talk with 'Bonky' Williams and Johnny Ross. The two of them had been friends of Danny's from school days. They were all about the same age and Bonky lived two doors away from Danny. He had got his name when, as a youngster, he lost his eye in an accident. The glass eye that he wore was often removed and laid down in front of unsuspecting victims in The Globe. Eddie Kirkland had threatened to bar him from the pub on more than one occasion, but Bonky spent well, and any altercation was quickly overcome by the lad buying drinks for the offended party. Johnny Ross was slight and dark-skinned. He limped noticeably owing to a tubercular ankle which had developed when he was very young. Johnny Ross had been involved in a few shady activities, and he was known to the police. He lived in Bermondsey Lane and worked as a labourer in the local vinegar factory.

The Globe was packed and getting noisy and Becky's raucous laughter could be heard above the din. Bonky was getting drunk and his good eye roved around the bar. Johnny nudged him. ''Ere. Don't you start yer tricks. We don't wanna get chucked out of 'ere.'

Bonky grinned. 'It's okay, I'm jus' lookin'.'

Johnny turned his attention to Danny. 'What yer gonna do now yer 'ome, me ole son?'

'I dunno,' Danny replied. 'I've gotta sign on the Labour Exchange an' get me cards on Monday.'

'Take my tip, Danny, don't let 'em palm yer orf wiv any ole job. Tell 'em yer a nerve-case, an' yer gotta get somefink quiet. Tell 'em yer can't stand noisy jobs.'

'See if they've got a vacancy fer a shepherd, that's a quiet job!' Bonky piped in.

'You be careful, Danny boy, if yer get too lippy they'll suspend yer. Yer gotta be as crafty as they are,' Johnny warned him. 'You take 'is case. Go on, Bonky, tell 'im about you gettin' suspended.'

Bonky drained his glass and put a ten shilling note down on the table. ''Ere, get a round in, Johnny. We gotta cheer our ole mate up. 'E don't look 'is ole natural self.' He grinned and turned to Danny. 'Yer look sort o' different. You okay, son?'

Danny put his glass down and leaned back in his chair. 'I feel pissed. Mus' be outta practice. Tell us about yer gettin' suspended, then.'

Bonky laughed. 'Bloody scream it was. This geezer sends me fer a job at a glass factory down near Dock'ead. I goes inter the office an' there's a real darlin' sittin' down at the desk. 'Course I get me Woodbines out an' asks 'er fer a light. "We don't allow smoking in here," she says in a posh voice. Well straight away I've copped the needle. I'm sittin' there dyin' fer a fag, when the phone goes. "Mr Jones will see you now," she says in this snotty voice. So in I goes all meek an' mild. I've got me clean scarf on an' I've 'ad a nice shave. I even took me 'at orf. Well, I takes one look at this geezer an' straight away I don't reckon 'im. 'E's got shifty eyes an' 'e's wearin' a collar two sizes too big. Now, I'm standin' in front of 'im an' 'e ain't asked me ter sit down or anyfing. 'E asks me if I can count. "Yeah, 'course I can, mate," I tells 'im. "My name is Mr Jones," 'e ses, all posh like. When 'e tells me what I'm s'pose ter do I done me piece.'

'What did 'e want yer ter do then?' Danny asked, trying not to laugh.

'What did 'e want me ter do?' repeated Bonky. ''E wanted me fer a glass inspector! D'you know what a glass inspector does?'

'Well 'e inspects glass, I s'pose,' Danny said, his eyes widening.

'I'll tell yer what a glass inspector does,' Bonky went on. ''E sits in front of a machine all day long, an 'e looks at all the bottles goin' along the belt. They give yer an 'ammer, and when a bottle goes past that's got a flaw in it yer gotta smash it. Nine hours a day sittin' on this stool, waitin' ter smash bottles. I ask yer, 'ow could anybody stay sensible doin' a job like that? If I'd took that job, me uvver eye would 'ave gorn in a couple o' weeks.'

Danny burst into laughter. 'Did yer tell 'im ter poke the job?'

Bonky looked indignant. 'Gimme credit fer a bit o' sense, Danny boy. I 'ad ter play me cards right, didn't I? If 'e puts "Refusal" on me green card I'm in bovver at the labour office. I 'ad ter get 'im finkin' I'm stupid, see. I got me chance when this office gel walks in the office wiv some papers. This geezer gives 'er a right lecherous look like the dirty ole git 'e is, an' I takes me eye out, wipes it on me scarf, puts it back an' I lets me tongue 'ang out as I watches 'er walk out the office. Yer should 'ave seen 'is face. 'E must 'ave fought 'e was about ter take on a pervert. 'E looked jus' like ole Bert Adams did when I stuck me eye on the table one night when 'e was pissed. Anyway, 'e scribbles "Not Suitable" on me green card an' 'e ushers me outta the office like I've got galloping cock-rot, which suits me fine, 'cos I don't fancy gettin' suspended.'

Danny looked at Bonky with a puzzled expression. 'I fought Johnny said yer got suspended.'

'No, it wasn't that time. This was anuvver time.'

Danny breathed a sigh of relief as Johnny came back with the filled glasses, and when Bonky Williams went off to the toilet Danny shook his head at Johnny. 'Bonky's gettin' worse. 'E jus' gave me a real ear-'ole bashin'.'

Johnny laughed. 'If yer ask me, I reckon Bonky's goin' orf 'is 'ead. Twice last week 'e took 'is eye out. And once in front o' Mrs Brown from the Council. She went potty. I fought Eddie was gonna ban 'im fer sure.'

The hour hand moved around towards two o'clock and Danny was feeling the effects of the drink. Bonky had got himself involved in a conversation at the bar counter. A couple of latecomers whom Danny recognised as friends of his father walked over and shook hands, but Danny politely refused their offers of drinks; it was time to leave while he was still able. He finished his beer and made to get up.

Johnny looked up at the clock. 'You goin' already? It's only two o'clock.'

Danny nodded. 'Yeah, it's a long time since I've 'ad a good drink and I'm feelin' a bit pissy.'

'What about ternight? Fancy comin' out fer a pint? We're 'avin' a drink wiv Tony the bookie, up The Crown. 'E's 'avin' a bit of a knees-up at 'is place afterwards. There should be a few birds there, Danny boy. Tony always 'as good parties – if 'e's 'ad a good day then the booze is flowin'.'

'Okay,' Danny replied, 'if I get a couple of hours sleep this afternoon I might feel all right. I'll see yer at The Crown about 'alf-eight.'

It was warm and sunny as Danny left The Globe. Tooley Street was quiet and deserted on that Saturday afternoon, with the wharves and warehouses closed for the weekend. In the 'Pool' – as the adjacent stretch of the Thames between London Bridge and Tower Bridge was known – small ships pulled against their anchors on the high tide, and out in the mainstream laden barges tethered in groups lay low in the water. The high sun lit up the silent quayside and the tall, still cranes, and it shone down on the white stonework of the Tower of London. A few strollers peered down from the grimy old London Bridge, but Tower Bridge was empty, except for the lonely City of London policeman who stood impassively, hands clasped behind his back, gazing downriver. The scene was peaceful and quiet, although the more discerning onlooker would not have been fooled; there were signs of war preparations. Fore and aft of the moored ships the tell-tale shapes of mounted guns beneath their tarpaulin covers could be seen. One of the ships wore the scars of battle where cannon shells had pierced the metal plating high in the bow. For the present the ships rested at anchor, but the usual feverish activity would begin on Monday morning, and on the evening tide the Tower Bridge would raise its cantilevers in salute as the craft sailed out of the Pool to join the Atlantic convoys.

Dawson Street was noisy. A group of children were playing tin-can copper and a baby wailed in its bassinet. Aproned figures stood chatting in doorways, and outside number 14, old Charlie Perkins sat in his wicker chair, holding a clay pipe steady with a forefinger crooked over the brown-stained stem. His face was expressionless and he seemed oblivious to the noise of the children. To the street's inhabitants, the sight of Charlie sitting outside his front door was as familiar as the street lampposts and the railway arch at the end of the turning.

Danny walked unsteadily down the street and veered around Charlie Perkins's outstretched legs. The railway arch seemed to be floating before his gaze and he blinked a couple of times. At his front door he swayed and peered closer at the number. He pulled hard on the knotted door string and almost fell headlong into the passage. Lucy came out from the parlour, her face showing her disgust at his condition.

'You're drunk,' she muttered darkly.

Danny put his finger up to his lips and grinned lopsidedly. He opened his mouth to say something, but changed his mind.

Slowly and deliberately he climbed the creaking stairs and staggered into his bedroom.

It was after six o'clock when Connie carried a mug of tea up to his room and found him lying face down on the bed. She put the tea down on the chair and sat on the edge of his bed. The gentle pressure of her hand on his shoulder aroused Danny from the depths of sleep, and in his semi-conscious state he thought the hand on his shoulder was pushing him under the water and Danny called out in terror.

Connie ruffled his hair, 'Danny! Danny, it's me, Connie. I've got yer tea. C'mon, it's turned six.'

The bed springs squealed as Danny turned over and looked up at the concerned expression on Connie's face. His head was pounding and his mouth felt parched. He attempted a grin and Connie grinned back. 'Don't tell me, you've bin in The Globe, an' everybody bought yer a drink.'

Danny reached for his tea with a shaky hand and swallowed a mouthful before replying. 'I met Bonky an' Johnny Ross,' he said.

'That's strange,' Connie mocked, 'what are those two doin' in The Globe?'

Danny sat up against the bedrail and sipped his tea. 'Bonky Williams ain't changed,' he said. ''E's still messin' around wiv that glass eye of 'is.'

Connie shuddered. 'I can't stand them two. Johnny Ross is the worst. Dirty git wanted ter take me out last week. 'E said there was a party goin' on somewhere.'

Danny looked serious. 'You keep away from Johnny Ross. I don't want you ter get 'urt.'

'Don't you worry about me, bruv,' Connie laughed. 'I'm goin' steady.'

'Oh, an' who's the lucky feller then?'

Connie looked down at the floor, her cheeks flushing slightly. ''Is name's Jimmy Ellis, an' 'e's in the Navy.'

Danny showed mock horror. 'Not Jimmy Ellis?'

'You know 'im?' Connie asked.

'Know 'im? Course I know 'im, they call 'im "ugly Ellis".'

Connie looked angry. ''E's not ugly. Jim's good lookin', an' 'e's very nice.'

Danny put his hand on her arm. 'I'm only pullin' yer leg. I've never met the bloke, but if yer say 'e's good lookin' I'll take yer word fer it.'

Connie stood up. 'You comin' down fer yer tea? There's fish an' chips keepin' 'ot in the oven. I can't stay 'ere chattin', I've got a date ternight.' She made for the door then turned. 'By the way, bruv, 'ave you bumped inter Kathy Thompson yet?'

'Not yet,' Danny answered, swinging his legs over onto the floor. 'Why d'yer ask?'

'No reason, 'cept I know yer used ter go out wiv 'er.'

'That was a long while ago,' Danny replied.

Connie went to say something, then changed her mind and walked out of the room.

Danny went down to the scullery and washed in the stone sink. The cold water revived him and the pounding in his head eased slightly. When he went into the parlour Lucy looked up from her armchair. 'Hello, how's your head?'

Danny put his hand up to his forehead. 'Thick,' he whispered.

Lucy got up. 'You'd better sit in the chair. I'll fetch your tea, it's in the oven.'

Danny sat at the table with his head resting on his hands. When Lucy came back with his meal Danny sat up straight in his chair. 'Where is everybody?' he asked.

'Mum and Dad have gone over to see Dad's cousin in Guy's. She's very ill. And Connie's upstairs getting ready to go out.'

'You in ternight?' Danny asked as Lucy sat down facing him.

'Ben's coming round later. We're going up West to see a concert.' Lucy answered, her forefinger drawing imaginary circles on the tablecloth.

Danny speared some chips on his fork and started eating. After a while he put down his knife and fork. 'You worried about Ben?' he asked. 'The tribunal I mean.'

Lucy folded her plump arms and leant on the table. 'Naturally I'm worried. You see, Ben's very sensitive, he couldn't hurt a fly. Apart from running the youth club, he's a regular church-goer. His parents were the same. He feels that killing is wrong, and he won't change his thinking. Ben won't put a uniform on. All right, I know you don't agree with his point of view, and I know you don't like him very much, but I hope to get married to him one day.'

Danny scratched his head and looked into his sister's dark eyes. 'Listen, Lucy, it's not that I don't like Ben, but 'e's different from me. I can't take 'im up The Globe fer a pint, 'cos 'e don't drink. I can't 'ave a conversation wiv 'im, 'cos we don't speak the same language. We're worlds apart. I know Ben's not gonna change, an' nor am I. Yer gotta see that. One fing's fer sure though, if you an' Ben wanna get married, you'll get no trouble from me. Ben's okay, and while we're on the subject I'll tell yer somefink else too. 'E ain't no different from the rest of us in one respect. Killin' people *is* wrong. The 'ole bloody war's wrong. The way Ben sees it is that if everybody 'eld the same views as 'im there'd be nobody ter fight the war. Trouble is, life ain't like that. Nuffink's gonna change. There'll always be some bloody maniac ready ter start a war, an' there's no shortage o' people ter do the dirty work. Maybe Ben's got the right idea, I dunno. Good luck to 'im anyway. 'E'll be all right at the tribunal.'

Lucy smoothed the tablecloth and leaned back in her chair. 'I've never heard you talk like this before, Danny. Everything was one big joke to you. You've got all serious.'

Danny pushed his plate away and picked up his teacup. 'I tell yer, sis, what I've seen of the war 'as made me fink. I lost a few good mates, an' I've seen what the war does ter people, but d'yer know what shook me most of all? I was trampin' along wiv our company, we were goin' up ter relieve anuvver regiment. Casualties were bein' brought back an' we got off the road ter make room fer 'em. Right where we stopped was a stone memorial. There was plenty o' names on that stone, I can tell yer. It was from the 1914 war. And there we was doin' it all again twenty-six years later. I got ter finkin', 'ow many more stones they gonna put up when this lot's over? I tell yer, Lucy, I wanted ter run as far as I could, away from what I was seein'. Maybe Ben 'as got the right idea – I only wish most o' the Germans agreed wiv 'im.'

Lucy stood up and playfully ruffled his fair hair. 'You know what Dad would say if he was here?'

Danny laughed. 'Put the kettle on,' he mimicked.

On the stroke of seven there was a knock on the front door and Danny went to answer it. A young sailor was standing on the doorstep. 'I'm Jimmy. Is Connie there, please?' he said with an eager expression on his face.

Danny looked out of his bleary eyes at the slim young man who was a few inches shorter than his six feet. 'I guessed who yer was. Connie's bin tellin' me all about yer bad 'abits.'

Jimmy was abashed. 'Oh!' he breathed, still looking wide-eyed at Danny.

Danny's face relaxed. 'C'mon in, I was only jokin'.'

The young sailor stepped into the passage and removed his cap to reveal a mop of wavy blond hair. His baby face turned towards the stairs as Connie came hurrying down and took hold of his hand. 'This is my 'orrible bruv, Danny,' she said, looking at him affectionately. ''E's bin out celebratin', Jimmy, so 'e can't see yer very well.'

The two shook hands and Danny motioned to the parlour. 'D'yer wanna cup o' tea?'

Connie put her hand on her brother's arm. 'Look, bruv, Jimmy's only got a few days' leave an' I'm claimin' all 'is spare time. Besides, I'm not gonna sit an' listen ter you two men talkin' about the war. C'mon, Jimmy, or we'll miss the big picture.'

Danny stood by the front door and watched as his sister walked up the turning holding on to Jimmy's arm, chatting and laughing. The young cockney smiled to himself. Connie was his favourite, and he hoped that nothing would ever happen to mar her happiness.

Chapter Five

The sun had left the room and slipped down behind the lop-sided chimney pots. Danny looked into the old faded mirror over the washstand and adjusted the knot of his tie. The clock showed twenty to nine. He patted down his hair with both hands and looked down at his polished shoes. His best grey suit felt tighter than it had when he left the hospital. He undid the buttons of the jacket and peered into the mirror once more. The fading light gave the room a sombre look and Danny felt a desire for company. He opened the door and heard his father's voice talking to his mother. He hurried down the stairs and put his head around the parlour door. Frank looked up from his paper and Alice stopped sewing.

'You're not goin' out again, Danny?' she asked, looking quite amazed.

'Leave the boy alone, Alice. 'E's turned twenty-one yer know,' Frank chided her.

'I know,' his wife retorted, 'but I'd 'ave thought 'e'd 'ad enough fer one day, 'spesh'ly in 'is condition.'

Danny grinned. 'Hush, Ma, people'll fink I'm pregnant or somefink.'

Frank chuckled. ''E'll know when 'e's 'ad enough, Alice. 'E'll fall over!'

Danny made to leave, then turned. 'By the way, 'ow was yer cousin, Dad?'

'Very weak,' Frank replied. 'Mind you, she's turned ninety, yer can't expect much.'

Danny dropped his gaze with a nod. 'Well I'm off folks,' he said quickly. 'Don't wait up, I might be goin' to a party.'

Frank leaned back in his armchair. 'All right fer money?'

Danny nodded. 'I'm okay, fanks. I didn't get a chance ter spend much terday.'

'So I 'eard,' Frank said, looking over his glasses at Alice.

The evening was still warm, with heavy storm clouds rolling in. It was still light enough to see the pavement in the blacked-out streets as Danny made his way to The Crown in Dockhead. His leg felt more comfortable now, and he had padded his chest with a few turns of bandage and a cotton wool dressing. At the outset he walked briskly but he became breathless as he crossed the Tower Bridge Road and he slowed his pace. It was fairly quiet as he continued on to Dockhead. A few couples strolled arm in arm along Tooley Street, and a number 68 tram rattled noisily past. Danny walked by a surface shelter with its sandbagged entrance, and it reminded him of Dunkirk. Farther on he saw the large grey spire of St James's Church showing up against the angry sky. His thoughts turned briefly to Alison. I should have written to her, he thought.

The Crown stood back from the main road. No light shone out, but sounds of merrymaking reached Danny's ears while he was still some distance away. He reached the saloon, pushed open the door and went in. The room was filled with tobacco smoke, and there was a strong smell of perfume.

Johnny Ross called out to him. 'Over 'ere. I fought yer wasn't comin'. Yer late.'

Danny grinned. 'I got a few hours' kip. I'm okay, as long as yer don't lean on me.'

Johnny pointed over to a tall, wavy-haired individual who

was talking to a young woman. 'That's Tony. Looks like 'e's pulled a bird.'

A barmaid came over and set some drinks down on the counter in front of Johnny, who pointed in Danny's direction. 'An' a mild an' bitter fer me mate, luv.'

The barmaid gave Johnny a sweet smile as she reached for a glass and proceeded to pull on the pump handle. Johnny's eyes looked down at the barmaid's low-cut V-necked dress and her eyes flickered at him.

'Pour yerself one,' Johnny said, winking at her suggestively.

Danny had been casting his eyes around the bar and suddenly he saw Kathy. His immediate reaction was to look away, but he found himself staring at her. She looked even prettier than the picture of her he had carried in his mind during all those months in France. He felt a surge of jealousy when he realised Kathy was not alone. She was talking to a well-dressed, thick-set man whose hair was combed smartly back from his forehead. Danny estimated the man to be in his mid-thirties. As he watched the couple Danny noticed that Kathy seemed to be disagreeing with her companion, she kept shaking her head and he was getting more agitated.

Johnny observed Danny's interest. ''Ere, cop yer drink, Danny boy, an' take yer covetin' eyes off 'er,' he said. 'That bloke spells trouble fer the likes of us.'

'Who is 'e?' Danny asked, still looking in Kathy's direction.

'That's Jack Mason. 'E used ter run the Elephant and Castle mob a few years ago. 'E done porridge fer GBH. 'E still runs wiv the mobs, so I'm told. That sort o' geezer don't go out of 'is way ter 'elp ole ladies across the road.'

Danny sipped his beer and paid little attention as Johnny Ross attempted to bring him up to date with the news in dockland. Kathy had seen him now. Her eyes caught his and held his gaze for an instant, then she deliberately moved around slightly so that she was out of Danny's line of vision. Her stocky companion was still in view however, and Danny could see him nodding his head vigorously. More people crowded into the bar and soon he could not see either of them. It was getting stuffy in the saloon bar and presently Johnny nudged his pal. 'Let's move inter the uvver bar, there's more room in there,' he said.

The small room that separated the saloon from the public bar was mainly used for darts. A few regulars sat around against the wall, and customers came through to use the toilets. Danny bought more drinks and leaned against the counter.

Johnny jerked his thumb in the direction of the clock. 'We're goin' roun' Tony's soon's the pub closes. We'll take a crate wiv us, jus' ter show we're willin'. By the way, Elsie said she's comin' round later.'

'Who's Elsie?' Danny asked.

'Elsie's that darlin' be'ind the bar. 'Er ole man's doin' bird, an' Elsie's lonely.'

Danny shook his head and grinned. 'You'll be lonely if 'er ole man finds out.'

Johnny shrugged his shoulders. 'Elsie's ole man's doin' a long stretch. From what she tells me, 'e was always playin' around 'imself.'

'That makes no difference,' Danny persisted. ''E mus' get visits. Somebody's only gotta grass yer up an' 'e can soon get one of 'is mates ter sort yer out. It wouldn't be the first time it's 'appened.'

'Don't worry, Danny boy, Johnny Ross can look after 'imself. 'E don't scare me.'

Danny Sutton raised his glass. ''Ere's to yer, Johnny. I 'ope yer stay 'ealfy.'

Johnny clinked his glass against Danny's. 'Nice ter see yer 'ome in one piece. Now yer gotta start earnin' some shekels. First of all though, yer gotta get fixed up wiv a bird. Yer don't wanna start mopin' about, do yer?'

Danny grinned and looked back into the crowded bar. Johnny puffed hard. ''Ere, 'old up! You ain't finkin' o' takin' up wiv that Kathy again, are yer? I'd leave well alone. She's got a villain on tow, an' as it 'appens them two are comin' ter the party. We don't want claret all over Tony's carpet, 'e would get the needle.'

'Don't yer worry, Johnny. I'm finished wiv fightin', an' I've got me discharge book ter prove it.'

It was almost closing time when Kathy walked into the small bar. Her cotton dress hugged her figure and Danny noticed how her large brown eyes seemed to sparkle as she gave him a smile. ''Ow are yer, Danny? Connie told me you was 'ome.'

'I'm fine, an' you?'

'I'm okay.'

Danny shuffled uncomfortably. 'Johnny tells me yer might be goin' ter Tony's party.'

'Yes, I'm just off ter powder me nose,' Kathy laughed.

'I'll see yer there then. We can 'ave a chat,' Danny said, catching Johnny's dark look.

Kathy began to look uncomfortable. 'Matter o' fact I'm wiv somebody,' she said.

'That's okay,' Danny said with a shrug of his shoulders. 'We can still say 'ello, can't we?'

'Course we can,' Kathy said as she walked off to the ladies' room.

The loud voice of the barman calling time spurred Johnny into action. 'C'mon, me ole son. Give us an 'and wiv the crate.'

Danny reached into his pocket and Johnny stopped him. 'There's nuffink ter pay. The guv'nor owes me. I done 'im a favour last week. 'E's gettin' off lightly.'

The crate containing a dozen bottles of light ale was passed over the counter, and they each took hold of a handle. 'C'mon, Danny, let's get roun' there, it's only in the next turnin',' Johnny said, winking at Elsie as he walked to the door.

Outside the night was dark, with a waxing moon peering out from heavy cloud. Johnny limped along on his bad ankle and Danny too found himself limping.

Johnny started giggling. 'You know what, if the birds could see us two now, we'd 'ave as much chance of pullin' 'em as Biff Bowden's dog's got of winnin' the Grey'ound Derby.'

'I wouldn't worry,' Danny laughed, 'yer don't 'ave ter do it standin' up.'

'Don't you be so sure,' Johnny countered. 'Elsie likes it standin' up!'

Three stone steps led up to Tony Allen's house in Dock Street. The front door was ajar. It looked impressive with its varnished surface and brass knocker. Once inside the two men put the crate down in the hallway, and Danny looked around. 'Christ! It makes a change ter see an 'ouse wiv electric light,' he said, standing on one leg and flexing the other.

Tony had already heard them and he came out into the hallway and nodded to Johnny. 'Is this Danny?' he said, holding out his hand. 'Johnny told me about yer bein' at Dunkirk. Must 'ave bin 'ell. You just enjoy yerself, son. 'Elp yerselves ter drinks.'

'Let's go an' chat up the birds, Danny, before Elsie gets 'ere,' Johnny grinned.

In the large room there was a piano at one end, and there were gilt-framed pictures of mountains and lakes around the walls. Easy chairs were spread about the room. The red carpet was thick underfoot, and heavy velvet curtains kept the light in. A Japanese fire screen hid the hearth, and up on the high mantelshelf there were iron statues of rearing horses. The centrepiece was of gilt, and it caught Danny's eye – nude figures were draped in various poses around the clock-face, and the whole piece was mounted on a marble plinth. Johnny noticed that his pal was staring at the ornament. 'Yer don't get somefink like that on Cheap Jack's stall, do yer?'

'All this mus' be werf a fortune,' Danny remarked, his eyes moving around the room.

'Yeah, Tony's got a lot o' contacts apart from 'is bookie's business,' Johnny informed him. 'In fact, 'e's gonna put a bit o' business my way later. I'll tell yer about it termorrer – we can't talk 'ere.'

The room was getting full and the piano player began to tinkle away on the keyboard. People started singing and the drinks flowed. Elsie flounced in looking hot and bothered in her fur stole. She came over to Johnny and kissed him on the mouth. Soon after, Kathy came into the room escorted by Jack Mason. The two looked serious-faced, though Kathy relaxed slightly when Tony Allen went up to them. Danny sat in one corner of the room, his drink held in his hand. Johnny was joking with Elsie and occasionally he slid his hand over her behind as Elsie snuggled up to him. And when the piano player started playing a waltz she dragged Johnny into the centre of the room and almost smothered him in her ample bosom as she danced around dreamily. Danny watched the pair gyrating, and then his eyes turned to Kathy again. She was over in the far corner of the room, looking stern as she sat cross-legged in an armchair. Her escort seemed to be ignoring her as he talked animatedly with Tony and two other men. Danny tried to catch her eyes but she appeared to be avoiding his stare. A few more couples got up to dance and someone pulled Kathy into the centre of the large room. She waltzed around, looking bored with the whole procedure, while her partner acted as if he were taking part in a dancing contest. A middle-aged lady asked Danny if he would care to dance, but with a brief smile he told her that he had a stiff leg, and immediately he regretted having said it. The lady showed concern and started to explain her own medical history, but then someone grabbed her and whisked her off into the dancing group. Danny got up and refilled his glass. As he walked back to his chair Kathy and her partner danced near to him. Kathy's eyes met his, and she raised hers to the ceiling in anguish as her feet were stamped on yet again.

Danny sipped his drink and looked around; everyone seemed to be with someone. Two girls who had walked into the party unescorted were now chatting happily with a group of young men. Danny began to wish he had stopped at home. The piano player broke off to get a drink and Kathy resumed her place in the armchair. Jack Mason looked around briefly and then carried on talking with Tony Allen.

Another ten minutes and they can stuff this party, Danny thought as he finished his drink.

'What's wrong wiv yer leg then, luv?' somebody asked him.

Danny looked around to see a large lady leaning over his shoulder. Her face was flushed and he could smell strong perfume and see the sweat lines running down her heavily powdered face. She was grinning, with her thick-painted lips parted to show large teeth.

'Somebody put a bullet frew it,' Danny said sharply.

'Good Gawd! You a soldier?' she asked.

'I was till I got this,' Danny replied.

'Why, you don't look old enough ter be a soldier, does 'e Muriel?'

'No,' Muriel said, without taking her eyes off the bald-headed suitor by her side.

The big lady tut-tutted and lost interest in Danny's wounded leg. She returned to Muriel's crowd, to Danny's relief.

Over in the far corner Kathy was shaking her head at Jack Mason and she looked distressed. Jack gesticulated with a wave of his arm and turned his back on her and Kathy suddenly got up and made for the door. Danny watched as she took her coat down from the clothes-rack, said something to the woman who had been serving the drinks, then quickly left. Danny stood up and with a quick glance in Jack Mason's direction he put his glass down on the sideboard and walked casually towards the door. Danny walked out into the hallway and let himself out into the street. It was too dark to see far but he could hear Kathy's footsteps up ahead. Quickening his pace he got closer. Kathy's high-heeled shoes clicked faster on the pavement and Danny called out, 'Kathy! It's me! Danny!'

Kathy continued walking. 'Leave me alone, Danny! I'm goin' 'ome!' she called out.

'Wait, Kathy! I can't walk fast! I wanna talk wiv yer!'

The footsteps halted and when Danny reached her he was panting. He saw the tears falling down her cheeks and her eyes shining in the darkness.

'Let me walk yer 'ome at least,' he pleaded.

Kathy dabbed at her eyes with a small handkerchief and smiled through her tears. 'It looks like you need somebody ter see *you* 'ome,' she said.

Danny put his hands into his trouser pockets and fell in beside her. 'I'll be okay in a minute. It was stuffy in that party, I wasn't enjoyin' it one little bit.'

'Nor was I,' Kathy said.

'I could see that. Is Jack Mason your steady bloke?'

'Do you mind if we don't talk about Jack Mason?' Kathy said sharply.

'All right, let's talk about me then,' Danny grinned. 'Let's see, I'm a war 'ero, an' I'm off ter see the King next week ter get me Victoria Cross! King George'll say: "'Ow did yer manage ter be so brave?" an' I'll say: "It was nuffink, Your Majesty, we're all the same in Bermon'sey".'

Kathy laughed aloud and took his arm. 'Was it really bad in Dunkirk? I'm sorry, it must 'ave bin terrible. What I meant was, was it bad fer you? Gettin' 'urt like yer did.'

Danny pulled up his coat collar against the cool breeze and shrugged his shoulders. 'Tell yer the trufe, Kathy, I was out cold when I got pulled out o' the water. I don't remember anyfing till I woke up in the 'ospital. I found out later that some feller 'eld on ter me, even though 'e couldn't swim a stroke 'imself. 'E supported the pair of us by clingin' on to an upturned boat. If anybody deserves a medal 'e does, I wouldn't be 'ere if it wasn't fer 'im.'

The two reached the end of Dock Street and turned into Dockhead. Although the night was dark, the half-hidden moon seemed to bathe the streets in a faint light. They approached Shad Thames, a narrow turning where wharves and warehouses loomed high and sombre. Danny chuckled, and Kathy pulled on his arm. 'What's wrong?'

'Jus' somefing I thought of,' Danny said, still chuckling.

'C'mon then, let us in on the joke.'

'All right,' Danny said, leaning his head in her direction, 'when the lads used ter pull the birds – sorry, girls – they used ter say to 'em, "'Ow would yer like ter see Butler's new crane?" They'd tell 'em all about 'ow big an' tall it was, an' they'd take 'em down ter Butler's Wharf in Shad Thames.'

'I see,' Kathy grinned, shaking her head in mock disgust. 'All those dark alleyways an' dark doorways, I see. An' I s'pose you took quite a few girls down there?'

'Not many,' Danny smiled.

'Were they disappointed they never got to see the new crane?'

'You'll 'ave ter ask them,' Danny said with a shrug of his shoulders.

Kathy was quiet for a second or two, then she pulled on his arm again. 'I s'pose you was finkin' about askin' me ter come down an' see the crane?'

Danny put on his innocent look. 'No. But it is a short-cut that way.'

The two veered off and walked down the deserted Shad Thames. High wharves towered above them as they walked the cobbled lane. Various smells hung in the night air – the aroma of spices and the eye-watering tang of pepper mingled with other more obscure odours. Shad Thames was full of pungent, exotic wares, and the loneliness of the place made them shiver. Kathy clung tightly onto Danny and he could feel her body pressing onto his arm. He looked at her and in the half-light could just make out her dark hair, pale complexion, and her full lips, and he shivered.

Half-way along the lane Danny stopped, took his hands from his pockets and turned to face Kathy. Without saying a word he moved in close to her and clasped her shoulders. She did not resist as he pulled her to him and kissed her on the lips. Her mouth opened beneath his as the kiss became more urgent. For some time they stayed locked in an embrace, then when they moved apart Danny took her hand and led her the few paces into a doorway.

The night was silent and they could hear their own heart-beats. Kathy put both arms around his neck and Danny could feel her slim body against his chest, and her thighs touching his. His hands sought her, opening her coat, and moved gently over her soft, smooth breasts. He bent to kiss her neck, and Kathy shuddered, her head held back as his lips moved over her throat. She could no longer think clearly, there was only the urge to meet his caresses and feel his passion. She needed him to love her more than anything in the world.

Together they drew back into the deepest shadows of the doorway, and their breathing became a rhythmic panting.

'Love me, Danny! Please!' she whispered harshly in his ear.

For a while neither of them spoke. Then finally Kathy moved away from his embrace. She buttoned up her coat and took his arm. 'I've wanted you to do that ever since that Saturday night before you went away, Danny,' she said.

The young man looked at the girl who stood with him in the dark recess and his face relaxed into a smile. 'You don't know 'ow many times I thought about that night since I left,' he said quietly.

They started walking again, their footsteps echoing along the silent and deserted lane. They were silent as they turned from Shad Thames into a side road and continued on past the huge brewery. The smell of hops hung in the air, and as they came out once again into Tooley Street rain started to fall. Each was thinking about the suddenness and the fantasy of the experience they had shared only a few minutes ago. Danny could not get the picture of Jack Mason out of his head, it hung like a dark cloud over him, and he was tortured by a feeling of possessiveness. Yet he knew that Kathy was not about to become his; he could sense her inner conflict as she walked beside him to the corner of Clink Lane. She held his arm tightly, but at the same time she had become distant and rigid.

Kathy stopped a few doors away from her own house. 'We'd better say goodnight 'ere. I don't want ter let me dad know I've bin out this late.'

Danny looked skywards and felt the rain beginning to fall on his face. 'What about us, Kathy? Can I see yer again?'

The young girl sighed deeply and put her hands up onto Danny's coat lapels. 'It's no good, I'm goin' steady wiv Jack Mason. Let's leave ternight fer memories. It's somefink I'm never gonna ferget, really, Danny. It was special ternight.'

Danny's face darkened. 'You frightened of 'im?'

'Who, Jack? 'Course not. All right, me an' 'im 'ad a bust up, but I don't wanna worry yer wiv me troubles. It's not your concern anyway.'

'That's just it,' Danny replied, taking her by the shoulders and squeezing her tightly. 'It is my concern. Only a little while ago we made love. It was great, we're good tergevver. We can make a go of it again.'

Kathy resisted his attempts to pull her close to him. 'Listen, you've bin frew a terrible time. You're gonna find yer feet again soon, an' when yer do you'll see this as . . . just an experience. Let's jus' remember ternight. We'll still see each uvver about, an' when we meet in the pub or in the street, we'll look at each uvver an' there'll be somefing special there. Let's leave it at that, Danny. Any uvver way an' it's gonna be trouble an' 'eartbreak fer both of us.'

Danny tried to pull her towards him but Kathy pushed him away. 'No, Danny. Look, I've gotta get in, my dad's givin' me a bad time as it is.'

Danny relaxed his grip and Kathy kissed him suddenly on the lips and turned away. He watched her trim figure disappear into the darkness.

Chapter Six

Sunday the 30th of June 1940 dawned clear and dry after the night rain. The sun rose early, and outside the Globe the winkle stall was set up ready for trade. The paper shop in Tooley Street sold out of the *News of the World* early, and all the local church bells remained silent. People gathered outside their tumble-down houses in the backstreets to discuss the progress of the war, while across the English Channel the German High Command were drawing up plans to invade.

The Sutton household was awake early as usual. Frank polished his Sunday best shoes in the yard, and Maggie brought her two children around to see Danny. Both Terry and Reggie tore up the stairs and bounded onto Danny's bed, demanding to see his 'soldier's gun'. Alice was already peeling the potatoes in the scullery sink, and Lucy was on her way round to meet Ben and then on to the Methodist church in Tower Bridge Road for morning service. The Sabbath in Dawson Street was a day when the doorsteps gleamed white, lace curtains looked freshly starched and, weather allowing, old Charlie Perkins put his wicker chair outside number 14 and prepared himself for another day's hard thinking. Crazy Bella appeared and reappeared at her front door, and the kids were their normal noisy selves – even noisier when the toffee-apple man cycled into the street. In a way it was just like any peace-time Sunday, except that during the previous week everyone in the turning had had a leaflet tucked into their letter boxes, and the street folk now had time to talk about it.

Mr and Mrs Brightman stood at their front door and listened to Granny Bell's furious outburst. 'I tell yer, Flo, if I'd 'ave caught the cow-son I'd 'ave given 'im what for. Fancy comin' round 'ere wiv that leaflet an' fright'nin' the bleedin' life out of us all. All this talk about us bein' invaded – scaremongerin', that's all it is. Them bastards 'ave gotta get 'ere first. D'yer fink our boys are gonna stan' back an' let 'em come 'ere? Course they ain't. Anyway, can yer imagine them Germans walkin' down this street an' catchin' a dekko of ole Bella? She'd scare the daylights out of 'em. They'd soon piss orf.'

Mrs Brightman wasn't so flippant about the leaflet. 'Well I dunno, Granny. Me an' Maurice 'ave bin talkin' about evacuatin' the kids, ain't we, luv?'

Maurice Brightman nodded, and by the time he had thought of a response, Granny Bell was off again.

''Vacuation my foot! What d'yer wanna send yer poor little mites away for? Strikes me you people wanna get rid of yer kids. Nobody sent their kids away in the last war, and we 'ad the Zepp'lins ter contend wiv then. They was 'orrible fings, like great sausages floatin' in the sky.'

Flo Brightman slipped her hands under her apron and pulled a face. 'Yer gotta understan', Gran, it wasn't the same in the last war. Fings are different now. I mean, look 'ow they bombed them towns in Spain. We saw it on the news at the Tower Kinema, didn't we Maurice?'

Maurice nodded and opened his mouth to speak but Granny Bell started in again. 'I ain't bin ter the pictures fer years, not since my ole man died, Gawd rest 'is soul. I read it in the papers though. I can't make 'ead nor tail of it. Them Spanishers are fightin' each uvver, ain't they?'

Maurice had read all about the Spanish Civil War and he was about to enlighten Granny, but she wasn't finished. 'I still say yer should keep yer children round yer. Anyfing could 'appen to 'em in the country. I remember ole Sadie Murgatroyd tellin' me years ago about those gypsies who stole a little boy from 'is 'ouse. Know what they done to 'im?'

Mr and Mrs Brightman shook their heads.

'They broke the poor little sod's legs, so 'e'd be double-jointed. They was gonna put 'im in a circus as an acrobat or somefink, accordin' ter Sadie Murgatroyd.'

The Brightmans left Granny Bell sweeping her front doorstep and went into their house to worry some more.

It was opening-time when Maggie's husband Joe called round for Frank, and the two of them took a leisurely stroll up to The Globe. Danny had promised to pop in later, but first he wanted to see his pal Tony Arpino. Connie had told him that the Arpinos had not been interned because they had taken out British citizenship long ago, but the Lucianis had not been so fortunate. Connie had said how upset Tony was about being parted from Melissa. It was commonly known locally that one day the two Italian families would be united through the marriage of Tony and Melissa.

As Danny walked towards Bermondsey Lane, where the Arpinos had their grocery shop, he was deep in thought. Last night still seemed unreal, it had all been so sudden. He desperately wanted to see Kathy again, but she'd seemed so sure about staying with Jack Mason. Maybe she was right, maybe he should leave things the way they were. Then he remembered he hadn't written to Alison and he decided to do so today for sure. If Kathy wouldn't see him then maybe Alison would. But it could be difficult. The Channel ports were out of bounds to normal travellers – it was in the morning papers – so he would have to find out when she could get leave, and maybe meet her somewhere. She might even come to London.

The Arpinos' shop was open when Danny arrived. Lou Arpino was piling tins of peas onto a shelf, and when he saw Danny Sutton step through the doorway he raised his hands above his head and knocked half a dozen tins onto the floor.

'Hey, Danny! How's a ma boy?' he called out, his olive face breaking into a wide smile.

'I'm okay, Lou. 'Ow's the family?'

Lou's dark eyes shone as he leaned over the counter and grasped Danny's hand. 'Hey, Mamma! Tony! Come a see what's a come in da shop.'

The buxom figure of Sofia Arpino appeared in the doorway at the back of the shop. Her raven hair was tied up in plaits which covered her ears, and she had a white crocheted shawl draped loosely around her wide shoulders. When she saw Danny she came around from behind the counter and took his head in both hands and planted a kiss on his forehead. 'Danny Sutton! It's good you come back. Didn't I say Danny will be okay, Lou?'

Lou Arpino put his arm around her shoulders. 'We see da papers an' we 'ear da news. Mamma cried, didn't you Mamma? She prays for your safety. It's a good to see you.'

Danny grinned, 'It's good ter see you two again. Where's Tony?'

Lou Arpino leaned his head around the door and called out to Tony. Sofia's face became serious. 'You heard about the Lucianis? Tony is very upset, he's not seen Melissa since they come to take them away. It's a very sad.'

Tony appeared in the doorway and his eyes lit up. He came over and threw his arms around the young cockney. 'It's great ter see yer, Danny boy. We all knew you'd be okay. Your Connie told us yer got wounded – 'ow d'yer feel now?'

'I'm all right, Tony. 'Ere, I'm sorry about Melissa an' 'er family. Are yer gonna get ter see 'er?'

Tony's face darkened. 'I don't know where they've all gone.

They're puttin' 'em all over the country. Melissa said she'd write, soon as she could. I've jus' gotta wait, nuffink else I can do.'

Danny looked at Lou Arpino. 'Can yer spare 'im fer 'alf an hour?'

Lou nodded and Danny put his arm around Tony's shoulders. 'C'mon, let's get a drink, an' I'll tell yer all about those French girls.'

The two walked out of the shop and Sofia dabbed at her eyes. Lou watched them as they sauntered up the street, and then he went back to his shelf-filling. Sunday customers came and went, and some passed by the shop, preferring to take their custom to the English shop owner further up the street. The war had already touched the Arpino family, just as it had the Lucianis.

In The Globe that Sunday midday the landlord felt uneasy. Eddie Kirkland had been in the business a long time and he had a nose for trouble. He had seen his share of bar brawls and right now he could smell one brewing.

At first he had paid no attention to the strange crowd of dockers in one corner of the public bar. It was not unusual for a strange group to come into the pub, and though there was a lot of rivalry between dockers from various wharves, it was nearly always good-humoured banter. Today it was different, however, and the big docker who seemed to be the ringleader was ranting off about conscientious objectors.

Eddie picked up his ears as the argument got more heated and glanced over to where Frank Sutton and his son-in-law Joe were standing. They seemed to be unaware of what was being said, but the discussion was getting louder.

'Well you can say what yer like, Bob,' the ganger was saying, 'but as fer as I'm concerned, anybody who says 'e's a "conchie" is a coward. The only people who can say that are vicars an' priests.'

'I dunno,' replied Bob. 'It's a free country. If yer got them principles about not fightin', yer should 'ave the right ter refuse ter put on a uniform.'

'Cobblers!' roared the ganger. ''Ow long's it gonna be a free country if everybody said the same? You'd 'ave the bloody Germans walkin' in. I bet they don't allow conchies in Germany. They'd lock 'em up or shoot 'em.'

'Don't talk silly, Ted, this ain't Germany. Yer can't compare us wiv them. You yerself could 'old the same views. 'Ow would you like ter be banged away?'

The big ganger was getting more irate. His bulging neck was red and he began to shout. 'Yer can fink what yer like, but in my book, anybody who's a conchie is a bastard coward. An' I tell yer somefing else, I only wish I was a bit younger. I'd be up that recruitin' orfice like a flash, never mind about bein' in a reserved occupation. I'd make 'em take me.'

Frank heard the commotion. 'Where's that loud-mouthed crowd come from?' he asked Joe.

'They're from The Surrey. I've seen 'em in The Crown a few times. That ganger's name is Ted Molyneaux. 'E was mouthin' off last time I see 'im. Yer wanna take no notice of 'em, 'e ain't werf gettin' yerself inter trouble over.'

Frank took a gulp from his glass and wiped his wet moustache on the back of his hand. 'You know what, Joe? I've lived in Dawson Street ever since me an' Alice got spliced more than firty years ago 'an' I've bin comin' in this boozer for all o' that time. You could say this was me local, couldn't yer?'

Joe nodded, wondering what Frank was getting at.

'I treat this pub like me own 'ouse,' Frank went on. 'I don't abuse the place, an' I don't go on upsettin' the people in it, but that don't meant I've gotta stand 'ere an' listen to that big, fat, ugly-lookin' bastard shoutin' 'is mouth orf, Sunday or no Sunday.'

Joe picked up their empty glasses. 'What yer 'avin', Frank? Same again?' he said, hoping to calm his father-in-law down.

Frank's face had turned white with temper, and Joe knew there would be trouble. He had worked together with Frank for some considerable time, and had seen him in a rage before. 'Frank. Ferget 'im,' he pleaded. 'What yer 'avin'?'

'I dunno as I wanna drink 'ere while 'e's shoutin' 'is face orf,' Frank replied, loud enough for the rival group to hear.

Joe was getting worried. He grabbed Frank's arm. 'Look, 'e don't know anyfing about Ben. You're takin' it personal. Ferget it. 'Ave anuvver drink fer Gawd's sake.'

It was too late. Ted Molyneaux looked over and then back at the crowd of faces around him. 'What's 'e goin' orf about? Can't a bloke 'ave a talk wiv 'is mates wivout somebody pokin' 'is nose in? Does 'e fink 'e owns the pub?'

Eddie had seen enough. He leaned over the bar counter and addressed the crowd of dockers: 'Now listen, I don't want no trouble 'ere, understood? Any fisticuffs in my pub an' you're barred, an' I'll get the law in quick an' all. Now drink up an' simmer down.'

Ted Molyneaux glared over at Frank Sutton, then he quickly finished his pint. 'Who's comin' down The Crown? I don't like the company in 'ere.'

Frank leaned one elbow on the counter. 'Go on, piss orf an' aggravate some uvver poor bleeder. Yer got too much ole bunny fer this pub, matie.'

The big ganger pushed away the restraining hands and made for Frank. Eddie vaulted the counter and barred his way. With a heave Ted Molyneaux threw the landlord aside and grabbed a chair with one hand. Joe Copeland held onto one of the legs as the ganger made to swing it at Frank's head, and at the same time Frank hit him full in the face. Molyneaux staggered back, blood streaming from his nose, Frank went after him, and the two fell in a heap on the floor. Joe tried to pull them apart but the ganger kicked upwards into his groin. Frank pinned him to the floor and was raining blows on his face when Eddie shouted for Arnold the potman, and he waddled over and lifted Frank off Ted Molyneaux as though he were a baby. Eddie hoisted the battered docker to his feet and shoved him towards the door as Frank struggled to free himself from Arnold's vice-like grip.

'Put me down yer bloody gorilla! Let me get at 'im! I'll swing fer 'im!'

Joe was sitting on a chair holding his crotch. 'Christ! 'E nearly ruined me!' he gasped.

The crowd followed their ganger out into the street, and Eddie gave Frank a blinding look. 'You're old enough ter know better. Yer shouldn't go gettin' inter scrapes at your age, it's bloody stupid.'

Frank grinned sheepishly and dusted his suit. 'Don't go tellin' Alice, she'll go potty.'

Eddie laughed aloud. 'You ain't got no chance. I bet somebody's already knockin' at your door. You'd better get orf 'ome before Alice comes in 'ere wiv 'er fightin' irons on.'

Frank looked over to where Joe was sitting. 'You all right, mate?'

Joe got up gingerly and leaned on the counter. 'Did yer see the size of 'is plates o' meat? I got one of 'em right in me 'alf a tea service.'

Frank laughed, 'C'mon, Eddie, fill 'em up. I got a thirst on.'

Ben Morrison climbed the wooden stairs and let himself into his flat in Tooley Buildings. For a while he stood in the darkness looking down into the empty street, the wharves and warehouses opposite ghostly in the dusk. Away down to his left were the premises of Messrs James Brown & Sons Ltd. He could read the gold lettering above his place of employment clearly. For six years he had been bookkeeper for that company, and until the war had broken out his employers held him in high esteem. However, things had changed dramatically at the start of hostilities, when Major Brown had asked Ben's intentions. When he heard of his bookkeeper's decision not to don a uniform, Major Brown, MC, DSO, became apoplectic. He made it plain that unless Ben had a change of heart and decided to fight for King and Country, then it would be better if he 'damn well cleared off'. Major Brown was aware of the tribunal hearing and Ben knew that he was on borrowed time.

As he looked down into the dark street his thoughts were troubled. He grieved for Lucy, who seemed to be taking the whole affair very badly, and he was grateful for the Suttons' friendly attitude. Alice Sutton was kindness itself, although Frank Sutton appeared to be slightly off-hand at times. Connie often chided him in a good-humoured way, but then it was understandable. She was worried about Danny, the news of his injuries had upset her and made her irritable. He knew that he must bear the burden. The church was important to him, and he hoped that one day he would have enough money saved to attend the theological college and become a Methodist minister. For the present though he had to get through the tribunal. He was aware that it might mean going to prison. The thought of being locked away terrified him, and he shivered as he stood deep in thought in his quiet flat.

Down in the street below Ben saw a young girl hurrying along. Coming towards her was a young man. They met and embraced, the young man put his arm around the girl's waist and the two tripped away happily into the shadows of the deserted wharves. Up above the roofs a crescent moon came out of the cloud, and in the distance Ben could hear the clatter of a tram. Footsteps on the stairs jogged him out of his reverie and he closed the curtains and lit the gas lamp. When he heard Lucy's distinctive knock, he opened the door. The two embraced, Lucy kissing him lightly on the lips. Lucy wanted Ben to hold her tight, to smother her with kisses, but Ben moved out of reach as he took her coat to hang it on the back of the door.

'I've been thinking, Lucy,' he said, pacing the room. 'Supposing I get through the tribunal okay, I'll still be forced to leave the job. I might get sent to another part of the country to do war work. I believe making weapons and ammunition is tantamount to fighting and I can't do it, it would be a betrayal of all my principles. Refusing work of that nature would mean I'd be sent to prison. I couldn't face it, Lucy, I couldn't.'

Lucy Sutton looked at the tormented figure before her. She saw his pale, worried face, his nervous hands that seemed to be forever fidgeting, and his deep-set blue eyes, and she was torn between strong passions. She wanted to go to him and shake him, and she desired him to come to her. She wanted him to forget everything for just one night, and desire her with the same intensity that made her tremble. She wanted to scream out, but instead she just looked at the pathetic figure who paced the floor in front of her.

She had made her decision when she left home that evening, and knew she would go ahead with what she had planned. She might fail, but Lucy knew it could not go on like this any longer. Slowly she stood up and walked to the window. With a quick movement she pulled back the curtains. Ben gasped, 'Lucy! The black-out!'

'Damn the black-out! Turn off the lamp.'

Ben stood rooted to the spot.

'Did you hear? Turn off the light,' Lucy said in a low and husky voice.

Ben reached up and turned the tap of the gas lamp. The room was plunged into darkness and Lucy moved towards the pale figure before her. Her hands reached for him and their bodies touched. Ben tensed, looking down at the round face, and in the dimness of the room he saw the desire in Lucy's wide eyes. She had her back to the window and her hair seemed to shine against the night light. Her lips were parted and her breath came quickly. Almost automatically his hands came up and stroked her hair. Ben felt its softness, and he closed his eyes and breathed in its fragrance. Lucy nestled close to him, her rounded figure soft to his touch, as Ben kissed her neck and trembled at the excitement. In the quietness of the darkened room above the wharves he could hear her rapid breathing. Her lips searched for his and her kiss was urgent and demanding. Ben felt out of his depth, and he could only gasp as Lucy pulled him down onto the hard floor.

Heavy, faltering footsteps in the street below carried up to the silent room. The drunken songster halted and clung to a lamppost for support, his broad Scotch accent ringing out as he struggled with a rendering of 'I Belong To Glasgow'. His singing died away in the night, and up in the small flat the lovers nestled close to each other, neither feeling the need to speak. For Ben the act of loving had been brief, over almost as soon as it had started; his body felt relaxed and heavy. For Lucy it had been intense; her passions had not been extinguished, rather they had cooled. For her it was a triumph, and she breathed slowly and contentedly as she lay against his chest. It was the first time for her, and she was content. There had been no expectations and no disappointment, only the knowledge that at last they had been able to step outside of their cloistered existence and express their love together. Lucy savoured the serenity of the moment. There would be other times. She was happy and she silenced his embarrassed concern with two fingers pressed against his lips. She rested her head against Ben's chest and listened to his quiet heartbeat.

Chapter Seven

Monday dawned dry and warm. The heavy, billowing clouds held rain and the air was clammy. The threatened storm finally broke at eight o'clock, with claps of thunder and frightening flashes of lightning. Raindrops beat against the windows in Dawson Street and water ran along the gutters in fast-flowing streams, spilling over the roof-top guttering and pouring out from the cracked and holed down-pipes onto the pavement below. The rain washed away the dust and the hop-scotch chalkings; it penetrated the ill-fitting roof slates and caused new stains to appear on the upstairs ceilings. The storm delighted the young children who watched as the growing puddle spread out rapidly over the cobbles. Wide-eyed and impatient, they waited for the rain to abate, and they made paper boats and loaded them with matchstick cargoes.

At number 26 Dawson Street, Danny sealed the envelope and waited. His letter to Alison explained the problem he had in getting down to Dover and suggested that they might be able to meet in London. He also penned a few lines saying how much he wanted to see her again, and he hoped that she would feel the same. It was with trepidation that Danny sealed the letter, after seriously considering tearing it up and starting afresh. Maybe Alison had forgotten all about him. With lots of patients to tend and all the chatting-up from homesick young soldiers, it would be understandable for her to have put him out of her mind. Three weeks had passed since he had seen her, and already the picture of her in his memory had faded. Could he hope that Alison would be interested in seeing him again? He wanted it to be so. He had to make the decision to forget all about Kathy. She was in his past now. Alison could figure very much in his future . . . In any case, it would only mean the cost of a stamp to find out, and he put the letter in his coat pocket.

Alice Sutton had a serious expression on her face as she cleared away the breakfast things. She had had words with Frank that morning before he set off to work. It was bad enough him getting into a fight, without ruining his only suit as well. Alice would be able to sew up the shoulder, but Frank had also put his knee through the trousers. When the rain stopped she would go around to see if Mrs Simpson could do one of her invisible mending jobs. It would probably mean a patch, but he would just have to put up with it. There were enough worries without Frank adding to them. There was Lucy, who had most likely got herself soaking wet on her way round to Ben. She had insisted on going with him to the tribunal this morning and would not wait for the rain to stop. Then there was Danny. He had only been home for a couple of days and already he had come home drunk on two occasions. Maggie's children looked like they were both coming down with something, and the front bedroom ceiling was dripping water. Alice Sutton sighed to herself and shook the tablecloth into the hearth. She was also concerned about the wagging tongues on the street. There had been the odd remark directed towards her about Ben, but she had shaken her head and walked on by when neighbours asked if her daughter's young man had received his call-up papers yet. There was another occasion when two neighbours who were chatting together at the greengrocer's shop raised their voices, saying that in ther opinion all 'conchies' should be sent to prison with hard labour. Alice had ignored the remark, which angered the two paragons even more. As she pottered about waiting for the rain to ease Alice Sutton felt worried. It was Lucy she was most concerned for. There would be much anger directed towards her daughter as time went on, and it would be bound to upset her. For herself she didn't worry. If the neighbours chose to adopt that attitude then they could all go and get stuffed. There were other more important things to worry about.

At nine-thirty the rain stopped and Danny walked up to the tiny post office in Tooley Street to get a stamp. It was not quite so oppressive after the downpour and the street looked clean. As he left the post office he saw a number 70 tram approaching and he ran up to the stop just as the tram shuddered to a halt. Danny climbed aboard and sat down on the lower deck. The short run had made him breathless and he realised with a pang of anger that he was far from being fully fit. He sorted out tuppence from a fistful of coppers and handed it to the bored-looking conductor who flipped off a ticket from a clip-board and slipped it into a ticket punch before handing it to Danny. The tram swayed and rocked its way along towards Dockhead and jerked to a stop once more. Danny could see The Crown public house lying back from the road and it made him think of that Saturday evening with Kathy. The tram moved off and swung around a sharp bend into Jamaica Road. Danny was brought out of his reveries by the conductor shouting 'Rovverhive Tunnel' in a sing-song voice.

The young cockney walked along Brunel Road, which ran alongside the approach to the road tunnel. At the end of the turning was the Labour Exchange building and Danny could see a small queue waiting outside. There was an entrance at the side of the building which Danny was directed to, and it opened into a hall where a few people were sitting around on wooden benches. A weary-looking individual sat at a desk at one end of the room and he sighed as Danny presented him with his papers. Once the preliminary questions were over, the young ex-serviceman was told to take a seat and wait.

'Got a snout, mate?'

Danny looked at the elderly character next to him and shook his head. The man turned his attention to the floor, hoping there would be an odd discarded cigarette butt lying around. The green linoleum offered nothing to his watery eyes and he turned back to Danny. 'Goin' fer a job, then?' he enquired in a squeaking voice.

Danny was about to say that he wasn't waiting for a tram when he saw something in the elderly man's face. The pale blue eyes were dull, and the lined, unshaven face looked thin and trouble-worn. The stranger's expression was apathetic and seemed in keeping with his general appearance – his shoes were down-at-heel and his clothes were shabby. Yet there was something else, there was a friendliness about his face, and Danny swallowed his hard words. 'I'm signin' on fer work. I'm just out o' the Kate.'

'I was in the last turn-out,' the man replied. 'Nineteen I was when they sent us ter France. I got gassed. Still get the wheeziness sometimes. Me doctor said I should pack up the smokin', but I told 'im straight, yer gotta die o' somefink.'

Danny smiled and looked up at the metal rafters in the high ceiling and at the poster-covered walls. One poster showed a ship sinking with the words 'Careless Talk Costs Lives' emblazoned over it. Another poster showed an air-raid warden wearing a gas mask and there was a list of instructions about what to do in the event of a gas attack. Another poster was headed 'Conscientious Objectors'. The poster was too far away for Danny to be able to read what was said below the heading, but his thoughts turned to Ben Morrison. He would probably be at the tribunal by now.

The elderly character had managed to scrounge a cigarette and came back grinning. He lit up and was immediately racked by a fit of coughing. When he had recovered sufficiently he wiped his eyes on a dirty handkerchief and nudged Danny. ''Ere, son, if the bleeders offer yer work at the lead mills, turn it down. I was there fer six months. It nearly finished me, I can tell yer. What wiv the stink an' the 'eat, I lost over a stone in weight. Can't afford ter lose that much, can I? My ole woman reckons I'm so skinny, I've gotta be out in the rain fer ages before I get wet. Me doctor told me ter go on oats, porridge I mean. Trouble is, me ole woman ain't much of a cook. She made us some this mornin' an' it looked like bloody cement. When I come ter fink of it, it tasted like bleedin' cement as well!'

'Mr Daniel Sutton!' a voice called out, and Danny looked up to see a bespectacled man beckoning from an open doorway.

'Good luck, son,' his new friend spluttered between fits of coughing as Danny got up from the bench.

The small office contained a desk, a filing cabinet and little else. More posters adorned the walls: grinning workers staring out from behind machines, their toothpaste smiles looking maniacal to Danny as he glanced at them. The wording urged everyone to join the struggle for victory. The official told Danny to take a seat and he himself sat down at the desk with a loud sigh. When he had made himself quite comfortable he took off his glasses and proceeded to polish them on a large white handkerchief. Finally satisfied, he put them back on and addressed himself to the papers on the desk.

Danny felt an immediate dislike for the man. He slumped down in his chair and glared. The official began his routine by first resting his elbows on the desk and tapping the tips of his fingers together, next he put his thumbs against his forehead in a display of deep concentration and started a low humming. Danny had an almost irresistible urge to scream some obscenity into the official's ear but he ignored the temptation and looked back at the posters.

'I see you are unfit for heavy work,' the man said at last. 'That makes it rather awkward for me to fit you in.'

'It makes it rather awkward fer me as well,' Danny said sharply.

'Quite, but I can't fit you in at the lead mills, and I can't see where I can send you. Most of the jobs I've got to offer are for fit men. Do you see?'

Danny could see quite clearly, and his temper began to rise. 'Look, I can't 'elp it if I'm not A 1. I didn't ask ter get shot at, an' I—'

The official stopped Danny by holding both hands up in front of his chest. 'You haven't got a trade, have you, Mr Sutton? You see I'm looking for skilled workers for munition factories, or for people to be trained to work lathes and milling machines. You don't fall into that category unfortunately.'

Danny's eyes focused on the official's rather bulbous nose and his thick-rimmed spectacles, which made his eyes seem like two large marbles. His long, thin fingers were tapping the paper in front of him in irritation, and Danny noticed the cluster of well-chewed pencils sticking out from a round tin. Suddenly the official grabbed one of the pencils and started to make notes. When he had finished he leaned back in his chair and sucked on the pencil, his eyes staring at his unskilled client.

Herbert Snelling had interviewed a few of these ex-service types recently, and in his opinion they were an insolent lot. After all, they shouldn't expect special treatment and, as he had remarked to his colleagues, most of them were probably making heavy weather of their disabilities. A few weeks in the lead mills would have got them back into shape. Sutton looked fit enough to do manual work. It was a pity the Ministry were so tolerant of those types. Everyone had to make sacrifices these days, as he had explained to his wife when she remarked that it was time she had a new coat. It was all so irritating, he mused as he chewed on the pencil.

Danny was getting more angry. He felt as though the official was expecting him to fall down on his knees and plead for a job with tears in his eyes and with his hands clasped together in anguish, just like in one of those old silent pictures. Danny had other ideas, although he was, too, aware of the consequences. After all, he had come here for a job, not to provoke a magistrate into giving him six months' hard labour for assault. Danny took a deep breath and sat up straight in his chair. 'Surely you've got somefink ter give us? There's gotta be plenty o' jobs about, now that everybody's gettin' called up?'

The official looked at Danny through his thick lenses and reluctantly pulled open the drawer of a small cabinet that sat at his elbow. He hummed tunelessly as he fingered through the small white cards until he found the right one. 'Here we are, Mr Sutton, here's something you could do. The Acme Glass Company are looking for glass inspectors. It's a sitting down job, no hard work.'

The young cockney's heart dropped. Bonky Williams had told him all about glass inspectors. He knew that he would not last more than a day at that job and he shook his head. 'Yer mean ter tell me that's the only job yer got fer me? What about all those vacancies frew the call-up? That's a rubbish job, it's soul-destroyin'. Yer must 'ave somefink else in that box.'

The official looked at Danny over his glasses. 'I don't think you understand. All those jobs you talk about are being filled by women. Yes, women. It releases the men for war-work and the forces, you see. We've got vacancies for manual workers, but you are disabled, aren't you?'

It was the emphasis placed on the end of the sentence that finally brought Danny to the boil. He got up and put his hands on his hips, his pale face flushed angrily and the corner of his mouth twitched. 'Now listen you,' he exclaimed, his voice trembling, 'I've bin sittin' 'ere like a naughty school kid who's waitin' ter get 'is arse caned! Yer bin pissin' me about wiv yer bloody papers an' yer stupid remarks. Anybody listenin' ter you would fink I wanted ter be disabled! D'yer know what it was like out in France? No, course yer don't!'

The official opened his mouth to speak but Danny shouted a tirade of abuse. 'If you fink I'm gonna sit 'ere an' listen ter you prattin' off wiv yer snide remarks, yer got anuvver fink comin'. What wiv yer twiddlin' yer poxy fingers an' eatin' yer bloody pencils, an' lookin' at me like I'm somefink the cat dragged in, an' then 'avin' the gall ter offer me a poxy glass inspector's job! I reckon yer takin' the piss!'

The official's face went white and the small cluster of purple veins on his temple started pulsating. He stood up and waved Danny to the door, 'I'm not going to talk to you any more. I shall put in a report about your behaviour. It will be for the manager to decide what's to be done.'

Danny leaned forward menacingly and the frightened Herbert Snelling backed away. 'I tell yer somefink else, four-eyes, yer can do what yer like, an' yer poxy manager can do the same. If yer fink I'm gonna sit in front of bottles all day wiv a 'ammer in me 'and, yer more stupid than I thought yer was.'

Mr Snelling waved his unhelpful client to the door again. 'We'll see what the manager has to say.'

'Get stuffed, an' tell yer poxy manager ter do the same,' Danny sneered as he stormed out of the office and into the coolness of the street.

Back in the office the harassed Mr Snelling sat down heavily in his chair. What was that he said about a hammer? he thought. What would a glass inspector be doing with a hammer? These ex-soldiers are getting worse!

Another member of the Sutton household was on her way to

encounter officialdom that Monday morning. Lucy slipped her arm through Ben's as they left Tooley Buildings and walked purposefully along the busy street. Horse carts were lined up outside the wharves and the bored nags were snorting into their nosebags. The narrow lanes that led down to the water-front were crowded as vehicles and carts were being loaded. Bundles of foodstuffs and other commodities were lashed tight and kicked out from loop-holes to hang suspended from crane chains. The loads were then slowly lowered onto waiting transport to the cries of: 'Up a bit! Whoa! 'Old it, yer silly bastard!'

The shouts of the dockers rose above the din of clanking cranes and revving vans as the working week began. Along the busy Tooley Street lorries and horse carts continued to arrive, and people were hurrying about their business. Well-dressed office workers carried brief-cases and bundles of papers, and heavy-booted dockers and stevedores moved about on the street. Trams clattered by with their warning bells clanging, and the sounds of the river trade reverberated down along the narrow side lanes. The signs of war were apparent in the busy dockland street. Men were pasting up stark reminders that 'Careless Talk Costs Lives' and about what to do in the case of a gas attack. A military convoy of trucks clattered past towing heavy guns, and a bored-looking policeman ambled along, a gas mask pack and steel helmet slung over his shoulder.

Lucy gripped Ben's arm tightly as they made their way to the magistrates' court for the tribunal hearing at ten o'clock. A few people were hanging around outside the court building as Lucy and Ben approached. Ben was silent, his stomach tightening as they climbed the few steps and entered the high-ceilinged hall. A flight of wide marble steps led up to a narrow balcony which circled the hall and gave access to the first floor courtrooms. Some people were sitting on polished wooden benches with worried looks on their faces, while others studied the court schedule. Ben motioned Lucy to the notice-board and saw that Ben's hearing was to be in court 4. His name was near the top of the list and he gave Lucy a wry smile.

'At least we should get it over with quickly,' he said.

They took a seat and watched as more people crowded into the hall and policemen moved among the crowd calling out names from their lists. Ben's name was called and he was directed to the upper floor. The lovers sat down close together, holding hands and gazing into each other's eyes. Lucy saw the fear in his face, and she smiled encouragingly. She felt that they now belonged to each other, come what may, and Lucy was determined to remain strong for both of them.

The courtroom was panelled in oak and the windows were high up so that the sun's rays did not penetrate down into the well of the court. Ben stood facing the five-man panel. The person seated in the centre announced himself as the chairman and each of the others introduced themselves in turn. Ben could sense the hostility as he waited for the chairman to begin. A sheet of paper was passed along from hand to hand, and he could only guess that it was his written statement to the panel. There was a slight mumbling from the back of the court and the chairman looked over his spectacles reprovingly. Ben knew that Lucy was sitting behind him and it gave him comfort.

'You are Benjamin Morrison of 16 Tooley Buildings, Tooley Street, Bermondsey?'

Ben answered in the affirmative.

'You registered on January the 6th as a conscientious objector, and subsequently presented this tribunal with a statement setting out your reasons for doing so?'

Ben nodded and was immediately rebuked by the chairman.

'You must answer. A nod will not do. Is that quite clear?'

'Yes.'

'Have you anyone to speak on your behalf?'

'No, but I sent in a letter from—' But the chairman interrupted him in mid-sentence.

'I'm aware of the letter, Mr Morrison, I was coming to that.'

Ben gripped the rail in front of him. The hostility was becoming obvious and he began to tremble.

The chairman glanced at the person next to him and the questioning continued. 'I have a letter here from the Reverend John Harris of the Tower Bridge Road Methodist Mission. He states that you are a regular attender at that church, and he goes on to say that you are a part-time youth club leader. Is that correct?'

'Yes.'

Another member of the tribunal took up the questioning. 'The letter also states that you intend to study for the cloth. Is that so?'

'Yes.'

'How long ago did you come to this decision?'

Ben coughed nervously. 'I first decided over two years ago.'

'Are you sure you did not come to this decision after the outbreak of war?'

'No, sir.'

'Can you provide this tribunal with any proof that would substantiate your assertion, Mr Morrison?'

'No, sir. You only have my word, as a Christian.'

'Mr Morrison,' the interviewer went on, 'do you consider it wrong for this country of ours to be at war with Germany?'

Ben's knuckles tightened on the rail. 'I consider it wrong for people to kill each other.'

'You think it is all right for the Germans to march into this country and kill our people? Because that is exactly what would happen if we did not defend ourselves.'

Ben looked hard at the questioner. 'No, I think it is wrong for Germans to kill, or for anyone to kill another human being.'

'I see, and are you conversant with the Holy Bible?'

'Yes.'

'Does the Bible tell you that killing is wrong?'

'Yes.'

'And does it not tell of how God led the Israelites into battle?'

'Yes.'

The members of the tribunal exchanged glances and the chairman smirked. 'Tell me, Mr Morrison, were you brought up in a Christian family?'

'Yes, both my parents were practising Christians.'

'Did your parents ever chastise you as a child?'

'I was punished for doing wrong.'

'Were you beaten?'

'No, I was sent to bed early, or had privileges taken away.'

'Are you prepared for the results of non-resistance?'

'I know I must take the consequences. I realise that.'

'Let me put this to you, Mr Morrison. God forbid the Germans ever get here, but in the event, if you happened to see a wounded German soldier lying in the street, would you render first aid?'

Ben felt himself being slowly forced into a corner from which there was no escape. He took a deep breath before answering. 'I feel that every human being has the right to receive medical assistance, regardless.'

'Regardless of what?'

'Regardless of the fact that most people see it as being wrong to aid the enemy. I feel sure in my mind that we are all one family under God.'

'Are you aware that the Royal Army Medical Corps picks up wounded soldiers from both sides in war, and that the medics are strictly a non-combatant corps?'

Ben sensed that the *coup de grâce* was not far off. 'Yes, I would expect that to be so.'

'Do you still say that despite what has been said you still object to wearing a military uniform?'

'I feel that a military uniform represents a willingness of the wearer to kill.'

The tribunal members conferred for a few seconds, and Ben looked around at the panelled walls. He did not turn completely round to face Lucy, but he felt for her and knew of the anguish she was suffering. He looked back at the tribunal members and saw the nodding of heads.

'Mr Morrison,' the chairman began, 'I suggest to you that you have been wasting our time. You have told us in the written statement that you intend to study for Holy Orders, but you cannot substantiate this. Reverend Harris also says in his letter that you intend to study for the Church. That is not a substantiation, it is merely a third party reiterating what you have said of your intentions – an indication of intent. You have provided no evidence of any communication between yourself and the Theological College. Reverend Harris does not tell us in his letter when you first confided in him about your intentions of taking Holy Orders. I put it to you that you first indicated your interest in the college after the outbreak of war. We have made note of the fact that you have stated you would succour the wounded. That is the role of the Royal Army Medical Corps. Therefore, the finding of this tribunal is that you will be called up into a non-combatant corps, subject to you passing the army medical. You will have to apply to be posted at the time of your medical. That is all.'

Chapter Eight

Alice Sutton sat in her small parlour talking to Annie Barnes. Annie was an old and trusted friend from the days when the two danced the ragtime and wept unashamedly into lace handkerchiefs each Saturday at the silent picture show. The two went back a long way, to the days of horse buses and wide summer bonnets, the days of hard toil in the local tannery for a few shillings a week. Alice and Annie had lived in the same street since they both married, within a year of each other. Annie Barnes was a confidante, and for her Alice made an exception to her rule of keeping the family business away from gossiping neighbours.

'I tell yer, Annie, I'm fed up wiv the lot of it. I 'ad ter take 'is suit round ter Fran Simpson terday. You 'eard all about it, I s'pose?'

Annie nodded. 'Bit old fer fightin', ain't 'e?' she said, her florid face puckering.

'It's that bleedin' bitter, gets 'im real narky when 'e's 'ad a few,' Alice said, brushing an imaginary crumb from her dress and folding her thin arms.

Annie Barnes looked out of the window from her easy chair and saw the deepening redness settling over the chimney pots of the houses opposite. The evening was warm, and the lengthening shadows lent a tranquillity to the neat and tidy parlour. Outside in the street a few children played, their happy voices carrying into the house as they made the most of their games before being called in to face a scrubbing brush and Lifebuoy soap which tortured the eyes and stung the skin. In the quietness the metallic ticking of the clock on the mantelshelf sounded unusually loudly. Annie stirred her tea thoughtfully and waited for her friend to begin again. Alice made herself comfortable and sipped her tea.

Unable to bear the suspense any longer, Annie Barnes broached the subject. 'Well, an' 'ow did young Ben get on at the tribunal?'

Alice put down the cup and folded her arms. ''E's gotta go in.'

'Yer mean 'e's gettin' called up?' Annie asked, surprise showing on her face.

'From what Lucy told me, they was right gits. They've told Ben 'e's gotta go in the non-compatible corps or somefink,' Alice answered.

'Yer mean like the medical blokes who look after the wounded?'

'That's right. Ter be honest wiv yer, I can't see Ben doin' that sort o' job. 'E ain't cut out fer it.'

'Don't you fret about that, Alice. It's surprisin' the fings yer do when yer 'ave to. Look at Fran Simpson's eldest boy. Times I've seen 'im come 'ome from school cryin' from bein' bullied. 'E's a sergeant in the Coldstreams now.'

'I 'ope yer right, Annie. Poor Lucy's that cut up about it. From what she said, 'er Ben didn't 'ave much choice. If 'e'd 'ave refused they would 'ave locked 'im up and chucked away the key.'

Annie put the teacup back onto the table and reached inside her apron. She took out a tiny silver box and tapped on the lid with two fingers. 'Wanna pinch?'

Alice shook her head.

''Ow's your Connie? I saw 'er the uvver day with that young sailor, what's 'is name, Jimmy, ain't it?' Annie spluttered as the snuff took effect.

'Jimmy Ellis. 'E's a nice boy, got luvverly manners. 'Is leave's up ternight. I do 'ope nuffink 'appens to 'im, a lot of our ships are gettin' sunk. It's a right worry, what wiv one fing and anuvver.'

Annie smiled. ''E'll be all right. 'Fore yer know where you are 'e'll be 'ome on leave again.'

'I do 'ope so, Annie. All this trouble and strife, an' the worry of the invasion . . .'

Annie looked up at the window, as though she expected a German soldier to be peering in, then back at Alice. 'You don't really fink they'll get 'ere, do yer? I mean ter say, they've gotta come over the water. What's our boys gonna do, stan' by an' let 'em walk in?'

'I dunno,' Alice replied. 'I tell yer what though, that bleedin' pamphlet they pushed frew the letter box scared the daylights outta me.'

'What, that one about the invasion? My Bill tore it up, 'e said there was nuffink ter worry about, but I'm not so sure.'

Alice got up and picked up the teapot. 'Fer Gawd sake let's change the subject. Wanna 'nuvver cup o' tea?'

Annie took the refilled cup and went into her thoughtful stirring routine. ''Ere, Alice, I see your Danny this mornin'. 'E looked like 'e was in an 'urry. I see 'im runnin' fer a tram up the top.'

Alice shook her head. 'That boy's worryin' me. 'E 'ad a barney down the Labour Exchange terday. Apparently they offered 'im a job in some glass factory. I couldn't get the rights of it, but 'e went mad. Told the bloke down there ter poke 'is job. Gawd knows what's gonna 'appen now. I s'pose they'll suspend 'im fer six weeks, that's what usually 'appens when yer get lippy, or don't take the job they offer yer.'

'It's a bleedin' shame if yer ask me,' Annie remarked. 'Fellers are comin' back wounded an' what 'appens? They get some bloody jumped up git expectin' 'em ter take the first fing they offer. Bloody disgrace I calls it.'

'Yer gotta be fair though, Annie. That Danny's always bin 'ot 'eaded. It seems like 'e's got worse since 'e's come 'ome, 'e can be a cow-son at times.'

Annie sipped her tea. 'Still, yer gotta give 'im a chance, luv. After all, 'e's only bin 'ome a few days. It'll take time, an' there's no 'arm in 'im.'

Alice smiled at her friend. 'No, there's no 'arm in 'im, but I do wish 'e'd find a nice girl an' settle down.'

''E's sweet on young Kathy Thompson, ain't 'e, Alice?'

'I dunno, I fink she's goin' aroun' wiv that Jack Mason.'

Annie puffed, 'She wants ter keep away from 'im, 'e's a bad one, is Jack Mason. My Bill's told me a few stories about 'im.'

'It's 'er life, Annie. From what I can gavver, 'er farver leads 'er a dog's life. 'E's always drunk, an' 'e knocks 'is wife about. I see 'er the uvver day wiv a shiner.'

'It's enough ter drive the poor kid away, Alice.'

The street noises had died down and dusk began to settle over Dawson Street. The clock ticked loudly, and the two friends lapsed into comfortable silence, their conversation exhausted. Finally, Annie Barnes yawned and stood up. 'Well, luv, I better be orf 'ome. My ole man'll fink I've run away. What time is your lot comin' in?'

Alice looked up at the clock. 'Frank shouldn't be long, 'e went to a union meetin'. Connie an' 'er young man's gorn ter the pictures. Gawd knows what time our Danny'll walk in. That Johnny Ross called roun' ter see 'im an' they marched out wivout a leave nor bye. Lucy shouldn't be long, she's roun' Ben's place.'

Annie buttoned up her coat. 'You know, I envy you wiv your crowd. I often wish me an' Bill could of 'ad children. Still, it wasn't ter be.'

Alice went to the front door with her friend. 'I tell yer one fing, Annie, they're more bleedin' trouble now than when they were babies. At least yer could wash 'em an' put 'em ter bed. Yer knew where they were then.'

Annie Barnes started up the street. ''Night, luv.'

''Night, Annie.'

Most Monday evenings were quiet in The Globe. A few regulars either leaned on the bar counter or sat around with half-filled glasses at their elbows. In one corner two young men were engaged in earnest conversation, empty beer glasses on the table beside them testifying that the discussion was proving thirsty work.

Johnny Ross put his arms on the table and leaned forward, his dark, sallow features taking on a serious look as he made his point. 'Listen, Danny, yer wastin' yer time down the poxy Labour Exchange. Come on now, what's on offer down those places? All the good jobs are snapped up. If yer wanna sweat yer cods off, that's okay, but yer gotta fink of your condition.'

Danny Sutton drained his glass and put it down on the table with a bang. 'That's the second time I've 'ad that said ter me since I've bin 'ome. I ain't exactly due fer the knacker's yard yet, Johnny boy.'

The sallow-faced young man got up and moved to the bar with a pronounced limp; he pulled a thick wad of money from his back pocket and peeled off a one pound note. 'Two pints of ale, Eddie, an' one fer Yer Lordship.'

Eddie Kirkland gave the youngster an old-fashioned look as he pulled on the pump. 'You wanna be careful flashin' that roll in 'ere, Johnny boy. The law was in 'ere last night askin' questions about stolen cases of corned beef. Seems someone broke inter one of the ware'ouses in Tooley Street. They asked me if anybody 'ad offered me any bent cans, bent meanin' crooked. I told 'em, "What d'yer fink this is, a bloody café or somefink?".'

Johnny grinned slyly. 'It's all right, Eddie, I 'ad a win down the dogs.'

The landlord placed two frothing glasses of ale in front of his customer and picked up the pound note. 'This is a new one. What yer doin', printin' 'em?'

As Johnny carefully carried the drinks back to the table, the door opened and Biff Bowden walked in with Shady Lady in tow. 'Evenin' all,' he said breezily. 'Gi's a Guinness, Eddie, an' a nice arrowroot fer the next champion.'

Two old cronies in one corner were exchanging whispers and the one with the large walrus moustache nearly choked into his beer. 'Ere, Biff, what's that all over your dog's coat, flea powder?'

Biff gave the old man a wicked glance as he ordered the dog to sit. 'Don't you take the piss outta Shady. She's in trainin' fer the big race at New Cross. Them arrowroots are good fer 'er teef.'

'Won't do much fer 'er legs though, Biff,' Eddie butted in.

Biff Bowden took a saucer from his coat pocket and poured some of his Guinness into it. 'C'mon, Shady, get that down yer.'

The dog looked up at Biff with large, doleful eyes before lapping up the beer.

'Yer gonna kill that dog wiv kindness, Biff,' Eddie said, shaking his head sadly.

'All right, you can all laugh. One day she'll be a champion, won't yer girl?'

Shady Lady shook herself and a spray of powder dropped onto the floor. One of the old cronies jumped up in mock horror, took off his cap and brought it down sharply onto the table. 'Got yer!' he shouted.

'What's goin' on over there?' Eddie called out.

'Did you see that flea jump onto the table? Big as a tanner it was! Came orf as that mutt shook 'erself,' the elderly character exclaimed, grinning evilly.

Johnny put the beer down on the table and he raised his eyes towards the ceiling. 'It's gettin' like a nut'ouse in 'ere, what wiv them two, and that silly bastard Biff.'

Danny looked at the frothing pint of beer for a few seconds then he said: 'So yer reckon Tony Allen can fix us up wiv some work?'

'No sweat,' Johnny said with a confident nod of his head. 'I've told 'im all about yer gettin' wounded at Dunkirk, an' I said yer done lots o' different fings since yer left school. I told 'im yer used ter take bets fer ole Tubby Green down Dock'ead. I fink 'e'll fix yer up wiv a bookie's pitch round 'ere. I said yer can be trusted an' that's what counts wiv Tony. Anyway, 'e told me ter 'ave a word wiv yer an' let 'im know if yer was interested in workin' fer 'im.'

'When does 'e want an answer?' Danny asked, picking up his filled glass.

'No sweat. Come down New Cross dogs wiv me on Thursday, yer can 'ave a talk wiv Tony Allen there. What d'yer say?'

'What 'ave I got ter lose? Only me freedom. All right, Johnny, yer on.'

The pub door opened again and Bonky Williams staggered in.

'Look out,' Danny said out of the corner of his mouth, 'there's Eddie's favourite customer jus' come in.'

Bonky reeled over to the counter and blew hard as he leaned on the wet surface for support. 'Gi's a d-drink,' he hiccuped.

'Where you bin, spendin' all yer money in some uvver pub?' Eddie mocked.

Bonky's one good eye rolled around in its socket. 'I bin 'el-'elpin' Flash 'Arry wiv 'is s-stall.'

'Christ! Bonky, ain't you 'ad a wash? I can smell the fish from 'ere,' Eddie gasped.

'W-wash? Course I 'ad a wash. Wh-what d'yer fink I am? D'yer fink I-I'd come in 'ere all smelly an' dirty?'

Eddie put down a pint of ale on the counter and leaned back noticeably. 'Go an' sit down, Bonky, 'fore yer fall down.'

Bonky staggered over to where his two friends were sitting and almost fell into a chair. ''Ello, fellers, 'ow-'ow yer doin' then?'

'Bloody 'ell, you smell like Billin'sgate,' Johnny remarked, pulling a face.

'Don't you start. I-I've 'ad enough wi-wiv 'im,' Bonky spluttered, pointing in the general direction of the counter.

Danny picked up his pint. 'I'm finishin' this an' I'm off 'ome, Johnny. We can't talk any more. I might see yer before Thursday.'

Bonky had swivelled around in his chair and tried to fix the two old gentlemen with his eye. The man nearest wiped his moustache on the back of his hand and returned Bonky's unsteady look with a glare. Bonky's face creased in a lop-sided grin as he reached in his pocket for a handkerchief. His intention was not lost on the elderly gent.

'If you take that bloody eye out once more in front o' me, Bonky, I swear I'll knock yer uvver one out.'

Danny pulled Bonky around. 'Look, we're goin' 'ome. You be'ave yerself, or me an' Johnny'll take yer out an' drop yer in the nearest 'orsetroff, understood?'

Bonky's good eye tried to focus on Danny's face but his head drooped and he slowly raised his hand. 'It's okay, I'm-I'm goin' 'ome meself.'

Danny got up. 'C'mon, Johnny, let's walk the piss-artist 'ome. I'm ready fer the sack.'

*

Earlier that evening, Connie left the brewery where she worked as a telephonist and saw Kathy Thompson ahead of her on the pavement. Kathy was employed as a typist in a nearby seed merchant's offices. Connie hurried to catch up with her, and the two exchanged smiles and fell into step. Factory hooters were blaring out their end of day racket and tired workers were plodding homewards or joining the bus and tram queues. The sky was cloudless and the sun had started to dip down over the rooftops as the two girls from the backstreets reached Tower Bridge Road. They had been chatting away, and while they waited to cross the road Kathy looked at Connie as if to say something, but she stayed silent. Connie sensed her need to talk and she took Kathy's arm as they started to cross. ''Ow's yer love life, Kath?'

Kathy saw the impish look in her companion's eyes and she grinned. 'Don't ask me. Men – I'm fed up wiv 'em! 'Ow you doin'?'

Connie's face became serious. 'My feller's in the navy. 'E's goin' back off leave ternight.'

'Yeah, I've seen yer tergevver. Nice lookin' boy,' Kathy said. 'You two goin' steady?'

Connie nodded. 'Jimmy wants us ter get engaged when 'e's finished this trip.'

'What about yer folks?' Kathy asked. 'Will they mind?'

'I don't fink so. Me dad'll puff a bit, an' me mum'll give me a talk, but they won't try ter stop me.'

'I wish me dad was like that.' Kathy paused. 'Yer know I'm goin' out wiv Jack Mason?'

Connie nodded. 'Yeah, I do. Yer feller's pretty well known around here ain't he?'

'Yeah, 'e was in wiv all the big villains once. 'E works in partners wiv Tony Allen now. You know Tony Allen the bookie?'

Connie nodded. Just as they got to the corner of Clink Lane she asked, ''Ave yer bumped inter Danny since 'e's bin back?' She wondered what Kathy felt about Danny now and wanted to see her reaction – she knew that Danny was still keen on the girl.

Two spots showed on Kathy's cheeks and Connie didn't think it was due to the exertion of the short walk.

'I seen 'im on Saturday night. 'E was at Tony's party wiv 'is mate Johnny Ross,' Kathy said casually as she stopped at the street corner.

''E didn't tell me,' Connie pouted. 'But then that's Danny all over. 'E'd be makin' 'is weddin' plans 'fore 'e'd tell any of us.'

Kathy felt that their conversation was getting too painful. She moved into the turning. 'I've gotta go,' she said. 'I promised ter give me mum a bit of 'elp. See yer, Connie.'

Connie waved. ''Night, Kath.'

Chapter Nine

The week wore on slowly for Danny. There was no word from the Labour Exchange, and so he took to getting up late and spending his afternoons taking long strolls. Walking made him feel better, and he found that he was not becoming so breathless. His favourite path was to cross the Thames at Tower Bridge and walk to Tower Hill. The weather remained warm and sunny, and Danny would spend time gazing down from the massive iron bridge at the bustling activity along the waterfront. Somewhere amongst the swinging cranes and laden barges his docker father was working, and the young cockney felt a certain sadness for him. His father had toiled on that waterfront since he was a young lad; he had known the hardships of the strikes, and the scrambling for a day's work. He had become bitter and cynical, and he was quick to anger whenever he spoke about his job. Danny felt that his father understood why his only son had chosen not to follow in his footsteps and become a docker. Times were changing: the unions were slowly extracting better working conditions from the employers, and the safety rules which were being enforced meant less unnecessary accidents for the men. Nevertheless the work was still back-breaking, and it was never certain that there would be a full pay packet at the end of the week. Because of the war there was plenty of heavy work available at the moment, but Danny knew that it could not last for ever.

He remembered talking to Albert Sweetland back at Dunkirk. He had told his pal all about the money to be made if you took the opportunities, but right now Danny realised he was a million miles away from making any kind of fortune. His prospects were limited to becoming a glass inspector, or working for the local bookie, Tony Allen. He had been a bookie's runner before and it had not paid all that well. Johnny Ross was enthusiastic, though, and he had implied that there were a few profitable sidelines to be enjoyed once Tony Allen got to know and trust him. Maybe Johnny was right, he always seemed to have money in his pocket, and it did not come from his poorly paid job at the vinegar factory. Danny had made up his mind. He would see the bookie on Thursday evening and find out exactly what was on offer.

On this Thursday afternoon stroll Danny stopped as usual on the Tower Bridge and looked down at the flowing Thames. The day was hot, and the sun was shining from a cloudless sky. The usual stream of traffic rumbled over the bridge, and the laden barges were being manoeuvred into their berths. He was thinking about Alison, and wondered if she had decided to answer his letter. The possibility of meeting her again excited him. If she was eager to see him then she might even have written a reply already, and it could be on its way. He walked further until he reached Tower Hill, and there he sat down to rest on one of the iron-framed benches. Two soldiers ambled by wearing peculiar hats and displaying the word 'Australia' on their shoulder flashes. A sad-looking young woman pushing a pram passed by, and a few yards away a tired horse flicked the flies away with its tail and rattled the chains that tethered it to the cart. Although the afternoon was peaceful and warm, the signs of war were apparent everywhere. Opposite, a wall of sandbags reinforced a surface shelter, and along the road, a timber frame had been erected to protect the Naval Memorial.

The flint chippings in the paving stones caught the sun's rays and the scent of roses drifted up from the Tower Gardens behind where Danny sat. In the afternoon quiet, everything suddenly seemed unreal and frightening. Only a few weeks ago he had been struggling to stay alive during the fighting in France. He thought of Albert Sweetland, and how his life had been suddenly snuffed out on the beach. He thought of Oggy Murphy, the ugly misfit to whom he owed his life, and he felt a lump rise in his throat. Many of his comrades in the regiment had been local lads, a lot of them he knew very well. He had seen many of them fall, but there must have been others who had somehow struggled back to England. Danny promised himself that he would go round to the drill hall; they would probably have a record there.

A long tug whistle carried up from the river. Then it became quiet again, and as Danny eased his stiff leg he felt a dull pain in his thigh muscle. He decided he ought to start walking again. He stretched and set off down the sloping road, into Lower Thames Street and through the fish market. He strolled along steadily until he reached the Monument. For a short while he leant against an iron post and stared up at the high stone column, a reminder of the Great Fire of London. He recalled the time his father had taken him to the top of the Monument and pointed out London's famous buildings, and then carried him down most of the spiralling stone staircase. He felt sad and a sudden dread of the future possessed him. He thought about the wireless broadcasts he had listened to, and he wondered how long it would be before an invasion took place. What would happen to his family and the people in the little streets then? He'd seen the ravages of the German invasion of France and the thoughts of the same thing happening in London filled him with terror.

Two scruffy-looking characters came past Danny carrying

pieces of wood. They walked down the sloping street by the Monument and disappeared into an alley. Another individual in a filthy raincoat and boots tied up with string passed him. He carried a paper bag and a quart bottle of beer under one arm. Danny had often seen the 'up-the-hill' men before. They slept rough in the market alleyways and hired their muscle for a few coppers to the market porters. The vagrants' pennies were hard-earned as they threw their weight against the laden fish barrows and helped the porters negotiate the slippery cobbles. Their pittance bought them their basic necessities and a little beer, but that was all. The tramps dried off the wet fish boxes to use for fires and they slept warm, oblivious to the stench from the burning wood. The 'up-the-hill' men were as much a part of Billingsgate as the Monument and the white-frocked fish porters.

London Bridge swarmed with bowler-hatted City workers carrying rolled-up umbrellas and briefcases, and everyone seemed to be carrying a gas mask. As he walked among the throng Danny recalled his conversation with the old gentleman on the bus. He was right: everyone seemed to be walking with their heads held rigid, eyes directed to the person in front. The river traffic and feverish activity hardly merited a passing glance from the homeward-bound masses as they streamed over London Bridge and into the railway station.

The station clock showed ten minutes past five as Danny walked down into Tooley Street. Tea wouldn't be ready yet, he thought, so he decided to drop in and have a chat with Ben. He should be home from work by now, and from what Lucy had said he probably needed a bit of cheering up. The tribunal result must have been a shock for him, although Lucy hadn't said too much about it.

As Danny climbed the wooden stairs an elderly lady appeared from one of the flats and gave him a suspicious look. Danny smiled at her and she looked even more warily at him as he passed her. Ben's rooms were on the top floor, and when Danny reached the landing he was puffing hard. He waited for a short while and then rapped on the door. Ben looked surprised when he saw his visitor. But he smiled and stood back for Danny to enter.

'Glad to see you, Danny. Anything wrong?'

'No, I was jus' passin' an' I reckoned yer might wanna chat or somefink.'

Ben closed the door and motioned Danny to a seat. 'I'm just about to have a cup of tea. Would you like one?'

'Great,' Danny replied, making himself comfortable in an armchair.

Ben disappeared into the scullery and came back carrying two mugs of tea. He sat opposite Danny and put his mug down on the floor beside him. 'How's the job situation? Lucy told me about Monday morning.'

Danny grinned. 'I'm afraid I blotted me copy book. I 'spect they'll suspend me fer gettin' lippy. Still, I'm seein' somebody ternight, I fink there's a job in the offin'.'

Ben picked up the mug and sipped his tea. 'Lucy told you about the tribunal?'

Danny nodded. 'Bit of a shock, wasn't it?'

Ben shrugged his shoulders. 'To be honest, I wasn't surprised. As soon as I went in I could sense the atmosphere. At least I was given a choice. I knew that if I refused to go along with their requirements I would end up in prison.'

Danny looked at Ben's pale face and saw the fear in his eyes. 'Lucy was tellin' me you was gettin' some aggro from your boss. What's 'is attitude now you're goin' in the Kate Carney?'

'To be honest I'm not sure,' Ben said, scratching his head. 'He knows that I haven't changed my views and he thinks I've been frightened into putting on a uniform. He's an old soldier and doesn't look on me as being very patriotic.'

Danny put his mug down on the floor and crossed his legs. 'What 'appens if yer don't get inter the medical corps? The medics are not the only non-combatant lot. You could be in the stores or somefink.'

Ben's face became dark and he said quietly: 'I tell you, Danny, as much as the thought of prison terrifies me, I'd have to accept it. The only reason I'll agree to wear a uniform is if it's in the medical corps. All right, it's a compromise, but at least I'd be helping to save life, not taking it.'

Danny nodded, but he felt uncomfortable. He always did when Ben started to talk so seriously.

The noise of the homeward bound traffic and the grating sound of a tram carried up to the room, and Ben got up and closed the window. He came back and sat down heavily in the chair. He looked hard at Danny and folded his hands in his lap.

'Danny, I want to tell you something,' he said with deliberation, and his face was serious. 'You've been in action, you might understand. I'm scared of what's in front of me. I went into that hearing on Monday with all the wrong answers. I was prepared to stand up and say just why I felt I couldn't join the services, I thought I had it all worked out, but when they started asking those questions I began to shake. My stomach was in a knot and I wanted to be sick. I knew that Lucy was sitting there behind me, and I think it was only that knowledge that kept me from breaking down. I was scared then, and I'm scared now. I started to question my own reasons for being there. Was it really my beliefs? Or was it that I'm a coward? Do you know, I looked at those faces on the bench and I felt they could see right through me. They seemed to be smirking at my discomfort. They could tell I'd crack, I'm sure they could. I haven't slept properly since Monday, you know. I'm scared of pain and suffering, I can't bear to see anything suffer. Yesterday, Danny, a dog got run over below. It was yelping and whining, and instead of going down to see if I could do anything, I just sat in this chair until the yelping stopped. I finally looked out of the window and I felt ashamed. A young lad had picked up the dog and was struggling down the street with it. I don't think it was badly hurt, but I never even went to find out, I just sat there. How, for the Lord's sake, am I going to cope with the carnage in a battle? Tell me, Danny.'

Danny Sutton looked down at the floor. Ben's outburst had taken him by surprise and he felt inadequate. He didn't know what to say. As a medic Ben would be picking up wounded soldiers who were screaming in agony; he would be breathing in the stink of grisly butchery, and mangled bodies waiting to be laid to rest in makeshift graves; he would be shaking with a stark fear that turned his legs to jelly and twisted his stomach into a tight knot. Could Danny explain how it felt when the bullets whistled past and thudded into flesh and bone, when the man beside you fell and you could expect to be the next to get shot? How could he explain the terror to Ben, sitting opposite him, his face white with worry? It was impossible. He could still feel it vividly, but he knew of no words which would help him. Danny looked up at Ben and saw the anxiety in his eyes.

He took a deep breath. 'I don't know the answer, Ben. I'm jus' like you, I get scared of silly fings. We're all human, ain't we? I can't stan' spiders. There's no reason ter be scared of bein' scared, that sort of reasoning only gets yer killed. You'll be okay, there'll be uvvers wiv yer. They'll all be scared, but they'll still do what they're s'posed ter do. You'll get the proper trainin', you'll be all right.'

Ben brushed his hand through his hair and sank lower in his seat. 'I hope you're right, Danny. I expect you think I'm being stupid, talking that way.'

Danny got up from his chair and stretched his stiff leg. He looked into Ben's eyes. 'I don't fink yer bein' stupid,' he said.

'I'm scared. We're all scared. You're no different.' He paused and looked down. 'Anyway, I'd better be orf 'ome. I'll get a rollockin' if I'm late.'

Ben saw his guest to the door. 'Thanks for dropping in, Danny, I appreciate it.'

Danny grinned. 'Yer'll 'ave ter come up The Globe wiv us an' 'ave a drink, even if it's only orange juice. We can 'ave anuvver chat, okay?'

Danny walked out onto the landing and Ben smiled at him. 'I never knew you were scared of spiders, Danny.'

Danny hunched his shoulders. 'I'm terrified of 'em. Keep it ter yerself though. If they find out in the pub they'll be puttin' spiders in matchboxes jus' ter see me shout out. Oh well, I'd better get 'ome fer me tea. See yer, Ben.'

'Cheerio, Danny.'

From the London docks and from other ports around Britain the ships assembled in convoy for the hazardous North Atlantic crossing. Tankers and freighters and the destroyer escorts left their home shores under cover of darkness and steamed out into the dangerous ocean. There was now a war at sea and U-boats were searching out the convoys. The destroyer escorts were increasing in size, and more U-boats were being sunk, but the losses at sea were still mounting as Convoy Q407 steamed into mid-Atlantic on the night of the 6th of July 1940. On board the accompanying destroyer, HMS *Prowler*, everyone was at battle stations. A tell-tale blip on the asdic had indicated that a submarine was in the area.

The look-out let his night glasses hang from the strap as he squeezed his eyes tightly against the strain of watching the water. The moon lit up the waves and a myriad stars shone down from a velvet sky. Although a full alert was in operation, an uncanny calmness seemed to surround the convoy. Other destroyers could be seen moving among the merchantmen and guarding the flanks of the stragglers. The look-out blinked and put his glasses up to his eyes once more.

The steady thump of the powerful engines and the roar of the sea were music to the seaman as he scanned the shimmering water. Ever since he was able to remember, the sea had held a fascination for him. He had seen those big ships come up the Thames, and he had watched as they slipped inch by inch into their berths. He had read the names on the sides and learned to recognise their national flags. At night he had scoured his small atlas and studied it until his eyes drooped; the ports around the world were magical names to the lad. He dreamed of becoming a sailor. When he got older his father took him to the Royal Docks in his van. There he stared open-mouthed at the great cargo ships from the Orient. It fascinated him to see those dark-skinned seamen who were not much taller than he come down the gang-planks carrying their white jugs of steaming water. His father had laughed and said they were going off for their tea. The young lad did not question his father, but it seemed strange to him that the little men should all go to the brick shed marked 'Asiatics' for their tea. What his father did tell him however was that the little men were Lascars, and that they were the only race who could stand the conditions in the boiler-rooms of those huge coal-burning ships. Sometimes in the Indian Ocean the temperature in the boiler-room could soar to one hundred and twenty degrees.

As he scanned the starlit sea the young sailor remembered the time he had been waiting on the quayside with his father at the West India Dock and saw one of those little men brutally kicked by a ship's officer. The Lascar had gone aboard without protest and the young lad had vowed that if he ever got to become a seaman he would treat those dark-skinned little men with kindness. He remembered how his father had laughed at his concern for the seaman, and had said that Lascars were a lazy lot who had to be thumped now and then or they wouldn't work at all. Now the sailor wondered how many of those little men were sweating away now down in the boiler-rooms of the merchantmen as they sailed across the danger area.

Spray soaked the hood of his duffle jacket and dripped from his steel helmet as the look-out searched the ocean from his position up on the bridge. He could see the merchantmen spread out to the horizon, and occasionally he caught sight of one of the escorts cutting in through the lines. His own ship HMS *Prowler* had dropped back to hurry on the stragglers, but now it was racing full-speed to take up the vanguard position.

The officer of the watch called out to him, 'You awake, Ellis? We've picked up a signal.'

Chapter Ten

Alice Sutton brushed the crumbs from the red and white checked tablecloth as she set a place for her husband Frank. She glanced over at Connie, who had her head buried in the evening paper. Alice banged a knife and fork down hard and then gave her daughter a sharp look, but Connie seemed completely absorbed in the news. Alice came round the table purposefully and tapped Connie on the shoulder. 'What's goin' on 'ere ternight, girl?' she asked curtly.

Connie looked up in surprise. 'What d'ya mean, Mum?'

'Danny's what I mean. 'E rushes in 'ere like the devil's after 'im, rushes 'is tea down, an' scoots orf out again. All I got from 'im was, "I might be late, I gotta bit o' business ter see to". What the bloody 'ell is goin' on 'ere?'

Connie shrugged her slim shoulders. 'Search me, Mum. I s'pose 'e's gone off ter New Cross. Danny always used ter go on Thursdays, didn't 'e?'

Alice puffed and folded her arms. 'I'm sure I don't know, what wiv one an' the uvver of 'em, they take this place fer a coffee shop.'

Connie put down the paper and gave her mother a smile. 'You still mad at Dad?'

Alice fought against letting her face relax. 'I've warned yer farver. I ses to 'im, "If yer come in 'ere ternight smellin' o' beer an' yer don't eat yer tea up, I'm gonna let you 'ave it".'

'What, 'is tea, Mum?'

'No, I'm gonna give 'im a piece o' me mind. I'm fed up wiv keepin' 'is tea 'ot. An' don't you be so lippy, my girl.'

Connie gave her mother a special smile, and as she looked at her Alice felt herself starting to grin.

'Sit down, Mum an' I'll make us a nice strong cuppa,' Connie said laughing.

Danny walked briskly under the railway arch and crossed the street into Bermondsey Lane. He was taking the back-streets to the Old Kent Road where he could catch the tram to New Cross. He had to pass the Arpinos' shop and so he decided to look in on Tony. They had often taken a stroll to the dog meetings together before Danny had been mobilised. The clock in the chemist's window showed 6.30 – if he hurried he'd catch the first race. Tony was inside the shop talking to a couple of tall, burly characters as Danny looked in.

'Fancy the dogs, Tony?' Danny called out from the door.

'Sure fing,' Tony said quickly. 'Walk on, I'll catch yer up.'

Danny strolled slowly on towards Tower Bridge Road and soon Tony caught him up. 'We got trouble I fink, Danny,' he said with a backward glance. 'Did yer see those two monkeys I was talkin' to? They've bin doin' the rounds of all the shops round 'ere this last few days. They're talkin' a lot a nonsense about us joinin' a shopkeepers' federation. I've jus' told 'em ter come back when me ole man's there. It's no good them talkin' ter me muvver, she won't know what they're on about anyway.'

Danny frowned at him. 'Sounds like the ole protection racket ter me, Tony. Yer wanna be careful, somebody tried ter pull a stroke like that in Tower Bridge Road a few years ago.

Me ole man told me about it. This geezer got a right goin' over. Yer wanna make sure all the shopkeepers stick tergevver. It's the only way ter beat 'em.'

The two friends crossed into Tower Bridge Road and walked up until they reached The Bricklayers Arms. They stood chatting together at the tram stop.

'I've gotta see that Tony Allen while we're at the meetin',' Danny was saying. 'Johnny Ross 'as 'ad a word wiv 'im about me doin' a bit o' bookkeepin'.'

Tony laughed. 'You workin' in an office? Do me a favour, you'll get the right bleedin' 'ump in no time.'

'I'm talkin' about takin' bets, yer berk,' Danny replied with a grin.

Tony winced. 'Yer wanna be careful there, Tony Allen's got 'is fingers in a lot o' pies. Yer might get in over yer 'ead. An' anuvver fing, yer wanna be careful o' that Jack Mason. 'E's in wiv Tony Allen. One nasty bastard that is.'

'Don't worry, Tony, I'll be cute. At least it'll be better than what that ponce at the Labour Exchange offered me on Monday.'

A young woman joined the queue and Tony gave Danny a nudge. 'That's a bit of all right!' he said, his eyes widening.

The woman turned round and gave Tony a cold stare. Tony smiled back at her with a ridiculously innocent look on his face. A number 38 tram pulled up at the stop and the queue boarded. Tony winked at his pal and followed the young woman onto the top deck. As the tram rocked and swayed in the tracks Tony continually glanced over to where she was sitting. At first she ignored him, but as he kept on looking at her she began to wonder whether he was a complete nutcase. But by the time the tram reached New Cross railway arch the two were exchanging smiles.

Danny nudged his friend, 'C'mon, Casanova,' he said, 'this is our stop.'

The first race had just started as the two entered the stadium and climbed the steps into the stand. People were milling around and a roar went up as one of the dogs was bundled over. Dog number 6 went out in front and held the lead until the finish of the race.

'Not much of a price that,' Tony remarked, looking at the odds on a bookie's stand in front of them.

Danny was searching the crowd with his eyes when Tony gave him a nudge. ''Ere, look at this.'

Danny glanced down at the race card in Tony's hand and saw that Shady Lady was entered in the third race. He grinned. 'That'll be a rank outsider, they'll prob'ly give yer two 'undred ter one on that.'

Tony looked up at his pal. 'Biff Bowden told my ole man ter get a few bob down on it next time it runs.'

Danny laughed aloud. 'It'll be too pissed ter run. If it gets out o' the trap it'll prob'ly fall asleep 'alf way round, or keel over wiv its legs up in the air.'

The dogs were parading for the second race and Danny handed Tony a ten shilling note. 'Do us a favour, Tone, stick this on number 4 dog. I wanna look out fer Tony Allen.'

Tony Arpino trotted down the steps to the trackside and while he was gone Danny scanned the crowds again. He finally spotted Tony Allen by the track talking to Jack Mason. Then he saw Kathy. She had just walked up to them and he saw her hand Jack Mason something. Danny had forgotten the race completely and his eyes stayed on Kathy as she took her escort's arm when the bell sounded. The mechanical hare was building up speed and as it passed the traps the dogs shot out and went into the first bend in a bunch. Slowly the number 4 dog gained ground. Danny turned back to Kathy and saw her jumping up and down excitedly. When he looked back at the race he saw that his dog was now being overtaken.

Tony came back as the dogs crossed the finishing line and

pulled a face. 'Oh well. There's still Shady Lady,' he said, but without much enthusiasm.

Danny pointed the bookie out to Tony. 'I'm goin' down fer a word. Comin'?'

Tony shook his head. 'You go on, I'll stop up 'ere. I'll see yer later.'

Danny Sutton walked slowly down to the trackside and held out his hand. ''Ello, Tony, remember me? Me mate Johnny Ross told me ter come an' see yer.'

Tony Allen shook Danny's hand. ''Course I remember yer. This is Kathy an' Jack, they're both good friends o' mine.'

Danny shook hands with Jack Mason and was unsettled by his limp, clammy grasp. He smiled at Kathy, who nodded back without a flicker of recognition in her dark eyes. Tony Allen studied the card for a while and then looked at Danny. 'Tell yer what,' he said, 'I'm just away ter put a few bob on number 6 dog. We'll 'ave a drink in the bar after the race, okay?'

Danny nodded. 'I'll see yer there then.'

Jack Mason looked at Kathy. 'I won't be long. I'm goin' wiv Tony,' he said shortly.

Danny watched the bookie walk away with his associate, then he turned to Kathy to find her smiling at him. 'I didn't expect ter see you down 'ere,' she said. ''Ave yer bin offered a job?'

Danny nodded. 'Johnny Ross put the feelers out fer me.'

Kathy put her hand on his arm. Danny felt her warm fingers and he looked into her eyes. He could see that she was anxious. 'Do yerself a favour, Danny,' she said seriously, 'don't 'ave anyfing ter do wiv Tony Allen or Jack. Don't ask me why, jus' say no, an' walk away while yer still can. You get in wiv that crowd an' you'll regret it.'

Danny reached down and took her hand in his. 'You concerned fer me? I . . .'

Kathy stopped him. 'Don't start that again, Danny, I meant

what I said. Yes, I'm concerned fer yer. Jus' take my advice.'

Danny searched her dark eyes. 'Yer know I still want yer, Kathy, yer must know that.'

'Don't, Danny, don't. Please. It's too late fer us now, fings 'ave changed since then. It's too late.'

Danny squeezed her hand until she winced. 'Look, Kathy, it's not too late. You're not married to 'im. Come out wiv me termorrer. I'll tell 'im if yer like.'

Kathy shook her head and tears came into her eyes. 'It is too late, Danny. I 'ad a big row wiv me dad. 'E chucked me out. I'm livin' wiv Jack now.'

'Christ! What did 'e do that for?'

Kathy looked down at her feet. 'I'm 'avin' a baby. It's Jack's. When I told me dad 'e went mad. Mum tried ter stop 'im goin' fer me an' she got a good 'idin' too.'

Her words stunned him. It felt as though icy fingers had suddenly gripped his insides. Feelings of anger and pity rose up in Danny's breast as he stared in despair at the slim girl in front of him.

'Yer mean yer ole man gave yer a pastin', wiv you 'avin' a baby an' all?'

Kathy gave him a weak smile. 'Yer know 'ow my farver gets when 'e's 'ad a drink. 'E gave me ten minutes ter pack an' get out. I went roun' ter Jack's place, I 'ad to. Anyway, Jack's bin wantin' me ter move in wiv 'im fer a while now.'

Danny shook his head sadly. 'Why didn't yer come roun' ter see me? I'd 'ave 'elped yer, you know I would.'

Kathy blinked back her tears. She looked into his worried eyes and felt a strong urge to collapse into his arms, but she breathed out deeply and pulled her hand away from his. 'Be sensible, Danny,' she said. 'I'm 'avin' 'is baby, I'm sleepin' wiv 'im. 'Ow could I possibly come runnin' round ter your place an' say, "take me in, I've bin chucked out 'cos I'm pregnant"? It's not your baby.'

'I wish it was, I wish you'd 'ave told me before. I wouldn't 'ave took advantage.'

Kathy smiled at him. 'Don't be silly, you didn't take advantage. I wanted it as much as you. Yer know that, don't yer?'

Danny's mouth twitched. 'Kathy, come with me, the baby don't make no difference. Leave 'im. 'E'll be no good ter yer.'

'Don't, Danny. Please.'

He gazed round the stadium in dismay. Kathy saw a hollowness in his eyes and she said anxiously, 'You'd better go now, luv. Please. They'll be back soon. I'll see yer in the bar later.'

The third race was about to begin. Danny walked back morosely to his friend and they stood waiting for the off. Tony sensed that there was something wrong with his pal but he refrained from asking questions. The bell sounded and five dogs bounded from the traps, but one dog had not moved.

'I told yer she'd be pissed, didn't I?' Danny shouted.

Tony grabbed his pal's arm. 'It ain't Shady! Look, she's in the lead!'

Shady was dashing round the track, to the roar of the punters. The rest of the field was left far behind as Shady Lady increased her lead. On the final straight she was ten lengths clear, and she romped home to the cheers of the surprised spectators. The bookmakers, who had expected a run on the money if the hot favourite had won, were openly smiling.

'Bloody 'ell! It done it! It bloody well done it! She won!' Tony shouted.

Danny looked at him. 'You didn't back it, did yer?'

Tony Arpino was beaming. 'Yep, I 'ad a dollar on the nose! Jus' fer luck.'

The numbers tumbled about on the totaliser and when they settled the crowd gasped. The forecast was over ten pounds. Tony Arpino rubbed his hands together with glee. He had backed Shady Lady at one hundred to six.

The bar at the rear of the stadium was packed. Danny stood

facing Tony Allen in one corner and Jack Mason was with Kathy some way off, talking to Johnny Ross, who had just walked in. Danny was listening to the bookie.

'I've 'ad a word wiv Bernie Marsh,' Tony Allen said. ''E told me yer was ter be trusted. That's good enough fer me. 'E told me yer run a good book fer 'im. Yer see, I've got a few little earners goin'. Play yer cards right an' I might be able ter put a few bob your way. Fer a start yer can take the bets on me Clink Lane pitch.'

Danny nodded. 'Is it the usual set up?'

'Yeah, the rozzers won't worry yer. I pay their guv'nor orf each week. When they've gotta make a pinch they let me know an' I get somebody ter do the honours. It works the same as it did wiv Bernie. We put a couple o' bets in the geezer's pocket an' 'e makes sure 'e gets caught. We pay the fine an' everybody's 'appy, includin' the coppers.'

Danny had already made up his mind. He gave Kathy a furtive glance and then looked at Tony Allen. 'When do I start?'

'Next Monday. I'll put one o' the lads wiv yer fer a few days, until the punters get ter know yer. You'll be all right, I'll do the business at the Labour Exchange, I know the geezer there. 'E'll give us yer green card fer me ter sign. For all intents an' purposes, yer workin' as a bookkeeper's clerk. That okay?'

Danny nodded. 'Fanks, Tony. I know the game, yer can count on me ter do the business.'

Tony Allen smiled and downed his Scotch. 'You'll be all right. Be straight wiv me an' I'll look after you.' He reached into his pocket and drew out a thick wad of money. He handed Danny a five pound note. ''Ere. Take this on account an' enjoy yerself. Yer can pay me back when yer flush.'

Danny tried to refuse but the bookie pushed the white note into his hand. 'You'll find out I look after my boys if they're straight. Go on, take it.'

*

Early that evening Frank Sutton came home to number 26 Dawson Street and walked through the front door without stumbling over the coconut mat that was spread out along the length of the passage. He went out into the scullery and gave Alice a peck on the cheek before rolling up his sleeves and scrubbing his hands with a stiff brush. 'Is Danny out?' he asked, taking a towel from the back of the door.

Alice nodded. ''E wasn't in five minutes. Gone on some business, so 'e said.'

'I thought I caught sight of 'im goin' under the arch as I come in,' her husband said. 'What's fer tea, Alice?'

'Boiled bacon an' pease puddin'. I know it's yer favourite. Now get in there an' get yer feet under the table. I wanna get cleared up early ternight, I'm goin' round ter see Maggie. The kids 'ave gone down wiv the measles.'

Lucy and Connie were both sitting in the small parlour when their father walked in. Lucy was reading and Connie was sitting on an upright chair, one knee drawn up under her chin.

'Bloody 'ell, what's that yer usin'?' Frank exclaimed, pulling a face.

Connie grinned. 'It's nail varnish, Dad, I'm makin' meself pretty.'

Lucy looked up quickly and put her head down again into her book. Frank sat himself at the table and picked up a knife and fork. Connie gave him a cheeky smile. 'You're 'ome early, Dad.'

Her father fixed her with a telling look as Alice put his tea in front of him and he began to eat in a deliberately sober manner. Connie winked at her mother who grinned back and walked out of the parlour with her head in the air. Frank ate his tea in silence and when he had scraped the last morsel from his plate he leant back in his chair and sighed contentedly. Lucy had gone to help her mother with the dishes and Connie sat with both feet outstretched and her arms behind her head. Frank hooked his thumbs through his braces and burped loudly.

''Ow's yer young man, Con? You 'eard from 'im yet?'

'Give 'im a chance, Dad. 'E only went back on Monday night. 'E's prob'ly gone straight ter sea. 'E won't 'ave much time ter write any letters.'

Frank nodded. 'Don't s'pose 'e will, girl. What boat is 'e on?'

Connie raised her hands in mock horror. 'Yer musn't call 'em boats, Dad, they're ships. Jimmy's on a destroyer. 'E's bin on convoy duties.'

''E's doin' a good job, Connie. It can't be very nice out there on the water. Mind you, though,' Frank went on, 'we've always relied on people like your young man. It's in our blood, the sea. We're an island. Wivout ships we're done for, an' wivout a navy we'd be a plum pickin' fer every little dictator that fancied 'avin' a go at us.'

Connie looked at her father with a saucy grin. 'Look at Sir Francis Drake. 'E sorted 'em out, didn't 'e?'

Frank felt he was wasting his time trying to talk seriously to his daughter this evening. 'Don't sit there mockin' yer ole dad, go an' get us a cuppa.'

The clock struck ten. Connie had gone up to her room, and Alice had just returned from visiting Maggie's children. She was sitting in the easy chair listening to the wireless. Frank shifted his position yet again and stretched. 'What's our lad up to then, Muvver?' he asked suddenly.

Alice folded her arms as she usually did when she had something to say. 'I dunno, Frank, but that Johnny Ross was round 'ere on Monday. 'E was eager ter see our Danny. I don't trust 'im, an' 'e's in wiv a bad lot. I 'ope Danny don't get too much involved wiv that crowd.'

Frank looked into the empty hearth. 'Yer can't wipe 'is nose now, Muvver. After all, 'e's over twenty-one. 'E's gotta make 'is own decisions.'

'I know that, Frank, but yer can't 'elp worryin', can yer?'

'No yer can't,' Frank said, straightening up in his chair. 'An' yer can't 'elp gettin' firsty, neivver. 'Ow's about me an' you poppin' up The Globe fer a quiet drink?'

Alice tried not to look too eager. 'Oh, all right then,' she said. ''Ang on, I'll get me coat.'

Chapter Eleven

Early on Saturday morning the postman delivered two letters to number 26. Danny was still fast asleep, but Connie was up and about. She took the letters out into the scullery and raised her eyebrows when she spotted a Dover postmark on the letter addressed to Danny. The other letter was for Lucy, but she had already left for work. Connie's sister was employed as a secretary to the manager of a manufacturing tailors who had their offices in Tower Bridge Road. Since the outbreak of war her firm had been working on a government contract to supply uniforms to the armed forces, and now everyone was working regular overtime.

Connie took Danny's letter up to his room with a cup of tea and shook him gently. Danny mumbled something unintelligible and pulled the clothes over his head. Connie shook him again without success and left the letter with his tea on the chair beside his bed. Alice had gone to the market and had left Connie the washing to peg out in the backyard. Outside the sun was shining and children's voices sounded in the street. Presently she heard the cry of the rag-and-bone man as he pushed his squeaking barrow into the turning. She went in and picked up the rag bag lying at the foot of the stairs and went to the front door to await Old Jerry.

For as long as anyone could remember, Old Jerry had trundled his rickety barrow around the backstreets of dockland. Where he came from or where he lived was a mystery. He was bowed and weatherbeaten, with a beer-stained moustache and bushy eyebrows. His faded blue eyes glared out from under a greasy trilby and he wore a tattered grey raincoat without buttons that was tied around his middle with string. It was filthy and he wore it in all weathers, and underneath he carried a money pouch, a spring balance that was rusting and did not work, and a roll of money secured with an elastic band. The most striking feature of Jerry's appearance was his brown boots. They were always clean and polished, which led some people to believe that he was an old soldier.

The barrow that Old Jerry pushed around the back-streets looked as worn out as its owner. The wheels squeaked and the shafts looked ready to fall off. It was piled high with rags, bits of old iron and an assortment of empty glass jars. How he managed to get a living from such rubbish was a puzzle to the local folk, but they were aware that Old Jerry was never short of cash. He struck a hard bargain and the locals learned not to haggle. He swore that his spring balance was correct to the ounce, and if it was ever doubted the bag of rags would most likely be deposited on the pavement and Old Jerry would be off, mumbling under his breath. Connie knew this as she walked up to his barrow and handed Old Jerry the rags her mother had sorted out the previous night. He fished out the spring balance and hooked up the bag, he squinted at the reading then tossed the bundle on his barrow before counting out three pennies and one sixpence.

Later that morning Danny took a leisurely stroll up to The Globe. A small boy cracked a whip against a spinning top and chased it happily, another couple of lads were setting up their firewood pitch, and women carried laden shopping baskets into the turning. Danny contentedy mulled over the letter he had received from Alison. It had really cheered him up after hearing Kathy's news at the races to know that Alison had been granted some leave and she was intending to come up to London next Sunday morning and stay over until Monday, when she would catch the night train to Cardiff to see her folks. And he smiled to himself as he walked into the pub.

The Globe was busy as usual with its regular clientele of dockers, stevedores and shoppers who called in for a 'livener'. Eddie was chatting to Biff and when he saw Danny he came over.

'Jack Mason's in the saloon. 'E was askin' if yer come in 'ere on Sat'day mornin's. I fink 'e wants a word wiv yer.'

Danny ordered a pint of ale and Eddie nodded to the connecting door. 'If yer wanna go frew I'll 'and yer beer round.'

'Fanks, Eddie,' Danny said. 'I'd better see what 'e wants.'

Jack Mason was talking to a couple of burly men and when he saw Danny walk into the bar he came over to the counter. 'So yer joined the firm then?' he said with a slight smirk on his bloated face.

Danny nodded. 'Me pal Johnny Ross spoke fer me. I used ter be Bernie Marsh's runner.'

'Yeah, so Tony Allen tells me,' Mason said, beckoning the barmaid over.

Danny sipped his drink while the bookie ordered another Scotch. He noticed how the man's deep-set eyes seemed to dart around nervously. He was a snappy dresser, Danny noticed. His suit looked expensive and was immaculately cut; his crisp white shirt made his swarthy complexion seem even darker, and his black patent shoes looked like they were from a West End shop. Danny watched as Mason took a swig from his glass and his eyes were drawn to the small, crescent-shaped scar in the corner of his mouth.

Mason laid a fist on the counter and leaned towards the young cockney. 'You're a mate o' Rossy then, are yer?'

'I've known 'im since we were kids. We went ter school tergevver,' Danny replied.

The villain's eyes seemed to bore into him and Danny felt uneasy. 'Trouble wiv yer pal is, 'e can't keep 'is mouth shut. I 'eard 'e was in 'ere the uvver night chuckin' 'is money about. Yer wanna tell 'im ter watch it. It don't do ter let people know yer business. Yer never know, the law might be in 'ere.'

Danny felt his dislike for the man growing as he listened. Jack Mason stared into his face. 'Jus' ter put yer in the picture,' he said, 'I'm what yer might call Tony Allen's right 'and. It's my business ter look after 'is interests. There's bin a few geezers in the past that's tried ter come it and I've 'ad ter sit on 'em, if yer get me meanin'. I 'ope you ain't got no fancy ideas?'

'Yer don't 'ave ter try an' put the fear in me. I'm pleased Tony Allen gave me the job, I'm not out ter take liberties,' Danny said.

Mason grinned crookedly. 'No offence, son, jus' tellin' yer, that's all.'

Danny finished his drink and Jack Mason pointed to his glass. 'Wanna top up?'

'No fanks, I've gotta meet somebody,' Danny lied.

Mason put his elbow on the counter and looked at Danny, a menacing expression on his face. 'Kathy tells me yer know 'er.'

Danny felt his stomach tighten, he was afraid of what Kathy might have said. 'Everybody knows everyone else round 'ere,' he said dismissively. 'Kathy, Johnny Ross an' me was all in the same class at school. As I was sayin', we all grew up tergevver.'

Jack Mason continued to fix Danny with an intimidating stare. 'Me an' Kathy are goin' around tergevver. Jus' so's yer'd know.'

'Yeah, I know,' Danny replied, returning the stare.

Jack Mason suddenly relaxed. He picked up his empty glass and looked in the direction of the barmaid.

Danny felt it was time he got away from him. 'Well, I'm orf. I'll see yer around,' he said, walking from the saloon bar and out into the warm sunshine.

Danny walked along Tooley Street; as usual on Saturday afternoons the area was almost deserted, the wharves were locked and only a few locals ambled by. In the sudden quiet Danny had time to think. He would have to be careful of Jack Mason, there had been a distinct warning in his tone when he mentioned Kathy. Maybe someone had seen him leave the party about the same time as Kathy and told Mason, but it seemed unlikely. It was more probable that Jack Mason was suspicious of him for another reason. It was obvious the man did not like Johnny Ross, and it was Johnny who put in a good word for Danny to the bookie.

As he turned into Dawson Street he saw Johnny Ross coming along towards him. Johnny was limping noticeably and he wore a large grin. ''Ello, Danny, goin' 'ome already? I was comin' up The Globe fer a chat wiv yer. What's the matter?'

Danny scowled. 'I jus' got lumbered wiv Jack Mason. After five minutes in 'is company I was glad ter get out inter the fresh air.'

'I told yer about 'im didn't I?' Johnny said with a confirming nod.

Danny pulled on his pal's arm. 'By the way, Mason told me ter give yer a bit of advice.'

'Oh yeah, about what?' Johnny asked, looking serious.

''E reckons yer should be more careful about flashin' yer money in The Globe.'

'Well somebody must 'ave told 'im, 'cos 'e wasn't in the pub,' Johnny said indignantly. 'An' I bet I know who it was. I bet it was that barmaid of Eddie's. Mason took 'er out a few times. She's still sweet on 'im, I can tell.'

Danny shrugged his shoulders. 'It don't matter who it was. Johnny boy. Be careful, or they'll stop yer little earners.'

Johnny Ross grinned. 'Don't worry, Danny. I've got a nice little touch comin' up. I'll tell yer about it later. Take it easy. I'll see yer soon.'

Danny stood beside his front door and watched his pal hobble up the turning. It looks like I've gotta look after both of us, he thought as he pulled on the door string.

The bows of the destroyer rose and dipped into the heavy swell, and up on the bridge Ordinary Seaman James Ellis wiped the salt spray from his face and stamped his numbed feet on the wet steel deck. His eyes were begining to play tricks with him and he blinked hard. 'Christ! Where's that dopey git wiv me cocoa,' he mumbled aloud as more spray lashed his raw face. Lofty Boulter was struggling for'ard and Jimmy could see him leaning into the wind, his hand protecting the steaming hot cocoa.

'Bloody 'ell, Lofty. It's about time. I was givin' you up.'

Lofty Boulter grinned and handed over the beverage. 'Fink yerself lucky, Jimmy boy. I nearly went over on me arse a couple o' times.'

Jimmy Ellis gulped the drink and felt the warmth penetrate into his stomach.

Lofty pulled his duffle coat up around his ears and leaned on the guard rail beside his pal. 'What a poxy night,' he groaned, ducking as the spray flew up from the bows. 'I knew it was a mistake ter sign on in the Andrew. I could 'ave joined the Brylcreem mob an' got meself a nice little WAAF ter keep me warm on nights like this.'

Jimmy handed back the empty mug and took another scan of the dark horizon. 'D'yer ever get scared on these patrols, Lofty?' he asked after a while.

'You tell me when I'm not,' his pal replied. 'I don't like

these cat an' mouse games wiv the U-boats. I don't like what I can't see. I know very well there's a bloody German down there somewhere jus' waitin' fer the opportunity ter stick a tin fish inter the first ship 'e can. I tell yer, Jimmy, it gives me the creeps.'

The *Prowler* continued the 'cat and mouse' manoeuvres and was now sweeping a wide arc ahead of the convoy. Clouds were gathering below the cold stars and spots of rain fell on the steel deck.

'Funny 'ow the weavver changes at sea,' Jimmy remarked, wiping his face on the back of his hand.

'Yeah, it's somefink yer can't predict, mate,' Lofty answered, bracing himself against the bulkhead and digging his hands deeper into his jacket pockets. 'I read somewhere that the sea's like a woman. It's right, I s'pose. Women are unpredictable, at least a few I know are. Yer fink yer got 'em sussed out, an' they kick yer right in the cods. Now you take this girl I used ter know. Rachel 'er name was. She was a good-lookin' sort, an' all the lads round Balham fancied 'er. I was cartin' 'er out fer a spell before I joined up. D'yer know I tried me 'ardest ter get 'er inter bed but she wasn't 'avin' any of it. All I got out of 'er was, "let's get engaged, Freddy". Well, I thought ter meself, play yer cards right, Freddy boy, an' you'll crack it, so I ups an' ses, "Yeah, all right" an' I got 'er a ring. Cost me a few bob as well. I took 'er out fer a good piss-up on the night we got engaged, but it didn't make no difference. "Wait till we're married", she said. Anyways, this went on an' on until I was gettin' like a dog wiv two dicks an' a double line o' trees. Frustration, Jimmy boy. That's what I was sufferin' from. Well, one night we 'ad a right ole barney. I called 'er a frigid prune, an' she called me a lecherous git. She threw the ring at me an' it dropped down a drain 'ole. Off she stormed an' next day I joined up.'

Jimmy grinned as he wiped the eye-piece of his night

glasses. 'So that's why yer joined the Andrew then. 'Ave yer seen anyfing of 'er since?'

Lofty shifted his position against the rail and leaned closer to his pal. 'Yer never gonna believe this, Jimmy, but after our last trip I bumped into 'er in the Balham High Road. She was in the club. Honest. She was out 'ere,' he said, gesticulating with his hand held out in front of him. 'Bloody pregnant, an' there's me couldn't get a look in.'

'She wasn't married, then?' Jimmy said.

'Married nuffink. She ended up wiv this geezer who 'ad a shop in the Balham market. Right flashy sort o' bloke 'e was. As I said, women are unpredictable. They're like the weavver.'

Lofty left the bridge and Jimmy Ellis put the glasses to his eyes for the umpteenth time. He could see the fitful moon playing down on the rolling sea and the distant stars as they broke from the rain clouds. Away to starboard he saw the billowing smokestack of a small freighter, and the oil tanker that had been running abeam for some time. He was looking forward to the warmth of the mess when his spell of duty was over and his thoughts turned to that last night in London. They were sitting in the back row of the stalls and Connie had snuggled up close. He couldn't remember the film, but he recalled the fragrant smell of her body and how her red lips had searched out his in the darkness as they whispered promises and everlasting love. They had walked slowly and sadly to London Bridge Railway Station where he was to catch his train to Chatham. Connie had given him a small locket as a good-luck charm and he wore it around his neck. He had wanted to take her in his arms and make love to her, but there had been no time. Connie had suggested that they see her father when he returned home, and then they could have all the time in the world.

Bright flashes suddenly blinded the look-out as torpedoes exploded in the dark. The silence was shattered. A freighter lay dead in the water and her crew were scrambling into lifeboats. The tanker was burning as its bow rose up out of the water and it began to sink stern first. The wild sea was full of flotsam and bobbing lifeboats. Oil was burning on the water and the other ships became shrouded as the convoy put down a smokescreen. The *Prowler* was speeding forward into the smoke and the surrounding chaos had dissolved into indistinct shapes.

Suddenly Jimmy Ellis saw the ugly wet shape of the U-boat dead ahead and he could read the number 107 clearly on its conning tower. The destroyer ran straight into it and the sound of crunching steel plates was like a scream out of hell. The *Prowler* rose up on the hull of the sub and then settled back in the water. Oil bubbles broke the surface as the 107 went down to the depths and then a fountain of water rose level with the bridge. The destroyer was beginning to swing around when a torpedo exploded amid-ships. Ordinary Seaman James Ellis shut his eyes as he felt the cold sea smash into him and close over his head.

When he struggled to the surface the *Prowler* had gone. Only pieces of wreckage remained. His thoughts were of Connie and he called her name aloud, but he was alone in the angry sea. He hoped that he would spot other survivors, or a lifeboat, but he soon realised that none had been launched, it had all happened too quickly. He tried shouting but he felt too shocked and tired and though his life jacket was keeping him afloat, the coldness was beginning to numb his body. In the loneliness of the vast ocean Jimmy waited for the end to come. He felt a strange sense of calm. His eyes were starting to close and he saw his pal Lofty walking down the street with a dark-looking girl on his arm. Lofty smiled at him and was gone. In his confused mind he saw the large ocean-going ship coming up river. 'Look, son! Can yer see it, Jimmy? 'Ang on, I'll lift yer on me shoulders. There you are, see it now?'

Chapter Twelve

The second week of July remained warm and sunny, but now the street drains began to smell and the pavements were hot and dusty. The council water cart plied in and out of the backstreets laying the dust and swilling the drains while children jumped in and out of twirling skipping ropes and chased marbles along the gutters. In Dawson Street, old Charlie Perkins sat watching the daily spectacle. Charlie's leathery features were composed and serene; from time to time his eyes drooped and his head nodded. The children of the street left him alone and Charlie gave them little thought. When little ones chased a bouncing ball or a skidding marble they passed him as they would the lamppost, for Charlie was inscrutable.

In the next street Danny started his job as street bookie. His pitch was in an ever-open doorway at number 18 Clink Lane. The little turning looked very much the same as Dawson Street, with two rows of terraced houses and a railway arch at one end, but unlike Danny's road there were a couple of tiny shops wedged between the tumbledown houses. In Sadie Frost's window flies buzzed around sticky toffee apples and Liquorice Allsorts and crawled over boxes of wine gums and sherbet dips. A little way along on the other side of the turning was a boot mender, where Sammy Hopgood sat for most of the day with a line of brads clenched between his teeth as he concentrated on shaping and nailing new leather onto wornout footwear. The tap-tap of Sammy's heavy snobbing hammer continued constantly throughout the day. A few doors along from Sammy's was Mrs Coombes's house. Her brood was large and fatherless – Reg Coombes had met with a fatal accident at the tram depot when his youngest was only a few months old, and his wife Ginny had been left to bring up their seven children. Ginny's door was always open – there were so many comings and goings at number 18 that she found it easier that way. Tony Allen was quick to take advantage of the fact, and it suited him to have a bolthole for his bookie when the police dashed into the turning for a pinch. The arrangements suited Ginny as the payment she received for her co-operation paid her rent and bought a few bits and pieces for her children.

The week had started well for Danny. Most of the street folk knew him, and his helper Tubby Smith was able to clue him up about a few awkward punters. On Wednesday Danny was left on his own, but on Thursday Tony Allen popped into the turning with a worried look on his face. 'They've got a new Chief Inspector down at Riverside nick. I've just 'ad Fat Stan come in ter see me, 'e reckons the Chief's wavin' the big stick. They've got some raids set up fer termorrer. The dice players are in fer it an' so are we.'

Danny winced. 'Bloody 'ell, they ain't given us much time ter get used ter the job, 'ave they?'

Tony Allen nodded. 'Don't worry, Johnny Ross is gonna 'ave a word wiv Bonky Williams. 'E might do the honours fer us. You know this Bonky, don't yer? Is 'e reliable?'

Danny thought about it. Bonky was okay, but things always seemed to go strangely haywire when he was involved. He could be a walking disaster. Suppressing his fears Danny nodded. 'Bonky's a good lad, 'e'll know what ter do.'

That evening a subdued family sat down to their tea at

number 26 Dawson Street. Lucy had come in with the news that Ben had been summoned to a medical and Connie was upset too – the news broadcasts reported heavy sea battles in which there had been many losses. She picked at her meal and then left the table hurriedly. Later, Danny listened at her door and heard her crying. He tapped gently and walked in. Connie's face was wet and puffy, and her eyes were red. Danny sat on the edge of her bed and picked at the counterpane.

'Don't yer worry, Con,' he said quietly, 'Jimmy's all right. 'E'll be 'ome soon, you see if 'e's not.'

Connie dabbed at her eyes. 'I 'ad an 'orrible dream the uvver night. I dreamt Jimmy was callin' me. I saw 'im plain as day, but I couldn't move. 'E was in the sea an' 'e 'eld out 'is 'and. I tried ter reach 'im, but it was no good. It was really 'orrible, Danny.'

Danny put his arm around her shoulders and she buried her head in his chest. He could feel her sobbing gently as he stroked her fair hair.

''E'll be all right. In any case, you shouldn't take notice o' dreams. 'Ere, I've got somefink ter make yer laugh. The police are gonna do a pinch termorrer, and who d'yer fink's gonna get nicked?'

There was concern in Connie's eyes as she looked up at him. 'Not you?'

Danny laughed aloud. 'Not me. They've set Bonky up fer the pinch. 'E'll get six months 'ard labour if 'e takes 'is eye out in front o' the magistrate.'

Connie laughed, and for a moment her face relaxed, but then she went quiet again. After a while she looked up. 'Danny,' she said, 'who was that letter from, or is it a closely guarded secret?'

Danny leaned against the bedrail. 'It's no secret from you. I met a nurse in the 'ospital at Dover. 'Er name's Alison an' I'm seein' 'er on Sunday. She's comin' on leave. But don't tell the others – I don't want 'em ragging me!'

Connie grinned. 'What's she like? Is she pretty?'

Her brother pursed his lips. 'She's fat and cuddly, with bright ginger 'air. I've never took a fat girl out, it'll make a nice change.'

Connie threw her pillow at him and Danny caught it. 'No, she's pretty – like you,' he said, tossing the pillow back at her.

Bonky Williams was feeling important. He paced up and down Clink Lane with a smirk on his face and his hands clasped behind his back. He had had a 'Trotsky' haircut and a shave, and he had put on his best coat, even though the morning was warm.

Danny had just finished paying out a punter when Bonky strolled by. He called out sharply, 'Don't go wanderin' too far, you're s'posed ter be on 'and.'

Bonky grinned and scratched his cropped head. 'Don't worry, I know what ter do.' He had been given two one pound notes to pay the fine, and two more for his trouble, and a few fake betting slips to put in his pocket as evidence.

In Riverside Police Station Detective Constable Stockbridge – Fat Stan – was feeling irritable. On the rare occasions he had to arrest the bookies his income had suffered. He was on the take, but he was proud of his integrity, and it was unthinkable for him to go around nicking the bookies and still hold his hand out. It wasn't right, he rued. Why did that bloody inspector have to go and get caught peeping through the dormitory windows at the hostel for young women? Bloody old pervert. Now there was a new chief at the station, and he had turned out a right bleeder.

Fat Stan mumbled angrily to himself as he raised his considerable bulk from the canteen chair. 'Better get goin'. Musn't ferget me ole Rennies.'

At eleven-thirty a police car pulled up at the end of Clink Lane and Fat Stan got out. At the other end of the turning a police constable stood in a concealed position under the railway arch. Danny had spotted the car draw up and he shouted out to Bonky. ''Old tight! 'Ere they are!'

Bonky Williams was ready. He was determined to make the pinch look genuine. As Danny slipped into Ginny Coombes's passageway and slammed the front door, Bonky did a quick shuffle. Fat Stan came waddling down the street and already he was puffing. Bonky took off in the direction of the arch, with Fat Stan in hot pursuit.

'Stand still yer soppy git,' the fat policeman gasped. ''Ow am I s'posed ter catch yer?'

Bonky looked over his shoulder and grinned evilly as he trotted on.

PC Entwhistle was observing. He had been told to stay put under the arch and just observe. No one had told him that a dangerous-looking character would be fleeing from the strong arm of the law, and in his direction. PC Entwhistle braced himself. It would be a feather in his cap if he was able to apprehend a dangerous criminal. Fat Stan was a few yards behind Bonky and puffing like a concertina. His face was scarlet, and he was concentrating on what he would do once he got the idiot to the station. PC Entwhistle suddenly jumped out in front of Bonky, but he ducked neatly under his outstretched arm and carried on running through the arch. But Fat Stan could not stop in time and he crashed into the startled constable. They fell in a tangle of arms and legs.

'Get yer big feet orf me chest, yer stupid oaf,' Fat Stan gasped out. 'Yer've let 'im get away. The chief'll 'ave me guts fer garters.'

'Sorry, sir,' PC Entwhistle blurted out, attempting to get Fat Stan up from the ground.

'Don't worry about me! Get after 'im fer Gawd's sake!' Fat Stan screamed.

The crestfallen constable ran through the arch and looked

both ways. Bonky had disappeared. As he stood nibbling at his chinstrap PC Entwhistle felt a tap on his back.

'Excuse me officer.'

He turned around and saw a little old lady standing there looking very flustered.

'What is it, madam?'

The old lady took out a lace handkerchief and dabbed at her eyes. 'It's me Bertie, I'm afraid 'e's gorn.'

'Gorn, madam? You mean 'e's dead?'

'Oh, I do 'ope not,' replied the diminutive old lady, dabbing at her eyes again.

Fat Stan had now reached the constable and had just opened his mouth to bark out some choice profanities when he saw the old lady standing there. He slapped his hand to his forehead in frustration. 'Christ!' he muttered, tramping off past them along the road.

'I'm afraid it was my fault,' the old lady went on. 'You see Bertie was naughty. I didn't give 'im any supper last night. 'E smashed me best vase, you see.'

PC Entwhistle took out his notepad. Things were going wrong for him today, he decided. Maybe if he could solve the mystery of Bertie it would redeem him in the eyes of his superiors.

'Please 'elp me find 'im, Officer. I'm frightened 'e'll kill 'imself,' the old lady sobbed.

'Don't worry, madam, we'll see what we can do,' the constable said, sucking on his pencil stub. 'I'll need a few particulars. Now then, full name, age, and description.'

The old lady sighed. 'Bertie Smith. 'E's about two, an' 'e's blue and yeller.'

PC Entwhistle bit through his pencil. 'Blue an' yeller?' he echoed incredulously.

'Well, sort of. 'E sings luv'ly, 'cept last night when I scolded 'im. What 'appened was, I let 'im out of the cage an' 'e flew inter me best vase, an' it smashed. "There will be no need fer you ternight", I said and Bertie knew I meant it.'

'Just a minute, lady,' the constable said, puckering his forehead. 'You're talkin' about a bird?'

'Of course. Bertie's my little budgie. I left the scullery door open an' Bertie jus' flew away. I 'ope those nasty cats 'aven't got 'im.'

PC Entwhistle put his notepad back into his breast pocket. 'I'll keep me eye open, madam,' he said with a frown. 'What's your address?'

'A hundred an' eleven Bermon'sey Lane. I'm on the top floor. You'll 'ave ter give two knocks, an' if 'er downstairs answers yer'll 'ave ter shout. She's very deaf yer know.'

'All right, madam, leave it ter me.'

'You'd better write it down, Officer, you might ferget.'

'I won't ferget, madam. One blue an' yeller budgie, answers ter the name of Bertie Smith. Okay?'

Satisfied that she had done everything possible to secure Bertie's return, the old lady toddled off. PC Entwhistle blew out his cheeks. He was only half-way through his shift, he had already allowed a criminal to escape, and now he was saddled with a missing budgie report. A policeman's lot is not always a happy one, he thought grimly.

Fat Stan was fuming. He stood against a wall while he recovered his breath and cursed the stupid idiot he had been chasing, and he cursed the constable who had caused him to lose his pinch. When he felt less exhausted Fat Stan walked slowly back to Clink Lane railway arch. The constable was still waiting there, hands behind his back. Stan gave him a blinding look. Bloody war, he thought to himself, they're taking anyone on the Force these days.

'No luck, sir?' Constable Entwhistle asked.

'Does it look like it?' Stan sneered.

At that moment Bonky decided it was time to give himself

up to justice. He had realised there was a slip-up in the proceedings when he trotted out of the arch. His pursuer was not behind him. Puzzled, Bonky had popped into the little tobacconists on the corner of Bermondsey Lane for a packet of Woodbines. He knew the shopkeeper, and they began to chat away. Now, as he stepped from the shop and saw the two policemen standing by the arch, Bonky could see by the expressions on their faces that all was not well. He ambled up to them and took the betting slips from his pocket. ''Ere, you'd better 'ave these,' he said, looking sheepishly at Fat Stan.

PC Entwhistle reached for his truncheon, just in case Bonky should cut up rough.

'All right, all right, I'll deal wiv this,' the fat detective growled, taking a handful of Bonky's best coat in his grasp. 'C'mon you, jus' wait till I get you down the nick.'

As quick as a flash Bonky put his hand up to his face and called out, 'Mind me eye.'

As Fat Stan steered him along Clink Lane Bonky brought his bunched fist down from his face and slowly unclenched it. A glass eye stared up at Fat Stan.

The detective gagged. 'Put that bleedin' eye in yer pocket,' he shouted, his face white. 'An' don't give me any more trouble. You're already on a good 'idin' when I get yer down the station.'

Bonky walked on passively beside the puffing detective. The police car had gone and Fat Stan cursed. 'That's anuvver one I owe yer, makin' me walk all the way ter Dock'ead.'

Bonky was beginning to feel depressed. Two pounds had seemed a good bargain when Johnny Ross put the deal to him. Getting a good hiding wasn't in the deal. 'Jus' wait till I see that cripple bastard,' Bonky mumbled.

'What's that?' Fat Stan spat out.

'Nuffink, jus' finkin'.'

'Well keep yer poxy thoughts ter yerself.'

Behind lace curtains at number 18 Danny sat with Ginny Coombes. They stared out into the street for a time before Danny spoke. 'I can't understand it. Fat Stan should've got 'old of Bonky an' brought 'im back by now.'

'Maybe they've gone round Dawson Street,' Ginny suggested.

'They wouldn't do that, unless Bonky's playin' a funny game. Yer never know wiv 'im. I don't know why Johnny lined 'im up. 'E should 'ave known. Jus' wait till the guv'nor finds out, 'e'll skin Johnny alive.'

Ginny shook her head. 'That Bonky's as nutty as a fruit cake.'

Danny looked up to the top of the street just in time to see the police car drive away. 'That's done it,' he groaned.

'What's that?' Ginny asked.

'The police car's pissed off.'

Ginny looked through the curtains. ''Ere they come. The fat git's got Bonky by the scruff of 'is neck. 'E must 'ave upset 'im.'

Danny peered through the curtains. 'Blimey! Look at that tec's face. Bonky's in fer a rough time at the nick. 'E can be right evil when 'e's put out. I remember Tony Arpino tellin' me about one of 'is Italian mates. That fat bastard gave 'im a right goin' over down the station.'

'There's nuffink we can do,' Ginny said.

Danny thought for a few seconds. Suddenly he clicked his fingers. 'I've got it!' he shouted. 'Quick! Got any pills?'

'Pills? What pills?'

'Any sort,' Danny said impatiently as Bonky and his captor drew level with the window.

'I've only got these, they're cascara.'

Danny grabbed the three little white pills from Ginny's hand and ran out into the street. Bonky and the detective were almost at the corner shop when he reached them. 'Excuse me, mate,

I've bin lookin' everywhere fer 'im,' Danny said, pointing to his pal.

Fat Stan gave Danny a wicked look. 'Yer can't talk to 'im, 'e's nicked.'

'I've got 'is pills 'ere, 'is landlady told me ter give 'em to 'im,' Danny said. ''E went out wivout 'em. They're fer 'is 'eart. 'E as ter take these every day, or 'e's likely ter go off jus' like that.'

Fat Stan looked at Danny suspiciously. ''Is 'eart didn't stop 'im runnin' away from me. The bastard nearly gave *me* an 'eart attack tryin' ter catch 'im.'

Danny shook his head sadly. ''E'll never learn, Officer. One o' these days 'e's gonna do it all wrong.'

Bonky was listening to the conversation with a pained look on his face. He wondered whether or not to have a heart attack there and then. He decided against it when the fat detective released his coat collar and took his wrist instead.

The rest of the journey to Riverside Police Station was slightly more civilised. Fat Stan did not want any complications at this point. Bonky for his part walked on quietly. After a while he thought he ought to show some distress.

'Can we slow down a bit, sir?' he asked with a grimace. 'I'm gettin' a pain in me chest.'

Fat Stan slowed down and gritted his teeth in anger. 'Yer givin' me a pain,' he said.

They had reached the junction with Tower Bridge Road and Bonky spotted the drinking fountain. 'All right if I take me pills, sir?' he asked.

'Go on then, I'm not stoppin' yer, am I?' snarled the detective.

'I gotta take 'em wiv water, sir. They stick in me froat uvverwise.'

Fat Stan released his grip on Bonky's sleeve. 'Go on then, an' be quick about it.'

At last they reached the police station. Bonky's captor was in an ugly mood, now that his bit of sport was stymied by his prisoner's condition. He had realised the danger of slapping a heart case around in the cell, and he decided that the sooner he got rid of the idiot the better. Bonky co-operated as the formalities were taken care of, and he was bailed to appear the following day on a charge of street gaming.

As he walked home Bonky felt relieved, but by the time he reached his home in Dawson Street the relief had turned to pain. After frequent excursions to the toilet Binky was cursing Danny viciously.

'Couldn't 'e 'ave given me some Dolly Mixtures instead?' he groaned aloud. 'That fat pig wouldn't 'ave known the difference.'

Chapter Thirteen

Waterloo Station was a sea of colour as uniformed figures in Air Force and Royal Navy blues mingled with khaki. Every now and then there was a poignant glimpse of innocent bright summer dresses and waving summer bonnets as the military mingled with the civilian population, hurrying to and fro or waiting around on the noisy concourse. Announcements came over the tannoy scratchy-voiced and flat, and only when a train was re-routed to another platform did any passion appear in the tone. Among the milling passengers hurrying from the platforms or rushing to their trains, there were many who were just waiting, lolling around on hard benches, on bulging suit-cases and on piles of kitbags and military packs. The big clock that hung from the arching girders clicked away the minutes of Sunday morning above the crowds. Harassed parents watched the clock as though it might suddenly spin, their stern glances defying their children to drop any ice cream down their best clothes. Their eyes darted from their tickets to the clock that hung high above them, and then to the platform number, almost in disbelief that everything was as it should be. Surely the suitcase clasp would snap and scatter clothes everywhere? Or little Mary would be sick, and young Billy would wander off just when the train arrived? But no, young Billy and little Mary were still there, looking perfectly happy. The noise of the protesting steam engines made them laugh and cover their ears, the soldiers and their guns were fascinating and soon they would be sitting in a big train watching the world whiz by.

One young man watched the clock and eyed the soldiers with interest. There were five minutes to go before Alison's train arrived at the station, and Danny had spent the last fifteen minutes pacing up and down, watching as groups of servicemen mustered by the platforms on their way to strengthen the garrisons along the South Coast. He felt some regret at not being a part of what was going on, and at the same time he was very relieved. He had been shot at, shelled and dumped in the sea, and he considered himself to have been very fortunate. If that shell fragment had been a little to one side he would have perished. He caught sight of a soldier with a Middlesex shoulder flash and he wondered how Oggy Murphy was. It seemed strange that he had only known the man for a very short time and had hardly spoken more than a few words to him, and yet he felt so close to him. They would probably never meet again but Danny knew he would often think of him and he would always wish him well, for he owed his life to that ugly gypsy.

Slowly the minute hand crept around to one-fifteen, and Danny saw the billowing white smoke way down the line. The announcer's voice crackled as he called out: 'The one-seventeen from Dover is now approaching platform three.' Danny walked slowly towards the ticket barrier and watched as the train came to a stop. Doors flew open and the platform was filled with hustling travellers as they struggled with luggage and kitbags. It was some time before he saw Alison. She was coming from the far end of the train and Danny could see her short dark hair bobbing around her ears as she walked briskly to the barrier. Danny had time to study her before she spotted him. She looked slightly slimmer than he remembered and she held her head high. The cotton half-coat which she was wearing over her summer dress was unbuttoned. Her feet look tiny in those high heels, he thought. She was holding a shoulder bag with one hand and in the other she was carrying a small suitcase. Her complexion was rosy and Danny was instantly captivated by her expression. She looked prettier than he remembered and he felt his heart start to beat faster.

Alison saw him and her face broke into a warm smile. There was a delay at the barrier before she joined him and put down her suitcase. Danny held her arm as he kissed her softly on the cheek and she replied by squeezing his hand.

'How are you, Danny? You look very well.'

Danny flushed slightly as he grinned. 'I'm fine. No pain, no aches. It's nice ter see yer again. I've bin finkin' about yer.'

Alison displayed her even white teeth. 'I bet you've not given me a thought, with all your old girlfriends clamouring round their hero.'

Danny pulled a face and looked into her large dark eyes. 'They've not come knockin'. Still, I might 'ave bin out at the time.'

They laughed and Danny picked up her suitcase. 'Would yer like a cuppa or a drink? They're open till two.'

Alison smiled. 'A drink would be nice.'

They walked quickly from the station and down the steps that led into Waterloo Road. They passed the Union Jack Club and took a side turning. Danny steered Alison through the door of The Bell and looked for a place to sit. He put her suitcase down and pulled out a chair from under an empty table. 'What d'yer like?'

'I'd like a shandy please.'

Danny soon returned with the drinks and they sat facing each other. Alison had a sip of her shandy and then took out a powder compact from her handbag. 'I must look a proper mess,' she said, opening it and peering into the mirror.

'You look fine,' Danny replied, aware that his voice sounded strange.

For some time they talked. Danny told her of his new job and made her laugh when he told her about Bonky Williams's arrest. Alison told him that the pressure at the hospital had eased since Dunkirk, but that there were still some nasty cases to deal with due to accidents during training. Danny felt relaxed with her and asked her several questions about herself, but Alison quickly switched the conversation around to him. She liked the way he smiled self-consciously and the way his fair hair seemed to curl above his ears. She liked his warm manner and his blue eyes which seemed to bore into her at times. She knew that she would have to be careful. It would be quite easy to fall for someone like Danny, but it was too soon. She wanted breathing space and a friendship, not another romance now.

Danny looked into her eyes and liked what he saw. She was so different from Kathy. Mystery shone in the depths of her eyes. She was alluring yet seemed somehow unobtainable. She both confused and attracted him, drawing him close yet keeping him distant. He felt no such conflict with Kathy. Their years together had built up between them an easy assurance, and implicit knowledge. It was a feeling of familiarity. But with Alison there was something that churned his insides, a challenge to be met. And there was a sense of urgency and it worried him. He would have to be careful, his impatience might be seen as a sign of immaturity, and Danny was anxious not to create a wrong impression. He realised then that he wanted her and he hoped she felt the same. He looked at her sweet face and imagined he was loving her. He could picture those dark eyes mirroring her sensations as he held her to him. He wondered what locked-up passions would be released if he were able to reach her intimately and love her completely. Alison had flushed at his intense look, and turned her face away. Danny suddenly smiled and shook his head. 'I'm sorry, I was staring. You look a sight fer sore eyes.'

Alison laughed. 'I bet you say that to all the girls.'

They had been talking over empty glasses for some time without realising. When Danny noticed he reached for them but Alison stopped him. 'I must get going, Danny, I promised my mum I'd look in on her old friends in London. They've got a dairy in Southwark Street. They said they'd put me up if I wanted to.'

Danny grinned. 'That's not far from where I live.'

'I know,' Alison replied.

Danny reached across the table and put his hand on hers. 'Look, can I see yer ternight?' he asked. 'We could go fer a stroll, or a ride up West.'

'I'd like that, but I really must make a move now or they'll be worried. They know what train I came up on. I wrote and told them.'

Outside the day was bright and warm. Alison took Danny's arm as they walked down Waterloo Road. 'D'yer wanna get a bus?' he asked.

'Let's walk, it's a lovely day,' Alison said, and then added with concern, 'that's if you're feeling up to it?'

Danny threw out his chest. 'I'm as fit as a fiddle. It's not a long walk anyway. I know the back doubles.'

They walked on and turned into the Cut. The wide market street was almost empty today and the shops were shuttered. A jellied eel stall stood outside a pub, and further along a circle of Salvationists were playing 'Onward Christian Soldiers'. A few children and some old men from the lodging house in Blackfriars stood listening to the music as Danny and Alison walked past, and one of the Salvationists held out a copy of the *War Cry*. Danny dropped a sixpence in the collection box and politely refused the magazine. 'If I take that 'ome me dad'll start ter worry. We've got one

religious member of our family wivout me startin' ter go all
'oly.'

Alison was curious, and so Danny explained all about Lucy
and Ben. In return Alison told him about her upbringing in
Wales. She told him of the huge family bible, and how all the
births and deaths were recorded inside the cover. She said that
there were pubs which would still not allow women inside and
remained closed on the Sabbath.

'Sounds a mis'rable place on Sundays if yer ask me,' Danny
said, pulling a face. 'What d'yer do fer amusement?'

'Oh, we get by. There's a lot of big families in Wales,' Alison
chuckled. 'Then there's the choirs. Welsh people love to sing,
but you know that already.'

Danny nodded. 'Me mum loves ter listen to 'em on the
wireless.'

Alison's face took on a look of sadness as she spoke of her
dead father. 'My dad was in a choir. He went to a local Baptist
mission every Sunday evening. I remember when I was little
Dad always sang as he cleaned his boots in the backyard on
Sunday mornings. He said it was good practice. He had a
beautiful voice. It seems such a long time ago now, but I can
still remember him clearly.'

They had reached Southwark Street and Alison pointed to
the shopfront a little way ahead. 'There it is, Morgan's Dairies.'

They walked across the street and Danny put the case down
by the door. 'When shall I call round? Will seven be okay?'

'Can you make it eight? I must spend a bit of time with
them,' she said.

Danny grinned and raised two fingers to his forehead.
'Okay, ma'am. See yer then.'

The smell of roast lamb and baked potatoes drifted up the
passage as Danny let himself in. In the front parlour he saw
the prone forms of his father and Joe Copeland sprawled out in

the easy chairs with Sunday papers lying opened on their laps. Both had their mouths gaping and Frank was snoring. Danny walked out into the scullery and found his mother and Maggie washing up the dinner plates. Alice gave her son a long hard look. 'And where might you 'ave bin? I've 'ad yet dinner in the oven fer ages.'

Danny gave his mother a peck on the cheek. 'Sorry, Ma. I met somebody.'

'I guessed as much. You know I put the dinner up as soon as yer dad gets in from The Globe. 'Im an' Joe 'ave 'ad theirs an' fergot about it.'

Danny glanced at Maggie and pulled a face. 'I was waitin' fer a train at Waterloo. I was meetin' this nurse an' I walked her . . .'

Alice looked surprised. 'A nurse yer say? Was that someone yer met when yer was wounded?'

''S'right, Ma. She's a Welsh girl an' she's stayin' in London till termorrer night, then she's off ter Cardiff. I'm gonna show 'er aroun' town ternight.'

Maggie picked up a pile of plates and bent down to put them in the cupboard of the dresser. 'Are yer gonna bring 'er 'ome, Danny?' she said, winking at her mother.

'I dunno. I might do. Yer'll 'ave ter wait an' see, won't yer?' Danny replied offhandedly.

Maggie grimaced. 'Sorry fer breavin'.'

Alice handed her daughter the tea tray. ''Ere, take this in the front room an' wake them two piss artists up. Wiv them two sprawled out there's no room fer anybody else in there. 'Ere you are, son. Take yer dinner in, an' don't spill the gravy. When yer finished yer can tell me all about yer nurse.'

Joe and Frank were rousing when Danny walked into the parlour. Maggie gave her husband a cold stare and started to pour the tea. Frank sat up and rubbed his hand over his face. 'Ello, son. I reckoned yer might 'ave come up The Globe. We 'ad a good session, didn't we, Joe?'

Maggie handed her father a cup of tea. ''E 'ad ter meet somebody, didn't yer, Danny?'

The young man buried his head over the plate and sawed away at the meat, but Maggie's remark was lost on the drowsy pair anyway. Frank yawned and stirred his tea with deliberation. 'I was talkin' ter Eddie Kirkland. 'E said Biff Bowden's dog's runnin' at Catford next. 'E said ter ask yer if yer got any more o' them pills. 'E said they made Bonky Williams run like nobody's business. What's that all about then? Eddie wouldn't tell me, 'e said ter ask you.'

Danny told them the full story and the two older men burst into laughter. Alice had come into the room just in time to hear Maggie voice her disgust. 'I reckon yer done a silly fing. Fancy givin' 'im cascara. Yer could 'ave made poor ole Bonky really ill.'

Danny cut a potato in half and held one piece on the end of his fork, ''Ow the 'ell was I ter know the stupid idiot would take 'em. 'E could 'ave made out.'

'What, wiv the copper breavin' down 'is neck? Strikes me you men are all the same. You ain't got no savvy.'

Joe Copeland laughed aloud. 'C'mon, Maggie, what about the time you an' Lil Franklin put gin in your forelady's orangeade at the party?'

Maggie sniffed. 'That was different, we all detested 'er. Bonky is s'posed ter be 'is pal,' she said, jerking her thumb in Danny's direction.

'Well 'e is, sort of,' Danny said, chewing on the potato. 'Anyway, what's a dose o' the runs between friends. I mean, it could 'ave bin worse. That fat git of a tec looked like 'e was gonna give poor ole Bonky a right goin' over when 'e got 'im ter the nick. If it wasn't fer me Bonky could well be walkin' around wiv a couple o' cracked ribs – at least.'

Maggie was beginning to see the funny side of it but she kept a straight face and walked back out into the scullery.

Danny looked around. 'Where's the kids?'

Alice was folding the tablecloth. 'Lucy an' Ben 'ave took 'em up Black'eath. Ben's made 'em a kite,' she said, brushing her hand over the table.

'Connie wiv 'em, Ma?' Danny asked as he leaned back in his chair and rubbed his stomach contentedly.

Alice Sutton became serious. 'No, she's gone round ter see Jimmy Ellis's mum. Somebody told 'er they 'eard ole Lord 'Aw-'Aw on the wireless last night. 'E was goin' on about our ships gettin' sunk, an' 'e give out some ships' names. People should 'ave more sense. I dunno what they mus' be finkin', worryin' the poor little cow like that.'

'Jimmy's ship wasn't mentioned, was it, Ma?' Danny asked.

'No, but she's all worried. She's gone round ter see if 'is mum's 'eard from 'im.'

Frank Sutton was nodding off to sleep again and Joe was trying to fold the paper without much success. Danny got up and stretched. 'I'm gonna go up an' 'ave a read of the papers, Ma. When I get married can I still come round fer me Sunday dinner? That meal was 'andsome.'

Alice smiled. ''Fore yer go upstairs, I wanna 'ave a word wiv yer. In the scullery.'

Danny followed his mother out into the tiny backroom. Alice folded her arms and looked at him. 'What's she like?'

'What's who like?' Danny smiled.

'You know who I'm talkin' about. The nurse. What's she like?'

'She's pretty, Ma. She was the nurse who looked after me at Dover 'ospital.'

'Why don't yer bring the girl 'ome ter meet me an' yer dad? We could fank 'er fer lookin' after yer, couldn't we?'

'I dunno about this visit, she ain't got much time, but I'll try an arrange it fer next time she comes, okay?'

Alice Sutton looked into the faded mirror that was hung on

the wall by the yard door. She pressed and patted her hair and her eyes caught Danny's in the reflection. 'You know you ought ter fink about settlin' down wiv a nice girl, Danny. Me an' yer farver don't like the idea of you workin' fer that bookie. You ought ter see about gettin' yerself a decent job. That Tony Allen's got a bad name, 'e gets in wiv a nasty crowd. I 'eard yer farver an' Joe talkin' last night. The police 'ave got their eye on 'im, they fink 'e's in on the black market game.'

Danny puffed. 'Look, Ma, it's only people talkin'. If the law knew or suspected anyfing they wouldn't broadcast it, would they? Some people are jealous of what 'e's got. 'E ain't a bad bloke. 'E give me a job, didn't 'e?'

'I ain't sayin' 'e's a bad bloke, Danny, but that Jack Mason is a rotter. I've 'eard a lot about 'im. Some of them uvver blokes 'e goes wiv ain't very nice either. Jus' you be careful, that's all I'm sayin'. We don't want ter come visitin' yer in prison. The 'ospital was enough.'

Danny put his arm around his mother's narrow shoulders. 'I'll be very careful, Ma, I know what I'm doin',' he promised.

Up in his bedroom Danny kicked off his shoes and sprawled out on his bed. The room was cool and quiet. He lay with his hands clasped behind his head and stared at a crack in the ceiling, thinking about Alison, going over their meeting in his mind. He let his eyes follow the line in the ceiling and his thoughts drifted. He found himself comparing her with Kathy. They were both pretty and both nice to be with, but they were so different. With Kathy it was easy to read her thoughts, and he thought of that Saturday night. Then he remembered the night at the dog track when she had told him in no uncertain terms that they must not see each other again, yet he was sure she wanted him to. He was sure too that Kathy was desperately unhappy with Jack Mason. She had realised her mistake but she was stubborn and was determined to stay with him, especially now with a baby on its way. Alison on the other hand was mysterious, she had a way of switching the conversation away from herself and he wanted to know more about her.

He followed the line in the ceiling and noticed for the first time that it was starting down the wall. The gaff's falling apart, he thought to himself as he twisted onto his side and bunched up the pillow. Through the bedroom window he could see chimney stacks and cracked chimney pots standing out stark against the sky. The view was too familiar and he rolled over again. Maybe he was being too impatient. No doubt Alison would relax a little more and talk about herself in her own good time. Perhaps he was comparing her too much with the girls he had known before – after the first five minutes most of them had given him a potted life history. Maybe Welsh girls were different. Alison had told him something of her life in the Valleys and about her father, but there seemed to be a curtain which she pulled down when he prompted her to talk about herself, and about her life at the hospital where she was working, and her social life. Maybe he was expecting too much of her, he thought. There would be time enough tonight to talk more.

He would take Alison up West, maybe they would stop off at The Globe on the way back and he could show her off to his pals. The only problem with that idea, he suddenly realised, was Bonky Williams. Bonky was still a little offhand with him over the cascara episode and it would be just like him to get up to one of his tricks. It might be a better idea to pop in at The Horseshoe in Bermondsey Lane. He could show Alison off to Tony Arpino, who was always to be found drinking there.

Danny drifted off to sleep, while down in the tiny parlour below things were rather subdued. Frank and his drinking partner Joe were also sleeping off the effects of their Sunday drinking session. Their snores had driven Alice to her friend Annie Barnes's house while Maggie sat alone in the scullery. The *News of the World* lay open at her elbow as she fretted over her two children. Maggie had just read that Churchill was going on the air that night to deliver an important speech. She was convinced that she would be doing the right thing by the children in getting them out of London, but she and Joe had had words about it the previous evening. He thought she was being hysterical and he didn't seem to realise that it wouldn't be long before the whole war blew up around them. All the papers said that British cities could expect severe air attacks and there would almost certainly be heavy casualties. What if anything happened to her children? Joe had got angry with her and stormed off to the pub saying that if the kids were sent away from London they could get ill treated. What then? Maggie sighed and picked up the paper again. She started to read an article about a bishop and a chorus girl. It all seemed very familiar to her and she turned the page. Joe's snoring carried out to the scullery and Maggie threw down the *News of the World* and walked out into the backyard.

Chapter Fourteen

On the stroke of eight Alison left the dairy and saw the figure of Danny Sutton sauntering along in her direction, looking very smart in a grey suit. Danny saw her walking towards him and he quickened his step. He kissed her on the cheek as they met and he could smell her freshness. Alison's hair shone and her face looked rosy. She was wearing a printed dress that hugged her slim figure and accentuated her small rounded breasts. She carried a cardigan over her arm and a small handbag was slung over her shoulder. Danny smiled at her as they started towards London Bridge Station. 'You look very nice,' he remarked.

Alison was aware of his strong clasp and she felt strangely excited. 'You look rather smart,' she said softly as they strolled on, shoulders touching.

The electric train rumbled over the railway bridge that spanned the Thames and slid into Charing Cross Station. Danny and Alison alighted and walked out into the Strand. The evening was warm and pleasant, and a slight breeze was blowing. They skirted pigeon-infested Trafalgar Square and stood for a while hand-in-hand, gazing down on the fountains that spurted up from artesian wells, the couchant lions guarding the high column and the war-scarred admiral, Lord

Nelson. And other young couples were sitting around the fountains or strolling among the strutting birds, servicemen and women and nurses still in uniform mingling in a colourful throng. Children chased the pigeons and dipped toffee-smeared hands in the cold water, while souvenir sellers plied their tin badges and tiny Union Jacks. The base of the column was boarded up; and at the north end of the square the imposing National Gallery was ready for war, a wall of sandbags reaching high up the stone pillars. Scurrying clouds seemed to brush the head of the august admiral and a pink evening light softened the fronts of the stone buildings. Starlings chattered noisily in the trees and flew away in wheeling formations as a taxi-cab backfired in the Mall.

For a time the young couple merely stood and took in the scene without saying a word. Danny felt at home here. He remembered his childhood, when for a penny ticket on a number 36 tram he would set off to see the sights of London. He was proud of his knowledge of the capital, and when Alison asked him about their famous surroundings he was able to elaborate on some of the finer points.

'See those lions? They were designed by a bloke called Lan'seer. That column is 145 feet 'igh. See over there? That's St Martin's in the Fields. They 'ave lunchtime concerts there nearly every day.'

Alison leaned against his shoulder and watched his face as he talked. She noticed the occasional nervous twitch of his lip, and she liked the way he laughed aloud. Danny was beginning to intrigue her, and she wanted to savour the feeling. Her racing thoughts worried her and a spasm of excitement passed through her. 'Let's walk on, Danny,' she said, squeezing his hand.

'Okay, let's go this way. We can go ter Piccadilly Circus. I used ter do this walk when I was a kid,' he grinned.

In the Charing Cross Road they stopped to have a drink.

The pub was full of weekend visitors and all the seats were taken. When Danny finally managed to get served he steered Alison into a corner and they stood very close while they sipped their drinks. The pub was noisy and bustling. An elbow caught Danny in the back and he gave the customer a long hard look. Alison giggled, finally drawing a reluctant grin from her escort.

'Let's get out of here. I want to see this famous Piccadilly Circus you've been telling me about,' she said.

'Okay, but there ain't any Eros. The statue's bin took away fer safety.'

Alison slipped her arm in his as they strolled leisurely through Leicester Square. They sat on a bench for a while, idly watching passers-by, and then made their way into Piccadilly Circus where they climbed onto the memorial steps.

Danny pointed in the direction of Shaftesbury Avenue. 'I know a nice little café over there. Shall we get somefink to eat?'

Alison nodded and held his arm tightly as they dodged through the traffic and walked to a side street off the Avenue. Luigi's Café was quite full, but they found a table for two beneath the arch of the stairs, and after consulting the crudely worded menu they decided on a meal of egg, bacon and chips. Danny grinned slyly when he ordered two large teas and when they arrived Alison put her hand up to her mouth and giggled at the absurdity.

'They're big enough ter drown in, ain't they,' he laughed, grasping the huge mug in both hands.

When they had finished their meal they sat for a while, chatting happily together as customers came and went. Finally they left the side street café and walked out into the late evening air.

Danny slipped his arm around Alison's slim waist as they skirted the Piccadilly Circus and sauntered into Regent Street.

Danny could feel her body brushing his and her softness troubled him. He wanted to reach out and hold her, he wanted to wrap his arms around her and kiss her soft neck. He looked down at her and it seemed to him that she was gently mocking him. She had a guarded look that dared him to reach out for her and yet seemed to warn him off. There was a strangeness about her – she appeared to be worldly-wise, confident and discreet, but he wondered if it was panic in her dark eyes. Was there something in her past that made her wary of him, or was it just her mystique? He was determined to respond to the challenge. His thoughts tumbled over and over in his mind as they walked on silently. The curve of Regent Street spread out before them and Alison pulled on his arm suddenly. The strap of her shoe had come undone and as she stooped to fasten it she sighed, 'My feet are beginning to ache, Danny. Can we get a bus back?'

Danny pointed to a nearby bus stop. 'A 53 stops 'ere. It goes ter the Old Kent Road.'

After a ten minute wait Danny and Alison exchanged smiles at the welcome sight of an approaching 53 bus, and soon they were passing over Westminster Bridge. They sat close together on the back seat, looking out at the flowing River Thames. Danny sighed. 'That's a nice sight. I've swum in there many a time. We used ter dive in orf the barges near where I live. I tell yer, Alison, there was a time not so long ago when I didn't ever expect ter see Ole Farver Thames again.'

Alison was quiet for a while and then she looked at him closely. 'Tell me, Danny, does it still worry you, Dunkirk?'

Danny shook his head emphatically. 'I used to wake up some nights in a cold sweat, but I'm okay now. I still fink of the lads I left be'ind there though.'

Alison squeezed his arm. 'I'll never forget that night they brought you in to the hospital. I didn't think you were going to pull through. Do you still get any pain from the wounds?'

Danny grinned. 'I've told yer, I'm fit fer anyfing 'cept a cross-country run. I'm still a bit breafless at times, that's all.'

'What about your mates, Danny? Do you see any of them?'

'Yer mean the ones who made it back? I ain't bin roun' the drill 'all since Dunkirk.'

Something in his tone surprised Alison and she looked round to see that his face had become dark. Her questioning eyes encouraged him to continue. 'The drill 'all is only a few minutes from my 'ouse,' he went on, 'but I can't seem ter face goin' there. They'll 'ave records of who made it back but I jus' keep wonderin' about the lads. D'yer fink I'm bein' stupid?'

Alison laid her head on his shoulder. 'Of course I don't. It's only natural I suppose. Names on a scroll are so final, perhaps that's why you can't face it. Maybe you expect to see your mates in the street. What you have been through must have left some scars. Don't worry about it, one day when you're good and ready you'll go and find out for sure. In the meantime you've got to give your mind the opportunity to adjust to the terrible things you've been through. Give it time.'

Danny's face relaxed slightly and he pressed his shoulder against her as the bus headed for the Elephant and Castle.

Danny had attracted the attention of a small passenger on the seat in front. Enquiring eyes stared into his and dirty hands gripped the seat rail tightly. The tot's lank blond hair hung down to her shoulders and a button nose twitched. Danny winked at the child, but she ignored his gesture. He folded his arms and closed his eyes, then slowly he opened one eye then shut it quickly. Still the child did not respond. Alison watched as Danny tried to bring forth a smile. He made faces and rolled his eyes but the child just stared at him, her pale eyelids heavy with tiredness, and as the bus jerked to a halt the child rocked back in the seat and was scooped up by her mother who cuddled her and crooned into her ear. Blond hair cascaded over her face, and presently she fell asleep. Alison watched Danny smiling.

At the Bricklayers Arms the large woman and her daughter got off the bus in front of Danny and Alison. Her child slept on peacefully. Danny took Alison's arm as they crossed over into Tower Bridge Road and walked along the quiet thoroughfare. The night was closing in quickly, birds slumbered in the tall plane trees and stars twinkled down from a velvet expanse. They walked for a while until Alison broke the silence. 'I've really enjoyed this evening, Danny,' she said.

'It's bin 'an'some,' he replied. 'I was goin' ter see if yer'd like ter meet me mate Tony Arpino, but the pubs are shut by now. By the way, what time yer s'posed ter be in by?'

Alison shrugged her slim shoulders. 'I've got a key. The Morgans run a dairy, don't forget. I expect they'll be snoring by now.'

They walked through a maze of drab grey backstreets and alleyways as the moon rose over lop-sided chimney pots and blue-grey slated roofs, and at last they reached Southwark Street. They halted at the dairy where there was a dark recess beside the shop front and Danny could see the empty milk carts through the slatted gates. The shadows closed round them as they moved together and held each other closely. Danny could smell the fragrance of Alison's hair as he bent down and kissed her open mouth. Her breathing came faster as she responded to his embrace and her fingers stroked his fair hair while Danny's searching hands ran down her back. Alison rested her head on his shoulder and he kissed her ear, his mouth moving down onto her smooth, soft neck. But suddenly Alison tensed; she stepped back from his embrace and put both hands on his shoulders. 'You don't like wasting time, Danny. Let me catch my breath,' she said quickly.

'I've wanted to do that ever since I saw yer at the station.

You're really somefink, d'yer know that?' Danny said smiling.

'Go on, I bet you say that to all the girls,' Alison chided.

Danny's face became serious and she felt his grip tighten. She could not trust herself to relax with him now that the first barrier was down. Her body cried out for him but her mind was troubled. It must not be like the last time, she vowed. Her painful memories had been kindled by his kiss and his searching hands had stirred her stifled feelings. She needed time to find herself again, there could be no hurried love until she was absolutely sure of herself. She knew in her heart that it would be so easy to give herself to him there and then. She tingled at his touch, but she needed to be certain that there would be an understanding, she had to make him see somehow. It was important for them both and she had to tell him everything.

Danny gazed down at her and saw her eyes misting over. He pulled her gently to him and they remained quiet for a while, both content to let their early passions abate. Alison felt his arms relax their hold on her. 'I must get in. It's been a lovely time, but I'm feeling very tired, Danny. Do you mind?'

Danny moved back and his hand went up to adjust his shirt collar. 'What about termorrer? I mus' see yer again before yer catch your train 'ome.'

Alison looked into his pale blue eyes and saw the urgency there. 'Yes, I'd like that.'

Danny's face relaxed into a huge grin. 'Look, I'm takin' bets up until about one o'clock. We could 'ave all afternoon tergevver. What d'yer say?'

'That would be nice.'

'Okay, I'll come round fer yer at two o'clock.'

Their goodnight kiss was soft, and Alison watched him as he walked off into the darkness.

*

The figure standing in the dark doorway changed position to ease his aching foot and peered impatiently at his small silver pocket watch. It was half past midnight and the beat policeman had just appeared from Shad Thames. He turned left and walked slowly towards Dockhead with his hands clasped behind his back. Johnny Ross moved out of his hiding place and saw the tall figure of Con Baldwin coming towards him. The approaching figure jumped nervously as Johnny hissed at him. 'Over 'ere, Con. It's okay, the rozzer's gone.'

Con joined Johnny and they quickly crossed Tooley Street and walked into Shad Thames. The narrow cobbled lane was deathly quiet as they reached an arched doorway. Con took out a crowbar from beneath his coat and inserted it into the heavy brass padlock. Johnny held his breath. Had Ernie Baines done his job properly? If he had, the padlock would spring open under a little pressure. Con grunted with satisfaction as he removed the padlock and slipped the hasp. The heavy oak door creaked as it opened and they stepped inside.

''Urry up,' Con hissed, 'I'll give yer five minutes an' I'll knock on the gate. Fer Gawd's sake don't move till I give yer the signal.'

Johnny disappeared into the warehouse and Con stepped back into the lane and gingerly closed the warehouse door. He replaced the hasp and levered the doctored padlock back into place. Satisfied with his efforts he walked along Shad Thames and passed by the gate of the adjoining warehouse. He was ready to adopt a drunken pose should the policeman appear again, but he need not have worried – PC Harriman was hurrying on to the road works in Jamaica Road, where old Bill Jones the council night watchman was busy brewing up some fresh tea over his coke brazier.

Johnny climbed the dark stone staircase to the roof. At the top of the stairs he put his weight against the iron fire door and it clattered open. He was now standing on the flat roof of the warehouse and he swallowed hard as he shut the door behind him. Johnny was only too aware that there was no way back. The door could only be opened from the inside. Ernie Baines had gone over the plan with him until Johnny was convinced he could find his way around blindfolded. Above him was the wide darkness of the night sky, and the fire escape staircase loomed up ahead. Johnny ducked low as he limped down the iron steps that ran down the outside of the building into the yard below. Ernie Baines has come up trumps this time, he thought. The laden lorry was there, standing by the massive iron-plated gate. Johnny hobbled quickly to the yard office, took out a scarf from his coat and wrapped it around his hand. Looking over his shoulder as though he expected to be seen he punched out the small glass panel of glass nearest to the door lock. As he left the office holding the bunch of keys Johnny heard a soft tap on the wicket gate. He threw the keys under the gap below the gate and soon Con Baldwin was in the yard beside him. While Johnny sorted out the keys for the main gate Con jumped up into the lorry cab and checked that the ignition key was there. Johnny beckoned urgently to him and the two of them pulled the heavy gate open. There was one more task left to do before they drove away. Johnny went over to a sand bin opposite the warehouse and lifted the lid. Con started up the lorry, drove it over to the gateway and stopped, then Johnny limped across the lane carrying a coiled length of rope that was knotted every couple of feet. Clambering up onto the cab roof he looped the rope over the spiked tips of the gate then hurried down into the cab as Con drove off.

They drove the stolen lorry steadily along Dockhead. It was not unusual for lorries to use that route at night, traffic from all over the country began to arrive in the early hours ready to load and unload at the wharves and docks. Con and Johnny were confident that their cargo would be stowed safely before the theft was discovered. They could feel the gods of fortune smiling down on them as they reached their destination without being stopped. The warehouse theft went undetected until after Ernie Baines arrived for work and switched padlocks.

Before he went off duty PC Harriman found himself having to answer some awkward questions. He should have patrolled Shad Thames once more before he finished his rounds, but the place gave him the creeps and he had opted out of his responsibilities in favour of another mug of old Bill's tea. The Station Inspector called in Detective Constable Stanley Stockbridge after he had finished with Harriman. 'I'm going to lay it on the line, Stockbridge,' he said, 'I want you off your fat arse and on your way to Sullivan's Wharf at Shad Thames. The guv'nor there has reported that a lorry's gone missing from his yard. Apparently they got in using a rope, they lassoed the spikes and shinned over the gate. On your way, Stockbridge.'

Later, a phone call from Limehouse Police Station informed him that a lorry belonging to George Sullivan and Sons, Wharfingers, had been found abandoned in a lorry rank outside the West India Docks.

'It wasn't exactly abandoned,' the desk sergeant explained. 'One of our constables found a couple o' Chinese seamen asleep in the cab. They had adopted the vehicle. Their dabs were all over the cab.'

'Can't we nick 'em for theft?' Inspector Flint asked.

'No chance,' was the reply. 'We're charging the two of 'em for an affray in a gambling house in Pennyfields. They sliced another Chink's ear orf during an argument over a game of Mah Jong.'

Inspector Flint shook his head sadly and looked out of his office window. Down below he could see the activity in the local timber yard. Two men were leisurely stacking pine planks while another worker lolled against a covered pile, busily engrossed in rolling a cigarette. Inspector Flint returned to his desk and picked up a pile of papers. That stupid fat Detective

Constable had better come up with something pretty quick, or it's back on the beat for him, he vowed. Inspector Flint was determined to 'ginger up' the station, as he put it. Already he had made some drastic changes in his efficiency campaign. Had Inspector Flint been gifted with X-ray vision he would have made more progress, for down in the timber yard behind a stack of deal boards, and out of sight of the station window, were three tons of corned beef and eighty cases of canned peaches.

Chapter Fifteen

On the Monday morning of the 15th of July 1940 all the daily newspapers carried a front page report of the Prime Minister's address to the nation. In the backstreets of dockland the speech was being discussed on doorsteps, in the corner shops and behind crisp lace curtains in the small parlours. Winston Churchill had seized the attention of almost everyone when he delivered what the papers were calling his masterful speech. Pubs had stopped serving to listen, and those with no wireless set had crowded round their neighbours'. The dire warning frightened the wits out of Granny Bell, as she confessed to the Brightmans. ''E fair put the fear o' Gawd inter me last night,' she said. 'What wiv 'im goin' on about fightin' 'em in the streets. 'E said they're comin' any day now, by all accounts.'

The content of the Prime Minister's speech had an effect on Maggie Copeland too. She was now more than ever determined to see that Joe would allow the children to be evacuated from London. 'Even 'e said it. London's gonna be laid in ruins before we'd surrender.'

Joe licked a dob of marmalade from his finger and shook his head in anger. ''Ow many times we bin over this? I've gotta get ter work, I ain't got no time ter argue wiv yer.'

171

Maggie threw down the morning paper. 'It's in there. Read it, sod yer! Read it!'

Joe pulled a face and picked up his teacup. Maggie saw that she was getting nowhere with him and she sat down and pulled the paper towards her. 'Listen ter what it says. "Be the ordeal sharp or long, or both, we shall seek no terms, we shall tolerate no parley. We may show mercy, but we shall ask none." You listenin'?'

Joe tried to hide a smile but Maggie saw his face and she got even more angry. She ran her finger along the type. 'There's more: "London itself, fought street by street, could easily devour an entire hostile army, and we would rather see London laid in ruins and ashes than it should be abjectly enslaved." What about that then?'

Joe felt the toast sticking in his throat and he realised he was late for work. 'Look 'ere, luv, we'll talk about it ternight, okay?'

Maggie was having none of Joe's procrastination. 'We'll talk about it now, or I'll leave yer, Joe, I mean it!'

Joe Copeland saw the determination in his wife's eye and he pointed to the teapot. 'All right, you win. Pour me anuvver cuppa, an' we'll talk.'

'I thought you was late for work?'

'Sod work. Let's talk.'

When The Globe opened Danny Sutton was the first one through the doors. He was soon joined by Johnny Ross who looked particularly pleased with himself.

'You look like you jus' found a fiver stickin' ter yer shoe,' Danny remarked.

Johnny winked and called Eddie Kirkland over. ''Ere, Eddie, give me an' me mate a drink, an' 'ave one yerself.'

The landlord of The Globe pulled a face. 'Leave me out, Johnny. We 'ad a late session last night. Biff Bowden was in 'ere wiv some of 'is cronies. Even 'is dog got pissed.'

The joke was lost on Danny, who sipped his drink thoughtfully. Johnny watched as Eddie moved away to serve an old gent who had just walked in, then he leaned over close to his pal. 'Done a bit o' business last night, we did. Might be able ter put some easy money your way.'

Danny was used to Johnny's boasting and he ignored the remark. Johnny looked around to make sure they were not being overheard and he put his hand to one side of his mouth. 'We knocked over a ware'ouse. Got a lorry load o' tinned stuff. Most of it's spoken fer, but we've gotta punt the rest. I'm seein' a bloke later terday. Fancy givin' us an 'and? I'll row yer in fer a few bob.'

'Sorry, Johnny, I've got a date. I'm seein' 'er soon as I'm finished takin' the bets.'

'Oh yeah? An' who's the lucky little bird then?'

Danny leaned back and folded his arms. 'Anybody ever told yer you're a nosy git, Rossy?' he said, his pale eyes glinting.

Johnny grinned. 'All right, all right, I'm only tryin' ter be sociable.'

'She's a nurse I met when I was in 'ospital. I took 'er out last night. She comes from Wales, an' she's on leave,' Danny said, hoping to satisfy his pal's curiosity.

'What's she like?' Johnny prompted.

'She's a little darlin'.'

'Does she do a turn?'

'Bloody 'ell, Johnny, you don't stop, do yer?' Danny exclaimed as he picked up the empty glasses and walked over to the bar.

When he returned Johnny was ready with a suggestion. ''Ere, if yer wanna place ter take 'er, yer can use my drum. I'm goin' up town ternight ter celebrate me good fortune. I won't be 'ome – if yer know what I mean.'

Danny sat down and sipped his pint thoughtfully. There would be little time before Alison caught her train to Cardiff but then it might be some time before he could see her again. Trouble was, if he accepted Johnny's offer, everyone in the pub would know within a day or two. But it wouldn't hurt to take the key, just in case. 'Okay,' he said at last.

'Okay what?' Johnny said absently, fixing Eddie's barmaid with a malevolent stare.

'Okay, I'll borrer yer key,' Danny said.

Johnny fished into his coat pocket and pulled out a key on a length of string. 'There we are. The only fing is, don't go blamin' me if yer put 'er in the pudden club.'

Danny finished his drink then glared at Johnny. 'I ain't cut out ter be a daddy. What do I do wiv the key when I'm finished wiv it?'

'Leave it wiv Ginny Coombes. yer can spin 'er a yarn, she don't 'ave ter know what yer borrered it for. I can call in fer it termorrer.'

'I won't tell 'er if you don't,' Danny mocked as he stood up to leave.

Johnny gripped his pal's arm. 'You sure it's a nurse yer takin' out, an' not Kathy Thompson?'

Danny looked down at his friend with a murderous stare. 'Yer gonna get yerself in a lot o' trouble wiv that tongue o' your'n. No it's not Kathy Thompson. She's not my concern since she shacked up wiv Jack Mason.'

'Sorry, Danny,' Johnny said. 'Water under the ole bridge, eh? By the way, she was in 'ere fer a spell last night.'

'Wiv 'im?'

'Yeah, but they went out early. I was in the piss 'ole an' I 'eard 'em naggin' each uvver as they went by the winder.'

Danny walked to the door. 'See yer aroun', Johnny, an' fanks fer the you know what.'

*

Joe Copeland was not the only member of the Sutton family who missed work that Monday morning. Connie had opened the paper and seen the heading: 'Destroyer sunk'. Her heart pounded as she read on. 'The Destroyer *Prowler* (Lt Cmdr W. Bass) has been sunk by a torpedo in the North Atlantic, it was announced by the Admiralty last night. There are reports of some survivors. The *Prowler* was launched at Greenock in 1935 and carried a complement of 145 officers and men. She had a speed of 36 knots and was armed with . . .' Connie could read no more. Her eyes were swimming and she dropped her head onto the table. Almost immediately there was a knock on the door and sounds of someone in distress.

Alice Sutton came into the parlour looking white and shaken. 'Connie, luv, it's Missus Ellis. She's 'ad a telegram. It's Jimmy.'

The plump figure of Mrs Ellis followed Alice into the room. Her eyes were red from crying and her face was ashen. In her shaking hand she clenched a plain, buff-coloured envelope. Alice led her to a chair and Mrs Ellis sat down heavily. 'It came late last night. I couldn't come roun' before, I was too upset.'

Connie bit on her knuckles. 'What does it say? Is Jimmy—?'

Mrs Ellis held out the telegram. 'You read it, Connie.'

The young girl took out the buff slip with shaking hands and read it quickly. 'It only says about 'is ship bein' sunk an' they'll keep yer informed when there's more news. I've jus' read that much in the paper,' she blurted out.

Mrs Ellis dropped her head and sobbed. Connie got up and went over to her. She knelt down and clasped the distressed woman's hand in hers. 'Listen, Missus Ellis, Jimmy's gonna be okay, I know 'e is. We've jus' gotta wait.'

'And pray,' Alice said as she laid her arm round Mrs Ellis's shoulders.

*

Ben Morrison had received a letter that angered and shook him. Now, a week old, it rested behind the mantelshelf clock, but still a fury burned inside him whenever he saw it. Lucy had argued with him to destroy it, but he was adamant. 'Those sort of letters are evil,' he had said. 'The writers should be exposed and locked up. I'm determined to find out who wrote it, however long it takes.' Lucy had given up the argument. There was no shifting him. More than the letter, she was startled by Ben's attitude to the affair. He had talked to her often of having compassion and understanding, and he had preached to her about the need for forgiveness and mercy, but he had changed since the tribunal hearing. He was becoming bitter and cynical, although in their most intimate moments together he was tender and romantic and Lucy found their lovemaking exciting. When Ben received the anonymous letter, however, he had shown her an anger that was alien to him. Lucy was shocked by his reaction and it worried her. She had come to the conclusion that he must be smarting from the taunts at work and the lack of any support at the mission; he must be feeling isolated and shunned. She sensed it in his growing need to be with her as much as possible, and she was more than willing to spend her time with him. One nagging worry, though, clouded Lucy's mind. Her period was overdue. It had never happened before, and she had always been as regular as clockwork. As she felt no different she put it down to worrying over Ben. She had wanted to tell him but decided to wait another week, and now he was preoccupied with the letter.

When the letter had first arrived Ben would not let Lucy see it, but she persisted until he gave in. The envelope bore a Bermondsey postmark and the message was hand-printed and badly constructed, although Ben was sure that was intentional. The letter vilified him. It condemned his pacifist views and called him a bastard. It went on to express the hope that Ben's family would be the first to get shot should the Germans arrive, and it ended by wishing him a syphilitic death, a plague on his offspring, and agony as they all burned in the fires of Hell. Lucy had been overcome when she read it and urged him to consign the evil thing to flames, but Ben had stubbornly placed it behind the clock.

Down below in Tooley Street the usual traffic was converging outside the wharves. Now and then a number 70 tram rattled along until it reached the foot of Duke Street Hill, where it waited until the next tram arrived. The points were then switched and the trams changed places. The area was noisy throughout the whole day. Vans and horse carts were called from their ranks into the wharves and onto the quays, more vans and carts arriving to take their places as the laden vehicles struggled past and drove away. The main topic of conversation on that Monday morning was the Prime Minister's speech. The carmen discussed it as they stood beside their vehicles or drank tea from tin mugs in the cafés; the dockers and stevedores chatted about it in the ships' holds and on the quayside. Almost everyone felt that what had been said needed saying. It had been spelt out, and at least everyone knew exactly where they stood.

The tall, stooping figure who walked along Tooley Street that Monday morning had known all along precisely where he stood. In 1914 he had stood on the street corner and watched the men march off to war behind blaring brass bands, and he had seen soldiers in their uniforms drinking and singing in the pubs before they sailed off to France. He had stood on the street corner and watched the parades as the ragged survivors were cheered and clapped upon their return. He had cursed his bad luck and envied the adulation the exhausted heroes received. A curvature of the spine, bad eyesight and flat feet had prevented him from joining up and being part of the parade. Embittered and envious, he had buried himself in his clerical job, and now he saw the whole process being re-enacted. There was a difference now, however, for this time he had found what he considered to be a worthwhile vocation. This time he was able to play a part, and as he walked towards the magistrates' court he smiled to himself. Who was it who said 'The pen is mightier than the sword'? Well he was making his own particular contribution to the war effort, and this morning he would begin a new episode. He would remain quiet and unobtrusive in the public gallery, and when the names were called and the addresses were read out, the slouching figure sitting on the polished wooden bench would decide on what action to take. It would not be a difficult decision to make, for he knew exactly where he stood.

Danny Sutton stood in Ginny's doorway. A few lucky punters had walked up to collect their Saturday night dog winnings and there was only one query.

'Look 'ere, son,' the old man said, 'yer must 'ave made a mistake. I 'ad a tanner each way on an 'undred ter seven. If it 'ad bin an 'undred ter six I'd 'ave copped 'undred tanners an' me place money, now wouldn't I?'

'Yeah, but it wasn't 'undred ter six, was it?'

'I'm jus' sayin' s'pose it was?'

Danny puffed loudly. 'Look, Pop, 'undred ter six is just over sixteen ter one. That means yer get sixteen tanners, not 'undred tanners. You'd get about eight an' fourpence plus yer place money.'

'But it wasn't 'undred ter six, it was 'undred ter seven.'

'That's what I'm tryin' ter tell yer.'

'Well my ole woman worked it out fer me. She don't make mistakes. She reckons she only ever made one mistake in 'er life.'

'Well she's made anuvver one, Pop.'

The old gent pocketed his winnings and walked off grumbling about the unfairness of it all. A short while later

Danny handed over the day's bets to Ginny and sipped the tea that she had made for him. ''Ere, Danny,' she said, 'I see that Thompson girl up the corner shop earlier on. I meant ter tell yer, she's got a nice shiner. D'yer reckon 'er feller give it to 'er?'

Danny gulped the hot tea in anger and felt it burn his gullet. 'That's an animal she's wiv, I'd take money on it.'

Ginny picked up a pair of torn trousers and searched for the cotton. 'I reckon she's a nice kid. Too good fer 'im. I don't know what she got 'iked up wiv that slob for.'

'I dunno, Ginny,' Danny said coldly, 'there's no accountin' fer taste.'

Ginny gave him a playful nudge. 'She'd 'ave bin better off wiv somebody like yerself. If I was twenty years younger yer wouldn't 'ave ter ask me twice.'

Danny grinned. 'You're all woman, Ginny, an' what's more yer make a luvverly cup o' tea.'

Ginny nudged him again and took his empty teacup. Danny watched as she rinsed the cup at the sink in the back scullery. She would still be a fine catch for someone, he thought. Her figure was still round and firm, and even with her hair pulled up untidily into a bun on the top of her head, Ginny looked attractive. Her skin was soft, and the few lines around her eyes did not lessen her good looks. Danny had to admit that he wouldn't say no to her in different circumstances.

Ginny put a fresh cup of tea down on the table beside him. While he sipped the tea she picked up the torn trousers and pulled the frayed material together. Occasionally her eyes moved up from her sewing and she watched him. Her husband had been gone almost three years and she felt a stirring in her belly. It was worse at night, when the solitude and the growing desire became an ache. The young man who had taken over the pitch figured in her fantasies. Her face would flush in the darkness as her hand reached over to the pillow beside hers.

Her desire was tempered by feelings of guilt; he was a mere boy compared to her, yet in her fantasies he was the one who climbed into her bed and loved her. The ache would then be drowned in a sea of passion, and in its wake a serene feeling would flow over their united bodies like an incoming tide. In the lonely silence the woman could do nothing about the salt tears that soaked her pillow. Her dead husband would come to fill her drowsy thoughts, and she always sought his forgiveness for her infidelity before sleep overtook her.

The sun was high as the carman climbed down from his dickey-seat and wrapped the wheel chain around the wooden spokes. As he strapped the nosebag over his nag's head the animal reared back. The carman spoke quietly to the horse and stroked its neck reassuringly. Normally he parked his cart in Tooley Street while he went for his lunchtime drink, but today the horse seemed nervous. Dawson Street was quiet in comparison to the main road, and before he went off to the pub the carman satisfied himself that all was well. The horse munched away at the oats and occasionally shook its head in an effort to get rid of the pain from its abscessed ear. Along the turning Crazy Bella was kneeling at her front door and putting the finishing touches to her stone step. She mumbled to herself as she gathered up the block of whitening and the house flannel. Across the street the Brightmans' baby slept peacefully in its pram by the front door, and a ginger-haired lad sat day-dreaming, his feet in the gutter. The sun shone down into the street and a pencil of bright light made young Billy Birkitt shield his eyes. He could see a glass marble lying in the middle of the cobbled roadway, and he got up to take a closer look. The marble was trapped between two cobblestones. Billy knelt down and tried to prise it loose with his fingers but it was firmly wedged there and the young lad ran back in his house and out into the backyard. He soon found the pointed stick that he used on the cat when it sauntered through his carefully arranged army of tin soldiers. He ran back to the middle of the street and knelt down to dig away at his prize. Crazy Bella was still wringing out her house flannel in the kerb. Up at the top of the turning, a horsefly flew into the infected ear of the cart horse throwing it into a frenzy of pain and fear. The horse reared up and bolted. The unladen cart with one wheel locked and its iron rim drawing sparks from the cobbles careered down the turning and gathered speed as the nag's hooves thundered onto the stones. Billy Birkitt had loosened the marble but was too absorbed to hear the horse charging down towards him. Someone screamed and Crazy Bella dashed out in front of the wild animal. She only had time to grab the little lad and throw him aside before one of the shafts of the cart hit her between the shoulderblades. Bella was trampled under the horse's hooves and the cart ran over her lifeless body. As if sensing what had happened the horse stopped at the railway arch and stood shivering, its head held down low.

At one o'clock the ambulance pulled into Dawson Street to take the body away. A hush had fallen over the turning. Every door was open and people were crying silently. Billy stood beside his mother, his head buried in her apron. Alice Sutton stood with Annie Barnes and Mrs Brightman, and together they watched the ambulance draw out of the backstreet.

When it had disappeared, Alice turned to her friend. 'Gawd rest 'er soul. She's at peace now, Annie. The poor cow couldn't find any while she was livin'.'

Mrs Brightman sobbed aloud. 'I seen it 'appen,' she said, 'She didn't 'ave a chance of savin' 'erself.'

Alice was staring at the screwed up flannel and the piece of whitening which lay beside the gleaming front doorstep. 'We'd better close 'er front door, Annie,' she said softly.

Chapter Sixteen

Danny Sutton stepped down from the tram and took Alison's arm as she alighted. Together they walked through the wide gateway into Greenwich Park. Danny had gone directly from Ginny Coombes's house to meet Alison and knew nothing of what had happened. His spirits were high as he took the young girl's hand and guided her towards the steep footpath that led up to the observatory. Only a few people were in the park and they strolled in pleasant solitude past banks of summer flowers in the shade of the leafy chestnut trees. When they reached the top of the hill and walked out onto the paved area they saw the silver band of river far below them. Cranes swung and dipped, tugs slid along with squat barges in tow, and down in the foreground the white stone Maritime Museum shone from the centre of an emerald carpet. Alison sighed and sat down on a wooden bench facing the view. She watched Danny's slim figure as he put one foot up on the low wall and stared down the grassy hill. After a short while he turned and walked over to the bench.

'What d'yer fink of the view? I reckon it's gotta be the best view in London,' he said.

Alison nodded. 'It's lovely here. It's so quiet and peaceful.'

Danny looked around. One old man sat nearby stroking a

mongrel that was tethered with a length of string, and away to his left he saw the gun emplacements with their protective walls of sandbags. ''Cept fer that yer wouldn't fink there was a war on, would yer?'

Alison was staring down at a tiny river craft that seemed to be bobbing about in mid-stream. A puff of smoke arose from its funnel and seconds later the muted hoot of a tug whistle reached her ears. The peaceful setting and the open sky made her feel ready for the talk she must have with Danny. Alison reached out her hand and as he took it she pulled him down beside her on the bench. 'I've got to get that train tonight, Danny,' she said. 'I'm going to miss you.'

The young cockney reached over and gently kissed her ear. 'I'm gonna miss yer, too,' he said. 'The time seems to be flyin'.'

'We should talk, Danny.'

'What about?'

'About us,' she said, her dark eyes opened wide.

Danny averted his gaze for a moment and stared down at his shoes. When he looked up again he said quickly, 'I want you, Alison.'

'I want you too, Danny, but I'm scared for us. We hardly know each other. In some ways we're like strangers. Well, almost.'

Danny gave her a kiss on the side of her mouth but Alison pulled away. 'Let's be serious, Danny, we've got to talk. It's important.'

'Listen, Alison,' he said, taking her hand in his, 'there's a bloody war on. Nobody knows what's goin' ter 'appen in the next few months. I fink we've got ter take what little 'appiness we can get, while there's still time.'

'That's just it, Danny. We can take, but what will we be able to give to each other?'

'Do I 'ave ter spell it out ter yer, Alison? I want yer because I luv yer. Not fer any uvver reason. Surely that's somefing, ain't it? Ter me that's what luv's all about.'

'You say the word easily, Danny. I can't find it that easy to say.'

'Yer mean yer don't feel the same way?'

Alison looked up at the thin clouds high in the sky and knew that she could not delay any longer. She must not allow herself to become trapped, there must be no sidetracking. She had to be bluntly honest. 'You ask me if I feel the same way. All right, now please listen to me. I want you. I want you to love me, but I don't think I'm ready for the strings to be tied. I don't want to be owned, I don't want to be tied down to a home and children yet, Danny. Marriage is what I'm talking about. There's got to be an understanding between us.'

'I'll go along wiv that, Alison,' he said, squeezing her hand in his. 'I want an understandin' too.'

The man with the dog got up and strolled off with his pet trotting along obediently by his side. They watched him in silence. Then Danny turned back to Alison and he could see that she was uneasy. She stared down at the gritted surface and moved the point of her shoe against the stone chippings, and when she looked up he could see the pain in her eyes. She sighed deeply and Danny felt he was about to learn something which he had been secretly dreading. As if to brace him, Alison put her free hand on his tensed arm and began.

'I think I told you that I came into nursing when I was nineteen, just over three years ago. When I finished my training I was sent to the hospital at Dover. At first I was worried that I'd made the wrong decision and it took some time before I realised that nursing was the only thing I really wanted to do. Maybe it came to me as I gained confidence, I don't know, but I was sure that nursing was going to be my whole life. I had been at the hospital for a year when I met a man at one of our hospital dances. He was a pilot whose family lived in the Midlands, and he was stationed on an airfield in Kent. His name was Wilfred Haggerty, though everyone called him Bill.

He was good fun to be with, and I must admit he swept me off my feet. Maybe it was because I was naïve and away from home for the first time in my life, I don't know. Anyway, we seemed to get on very well together. We began to see each other regularly, and after a couple of months he asked me to marry him. At first I was taken aback, I don't mind telling you. It was impossible for me to even consider it. We came from different worlds: he was an officer who had gone straight from Cambridge into the Air Force, and I was a twenty-year-old from the Valleys who was just starting out on a career – I had never even had a steady boyfriend before he came along. But Bill wouldn't accept that we were different, I couldn't make him see it. He was a persistent type, I'll give him that. By this time we were spending every weekend together, and most of the nights too when I was off duty and he could get away from the airfield. Bill was sure that after a time I'd change my mind and agree to marry him, and I must admit it was good at first. We were happy and he seemed content the way things were.

'We had been together about six or seven months when the rows started. I think it had a lot to do with the realisation that there was going to be a war. He was beginning to press me again to marry him – I suppose he knew that he would be in action soon and wanted something to hold onto. I know a lot of people wouldn't consider getting married the way things were, but Bill was different. And he began to get irritable. When I couldn't get to see him because of my duty rota he thought I was deliberately avoiding meeting him. We had some blazing rows and we knew we couldn't carry on like that. One weekend Bill asked me again to marry him, and in a weak moment I said I'd think about it, and he took that to mean that I'd changed my mind. He was so happy. Early next morning he gave me a lift on the back of his motorbike as far as the hospital. He left me and set off for his squadron.

'I'll never forget that day. Mid-morning the ward sister

called me into her office and broke the news: Bill had been killed in a road accident not far from his airfield. I was devastated. And worst of all, he died believing in a lie. He never knew, Danny, that I hadn't changed my mind. He never knew that it was all a lie.'

While Alison was talking to him, Danny's eyes were riveted on her. His face was set hard, and when her dark eyes filled with tears he could find nothing to say. Alison remained silent for a short while. When she had composed herself again she went on. 'You see, Danny, I've asked myself the same question a thousand times: how can I love a man and yet deny him marriage and children? That's what it comes down to. If I had loved him enough I would have married him and had his children. I would have given up nursing for him.'

Danny swallowed hard. 'But yer didn't 'ave ter give up yer nursin'. The kids would 'ave come later if yer both wanted 'em that much.'

'Bill loved kids,' Alison said, looking down at the river below. 'He wouldn't have been happy without them. I may be wicked to think it, but I had a feeling he expected something to happen to him if there was a war, and he wanted to be able to leave something behind. He wanted children to carry his name on. I'm sure in my mind he felt that way, although he didn't ever mention it.'

'I don't fink you're wicked ter 'ave them thoughts locked away inside yer. I fink yer stupid ter punish yerself. It wasn't ter be. If yer'd 'ave said yer'd marry 'im it still wouldn't 'ave prevented the accident, would it?'

'I know,' Alison replied, 'but it doesn't stop me asking myself the same question. Could I love a man enough to give up everything for him? Have I got that much love to offer? I feel I'd be trapped inside a marriage.'

'Only yer know that,' Danny said quietly. 'Yer said a little while ago that the word "love" comes easy ter me. I tell yer this. Maybe I can say it easy, but it's not an easy feelin'. It's a bloody 'ard feelin'. It grips at me inside. It's painful, an' it makes me feel terrible when I'm not wiv yer. It makes me want ter jump up an' shout me bleedin' 'ead orf one minute an' cry me eyes out the next. No, Alison, it ain't an easy feelin'.'

Alison had to smile through her sadness at the way Danny expressed himself. His flippant nature had intrigued her in the beginning, yet there was another side of him she was fast discovering. He seemed to have an intensity that he tried to cover up, but now his words revealed his strength of feeling. Her body suddenly ached for his. She wanted to know his love before she left that evening, and at that moment she also wanted his understanding desperately. He must give her the space she needed to adjust to a new relationship. She had tried to make him understand, to warn him not to expect too much, and now it was up to him.

The sun had passed its zenith and the brow of the hill was becoming less private as people arrived and children ran up to the bench next to where the young couple sat.

'Let's walk a while, Danny,' Alison said.

His face brightened. 'I know,' he said, 'let's go down ter the pier. There used ter be a nice coffee 'ouse there. We can get a drink.'

They left the hill-top view behind them and walked quickly down the grassy slope. In a few minutes they had reached the gate and crossed through into the busy road. They walked on past ancient-looking shops that displayed tattered books and faded paintings of ships in full sail. They saw the high-pillared Church of St Alphege ahead and when they reached the corner they turned down towards the pier. The little coffee house was still there, and soon they were seated comfortably in the shaded interior. An elderly lady came over and Danny ordered tea and cakes. The only other customer was a harassed mother who was trying hard to contain her young daughter. Cream oozed from a cake that the child held in her small hands, dripping onto the checked tablecloth and dribbling from her chin. Her mother smiled lamely at Danny and Alison as she attempted to clean up the mess while the elderly proprietor watched sternly from over her half-rimmed glasses. Soon hot tea in blue china cups and two large cream cakes were placed on the table beside the young couple.

Alison watched as Danny got into difficulty with his cake; he reminded her of a child in some ways. He was uncomplicated and straightforward, and his self-conscious grin pulled at her heart. There in the quiet, old-fashioned coffee house Alison felt she was being unavoidably drawn into a situation she had fought against. Why had she agreed to see him again? It would have been so easy to have said no in her letter to him, but she had been strangely attracted to the young patient and the chance of meeting him again had excited her. It was also an opportunity to test her emotions once more in the safe confines of a meeting that could only be brief. Even if their affair were passionate, it would certainly be short-lived. Time would not permit, nor would she. Now, as she watched Danny blowing on his tea, she felt ashamed. She wanted him badly but she could not fully trust herself, and yet she was using him to test her own emotional strength, and he was going to get hurt in the process. She felt a sudden panic and wanted to rush from the shop. She might experience love again, but in time she would have to walk away. What of him? Her thoughts tumbled around inside her head. Maybe she was being too presumptuous, he might merely be making a play to seduce her. He was young and good-looking, why should she assume he was in love with her? Because he had told her so? She realised it was getting more and more difficult to remain detached, a net seemed to be closing around her. Maybe it would be better to swim with the tide and allow events to bring her closer to a clear understanding of herself. That was the answer, she decided, and she felt an inner calm replacing her feelings of panic.

Out in the street the sun was dipping down behind the rooftops as they walked slowly to the tram stop. Danny had asked if he could escort her to Paddington Station that evening and she had accepted his offer gratefully. Now it was time to get back to the Morgans, to pack and to say goodbye to her hosts. As they waited for the tram, Alison couldn't help but smile to herself – she had been so preoccupied with her thoughts of an affair, of passionate love and heart-rending decisions, but in reality there had been little time and no opportunity. Soon she would be speeding towards her home town, and later there would be more agonising, more decisions to be made, she would be on her own again. Parted from Danny and back with her family, she would have time to think, to examine her feelings and to question herself again, and perhaps she would be able to discover some peace.

Danny looked along Greenwich Road. He could see the approaching tram away in the distance. His hand was clasped around the key that Johnny Ross had given him but he knew in his mind that he would not take Alison to the flat. It was too contrived. He realised that suggesting it might make Alison feel cheap and degraded. Maybe he was getting soft, maybe he was losing his nerve, and his confidence. Maybe Alison's disclosures had thrown him. In his heart he knew that such vanity was out of place. She had known love and was quite able to make up her own mind; it would not be a question of his taking advantage of a virgin. If she agreed to spend the night with him it would be her choice; she was an experienced woman and knew the consequences. Whichever way he looked at it he knew that the flat was out of the question. He was going to kick himself later, but that was the way it had to be.

The journey back to London Bridge was strained. Danny attempted light-hearted conversation but Alison was preoccupied. He sensed a disappointment and sadness, and his hand tightened on the key. He went over and over in his mind what Alison had told him of her affair with the pilot. His mixed feelings made him angry and regretful. He resented the pilot for having known her love, and he was upset because he could not bring himself to suggest that they use Johnny's flat. Danny felt inadequate and unhappy, and he was glad when the tram arrived at London Bridge. The short walk to Southwark Street was carried out in awkward haste, both struggling to make conversation, and when they reached the Morgans' dairy, Danny half expected Alison to change her mind about him going to the station with her. She kissed him lightly on the cheek. 'Thanks for this afternoon, Danny, and thanks for being patient. Can we leave at eight? My train goes at ten past ten.'

'I'll be on the dot,' he said, as she let herself into the dairy.

Detective Constable Stanley Stockbridge was in a foul mood. He had gone to Sullivan's Wharf and stood scratching his head at the scene of the crime. 'The bloody gate's more than twelve feet 'igh. Whoever it was must 'ave bin part monkey.'

The uniformed policeman nodded. 'Mr Sullivan's up in the office on the first floor, Stan. 'E's waitin' fer yer.'

'Well 'e can bloody well wait,' Fat Stan growled. 'I've gotta 'ave a decko round first.'

Accompanied by the policeman he walked into the yard and saw the broken window. 'When the fingerprint Johnny gets 'ere I want 'im ter go over that door 'andle.'

The police constable had already taken a look round the yard. 'Yer won't find anyfink there, Stan. There's grease all over the 'andle. The mechanic's bin in there 'alf a dozen times already.'

Fat Stan cursed. 'Didn't anybody try an' stop the silly bleeder?'

'Bit awkward really, Stan. The piss 'ole's at the back o' the office, an' the mechanic told me 'e's sufferin' from a weak bladder.'

'Christ Almighty! Ain't there anuvver piss 'ole in this place?'

The constable merely pursed his lips and stood with his hands clasped behind his back. Fat Stan looked up at the rope. 'That don't tell us anyfing. The sort o' rope yer can buy anywhere round 'ere. No keys bin found?'

The constable shook his head. 'Must 'ave took 'em wiv 'em.'

Fat Stan took the constable's arm and whispered in his ear. 'This is your beat. D'yer know any o' those who work 'ere?'

The constable's eyebrows lifted in surprise. 'D'yer suspect it was an inside job then, Stan?'

'I ain't made me mind up yet,' Stan growled. 'I'm off ter see this Mr Sullivan. You 'ang around, I'll talk ter yer later.'

A tall matronly figure in thick spectacles gave the puffing detective a disapproving look as she led him into the inner office. Mr Sullivan did not bother to get up. 'I'm Sullivan. And you are . . . ?'

'Detective Constable Stockbridge, sir. We'd better 'ave a description of the lorry an' its contents first orf.'

The wharf owner looked hard at the fat detective. 'They've found my lorry,' he said. 'It was parked outside the West India Dock. Empty, I might add, except for two orientals. They were asleep in the cab. They weren't involved, so I'm told.'

Fat Stan looked embarrassed. 'I didn't know they found yer lorry. The report must 'ave come in after I left. What about the load?'

Mr Sullivan pulled a sheet of paper towards him and scanned it while Fat Stan flipped open his notebook. The wharf owner scratched his ginger hair and moved his tortoiseshell spectacles up from the tip of his nose. 'Here we are. One hundred and twenty cases of Argentine corned beef. Brand name "Swan". Each case contained forty-eight sixteen-ounce tins. Then there were eighty cases of best Californian peaches, brand name "Sunrise". Same packing: forty-eight sixteen-ounce.'

Fat Stan was struggling to get all the information onto his small notepad. 'What about yer staff? Any ex-cons workin' fer yer?'

John Sullivan flushed indignantly. 'I don't employ that sort of person. All my staff have been with me for years. They are all honest, hardworking types.'

Fat Stan grunted. He was convinced that that particular species just did not exist. 'Who's responsible fer openin' up in the mornin'?'

Mr Sullivan beckoned to his secretary through the open door. In the outer office Monica Adams was straining her ears in an effort to catch the conversation. This would make exciting gossip at her weekly women's sewing circle. She got up quickly and adjusted her dress before tripping into the inner office. She smiled sweetly at her boss and gave the detective a cold look.

'Will you ask Basil to come in, Monica?' Mr Sullivan said peremptorily.

Miss Adams turned on her heel and Mr Sullivan beckoned the detective to a chair. 'Basil will be down in the warehouse, Officer. You might as well take a seat. Basil Bromley has worked for me for over thirty years and he's honest as the day is long. It was Basil who discovered the theft when he arrived to open up at seven-thirty.'

Fat Stan glanced through his notes. It wouldn't be the first time an esteemed and trusted employee had turned crooked. Basil Bromley sounded like the sort of name they gave to music hall villains. A trusted servant with keys to the wharf. It wouldn't be too difficult to set it up – a rope over the gate to allay suspicion, and Bob's your uncle. Basil would have got himself a buyer for the swag easily. There were plenty of crooked shopkeepers around the neighbourhood willing to put some corned beef and tinned peaches under the counter, what with the food shortages. They'd most likely charge double the price. 'Basil Bromley' he mumbled to himself and looked up at Mr Sullivan, but the boss was studying an insurance claim form and ignored him. Fat Stan went back to his notes and pencilled a cross beside the trusted employee's name. It would be a feather in his cap if he made a quick arrest. The new inspector was already reading the riot act out to his officers and Fat Stan did not relish the thought of pounding the beat. His feet wouldn't stand it. Basil Bromley, he thought to himself, I arrest you for the theft of five tons of corned beef and canned peaches. It's no good you struggling. I think we'll have the handcuffs on. That's all right, Mr Sullivan, no need to thank me. All in a day's work. How did I get on to him? Well, it was intuition, Inspector, I've got a nose for a villain. I can smell 'em a mile off. Very few of 'em get by me . . .

The sound of voices brought Detective Constable Stanley Stockbridge back to reality. The outer office door opened and he heard Miss Adams's strident tones. 'Go right in, Basil, Mr Sullivan's waiting for you.'

A white-haired, stooped old man walked painfully into the inner sanctum and leaned on the desk for support. 'I'm sorry, Mr Sullivan. Those stairs seem to take it out of me lately,' he said in a cracked voice.

Mr Sullivan smiled sympathetically and motioned Basil to a chair. Fat Stan looked at the pathetic figure whose suit seemed to be two sizes too large for his frail body while Basil peered at him over metal-rimmed spectacles and blinked owlishly. His sunken cheeks puffed in and out as he fought to regain his breath, and his bony hands made motions of washing. Fat Stan began to get the feeling that pounding the beat again was becoming a distinct possibility.

Chapter Seventeen

The tragedy in Dawson Street left a cloud of gloom that hung heavily over the small turning. There were no children playing in the street, and the few people who stood at their doors were talking in little more than whispers. While she lived, Crazy Bella had been ignored by most of Dawson Street's folk, but in death everyone had some anecdote to tell about the unfortunate woman.

'She 'ad a son, yer know,' announced Mrs Brightman.

Annie Barnes did not know. 'Go on with yer,' she said.

''S'right. 'E run away ter sea years ago when poor ole Bella lived in Tower Bridge Road. Wasn't much good by all accounts. I 'eard 'e was dead rotten to 'er. Brought 'im up all on 'er own as well.'

'Didn't she ever marry?' Annie asked, digging into her pocket for her snuff.

'Not as far as I know,' replied Mrs Brightman. 'Accordin' ter Granny Bell, she was a smart woman when she was younger. She used ter go up West quite a lot. She was always bringin' fellers back. Still, she wasn't doin' no 'arm. Granny reckons she was on the game, but I don't fink she was.'

'Somefing must 'ave turned 'er brain,' said Annie, shaking her head sadly. 'I've seen 'er up on London Bridge Station. She used ter give the toffs a lot o' verbal. I've seen 'er walkin' be'ind 'em City gents swearin' 'er 'ead orf at 'em.'

'I did 'ear that she 'ad 'er son by a well-ter-do feller. 'E wouldn't marry 'er but 'e gave 'er a few bob ev'ry week. That's if yer can believe it,' Mrs Brightman said, folding her arms under her apron.

Annie Barnes shivered although the evening was still warm. 'Did yer see that poor carman's face? White as a sheet it was. That copper was 'oldin' 'is arm.'

'Yer can't blame 'im, Annie. They reckon somefink frightened the 'orse. Yer can't foresee these fings. I say it was an act of the Almighty.'

Annie Barnes looked up the turning. 'There's young Danny Sutton goin' 'ome fer 'is tea.'

'What's 'e doin' now, Annie?'

''E's got the bookie's pitch in Clink Lane. I was talkin' ter Alice Sutton earlier on. She's all upset. 'Er Connie got some bad news about 'er chap. 'E's on the boats and 'is muvver come round cryin' 'er eyes out. They got a telegram ter say 'e's missin'.'

'Gawd Almighty, Annie! Whatever next?'

As the train jerked to a stop at Paddington Underground Station and the doors slid open, a tide of uniformed figures rushed out towards the exit stairs. Two young people who were holding hands and talking let the hurrying travellers pass them by. They were early, and they emerged onto the railway station almost reluctantly. Danny carried Alison's small suitcase as they came to the station departure board and studied the train times. A large clock over the display showed ten minutes to nine. Alison looked at Danny and at her case he was holding. 'I won't be a minute. I'm just going to powder my nose,' she said.

Danny eyed her slim figure as she walked swiftly towards the Ladies. Unlike Waterloo Station, he found Paddington depressed him. He watched servicemen pass to and fro, all laden with heavy equipment and rifles and all looking grim and tired. Tearful families and sweethearts waved handkerchiefs as a train grew smaller in the distance. The station tannoy announced yet another delay, and two porters began to argue over who should shift a heap of luggage the few yards to the nearby taxi rank.

Danny felt it was one of those forsaken days when everything went wrong. Back in Dawson Street everyone was mourning poor Bella, and Connie was shut up in her room crying. He had tried to cheer her up before he left to meet Alison, but on this occasion his playful chatter did no good. Now he was waiting to say goodbye to Alison, who seemed quite happy to be on her way home. As he stood beside her case a large lady in a mink stole and feathered hat dragging a tiny dog on a lead beckoned a porter over and addressed him with her high-pitched voice. The hysterical-looking dog sniffed at the case by Danny's feet and began to cock its leg. Danny quickly lifted the case and resisted a strong urge to drop it on the dog's head. He turned angrily and walked away.

Five minutes later he saw Alison emerge from the Ladies and talk briefly to a porter before walking over to him.

'What shall we do, Danny?' she said. 'We've got almost an hour before the train leaves.'

'This station's givin' me the willies. Let's get a drink.'

They walked out into Praed Street and found a little pub a short distance from the station. In the smoky atmosphere they sat in a corner sipping their drinks. Alison put her stout down on the table and ran her index finger around the rim of the glass. 'Tell me something, Danny,' she said, 'are you disappointed?'

Danny looked up into her dark eyes. 'About what?'

'About what I told you today in the park. And about us not having much time together.'

'No, I'm not disappointed,' he lied. 'What 'appened wiv you an' this Bill was yer own affair. As fer not 'avin' much time tergevver, I'm not really disappointed, I'm more sorry. It wasn't on the cards, was it?'

Alison fished into her handbag and took out a small mirror. While she was studying her reflection she said, 'I'm sorry too. Really sorry.'

Danny laughed mirthlessly. 'Now if I was an Arab sheik or somefink I'd 'ave carried yer off this afternoon. You'd 'ave bin a prisoner in my tent, an' I'd 'ave dismissed all the uvver wives while we made love.'

Alison stroked his hand and Danny felt the softness of her skin. She looked into his pale eyes and smiled. 'I don't want to be ravished by a sheik, Danny. A soldier boy will do – or should I say ex-soldier.'

They were silent for a while, then Danny said, 'Alison, do yer fink I'm a bit slow?'

The young girl laughed aloud. 'Slow, Danny? I think you're as sharp as a pin.'

'I don't mean that way,' he said quickly, 'I mean slow – you know – ter get goin'?'

Alison picked up her drink again and Danny had the feeling she was laughing at him. 'Of course I don't. Let's face it, Danny, we've not had any opportunity to . . . Well, you know what I mean.' She looked up at him and noticed the tell-tale twitch of his mouth. He put his hand into his coat pocket and laid Johnny's front door key down on the table in front of her.

'Yes we 'ave,' he said. 'A pal o' mine loaned me that key. 'E said I might wanna take yer to 'is flat.'

Alison looked surprised. 'Why didn't you?' she asked.

'I'm not sure,' he replied. 'It seemed wrong. It seemed like it was all arranged. What's more, the bloke that give me the key can't keep 'is mouth shut. If I tell 'im I used the flat, 'e'd be a walkin' *News of the World*.'

'Why did you take the key then, Danny?'

'It was the way I was feelin' at the time, I s'pose.'

Alison studied her long fingernails. 'Do you feel different now?'

'Yeah, I want yer twice as much,' Danny said quietly.

'Danny.'

'Yeah?'

'There's another train leaving at ten o'clock tomorrow morning. We could go to a hotel.'

Their eyes met, and for a moment they clasped hands, the noise and movement around them forgotten. Finally Danny smiled sheepishly and picked up the glasses. 'Let's 'ave anuvver drink,' he said.

Night was falling as they emerged from the pub. Taxis hooted and swerved in and out of the station and evening revellers sauntered through the busy street.

Danny took Alison's arm. 'Let's cross over,' he said. 'The side turnin's are the best bet.'

They found themselves in a narrow backstreet where almost all of the Victorian terraced houses offered rooms for the night. The first two places were full, but at the third attempt they were successful. A bleary-eyed man with his shirt-sleeves rolled back over his forearms span the register and watched as Danny signed them both in as Mr and Mrs Halleron. He handed Danny a key and called out, 'Beryl, take Mr an' Mrs Halleron up to number six.'

A fat woman with a cheery grin waddled up the carpeted stairs ahead of the young couple, and when she had recovered her breath she opened the door at the end of the landing. 'There you are, me dears,' she said. 'If there's anything else you want, you just tell hubby. Breakfast is from eight o'clock.'

The room smelled musty but it was clean. The curtains were drawn back and the bed with its white counterpane seemed to fill the room. Danny looked at Alison in the dimness and she stepped close to him. Their lips met and their bodies came tightly together. The kiss was long, and when they moved apart Danny pulled the curtains shut and switched on the light. A tall wardrobe of dark wood, an old chair, and a washstand were the only furniture in the room. Over the bed was a gilt-framed picture of Victorian Bayswater. The walls were covered with a floral wallpaper, and hanging from the ceiling above the bed was a tasselled shade around the light which gave out a pinkish glow. Danny opened a door which led, amazingly, to a private bathroom and Alison began to undo her suitcase.

'Look at this,' he called out to her, eyeing the large bath. 'This beats our ole bog in the yard. A real tub as well. We take our'n down from a peg be'ind the back door.'

When Alison went to the bathroom Danny turned off the light and opened the curtains. He sat on the edge of the bed and gazed at the moon. The room felt strange and he suddenly realised he was trembling. The bathroom door opened and he saw Alison standing on the threshold. He caught his breath as he saw her figure silhouetted in the dim light; her hair seemed to shine, and as she came over to the bed Danny noticed her small, firm breasts standing out beneath the white cotton of her nightdress. 'Christ! Yer beautiful,' he breathed as she sat down beside him.

'Thank you, kind sir,' she said with a coy smile.

Danny reached out and pulled her to him. She did not resist as he kissed her chin and neck, and when he pressed her down on the bed Alison shuddered with pleasure as his fingertips traced a very gentle ring around her taut nipple. After a lingering kiss Danny drew up on his arms and looked down at her flushed face and sighed deeply. 'I won't be long,' he whispered as he rose and went into the bathroom.

Alison climbed into the comfortable bed and pulled up the bedclothes. She had been aroused, and the desire for full love made her feel impatient. 'Come on, Danny, don't keep me waiting,' she whispered aloud.

Danny was standing in front of the wash-basin. He had washed down in cold water to ease the growing feeling that threatened to overwhelm him. He eyed his pale skin and looked at the thin white scar that ran from his right side to his sternum. He ran his trembling fingers through his fair hair and reached for the towel which he wrapped around his middle. From somewhere deep in the recesses of his mind a strange alarm was beginning to interrupt his thoughts. He was reaching out for the unobtainable, a mutual attraction was drawing them both like two moths fluttering around a brightly burning candle flame. He shivered as he turned out the light and opened the door.

Alison saw the slim figure come to her and remove the towel from around his stomach as he slipped in the bed beside her. She turned to face him and felt his fingers stroke her hair. She had wanted their love-making to be slow and gentle, but now as his anxious hands caressed her aching body she became impatient. Suddenly Alison sat up, and with one smooth movement she pulled the nightdress over her head and guided his trembling hands up to her naked breasts.

In the dark hotel room, with the moon gently streaming over the bed, they became lovers at last.

A cloud had covered the moon, and now monstrous shapes seemed to loom up in the shadows around the ghostly white counterpane which covered Danny and Alison. The wardrobe creaked and occasionally the distant sound of a train drifted in through the open window. The lovers lay close, their demanding passion spent. Alison rested her head on Danny's chest and gently ran her fingers down his arm. He held her close and watched the eerie light playing tricks around them. Danny could smell the fragrance of her hair and her warm body scent that had drawn him to the summits of pleasure. Now, his body calm and heavy, he whispered into her ear: 'I've never experienced anyfing so good. You was fantastic.'

Alison sighed and nestled even closer. 'I didn't want it to end. Was I greedy?'

'You was great.'

'So were you.'

Danny stretched out and yawned. 'It's funny really. 'Ere we are in a bedroom of a strange 'otel, an' only a couple of hours ago I was gettin' ready ter see yer off. I 'ad the feelin' yer wanted ter get on that train as soon as yer could. I was gettin' the 'ump on that station. I like comin's not goin's. I was jus' gettin' used ter the idea of a lonely trip back ter Bermon'sey when yer told me about the uvver train. Was that what yer was speakin' ter the porter about?'

There was no answer and Danny realised that Alison had fallen asleep. Her breathing was shallow and even, and as he eased her head onto the pillow she sighed and slipped her arm around him.

The early morning was dull and humid. When Danny awoke he found that the place beside him was empty. He sat up with a start and then dropped back onto the pillow when he heard the sound of water running in the bathroom. In a while Alison came into the bedroom fully dressed, her face fresh and pink. She squeezed his big toe. 'Come on, sleepy-head, breakfast started ten minutes ago.'

Danny got up and washed his face in cold water, grimacing at the puffiness under his eyes and the light stubble around his chin. He dressed quickly and went back into the bedroom. 'I'm gonna remember this room,' he said, pulling Alison to him. She held him at bay and smiled. 'Come on, let's get some breakfast,' she said.

Down in the dining-room two other couples sat at breakfast. A dark-skinned man was chatting incessantly to a woman who nodded at him between mouthfuls of egg and bacon. Another couple was utterly silent. Danny became intrigued as he waited with Alison for their breakfast to appear. The man was much older than his partner and he continued to glance at her while he ate. The girl returned his look occasionally with an angry glare. Whatever row had happened between them last night was spilling over into the morning, Danny thought. He saw the man point to the last piece of toast on the plate and in answer the girl with him nodded her head. The man picked up the slice of toast and dipped it into the yolk of his egg with a vengeance, the girl watching disdainfully as he greedily devoured the toast. It's a good job bedrooms can't talk, he mused.

Alison touched his hand briefly. 'Don't stare, Danny,' she chided him.

'You ought ter be sittin' where I'm sittin',' he whispered. 'There's a full-scale war of silence goin' on be'ind yer.'

Two portions of egg, bacon and tomatoes were placed in front of them with a plate of thin, crispy toast. The fat cheery lady who had shown them to their room came in carrying a tray with a small china teapot, cups and saucers, milk and sugar. She placed the tray on the table and smiled. 'I hope you both slept well?'

'I was off as soon as I 'it the piller,' Danny grinned, and Alison flushed slightly.

They ate their breakfast in silence. The other couples had left and the only other person in the room was a weary-looking girl who was busy laying fresh tablecloths on the cleared tables. She yawned as she carried a pile of plates out to the kitchen. Danny watched her exit with some amusement. ''Appy soul, ain't she?'

'I don't suppose she's got much to laugh about,' Alison answered, sipping her tea.

Danny could sense some irritability in her tone but chose to ignore it. He glanced at the wall clock. 'It's only jus' nine, we've got plenty o' time.'

'I don't want to leave it to the last minute, Danny. I don't relish standing in the corridor all the way to Cardiff.'

Danny gave her a quick look, surprised at her brusque tone. Maybe she was always sharp in the mornings, he thought. It was the first time he had been with her at this time of day. His sister Lucy was the same, it was almost impossible to get a civil word from her before midday. Danny felt a little confused. Though she had given him some insight into her feelings during their conversation in the park yesterday, she still remained mysterious. He sensed her sadness was never far from the surface. He had first begun to notice it back at the hospital in Dover when even in her light-hearted moments she had seemed to be under a shadow. He sensed that the loss of her pilot was only a part of it. Danny was sure it went deeper. She had told him of her fear that she was unable to give a total love but he was puzzled. Last night she had given herself with abandon. She had been willing and eager to lead them both to the heights and had succeeded without any hesitation, without any apparent anxiety. Maybe she desired the very thing she rejected, and snuffed out any chances of finding it with casual flings. Danny hated himself for even thinking that he might just be one of her brief affairs. She had told him that there had been no one before her pilot, but she might have taken lovers since. His thoughts tortured him and he felt a strong urge to get away from the hotel, to walk out into the dull morning and leave his twisted, confused feelings behind.

The weary maid appeared carrying clean folded tablecloths. Alison looked at Danny. 'We'd better get started,' she said. 'I think she wants to clean up.'

Danny settled the bill and they walked out of the side street and into the morning crowds at Paddington Station. Danny bought a platform ticket and walked along beside the carriages until Alison jerked on his arm. 'Here's an empty one.'

Danny climbed aboard the train and put Alison's suitcase on

the luggage rack. He stepped down again onto the platform and Alison joined him. 'I'll always remember last night, Danny,' she said. 'It was wonderful.'

'Don't ferget ter write. I can meet yer when yer come back ter London.'

Alison nodded but said nothing.

'I could come down ter Dover if they ease the restrictions, Alison.'

She touched his arm. 'Don't let's make any plans yet. I'll write to you, I promise.'

The railway guard walked along the platform, his green flag held ready. The lovers kissed and Alison pulled away from his grasp. As she climbed aboard the train the guard raised his flag. Danny stood watching as the train drew away, and he waved until Alison's head disappeared into the carriage. He thought about their conversation in the park, and the quiet moonlit room in the backstreet, and then turned on his heel to walk away down the platform.

Chapter Eighteen

Frank Sutton was prowling around the house waiting for Joe Copeland's knock. It was the time of day when Alice made her views known, and she chose this particular time for good reason. Frank could be argumentative and was inclined to 'argue the hind legs off a donkey', as she put it, so when she had something important to say or a telling point to make, Alice caught him when he was getting ready to go to work. Frank had to get to work on time or he would miss the 'call-on', so he didn't have time to argue with her. And then he would have all day to dwell on what she had said, and in the evening after a hard day's work, Frank would be too tired to argue. It was the way Alice made sure that she was listened to.

Today Alice had a point to make and she timed it to perfection. 'I don't mind Danny comin' and goin', Frank,' she said as her husband looked anxiously at the door, 'but 'is bed wasn't slept in last night. Gawd knows where 'e is, but I do know 'e was takin' this nurse out.' And she looked at Frank to check that he understood her.

Frank sighed as he looked through the curtains and saw Joe hurrying along the turning. 'I've told yer before, Alice,' he said. ''E's over twenty-one. I can't stop 'is sweets or smack 'is arse, now can I?'

'It ain't the point, Frank. 'E could 'ave told us 'e wasn't comin' 'ome. Somefink could 'ave 'appened to 'im. You'll 'ave ter talk to 'im, you're 'is farver.'

'I ain't got no time ter argue wiv yer, Alice. Joe's comin' along the street. Anyway, I don't s'pose 'e knew 'e was gonna stop out.'

'Well I want yer ter 'ave a word in 'is ear. 'E might take notice o' you.'

Frank opened his mouth to utter a choice profanity, but Joe's rat-tat stopped him. 'I'll see yer ternight, Alice. We'll talk about it then.'

Alice felt pleased with what she had accomplished. She reckoned that there was enough on her plate, what with Connie being all upset over Jimmy, and now Maggie springing it on her about sending the kids away from London, without having to worry about Danny's roamings. Young Tony Arpino had come round to see him and had had to leave a message. It wasn't good enough, Alice told herself, as she took the broom to the passage carpet. Frank will have to say something to him. Stopping out all night is asking for trouble. Danny might have got the poor girl pregnant. Worse still, he might be lying in some hospital. Her thoughts were beginning to make her feel panicky, so she decided the housework could wait. She would go over for a chat with her friend Annie instead. She scribbled a short message on the back of a brown paper bag and after looking it over she propped it up in front of the teapot in the centre of the kitchen table.

In The Globe Eddie Kirkland was having a chat with the subdued owner of Shady Lady, the dog who had broken the track record at Catford last Saturday night. After three consecutive nights of revelry, Biff Bowden was feeling the effects. His winnings had all but disappeared and he was being consoled by the landlord.

'You looked drunk as a sack on Sat'day night, Biff,' Eddie

said. 'Sunday night yer didn't look much better. Don't yer remember offerin' ter buy everybody a drink? Then there was those games o' darts at a fiver a time. No wonder you're skint.'

'Tell yer the trufe, Eddie, the weekend's a bleedin' blank. I don't remember much about it at all.'

Eddie grinned. 'Yer don't remember the ruckus last night then?'

'No.'

'Well I'll tell yer what 'appened. It must 'ave bin about 'alf nine when Bonky Williams walked in wiv a strange geezer. I've never clapped eyes on 'im before. Proper scruff 'e was. Anyway, Bonky starts 'is tricks in front of 'is mate – you know what Bonky's like. Last night 'e 'ad a black patch over 'is wonky eye. You was proppin' the counter up an' tryin' ter date our new barmaid, when up walks Bonky. 'E stan's next ter yer an' orders a drink fer 'im an' 'is mate. Now, when Carol puts the glasses down in front of 'im, dear Bonky opens 'is fist an' tells the girl to 'elp 'erself. Right in the middle of the coppers was 'is glass eye. Carol screams out, an' you, yer soppy git, knocks Bonky's 'and up in the air and the money goes everywhere. But Bonky ain't concerned about 'is money, 'e's more worried about 'is glass eye. We 'ad the customers on their 'ands an' knees lookin' fer it. You was tryin' ter organise the search an' yer offered a fiver reward. Bonky's copped the needle by this time, 'e wants ter crown yer wiv 'is pint mug, an' 'e would 'ave done if it wasn't fer our potman. 'E calms Bonky down an' we got you stuck away in the corner. Proper to-do it was.'

'Bloody 'ell, Eddie, I'm sorry about that. Did Bonky find 'is eye?'

'Yeah, Arfur found it. 'Course, that started it off again. The ole chap was doin' 'is nut 'cos yer wouldn't pay up the reward. Honest, Biff, you was as pissed as an 'andcart. If that bloody dog o' yours ever wins the Grey'ound Derby I'm gonna shut the pub up fer a week. I'm gettin' too old fer all this aggro.'

At noon Danny walked into the pub. His message from Tony Arpino had been that he should look in The Globe around twelve and that it was urgent. Danny was due at Ginny's at twelve-thirty, and it was on the half hour that Tony walked in looking agitated. 'Sorry I'm late,' he said breathing hard. 'I gotta see yer, Danny, there's trouble brewin' in our street an' I'm scared fer me ole man.'

Danny looked up at the clock. 'I'm due on me pitch, Tony,' he said. 'Walk round wiv me, we can 'ave a chin wag on the way.'

They left The Globe and walked towards Clink Lane. Tony seemed reluctant to begin. 'Look, Danny, I know yer in wiv Tony Allen's crowd, but . . .'

''Ang on a minute, Tone. I take bets fer 'im, that's all. I don't socialise wiv 'em. Least of all Jack Mason.'

'It's 'im I wanna talk ter yer about,' Tony said as he grabbed his pal's arm and halted.

'Go on, Tony.'

'Last time I see yer, Danny, I told yer about those two fellers what come round our street. Well they come back. They called in all the shops an' they give us all the spiel. It's a protection racket.'

'What's that gotta do wiv Jack Mason?' Danny asked.

Tony gave his pal a hard look. 'I'd bet a pound to a pinch o' shit 'e's be'ind it.'

'What makes yer say that, Tone?'

''Cos I've seen Mason wiv those two ugly gits, that's why.'

'Where?'

'Down New Cross dogs last Sat'day night.'

'It might 'ave bin a coincidence, Tony.'

'No chance. I was wiv Johnny Ross. 'E told me they're always tergevver. It don't take a Sherlock 'Olmes ter work it out, does it?'

Danny started to walk to Ginny's front door with Tony

falling in beside him. 'Tell me, Tone, 'ow are they workin' it?'

'It's the usual fing. Accordin' ter them, there's a team from over the water tryin' it on, an' we're bein' offered protection – at a price.'

'Ain't none o' the shopkeepers gone ter the police?'

'Leave orf, Danny, yer know the way they work. They've scared the daylights out o' most of 'em. 'Cept me farver, that is. 'E was gonna go roun' the nick, but me muvver wouldn't let 'im.'

Danny stopped at Ginny's house. 'I don't know what I can do, Tony,' he said.

The young Italian looked down at his feet. 'I know you an' Kathy were close once, an' I 'ear she still goes a bundle on yer.'

'So?'

'I also 'ear that Jack Mason's givin' 'er an 'ard time an' she'd leave 'im if she wasn't so terrified of the consequences.'

'Go on, Tony.'

'Look, Danny, I know it's askin' a lot, but can yer 'ave a talk wiv 'er? See if yer can get 'er ter find out when those two monkeys are comin' round again. She might 'ear somefink.'

Danny shook his head. 'I don't s'pose they'd tell Kathy anyfing, an' she can't very well ask 'em, can she?'

'All right, it's an outside bet, Danny, but she might just over'ear somefink. They might use Mason's place fer a get tergevver. We've gotta know when they're comin' back so we can be ready fer 'em.'

'Listen, Tone, even if the law grabs 'em, yer won't get Jack Mason. 'E don't do 'is own dirty work, 'e leaves that to 'is mugs. All right, they might try ter implicate 'im, but it's on the cards Mason's boys'll keep their mouths shut.'

Tony gave Danny an entreating look. 'I wouldn't ask yer, Danny,' he said, 'but I'm scared they're gonna do the ole man some 'arm. We want those gits o' Mason's right out o' the way, an' if the law don't pull Mason in I'll take care of 'im meself.'

'Don't be stupid, Tony. Jack Mason is an animal. 'E'd eat yer alive.'

'You let me worry about 'im,' Tony said, gritting his teeth. 'Will yer 'ave a chat wiv Kathy?'

Danny puffed out his cheeks. 'Okay, Tone, I'll see what I can do.'

Tony Arpino's plea only added to Danny's feeling of depression. His problems seemed to be piling up without any answers. When he had returned home that morning his mother had berated him about staying out all night, he was playing with fire in keeping a young girl out all night. Danny had ignored her and stormed out to The Globe but there was no one around. The street was in mourning for Bella and seemed uncannily quiet. Even old Charlie Perkins was forgoing his seat in the sun.

Danny stood in Ginny's doorway thinking about his brief liaison with Alison. He knew that she was not going to rush a letter off to him as soon as she got home, and he was sure that she was trying to tell him in a roundabout way that they were not going to get too serious. The chat they had together on the platform at Paddington Station made him feel that she was preparing him for a rejection. Why did it all have to be so complicated? It seemed as though a dark cloud was settling over everything, even Dawson Street and his own family. His sister Connie was walking around in a perpetual daze since she had heard about Jimmy's ship going down, and Lucy was getting very irritable and unapproachable. Even Maggie seemed to have lost her calm 'big sister' image and was wearing a constant frown.

Just as Danny was ready to finish his morning stint he saw Jack Mason coming down the turning towards him looking like he was about to burst a blood vessel. His face was flushed and he was clenching his fists, and as he got closer Danny could see the vicious look in his eyes. Mason stopped in front of Ginny's house.

'You seen that berk Rossy?' he blurted out without any greeting.

Danny felt dislike welling up inside him. 'I bin 'ere fer the last hour an 'alf, an' 'e ain't showed. What's wrong?'

'What's wrong?' Mason sneered. 'Rossy's s'posed ter be collectin' some gear from Tony, an' 'e ain't turned up. Tony's copped the needle an' I'm left ter do the errands. If yer see the cow-son tell 'im ter get 'imself roun' Tony's quick as 'e can, or I'll put one in 'is chops.'

Danny gave Jack Mason a sideways glance. 'I thought Johnny Ross was workin' at the vinegar factory?' he said.

'So 'e is, but 'e's signed on the panel again. That's why the job was arranged fer this week. I tell yer, son, if it was down ter me an' not Tony I'd give 'im the elbow. It ain't only 'is mouth that annoys me. The bastard's unreliable.'

Danny nodded. 'Okay, if I see 'im I'll pass the message on.'

Mason suddenly relaxed a little and he gave Danny an evil grin. 'You ain't seen nuffink o' that fat git Stockbridge round 'ere, 'ave yer?' he asked.

'Not since 'e nabbed Bonky Williams. Why?'

'Just askin'. By the way, 'ow's the pitch goin'?'

Danny forced a grin. 'Not bad. Biff Bowden's mutt cost Tony a few bob, but it's pickin' up a bit.'

Jack Mason rubbed the sweat from his forehead with the back of his hand. 'Well I'll be off. Yer keep yer nose clean an' we won't ferget ter put a little somefing your way later on.'

Danny watched as Mason hurried out of Clink Lane. A couple of weeks ago he would have been eager to work his way into the set-up, but now he felt that no good was going to come out of it. If he got involved any further in Tony Allen's organisation there would be no backing out. He thought over what Tony Arpino had said, and he realised he would have to be very careful in arranging a meeting with Kathy. Mason had a house in Dockhead and it was out of the question to go there to see her. Maybe Ginny Coombes could help him. She had seen Kathy at the shops in Tooley Street, she might know if Kathy ever came round to see her mother since her father threw her out. If she visited her mother at all it would have to be during the day when her father was at work. That would be the best time to catch her, he thought.

The warm, sunny weather continued throughout the rest of the week. Danny was constantly sullen and miserable. There had been no letter from Alison and no news for Connie, and on Saturday morning Maggie was reduced to a flood of tears as she bade farewell to her two children. Alice joined Maggie at the school gates and stood around with the rest of the local parents while their offspring were tagged with their names and given a bag of fruit and a packet of sweets each. The kids seemed excited at the new adventure, although a few tears were shed by the less adventurous ones. Buses arrived and the fond farewells began. There were last minute hugs and kisses, and a general dipping into handbags for handkerchiefs, and finally the parents walked away toward their homes in the backstreets looking sorrowful and apprehensive.

On Sunday morning Lucy joined Ben for the early service at the Methodist mission. When the Reverend John Harris climbed up into the pulpit in his white cassock, his greying hair flattened to his head with brilliantine, Ben whispered to Lucy, 'The organist is late.'

Lucy glanced up and gazed at the huge instrument with its multitude of gilt and blue pipes that stretched up to the rafters. She wondered how the minister was going to start the service, now that the usually dependable Mr Craddock was not in his place. The Reverend gripped the rail of the pulpit and beamed down benevolently at his flock. 'Good morning, brethren. While we are waiting for Mr Craddock let us begin this morning's service with a short prayer.'

Heads bowed and a silence reigned in the cold, sterile hall. When Reverend Harris lifted his head at the 'Amen' and saw Mr Craddock enter the back of the hall he was delighted. He had selected some rousing hymns for the service, and good old Mr Craddock had not let him down after all. The organist nodded to the congregation as he hurried to his place. His tall, stooping figure and flat-footed gait drew some sympathy from two elderly ladies who were sitting immediately in front of Lucy and Ben.

'Poor Mr Craddock, he's such a dear soul,' one of the ladies whispered.

Her companion touched her Sunday hat with the tips of her fingers and nodded. 'He's so pleasant to everyone. It's a shame. He seems hardly able to do the collection lately. I think it's getting too much for him.'

Mr Craddock had reached the organ and settled himself at the keyboard. He pushed up his pebble-lensed spectacles onto the bridge of his nose and squinted at the opened music sheet. He rocked back and forth a couple of times, then the opening bars of 'Onward Christian Soldiers' shattered the silence. The old ladies' kindly mutterings about Mr Craddock's health and humility were drowned out as the congregation sang with feeling.

Monday morning the 22nd of July dawned wet and windy. The recent glorious weather changed suddenly on the day Bella Corrigan was to be laid to rest. The horse-drawn hearse and its attendant coach stopped for a few seconds at the top of Dawson Street as a last respect, and in the coach Alice Sutton, Annie Barnes and Billy Birkitt's mother held handkerchiefs to their faces. Bella's neighbours stood silently by as the cortége passed along Tooley Street. Dockers doffed their caps, and a strolling policeman halted and gave a stiff salute. At noon the rain stopped and the sky cleared. The period of mourning was over, and in the early afternoon when Alice was hanging her black coat up in the wardrobe, she heard loud shouts and laughs in the street outside. Mrs Ellis came hurrying into the turning, beaming and waving a telegram. Her son Jimmy had been picked up and landed in Newfoundland. He was quite well and recuperating in hospital from his spell in the cold waters of the North Atlantic.

That lunchtime Danny was anxiously watching along Clink Lane. He had spoken to Ginny about Kathy and was told that she visited her mother every Monday during her lunch-hour. Danny was getting worried. Tony Arpino was pressing him for information, and he said he had heard that there would be a visit sometime during the week for a pay-off. It was ten minutes past one when he saw Kathy walking down the turning and he was shocked by her appearance. She looked tired and jaded, her usual bounce and vitality replaced by a leaden walk. Danny noticed the dark circles around her eyes as she got closer. He waved to her and Kathy smiled. ''Ow are yer?'

'Not so bad,' Danny replied, moving his hands in a rocking gesture. 'I need ter talk ter yer, Kath. Soon as possible.'

'I've got no time now, Danny, I'm jus' poppin' in ter me mum. I've gotta be back ter work by two.'

She looked at him and saw the anxiety in his eyes. ''E goes out most nights. I might be able ter get out fer a while ternight. I can't promise though.'

'Where can I meet yer?'

Kathy thought for a moment. 'There's a little pub down by the riverside – The Bell. D'yer know it? It's only five minutes from my place.'

Danny nodded. 'Yeah I know it. Is it okay there?'

'We'll be all right there,' Kathy assured him. 'It's a family 'ouse. None o' the villains get in there. I'll try ter get there by 'alf-eight, it should be quiet then. Okay?'

Danny grinned with relief. 'That's 'an'some. I'll be there. Try an' make it.'

'I'll do me best, Danny,' she said as she hurried back to the other side of the street.

She waved to him as she reached her mother's house.

It was a momentous Monday morning for Ben Morrison. He had his army medical and passed A1. He also saw the selection officer and asked to join the Royal Army Medical Corps, but he was not too encouraged by the officer's response. The man shrugged his shoulders. 'You'll be told in good time,' he said dismissively. Ben hoped desperately that his request would be granted. If not, he could only envisage a confrontation with the military and a spell in an army prison. He was troubled by something else too that had been niggling away at him for the past few days now. When he got back from his medical he went up to his flat and made himself a mug of tea. In the quietness of his room he took the letter down from behind the clock and sat for a while looking at the envelope. Was there something he had missed? he wondered. Was there something in the content that would identify the sender? Ben put his mug down and turned the envelope over. It was an ordinary kind that could be bought anywhere. His name and address had been printed in bold lettering: childlike but legible. Almost reluctantly he took out the folded sheet of paper that had one rough edge.

It was lined paper and had obviously been torn from an exercise book. The wording was upright and neat, and the spelling mistakes seemed to be more deliberate than natural. Ben stared at the letter until his eyes were tired. Maybe Lucy was right, maybe he should burn the evil thing instead of becoming obsessed with trying to identify the writer. After all, there were thousands of these sort of letters received every day by conscientious objectors, according to the newspapers. They were the product of sick minds. Ben sat for some time thinking

217

about whether or not to destroy the letter, then finally he folded the sheet of paper and replaced it in the envelope. He heard Lucy's familiar knock on his door and before answering it he put the envelope back behind the clock.

Chapter Nineteen

Danny strolled along in the cool of the summer evening until he came to Jamaica Road. He walked on for a while then turned off into a backstreet leading down to the river where moored barges rocked on the incoming tide. That particular stretch of the Thames was quiet, almost rural. A patch of green stood out across the river at Wapping where the ancient churchyard held back the threatening wharves and storehouses. At the river wall a lane ran along beside the warehouses until it narrowed into a pathway. It was there that The Bell stood. The pub had none of the trappings associated with riverside inns, apart from a couple of faded pictures of the *Cutty Sark*. The one long bar was sparsely decorated and the proprietors, an elderly couple, seemed content to keep it that way.

When Danny walked in he aroused no more than a casual glance from the few folk who sat around on hard chairs resting their beer on iron-legged tables. He ordered a pint and took a seat. Now and then a customer came in, but there was no sign of Kathy. Danny finished his drink and eyed the bar clock: five to nine. He decided to get a refill, and if Kathy had not shown up by the time he had finished his second pint he would leave. Danny was halfway through his drink when Kathy walked in. She came over and sat down with a sigh. 'I didn't fink 'e was goin' out ternight. 'E's only jus' left,' she said, breathing heavily.

'D'yer wanna drink? I mean, are you . . .' Danny began.

Kathy laughed. 'I'll 'ave a stout, Danny. It's all right, me doctor ses it's good fer me – an' the baby.'

Danny returned with the stout and watched while Kathy took a sip. When she put the glass down onto the table he leaned forward and put his hand on hers.

'Listen, Kath, I've got a big faver to ask. It's not fer me really, it's fer Tony Arpino. You know Tony.'

Kathy looked at him with a mischievous glint in her eye. 'I thought yer got me 'ere so yer could carry me off ter some exotic place,' she said smiling.

Danny squeezed her hand and grinned. 'Later, Kathy. Right now I want some info. Will yer 'elp me?'

'What is it, Danny?'

'There's a mob goin' roun' puttin' the squeeze on Tony's family, an' the rest of the shopkeepers in Bermon'sey Lane.'

Kathy stared at her glass. 'Yer fink it might be Jack's crowd?'

'Tony's pretty certain 'e's be'ind it, Kath. Can yer give us any idea if it is 'im?'

Kathy's eyes flared angrily as she looked at him. 'You've got a nerve. Do yer really expect me ter snitch on 'im?'

Danny returned her angry stare with a hard look. 'Listen, Kath, I wouldn't even think of it if yer was 'appy wiv 'im. Don't try an' tell me 'e don't knock yer about. Don't tell me yer 'appy wiv 'im.'

'There's such a fing as loyalty, Danny. I've made my bed an' I'm lyin' in it.'

'Yeah, an' yer 'avin' 'is kid, an' the cow-son's knockin' yer about.'

'I ain't said Jack's knockin' me about, Danny. You said it.'

'C'mon, Kath, it's yer ole Danny yer talkin' to. Tell me the trufe.'

'All right, maybe we do 'ave our ups an' downs. So do lots o' people. Yer can't expect me ter tell yer if 'e's involved, even if I did know 'e was – which I don't.'

Danny swallowed the rest of his drink and put the glass down heavily on the table. 'I didn't know if yer knew or not. I thought yer might over'ear somefing an' be able ter tell us when they're goin' roun' ter put the boot in.'

'Look, Danny, Jack's always got somebody callin' round ter see 'im. I don't stay in the room when they're talkin'. Even if I did over'ear somefing an' I told yer, Jack would know it was me. 'E'd kill me.'

Danny toyed with his empty glass. 'Yeah, yer right, I can't expect yer ter take that sort o' chance. Ferget I asked yer.'

Kathy's eyes misted and she stared at her drink. When she looked up at him Danny saw the torment on her pale face. He squeezed her arm gently. ''Ow yer feelin'? I mean bein' – you know—'

'Pregnant,' Kathy said, finishing the sentence for him. She got some looks from the people near to them. 'You don't 'ave ter be frightened of sayin' it, Danny. But to answer your question, I'm okay.'

Danny looked at her, his pale blue eyes showing concern. 'Why don't yer leave 'im? Surely there mus' be somewhere yer can go?'

Kathy sighed. 'I can't go back ter Clink Lane, and where else is there? I s'pose I could throw meself on the mercy of some women's 'ostel, but I ain't gonna bring a kid inter the world at one o' those places. No, Danny, I'm gonna stick it out, fer the baby's sake.'

Danny twisted his glass. 'I wish I 'ad me own place,' he said. 'Yer could stay wiv me.'

Kathy smiled. 'Yer mean yer'd take me in, an' me 'avin' anuvver man's kid?'

Danny became embarrassed. 'Yeah, well I'd be doin' it fer you, not 'im.'

'Danny, you're a luv'ly person. Why don't yer find yerself a nice girl an' get married?'

'Chance would be a fine fing,' he grinned. 'I don't seem ter be 'avin' much luck lately.'

'I wish we could put the clock back, Danny. Me an' you'd make a good team.'

'Yeah, we sure would,' he smiled.

They left The Bell together and strolled slowly along the riverside. The night was warm, with the pungent smell of mud rising from the foreshore. Heavy, dark clouds were drifting in, and they heard the water lapping and the moored barges creaking and thudding as they lifted on the tide. The two young people stopped on the corner of a small turning.

Kathy squeezed his hand. 'I've gotta leave yer 'ere, Danny,' she said. 'Take care of yerself. I'll be seein' yer around.'

Her kiss was soft and her gently rounded body pressed against him briefly. He watched her disappear into the dusk, wishing things could have been different.

On Tuesday there was new cause for gloom and a new topic of discussion around the backstreets and in the docks and wharves. Frank Sutton sat beside Joe Copeland on the quayside during a lull in the unloading. 'That's a bit much, Joe. Income tax up ter eight an' six, a penny on a pint, an' this bloody purchase tax they're bringin' in,' he said with a scowl.

Joe threw his wet cigarette stub into the water. 'I fink it's scandalous. I know there's a war on, but it's always us that gets it.'

Frank scratched his head. 'Well they've 'it the rich this time. That purchase tax is on lux'ries. What lux'ries do the likes o' you an' me 'ave?'

'Yeah, I s'pose yer right. Fancy puttin' the beer up though, it's bloody outrageous. After all, it's weak as piss as it is.'

Frank grinned. 'I reckon we ought ter change our boozer, don't you? I'm sure ole Kirkland's waterin' the beer. Why don't we try the brew over at The Castle?'

Joe pulled a face. 'I don't like that 'ouse. It's full o' nancy boys.'

Frank laughed. 'I know a few of 'em get in there, Joe, but they're all right. In fact they're a bit of a laugh. Ole Billy Farnsworth goes in there reg'lar. 'E's a scream. Bent as a nine-bob note 'e is. I see 'im the uvver day pushin' 'is sister's kid in a pram. When 'e see me lookin' 'e shouted out, "It's not mine!"'

The crane swung around and the dockers went back to work. 'We'll try The Castle if yer like, Frank,' Joe shouted as he grabbed a swinging rope, 'but if one o' them "iron-'oofs" tries ter kiss me on the lips I'm pissin' orf.'

The backstreet folk seethed at the budget news. The price of beer overtook the pending invasion as the main topic of conversation, and it caused long faces among the old gents who used The Globe.

'Now if we was workin', Bill, we'd get anuvver shillin' in the pound stopped. On top o' that, we drink about two dozen pints a week. That's anuvver couple o' bob out o' pocket. This rate, we're gonna suffer both ways.'

''Ow d'yer make that out, Fred? Me an' you ain't workin'.'

'I know we ain't, Bill, but when yer fink about it, if we was, an' we come in 'ere fer a pint, we'd 'ave ter fink twice about buyin' a drink fer anybody now we're gonna be worse orf. See what I mean?'

Bill turned his head and spat a stream of tobacco juice through the open door of the pub. 'It looks like we ain't gonna be drinkin' two dozen pints a week now, Fred.'

The gloom persisted throughout the week. Danny had still not heard from Alison, and Maggie was missing her kids. She was even more miserable when she listened to the street gossip. Rumours of evacuees being ill-treated were rife, and some of the parents were considering fetching their children home. Lucy too was very touchy. She was unapproachable in the mornings, and when Danny mentioned about Kathy having a baby she suddenly rounded on him. Only Connie brightened Danny's day. She was eagerly looking forward to being reunited with Jimmy, and she suggested that it would be nice if they could have a street party to celebrate his safe return.

'What d'yer fink, Danny boy?' she bubbled, her button nose screwing up and her deep blue eyes widening.

'Anyfing ter liven it up a bit, sis. The way fings are 'ere, I wish I was back in the army.'

Connie was alone with Danny in the front parlour. She had been concerned about her brother's depression and decided to try drawing him into conversation. 'What about that Alison, Danny? Ain't yer gonna see 'er any more?' she asked.

'I'm waitin' fer a letter, sis.'

'She still on leave then?'

Danny shrugged his shoulders. 'I don't fink so. She was s'posed ter drop us a line so I could meet 'er in London again.'

'Is that why yer fed up? You fink she's given yer the brush-off?'

Normally Danny was reticent about discussing his affairs, but Connie had a special way with him and he found it easy to talk to her. 'Yeah, I reckon so,' he said.

Connie pulled her legs up under her as she sat in the easy chair and sighed. 'I was 'opin' you'd get serious with Kathy. I fink she's nice. She likes you, I can tell.'

Danny winced. 'Yer know she's livin' wiv Jack Mason now?'

'Yeah, I know,' Connie replied. 'She's 'avin' a baby, ain't she?'

Danny was keen to change the subject. 'What about you? Are you an' Jimmy gonna get married?'

'Soon as we can, bruv. The way fings are, we don't want ter wait. D'yer fink that's right?'

'Them's my sentiments, Connie. Marry yer sailor boy. Grab what 'appiness yer can, while yer can. There's no sense in waitin'. Yer can wait fer ever.'

Connie's face suddenly became serious. 'Danny, can yer keep a secret?' she asked.

'Try me.'

'Promise yer won't let on ter Mum an' Dad?'

'Promise.'

'Lucy reckons she might be 'avin' a baby.'

'*What?*'

'She's pretty certain. Gawd knows what Mum an' Dad's gonna say when they find out, but they've gotta know before long.'

Danny puffed out his cheeks. ''E's picked a fine time ter get 'er pregnant.'

Connie pouted. 'It takes two ter tango, Danny. She's jus' one o' the unlucky ones.'

'Well at least she'll 'ave a better chance than Kathy. I can't see our ole man chuckin' 'er out like Kathy's ole man did.'

Connie got up and took her coat from behind the door. 'I've gotta get back ter work. See yer ternight, bruv.'

'Don't you get pregnant, Connie, fer Chrissake,' Danny said as she opened the door.

'Chance would be a fine fing,' Connie called back from the passage, slamming the front door shut behind her.

Danny put his feet up onto the vacant chair and closed his eyes to think. It was Friday, and since he had talked to Kathy he had been unable to contact Tony Arpino. On two occasions he had gone along to the Arpinos' shop in Bermondsey Lane, and each time Tony's father had told him that his son was up town trying to get some information as to the whereabouts of Maria and her family. Danny had bumped into Johnny Ross in

Clink Lane that morning and heard that Tony hadn't been to the New Cross dogs the previous evening. Johnny had been edgy, and asked if he could stand in Ginny's doorway while he talked. Danny grinned to himself when he recalled the conversation.

'I'm in the shite, Danny.'

'I know yer are. Jack Mason's bin lookin' fer yer.'

Johnny winced. ''E's gonna give me a good goin' over when 'e catches me. It's about somefink I done.'

'Bloody 'ell, Johnny, you're a walkin' disaster. What yer done now?'

Johnny peered out from Ginny's doorway to make sure he wasn't in any immediate danger and then he spoke in a low voice: 'Yer remember me tellin' yer about that load I 'ad away? Well, Tony Allen stuck it in 'is timber yard.'

'Not that one next ter the nick?'

'Same one. Anyways, 'e paid me fer the stuff, but 'e was left wiv a couple o' dozen cases 'e couldn't place. 'E wanted 'em out of 'is yard, just in case the law got sensible all of a sudden. That's what Jack Mason was gettin' all stewed up about. What 'e didn't know was that I was puttin' around tryin' ter get a buyer. There was no way I was gonna get lumbered wiv the gear. I must admit though, Tony Allen was fair about it. 'E'd already paid me fer the lot an' 'e said I could earn a dollar a case fer placin' 'em. Anyway, I got a buyer in Deptford. Fing was, I stuck a couple o' bob on fer me trouble. The bloke seemed 'appy wiv the price, but what I didn't know was that 'is mate a few doors away 'ad already bought some o' the corned beef from Tony. They got talkin' an' my bloke finks 'e's bin took on. 'E gives Tony a ring, an' I'm called inter the office. Tony went on about losin' 'is credibility an' I'm standin' there noddin' an' lookin' all sorry fer meself. The result was, I got a slap on the wrist an' told not ter do it again, when in walks that bastard Mason. 'Im an' Tony get at it, an' I'm told ter wait outside. I can 'ear 'em goin' orf at each uvver an' I'm gettin' scared. Jack Mason's ravin', an' I know I'm in fer a pastin'. So I scarpers quick, 'cos if Mason gets 'old o' me I'm gonna look like a sack o' coal – all lumps an' bumps.'

Danny had been horrified by Johnny's tale, and now he eased his position in the chair and wondered how he was going to locate his pal Tony Arpino. He would have to make him see that Kathy couldn't help him without putting herself in danger. Danny thought about his own situation too. Jack Mason appeared to be pulling the strings, if what Johnny had said was anything to go by, and Tony Allen wasn't into protection rackets, he felt sure. That was one of Mason's sidelines, and Jack Mason was a force to be reckoned with. The whole business was putting him in a very precarious position. Being the local bookmaker's runner was jeopardising his loyalty to his pal Tony Arpino. Danny thought about talking to Tony Allen but rejected the idea. It would only bring the bookie's minder down on him, and everything would then get very nasty. He was beginning to regret ever having became an employee of Tony Allen and Co.

Alice Sutton brought the news back with her Saturday morning shopping. There was to be a christening party in the street. Alice was full of it as she unpacked the week's rations and laid them out on the table.

'I'm so pleased for 'em, an' what's more it'll cheer us all up. I was talkin' ter Missus Mitchell, an' she said she was gonna borrer some forms an' some trestle tables from the church 'all. Everybody's invited. If the weavver stays fine the party's gonna be 'eld in the street. That'll be nice, Frank.'

Alice's husband was reading the morning paper and uttered an unintelligible reply. Alice stood in front of him with her hands on her hips. 'Frank, will you put that bleedin' paper down an' listen ter me?'

'I was listenin', Alice. What d'yer say?' he asked, scratching his moustache.

'I said the Mitchells are 'avin' a street party termorrer. Their baby's bein' christened.'

Frank chuckled. 'That'll be nice. We'll get Bonky pissed an' doin' 'is Nelson bit. Then we can carry ole Charlie Perkins up ter the top o' the turnin' ter stop any traffic comin' down.'

Alice tried to look stern. 'I don't want yer showin' me up, Frank Sutton. I remember the last street party. What wiv you an' Annie Barnes's ole man dancin' up the street in those red flannel drawers, an' the pair of yer grabbin' ole Granny Bell. Showed me up proper, yer did.'

Frank grinned. 'Blimey, Alice, that was a few years ago. That was when Charlie Perkins 'ad that set-to wiv 'is ole woman an' blacked 'er eye. On their weddin' anniversary as well.'

Alice shook her head. 'That was a different time. You 'ad them drawers on at the Brightmans' party.'

'No, yer got it wrong, girl. I know when I got dressed up, 'cos Charlie Perkins give me the drawers. They was 'is ole woman's, that's what the row was about.'

Alice conceded the point; it wasn't worth arguing when there was so much to do. She had to sort out her best dress, and maybe Maggie could do her hair up for her. Frank was still belabouring the point when Maggie looked in a little later.

'What's all this about red flannel drawers?' she asked as she walked into the parlour.

'Take no notice of yer farver, Maggie, 'e's comin' over all unnecessary in 'is old age,' Alice grinned as she smoothed down the clean tablecloth. Frank realised he was now outnumbered and decided it was time to retreat to The Globe.

Chapter Twenty

The Mitchells lived at number 17 Dawson Street. John Mitchell was a Scot who first saw the light of day in a croft, and had travelled down to London to seek work, and instead had found himself knee-deep in mud on the battlefields of France. By the end of the war he had risen to the rank of sergeant in the Scots Guards, and had been awarded the Military Medal. His friends reckoned that John Mitchell was a hero, but the dour Scot disagreed. The medal meant very little to him, and the jubilation had soon evaporated in the rush for work and the endless dole queues of the thirties. John Mitchell was lucky, he had got a job with a Bermondsey blacksmith who taught him well. When the next war began he was established in his own business with a young apprentice articled to him. He had also found a wife, a Bermondsey girl whom he doted on. He and his blond-haired Janie desperately wanted a child and, just when they had begun to despair, Janie became pregnant. John Mitchell hoped it would be a boy, who would of course follow him into the business. The birth was a difficult one, and when the tiny bundle was placed into his muscular arms John Mitchell swallowed his disappointment, and promptly fell in love when he looked at his daughter's puckered face. Janie allowed her husband to name the child and he picked the names Heather Louise: Heather, because he said the child smelled of the heather-covered braes; and Louise after his late mother. The Mitchells were a respected and well-liked couple who stayed in the street despite their growing business. Janie could not envisage leaving the turning she was born in and the folk she loved, and John Mitchell was happy to pander to his wife's wishes, and so they stayed. Sunday was going to be a big day in their lives, and everyone in the little backstreet was invited to the party.

The idyllic weather continued, and Sunday was bright and warm. The revelries began at lunchtime and The Globe was packed with back-slapping customers who threatened to overwhelm John Mitchell with their offers of drinks. The proud father had to refuse all but the first pint. The christening was at three o'clock, and for him the party would begin after the naming of Heather Louise. The landlord of The Globe was also being cautious. Biff Bowden was in full swing following Shady Lady's narrow victory at Catford and Eddie was watching out for the arrival of Bonky Williams. He was aware of the hostility between Biff and Bonky and realised that he would have to take on the role of peacemaker.

At one o'clock Bonky Williams walked in the pub, and as soon as he saw Biff Bowden standing at the bar his face became dark. Eddie did not miss the omen, and he hurried to serve Bonky. ''Ow the bloody 'ell are yer, me ole mate?' he cried.

'I was all right till I see that ugly bastard,' Bonky replied.

Eddie poured the stout carefully. 'It's a shame yer feel that way about Biff.'

'Why's that?' Bonky asked, eyeing the landlord suspiciously.

'Oh, nuffink.'

Bonky was hooked. 'C'mon, Eddie, why is it a shame?'

Eddie leaned over the counter in an exaggerated gesture of secrecy. 'If I tell yer somefink, can yer keep it ter yerself?'

'You know me, Eddie, I'm as tight as a drum.'

'I know that, Bonky, but can yer keep a secret?'

Bonky Williams puffed and slapped the counter in frustration. 'You gonna tell me or not?'

'Right, now listen carefully, 'cos I gotta whisper,' Eddie said, trying not to laugh.

Bonky gave the landlord a sideways glance. 'Look, I might be short on eyes, but me poxy 'earin' ain't affected.'

'Okay, Bonky lad. Biff Bowden's dog's goin' inter retirement soon.'

'What d'yer want me ter do, go roun' wiv a bleedin' collection fer it?'

'Now don't get all shirty, Bonky, jus' listen. Biff told me in confidence that Shady Lady is goin' fer breedin', an' when she 'as 'er first litter, Biff's gonna name the first pup "Bonky's Gem". What d'yer fink about that?'

Bonky Williams looked over to where Biff was standing, then back to Eddie. 'Cor! That's decent of 'im, ain't it?'

Eddie turned away and fiddled with the spirit optics until he had regained control of his facial muscles. 'I fink it's a nice gesture, Bonky. Ole Biff reckons yer a good sport.'

'Did 'e tell yer that, Eddie?'

'Sure did, mate.'

'Well I'll be! I fink I'll buy 'im a drink.'

'That'd be 'an'some, Bonky.'

'"Bonky's Gem",' ruminated Bonky 'Now that'd be somefing ter drink to!'

Eddie winced noticeably. 'Don't let on I told yer. Biff'll do 'is nut.'

'Don't worry, Eddie. Mum's the word.'

Bonky walked over to Biff and tapped him on the shoulder. 'Wanna drink, Biff?'

Biff, slightly the worse for drink, looked at the one-eyed character, his face contorted. 'Fanks, Bonky, I'll 'ave a pint of ale.'

Eddie stood at the counter, his fingers crossed behind his back, and when Biff looked in his direction he saw the landlord winking at him urgently. Old Arthur Smith saw the gesticulations too. ''Ere, Eddie,' he said, 'when yer get rid o' yer affliction can yer pour me anuvver pint? I'm dyin' o' thirst.'

Before The Globe had shut for the night, the Mitchells' christening party was in full swing. Charlie Perkins sat beside the crates of ale, his bony fingers tapping in time with the wheezing concertina, Granny Bell was doing a soft-shoe shuffle with her skirts held up to her knee, and the street folk clapped in unison. All the children were allowed to stop up late while the guest of honour, Heather Louise Mitchell, slept peacefully in her bassinet. All around her the merriment went on: Frank Sutton took his wife Alice out onto the cobblestones and held her firmly as he whisked her around; Joe Copeland was talking to John Mitchell, a pint glass clutched tightly in his large fist; and Maggie sat with Lucy and Connie. 'My two would 'ave loved this,' she said sadly.

Connie put her arm around Maggie's shoulders. 'I fink yer did the right fing, Mag. I got a feelin' it's gonna get really bad before long.'

Lucy nodded her agreement. 'It's only a matter of time. The children are much better off being out of London. I feel sorry for the little mites here, they're going to be in the thick of it.'

Maggie sighed. 'I 'ope I did do the right fing. It caused a right ole barney between me an' Joe.'

'Ain't you an' 'im talkin'?' Connie asked in her usual forthright manner.

'We're all right now,' Maggie replied. ''E soon got over it. I fink deep down 'e knew I'd done the right fing. 'E didn't like admittin' it though.'

Danny Sutton walked back from The Globe to the street party, his thoughts centred on his pal Tony. He felt ineffectual and useless, and it worried him. The two of them had run the streets together as kids and got into the usual scrapes. Now, when Tony asked him for help he was unable to do anything. The pints he had drunk were beginning to take their toll and Danny felt he was well on his way to getting drunk. Maybe he should sink a few more pints and blot out the depression that was gnawing away at his insides and tightening the base of his skull like a vice. Maybe he should tell the bookmaker to poke his job, and tell Jack Mason to get stuffed. Perhaps he could find rooms and move Kathy in with him. At least she would be away from that bullying bastard. He would have to give it some thought, but first he was going to join the party and drink himself into a state of sublime intoxication.

The young cockney heard the sound of the concertina before he turned the corner. Dusk was settling down around the merrymakers, and he could see the outlines of people dancing in the light that shone out from the gas-lit passages of the tumbledown houses. All the front doors were open, the black-out regulations apparently forgotten, and the street warden Archie Madden was waltzing around with the aged Mrs Jackson who owned the little sweetshop on the corner of the turning. Bernie Wright the concertina player was grinning widely as he stamped his foot in time to the melody he was squeezing out from his beloved instrument.

Connie came up to Danny and grabbed his arm. 'C'mon, bruv, I've bin waitin' fer yer. Let's 'ave a dance.'

John Mitchell and his Janie were passing among the guests, filling their glasses and exchanging pleasantries. Their pride and joy, Heather Louise, slept on as the music got louder and the raucous laughter filled the street. Charlie Perkins was rocking in his chair, with a pint glass in his hand and a toothless smile that infected everyone who looked at him. The war and the troubles that might come were far from the minds of the Dawson Street folk on that balmy Sunday night. They toasted

233

John and Janie and their baby, they drank the health of each other, and they remembered absent friends. The music rang out again, and the strains of 'Roses of Picardy' drifted through the backwater of dockland. John Mitchell felt a wave of nostalgia wash over him, and he remembered the Somme and Ypres. Danny was transported back in his mind to more recent battles. He thought of the young soldier who died at his side on the beaches, and the imperturbable gypsy Oggy Murphy who held him safely in the dark, freezing water off La Panne, and his eyes filled with tears.

The drinking carried on as the midnight hour came and went. Old songs were sung and the strains of 'Alice Blue Gown' and 'She's Only a Bird in a Gilded Cage' carried down the turning and echoed through the railway arch. Sleepy, happy children were hauled off to bed and their parents rejoined the revelry. Two lovers sat close together in the shadows and kissed tenderly. The girl was happy to be sharing the secret, and her beau was a little overcome.

'Tell me, Ben, are you happy for us? Are you really happy?' she asked.

He tried to answer but the lump in his throat prevented him, and he nodded, his glowing eyes answering her fully. She snuggled up to him and felt a slight shiver run down her back. He was fearful for the future, but the night was magical.

She could see the river from her bedroom window. The dark sky held no magic, only a foreboding. She had been happy that morning but the feeling was shortlived; the future held no happiness, only sorrow. She saw the days ahead as too burdensome to bear. Her head ached, and the dark swelling below her eye was tender to the touch. She raised her hand to her forehead and stared out into the night. It seemed that her whole life had been one of constant unhappiness; there were very few occasions when she had felt really happy and wanted.

She could count the times on one hand. She thought about the young man who had brought her brief happiness and tears welled up in her eyes. It was too late. She could have gone to him, but the baby inside her would soon come into the world and be a constant reminder of her past. There would always be secret thoughts which would eat into his mind and destroy any true happiness.

It was too late for tears. If only, she rued. If only there had been more time with Danny before he left. Maybe things would have been different. Maybe he would have realised just how much she cared for him and wanted him. Her anger and pride had led her into an impossible relationship with a man whose thin veneer of respectability and decency had peeled away so quickly to reveal the true character beneath. Why had she been so blind? Why had she been attracted to a man like Jack Mason? Why had she succumbed to his surface charm and not seen the real man beneath? Had she gone with Mason to punish Danny? Or to punish herself? It didn't matter now . . .

It was all too late.

The room became dark and Kathy drew the curtains. She turned on the small bedside lamp. The letter was still lying on the dressing table. It would not have been so bad had he tried to excuse his actions or say he was sorry. Instead the confrontation had been violent. She had found the letter quite by accident. It had fallen out of his pocket when he threw his coat over the back of a chair that morning. She had noticed it when she was tidying up, and now she wished that she had never read it. It was from a woman she knew slightly. She was a barmaid in one of the pubs in Deptford which Jack Mason used. It was a passionate letter, referring to the happy times they had spent together, and went on to say how she was missing him while on holiday, and how she looked forward to seeing him once more. Kathy recalled the shock and blind fury she had experienced as she held the letter in her shaking hands.

There were many things she had endured with him – the beatings and the rough, inconsiderate way he made love to her – but there was one thing she would not endure. She would not share him with another woman. She was having his baby and she tried to make him see that he owed her his loyalty. His answer was to tell her that he never wanted the kid and that she should have got rid of it like he told her. Her anger spilled over and she tore at his face with her hands, only to be sent sprawling by a cuff. He had stormed out in a vile temper at lunchtime and had not returned. Kathy had spent the rest of the day crying hysterically, but now, as the night drew in, she had composed herself.

With calm deliberation she went to the bathroom and filled a tumbler full of water and then placed it beside the bed. Next she undressed and put on her nightgown. She filled her palm with the contents of a small glass phial and swallowed the lot between gulps from the tumbler. She turned off the light and pulled open the curtains. The bed felt cool as she closed her eyes. The cold, distant stars twinkled through gaps in the cloud bank. After some time the soft moon shone into the room and lit up the prone figure on the bed, then the stars faded and the moon was covered once again by clouds. The pin-points of light went out, and a velvet blackness smothered her heavy eyelids.

Sadie Comfort sat in her comfortable front room listening to the evening service. Boss, her red setter, lay at her feet and looked up with large, doleful eyes. Sadie Comfort felt uneasy, and the hymn-singing on the wireless did little to relieve her. Maybe Albert was right when he said she should mind her own business and not get involved. After all, it was nothing unusual to hear banging and shouting next door. The man who lived there was a pig, in Sadie's estimation, although she thought the girl was very pleasant and polite. They seemed an odd match;

he was a lot older than her, and was always going out alone. He was prone to raise his hand to the girl and there were often tell-tale marks on her face. Albert said they had to sort things out for themselves, and as long as they didn't interfere with anyone else there was nothing to be done, but Sadie could not get rid of her uncomfortable feeling; something was wrong. Since that morning when she heard the row the girl had not made an appearance, which was unusual. The man had gone out though, and Sadie's horse-brasses had rattled as he slammed the door violently.

Sadie Comfort's eyes dropped, and the sing-song voice of the minister reciting the evening prayer sounded far away. Boss put his head on Sadie's foot and made her start. She looked down at the dog and saw the large eyes staring up at her enquiringly. Sadie yawned and looked up at the clock on the mantelshelf: ten past ten. Albert would be in from the pub soon and then she would feel better. Being left alone didn't normally worry her; Boss was a good house dog, and Albert was rarely gone for more than an hour. Tonight though was different, though Boss seemed restless, too. He had had his walk and his supper, and by now he should have been curled up asleep on the hearth rug. Albert would no doubt think she was being silly, but Boss knew there was something wrong.

At the sound of a key in the door Boss stood up and growled. Albert walked in and took off his coat. ''Ello, Boss, ain't yer asleep?' he said.

Sadie glanced at the clock. 'There's not bin a sound from next door, Alb. I'm sure there's somefink wrong.'

'We gonna start all that again, Sadie? I told yer, it's not our concern.'

'But there ain't bin a sound since 'e went out. I usually 'ear 'er movin' about, an' she nearly always goes out some time durin' the day. 'E could 'ave killed 'er fer all we know.'

'Ain't 'e bin back?'

'Nope. I would 'ave 'eard 'im. I would 'ave 'eard the door go.'

Albert scratched his head. 'It's a bit late ter go knockin' on 'er door. It'd frighten the life out of 'er this time o' night.'

Sadie got up. 'Look at Boss, 'e knows there's somefink wrong, don't yer boy?'

The dog gave a short whine and rubbed himself along Albert's leg.

'It's no good, Alb, I'll 'ave ter knock. I wouldn't get any sleep if I didn't.'

Albert sighed and followed his wife out into the street. He knocked on Mason's door. 'She's not answerin'.'

'Knock a bit louder, Albert.'

Albert rat-tatted. 'She must 'ave gone ter bed,' he said.

'She never goes ter bed early. Yer can normally 'ear 'er movin' about till late.'

'Look, Sadie, p'raps she felt tired an' got an early night?'

'No. I'm goin' fer the keys. She could be dead in there.'

Albert pulled on her arm. 'Yer goin' ter get yerself in trouble if yer not careful. She told yer ter mind the keys fer 'er. She didn't give yer the spare set ter go moochin' around 'er place when yer feel like it.'

'Well that's jus' too bad. Somefink's not right. I gotta find out, Alb.'

When Sadie returned with the keys Boss was trotting along at her heels. Albert opened the front door gingerly, with Sadie wide-eyed looking over his shoulder anxiously. The downstairs was in darkness and the only light came through the landing window. The moonlight shone on the steep staircase and lit up the gilt-framed picture at the head of the stairs.

'Kathy, yer asleep?' Sadie called out.

'That's a daft question, Sadie. If she is asleep she can't answer, can she?'

'Albert, take a look in the front room. She might be in there.'

Albert opened the door and switched on the light. Everything looked tidy. Breathing a sigh of relief, he turned the switch off and closed the door quietly. 'C'mon, girl, we'd better get goin'.'

'D'yer fink we should take a dekko upstairs first, luv?'

'Now listen, Sadie, yer told me the row was in the front room. That's when yer 'eard 'er scream when 'e thumped 'er. Now if 'e 'ad a done 'er in, 'e wouldn't 'ave carted 'er up the apples, now would 'e? She's asleep. If we go up it's gonna scare the bleedin' life out of 'er. C'mon, let's get back.'

'I s'pose yer right, luv,' Sadie conceded, and she turned towards the front door.

Suddenly Boss dashed between the two of them and ran up the stairs.

'Christ! Albert, get 'im quick!'

Albert Comfort raced up the stairs expecting to hear Kathy scream out, but when he peered into the dark bedroom he could see the outline of Boss with his front paws on the bed licking the face of the prone figure. Albert put on the light and quickly drew the curtains. The girl's face was pale and still.

'Gawd Almighty! She's dead!' he said aloud. 'Sadie! Quick!'

Sadie came hurrying into the room, fearful of what she would see, her mouth hanging open. She crept over to the bed and looked down at the wan face of the still woman. She saw the empty phial and the tumbler beside the bed.

'She's took an overdose!' she cried out. 'The poor cow's took an overdose!'

'Is she . . . ?' Albert whispered, stepping back a pace.

Sadie picked up the limp, cold hand and could feel no pulse. In desperation she looked around and saw the small oval mirror lying on the dressing table. 'Give me that mirror. Quick, Albert!'

Sadie held the mirror close to the girl's open mouth. 'She's still breavin'! Quick, run up the top o' the street an' phone fer an ambulance! While yer there yer'd better phone the police as well!'

Chapter Twenty-One

Monday the 29th of July began the same as any other Monday in dockland. The corner-shop owners had to listen to the customers' moans and groans, everything seemed in short supply. The greengrocers took a large share of the complaints. Bananas had disappeared entirely from the shops, stalls and barrows, lemons and oranges were fast disappearing too, and only home-grown produce could still be bought in quantity. Corner-shop customers in the area had read of the recent haul at Sullivan's Wharf and hoped that they would soon be able to purchase a tin of under-the-counter corned beef or peaches but knowing winks and vague gestures did no good. They finally realised that any goods that fell off the back of that lorry had not landed in the Tooley Street area. However, the odd luxury did find its way into a shopping bag, and the satisfied customer realised that all was not lost.

On that particular Monday morning the usual glumness was forgotten when the news of Kathy Thompson spread through the little backstreets. Alice Sutton heard it from Annie Barnes, who had just returned from getting her shopping.

'It's terrible, Alice, 'er poor muvver's goin' mad. A copper knocked on 'er door an' told 'er the news. I bet that bastard Mason's drove 'er to it.'

'Where they took 'er to, Annie?'

'Guy's. Missus Thompson's rushed up there. Gawd knows 'ow bad it is, what wiv 'er bein' in that condition.'

'Well she's in the right place. They're marvellous at Guy's, Annie.'

Annie Barnes nodded her agreement. 'She's 'ad an 'ard time of it, one way an' anuvver.'

It was Alice's turn to nod. 'You're right, 'er ole man's got ter shoulder the blame as well. 'E kicked 'er out when 'e found out she was carryin'. 'E's anuvver no good cow-son. 'E knocks Kathy's muvver black an' blue.'

'I tell yer, Alice, I wouldn't stan' fer it, if it was me.'

'Me neivver, Annie. I'd stab the whore-son when 'e was asleep.'

Danny did not hear the news about Kathy. He had left his house early to call in on the Arpinos' shop. As he walked towards Bermondsey Lane he tried to think clearly about what he was going to say to Tony, but he was still feeling the effects of the party. His head was pounding and his legs felt leaden. As he walked along the line of shops he could sense something was wrong. The usual array of goods was absent from the pavement outside the Arpinos' store. When he entered the shop, Danny stared in disbelief. The floor was littered with cans and packages, and one of the shelves had been yanked away from the wall. The grey marble counter had been smashed, and the large brass scales were lying on the floor. Lou Arpino stood amid the litter, his face grey with misery.

'Dey done ma shop, Danny. Dey 'urt ma boy Tony. Look at da mess. It's a no good, I'm tellin' you, Danny. Dey ruined me.'

'Where's Tony?' Danny asked, taking hold of the Italian's arm. 'Where is 'e, Lou?'

''E's in da back. See if ma boy's okay, Danny. Mamma's wiv 'im.'

Danny walked through into the back room and saw Sofia

bending over her son. Tony sat slumped in a chair, blood coming from a cut above his eye. Sofia was parting his hair gently with her fingers and Tony winced. 'It's all right, Ma, it's only a bump,' he said impatiently.

'Bloody 'ell! What 'appened, Tone?'

Tony Arpino looked up as his pal walked in. 'They done us, Danny. They done us proper. They was too quick fer us.'

Sofia held her hands up to the ceiling. 'Dey nearly killed our Tony,' she cried. 'Why dey do dis to us? We don't 'urt anybody. Why, Danny?'

Tony took his mother's hands in his. 'Mamma, it's okay. Yer go an' make Danny a cup o' tea. Go on mamma, yer forgettin' Danny's a guest?'

Sofia dabbed at her eyes as she disappeared into the kitchen, and Danny sat down facing his pal. 'Tell us exactly what 'appened,' he said.

Tony winced as he pressed the cut over his eye. 'We'd just opened an' they walked in large as life. Two of 'em there was. I ain't seen eivver of 'em before. They didn't say a word. One of 'em pulled the shelf over an' the uvver git took an' 'ammer from under 'is coat 'an smashed the counter. I jump the one wiv the 'ammer but the uvver bastard clobbered me over the crust. It looked like a pick-axe 'andle 'e 'it me wiv. I saw stars. Our pop tried ter grab the geezer that whacked me, but they pinned 'im ter the wall an' they told 'im 'e'd better fink again about not payin' up. They said they'd be back.'

Danny puffed out his cheeks. 'I come down 'ere a couple o' times last week lookin' fer yer. Did your farver tell yer?'

'Yeah, he told me. I'm sorry I wasn't 'ere. I was over Clerkenwell.'

'What yer bin doin' over there?'

Tony winced again as he felt the bump on his head. 'There's a lot of Italians live over Clerkenwell. They call it "Little Italy". Ain't yer never 'eard of it?'

Danny nodded. 'Course I 'ave. But what was yer doin' over there?'

Tony looked towards the kitchen, then lowered his voice. 'I ain't told Ma what I'm up to, but I've gotta do somefink, Danny. It was lucky she wasn't in the shop at the time. I bin ter see some people I know. Some o' Pop's family live over Clerkenwell. They 'ad the same trouble there a few years ago but they sorted it out fer themselves. This crowd round 'ere won't stick tergevver. Most of the shopkeepers ain't exactly friendly wiv us, I fink they reckon we're spies. They don't see us as bein' the same as them, but we're no different, Danny, you know that. Take me: I was born in Bermon'sey, I speak the same as you do. Me pop took out English nationality papers years ago. It's 'is country as well, but they can't see it. Anyway, all the shopkeepers 'ad a meetin' last week. Pop said we should all stick tergevver an' not pay up. 'Course, a few of 'em agreed wiv 'im, but most of 'em reckoned it was easier ter pay up an' avoid the aggro. What they don't seem ter realise is that this is jus' one foot in the door. Once that mob get us payin' up, they'll be pushin' the dodgy gear on us. All that under the counter stuff. Yer know what they're like, Danny.'

'Yer still ain't told me what yer was doin' over Clerkenwell, Tony.'

Sofia Arpino came into the room carrying a tray with two cups of tea. 'It's nice you come to see us, Danny. You stay wiv Tony. I mus' 'elp Papa clear up da mess.'

She left the room, and when she was out of earshot Tony leaned forward. 'Danny, I've looked up a couple of ole pals. They're gonna 'elp me take care o' Jack Mason. We're gonna give 'im a goin' over, an' if 'e don't get the message an' leave us alone, we're gonna get really nasty. Those two pals o' mine ain't no powder puffs. We can 'andle Jack Mason.'

Danny looked at his friend affectionately. 'Tony, yer me pal, an' I like yer family. I'd 'ate it if any of yer got 'urt. Yer don't know what yer lettin' yerself in for. Yer ain't dealin' wiv some ole plum. Jack Mason's got 'is fingers in everyfink, 'e knows a lot o' people. If yer not careful, yer gonna start anuvver war of yer own. There's bound ter be comebacks, it's a certainty.'

Tony's face was set hard. 'All right, yer tell me what we're expected ter do? If yer fink we're gonna pay up, yer wrong. We ain't gonna do it.'

Danny sighed and leaned back in his chair. 'I don't know the answer, Tone. I tried ter get Kathy ter come up wiv some info, but she was scared. Yer can't very well blame 'er, can yer? She's terrified of Mason. And I ain't gonna ask her again, it's too dangerous.'

An argument was developing in the front of the shop between the Arpinos. Sofia started to raise her voice and Tony looked at his pal and sighed in resignation. Danny put his hand on Tony's shoulder. 'Stay put, Tone. I'll give 'em an 'and ter clear the mess up. When yer feelin' up to it we'll 'ave a drink an' a long chat. Okay?'

It was a week since the warehouse break-in had been reported and Inspector Flint was getting impatient. There were no leads, and no information forthcoming from the usual informers. It was as though the whole load had vanished into thin air. Inspector Flint stood up from his desk and looked thoughtfully out of his office window. Down below people were moving around in the yard; timber was being neatly stacked, and two workers were loading deal boards on to a lorry. For a few moments he watched the activity. At times like this, it would be nice to have a job that ended when the five o'clock whistle went, he thought. That idiot Stockbridge is an incompetent ass. I seem to be surrounded with brainless idiots. Surely someone would have spotted that stolen gear being sold off by now? Apparently Limehouse nick was drawing a blank, too. Still, maybe the impossible has happened, maybe Stockbridge has got a new slant on the business. Anyway, it's about time I shook him up a bit, he decided, opening the door and screaming out for his subordinate.

Detective Constable Stockbridge was dreading the call. He had contacted all his snouts and filled up two notebooks with memoranda, and his feet were sore from all the walking. Stockbridge was convinced that the stolen cases had been unloaded locally and shipped out of the area. The lorry belonging to Sullivan's Wharf had been left in Limehouse to draw the scent away from Bermondsey, he told himself. If none of his snouts had seen anything, then there was nothing to see. They had never let him down before. Problem was getting that dopey git of an inspector to see how sensible his assumptions were. It was a pity that the inspector's predecessor had let his sexual hang-up become his downfall. If he had been a little more discreet, he could have pursued his pastime and still kept his job, there would then have been no threat of going back to the beat.

When he walked into the inspector's office, Stockbridge feared the worst. Flint had a face as long as a month of Sundays, and he was drumming his fingers on the polished surface of his desk.

'Well, Stockbridge, it's been a week now. What have you got for me?'

Fat Stan grimaced. 'It's quiet, sir, none o' me contacts 'ave reported anyfink. They've 'eard nuffink, an' there's no whispers about the local villains bein' involved.'

'Well someone broke into the warehouse, man, and it wasn't the bloody fairies. The lorry was found in Limehouse, okay? It was full of Orientals and Oriental fingerprints. The results are, the local police make a pinch and we've got sod all!'

Fat Stan winced. 'I reckon the stuff was unloaded in Bermon'sey, sir. There's loads o' railway arches an' yards round 'ere.'

'What about the lorry?'

'I fink it was a red 'errin', sir.'

'That's what the villains want you to think, Stockbridge. While I'm wasting manpower turning over the thousand and one likely sites in Bermondsey, they're knocking the stuff out in another area. Think about it, man. I'd be a bloody fool walking into, say that timber yard opposite, and telling them I'm looking for some corned beef! I'd be a laughing stock. No, Stockbridge, the stuff's being sold in the East End. What we've got to do is apprehend the thieves. Tell me, Stockbridge, you must know the local villains, have you got any suspects?'

Fat Stan thought hard. Tony Allen would be the most likely person among the local criminal fraternity to be involved, but Tony always played ball. His name had to be kept out of the frame. There was no way he was going to cut off his own private source of income by nailing Tony Allen. After all, no one had got hurt, and Sullivan was probably well insured against that very eventuality. Fat Stan realised, too, that he would now be able to put the squeeze on Tony Allen for a little more security against being named as a suspect.

'Well, sir,' Stockbridge began, 'there's a nasty little team tryin' ter put the clamps on the shopkeepers in Bermon'sey Lane. Me snout tells me they're not from this area. 'E reckons they come from over the water. Maybe they was involved in the robbery?'

Flint banged his desk. 'Cobblers! The other side of the water used to be my manor. The East End villains don't get involved outside their own patch. Take my word for it, Stockbridge, they're local villains who clobbered the warehouse, and they're local villains operating in Bermondsey Lane. Now you get out there and bring back something. I want action! Understand?'

Fat Stan understood only too well. His feet were already reminding him of the rigours of walking the beat.

*

Ginny Coombes spread margarine over a thick slice of bread and then smeared a thin coating of strawberry jam over the top.

'Now take that an' get out in the street wiv yer bruvvers an' sisters,' she said to her son. 'And mind the road.'

Joey Coombes grabbed the slice of bread in his grubby hands, a grin breaking out on his dirty face. 'Cor, fanks, Mum. Is Danny comin' roun' terday?'

''E comes round every day 'cept Sundays. Now get out from under me feet.'

Joey bit into the bread and a blob of jam stuck to his nose. He looked up at his mother with large blue eyes and said, ''Ere, Mum, 'ow much d'yer like Danny?'

Ginny glanced at her son enquiringly. 'What d'yer mean, 'ow much do I like 'im?'

'Well, Billy Brightman's mum said it's on the cards you an' Danny could get really friendly. What cards she talkin' about, Mum?'

Ginny hid her smile. 'Look, Joey, yer get out an' keep yer eye out fer yer bruvvers an' sisters. Don't stand there askin' stupid questions. I've got a lot o' work ter do.'

Joey took another bite from the slice and jam dripped onto his tattered pullover. 'Are we gonna 'ave anuvver dad one day, Mum?'

Ginny felt the question strike into her insides and she wanted to hug the child, but instead she swallowed hard. 'Your farver's dead, Joey. Yer can't 'ave two dads,' she said.

'I know that, Mum, but we could 'ave a pretend dad if yer got married, couldn't we?'

'Look, Joey, I am not goin' ter get married. I was married ter yer farver, an' I don't wanna get married again.'

'I wouldn't mind Danny fer a pretend dad,' Joey said as he made for the door.

Ginny felt tears welling up and she dabbed her eyes with the apron. Sleep had come slow last night, and she had been troubled by her guilty thoughts. Her lad had caught her off balance, and she was worried about the rumours. There was obviously gossip going around about her. She would have to be careful not to fuel the fire, but she knew that the backstreets did not allow for much privacy. Everyone lived in each other's pockets, the slightest impropriety was discussed and disseminated at one end of the houses until it became scandal at the other end of the row. News travelled fast in the backstreets. Word of Kathy Thompson's suicide attempt had spread around in minutes. The terrible news added to Ginny's own sadness, and she tried to blot out her dismay by working about the house. She got so involved that she forgot the time, and when Danny knocked on her door the kettle was not yet over the gas. When he walked in Ginny expected him to say something about Kathy, but he was cheerful.

''Ello, Ginny, I saw yer brood outside. School 'olidays started?'

Ginny pulled a face. 'I've got six weeks o' this. "Mum I fell over" an' "Mum gi's a slice o' bread". It'll be Mum this an' Mum that. It's a wonder I ain't grey.'

Danny smiled. 'Ginny, yer don't look a day over firty-five.'

Ginny suddenly became serious. He can't know she thought, he would have mentioned it. 'Danny, 'aven't you 'eard about Kathy?'

Danny's face took on an anxious look. ''Eard what, Ginny?'

'She took an overdose.'

Danny's face went white. 'Bloody 'ell! Is she . . . ?'

'They took 'er ter Guy's 'Ospital, Danny. 'Er next door neighbour found 'er. That's all we know.'

'I wanna go an' see 'er, Gin.'

'It's no good, they won't let yer in. 'Er muvver's up there wiv 'er, but they won't let anybody else in yet. Please Gawd she'll pull frew.'

'When did it 'appen, Ginny?'

'Last night. The police came round. I 'eard a commotion when I was puttin' the milk bottles out. It must 'ave bin well after twelve. I'm normally a-bed by that time, but last night I fell asleep in the chair. The kids wore me out yesterday.'

Danny sat down heavily in the chair. 'Did yer know she was carryin'?' he asked.

Ginny nodded. 'It was no secret, yer could tell anyway. That was why 'er ole man kicked 'er out, wasn't it?'

Danny nodded. 'What'll 'appen ter the baby, Ginny?'

'Gawd knows. If they manage ter pull 'er frew it's quite possible she'll lose the baby. It 'appened ter that girl in Tooley Buildin's only last year. She took an overdose. She was all right, but she lost the baby. Four months gone she was.'

Danny ran his fingers through his hair. 'Kathy's gonna be all right, ain't she, Gin?'

Ginny smiled. She had noticed how he reacted when she told him the news. She sensed there was something between them, it showed on the lad's face. 'She'll pull frew, Danny. If she gets over this okay it might be a blessin' in disguise. She can make a clean break from that 'orrible bloke. I knew all along no good would come out of 'er goin' wiv 'im. Did yer know 'e left 'is wife an' kid?'

'No, I didn't,' Danny jumped up, his face dark with anger.

Ginny picked up the teapot from the table. 'I'll make a cup o' tea, you look like yer could do wiv it.'

Danny suddenly felt drained, and sat down again. 'You ain't seen anyfink o' Johnny Ross, 'ave yer, Gin?' he called out, brushing his fingers through his hair.

'Not since yer spoke to 'im last Friday. What's 'e done now?'

'You know Rossy. 'E's upset Mason, an' I told 'im ter stay out the way fer a few days. If Mason or Tony Allen asks yer 'is whereabouts, Gin, yer don't know, all right? Cor, what a bloody mess.'

'Don't worry, Danny, I know Rossy's a bit of a cow-son, but I wouldn't wish that bastard Mason on me worst enemy. I won't let on.'

The morning punters walked up to Ginny's door with their 'tanner each-ways' and their 'shilling win doubles', and the backstreet rang with children's happy voices. Trains rumbled over the railway arch and the din of traffic carried down Clink Lane from the Tooley Street end. Women came in and out of the turning carrying shopping baskets, and the street knife-grinder treadled his whetstone and sent sparks flying. Joey grazed his knee and tears ran down his sticky face. Cigarette cards changed hands at the turn of a playing card, and another egg-crate was carried into the street by two youngsters ready for the weekend 'wood-chop'. Up above the grey slates and the crazily leaning chimneypots the sky was blue. Lazy clouds drifted on the summer breeze, and cooking smells wafted from open doorways. The midday sun warmed the flagstones and children, tired from their exertions, sat in the shade and talked of the coming hop-picking season.

'Bodiam? Where's Bodiam?'

'It's in Kent.'

'Is Kent very far?'

'It's 'undreds o' miles from 'ere. Takes hours on a train.'

'What's it like, 'op-pickin'?'

'It's smashin'. We go scrumpin' an' the gypsy kids show us where the rabbits are. We go crab-apple pickin' as well.'

'What's crab-apples?'

'They're tiny apples, an' if yer eat 'em yer get poisoned.'

'What yer pick 'em for then?'

'To aim at the rabbits.'

'Cor! Wish we went 'op-pickin'.'

'We sleep in 'uts, an' we 'ave straw beds. Fousan's o' spiders though.'

'Ugh!'

'Spiders can't 'urt yer – not like bugs.'

'We 'ad bugs. My mum got rid of 'em wiv a burnin' stick. They suck yer blood, bugs do.'

'There was a stag beedle down 'oppin'. They can sting yer dead.'

'Cor!'

They were interrupted by calls to dinner, and the street was quiet once more. Joey Coombes dipped a chunk of dry bread into his lamb stew.

''Ere, Mum, why don't we go 'oppin'?'

'We've never bin, that's why.'

'All the kids go 'oppin'. We never do nuffink.'

'Yes we do. We went ter Soufend once.'

'There's no stag beedles in Soufend.'

'Eat yer dinner, Joey.'

Chapter Twenty-Two

For three days and nights Kathy was in danger. On Thursday, as the first August dawn broke, she drifted from a misty greyness into the starched white of the hospital ward. Her eyes hurt, the pressure around her hand tightened, and the uncertainty was over. The pressure that had prevented her from floating away, that had kept her clinging on at the edge of death, became warm and comforting. Kathy blinked and focused her eyes. Tired, worried eyes stared back into hers, and she began to understand what had happened. She tried to speak but her mouth was parched. Gentle hands lifted her head and bitter liquid was held to her lips. Hearing words whispered and feeling a cool hand on her forehead, she sank back into a peaceful sleep that was free of dreams. The crisis was over at last.

Mrs Violet Thompson left the ward and walked wearily down the wide, stone stairs and felt the cool morning air rush at her face. The chapel door was open, and inside the quiet and solitude seemed to lift her spirits. The early rays of the sun hit the stained glass arched window and played on the tiny altar. For a time Violet prayed, then she raised her head and sat deep in thought. The heartbreak was not yet over. Soon she must go back and tell her daughter about the baby, though for the moment Kathy must sleep and recover her strength. It had been agreed with the doctor that Violet should break the news. She had also impressed on the doctor and nurses that no one else should visit her daughter, at least for the present. She was adamant that Jack Mason should not be allowed in under any circumstances, and when she'd explained her reasons they acquiesced.

For three days Mrs Thompson had walked back and forth from the hospital in a daze, but this morning there was a spring in her step. The usual band of neighbours would be waiting by their front doors. This morning she would be able to smile at them, and the good news would soon spread. Her only worry was Jack Mason's reaction. She had never spoken to him, but someone would no doubt pass on the news. Violet knew that her husband would not take Kathy back, and it was useless to argue any more, but she hoped that when her daughter left the hospital she could go to stay with her aunt in Ilford for a couple of weeks until the fuss died down. Violet decided she must write to her sister that very day.

As she turned the corner and walked into Clink Lane, Violet met her neighbours' solicitous looks with a huge grin. Pinched, morning faces beamed, and their hugs and tears caused the passing dockers to wave as they hurried to the call-on.

'She's gonna be all right, Fred. Tell Bill, won't yer?'

'Fank Gawd fer that, Vi.'

'We'll 'ave ter get 'er some flowers.'

''Ere, there's a tanner. Put me in.'

Violet looked anxiously down the street. 'I mus' go, luvs,' she said, 'I've gotta tell my Charlie 'fore 'e goes off ter work.'

Beaming faces grew serious and pitying looks followed Mrs Thompson down the turning. 'She's 'ad enough on 'er plate, what wiv one fing an' anuvver,' someone said.

'You're right. I 'ope this pulls 'im to 'is senses.'

'It won't alter the ugly git. 'E's disowned 'is own daughter, the rotter!'

'Well it might quieten 'im down fer a bit.'

'Yeah, fer a couple o' weeks, then 'e'll get pissed an' take it out on poor Vi, yer mark my words.'

'If that was me I'd open that Charlie Thompson. 'E's a no-good whore-son.'

'I said ter my Frankie only the uvver night: "Yer an' yer mates ought ter send the bastard ter Coventry". My Frankie only laughed. Yer know what men are like – all pals tergevver.'

Danny heard the good news as he was going down the street that morning, and before he started work he called in on Mrs Thompson.

'Come in, son, I'm jus' makin' meself a nice cuppa,' she said.

Danny sat in the scullery while Violet filled the kettle and stood it on the iron gas stove. 'Kathy's out of the coma, fank Gawd. She'll be all right now. She'll look a lot better when I go in, I'm sure.'

'Can I go in ter see 'er, Vi?'

'I'm sure Kathy would like ter see yer when she's feelin' a bit better, son. I'll tell 'er yer called round.'

Danny picked at the oil-cloth covering on the creaking wooden table. 'Any idea what made 'er do it, Vi?'

'Why, it was that whore-son, wasn't it? 'E's led 'er a dog's life since she's bin livin' wiv 'im. She should 'ave known better. Kathy's seen enough of it 'ome 'ere wiv me an' 'er farver.'

'What about the baby?' Danny asked.

Violet Thompson suddenly reached for her handkerchief and put it to her eyes. 'She lost it. She ain't bin told yet. I'm jus' 'opin' it don't upset 'er too much. That git Mason got 'is wish, didn't 'e? 'E wanted Kathy ter get rid of it right from the start.'

The kettle came to the boil and Violet filled a small china

teapot. Danny watched while the frail-looking woman busied herself about the scullery.

'What's goin' ter 'appen to 'er now, Vi?' he asked.

'She can't come 'ome 'ere. 'Er farver's washed 'is 'ands of 'er. I'm goin' ter write ter me sister in Ilford terday. She'll 'ave 'er there fer a couple o' weeks. We'll jus' 'ave ter see what 'appens then.'

Danny put a half-crown down on the table. 'Can yer take Kathy somefink in?'

'Fanks, son. I'll get 'er a nice bunch o' flowers. The neighbours 'ave bin real nice. They say in times o' trouble yer find yer real friends. And they've come up trumps round 'ere. Even ole Missus Johnson said 'ello this mornin'. I ain't spoke wiv 'er since me ole man clouted 'er boy when 'e broke me winder.'

While Danny sipped his tea Mrs Thompson studied him. Presently she said, 'Yer know, I often wondered about yer an' my Kathy. I fink everybody round 'ere expected the two o' yer ter get married one day. I mean, yer was always tergevver. Even when yer was kids. Why the bloody 'ell she got mixed up wiv that 'orrible bastard, I'll never know.'

Danny shrugged his shoulders. 'I got a letter from me sister, Con, while I was in France. She told me Kathy was goin' aroun' wiv 'im.'

Violet Thompson folded her arms and tucked her hands under her armpits. 'Did you an' Kathy 'ave a bust-up, son? 'Fore yer went overseas, I mean?'

Danny nodded. 'Yeah, we did, sort of, Vi.'

'Yeah, I guessed as much. I remember 'er comin' in cryin' one Saturday night. It was about the time yer got called up. I remember that night well. My Charlie followed 'er in. Pissed 'e was. 'E wanted ter know who it was she was wiv in the doorway. I told 'im ter leave 'er alone 'cos she was upset an' me an' 'im gets at it. I got a right ole shiner that bleedin' night.'

Danny finished his tea and put the cup down on the table. 'I wished we could 'ave patched it up, Vi. I tell yer, she's too good fer that bastard.'

Violet Thompson nodded. 'Trouble was, son, even when 'e turned bad, she stuck wiv 'im. And then 'e got 'er pregnant. There was a terrible row 'ere when me ole man found out. 'E went up the pub an' got blind drunk. 'E'd already told Kathy ter be out o' the 'ouse by the time 'e got back, and I made sure she was. 'E give me a good 'idin'. 'E was in a terrible state. So was I by the time 'e'd finished wiv me.'

Danny drank his tea and stood up. 'Fanks, Vi. I'd better get over ter Ginny's,' he said. 'Give Kathy me love. Let me know when it's all right ter go in, won't yer?'

On Friday morning the early breeze sent pieces of paper swirling down the street and billowing clouds raced across the sky. Danny came down into the parlour to find a letter with a Maidstone postmark addressed to him. He knew it was from Alison. He opened it and read through it quickly. He had been despairing of ever hearing from her again, and now it seemed she was eager to pick up the threads of their brief liaison. At first he had wanted to take up a pen and write back in anger, but he had read the letter through once more and felt the hot blood coursing through his veins. Their time together had been an exciting one, she had been hot, demanding and moody, which both excited and puzzled him. He realised that he would probably never really understand Alison. He felt she did not fully understand herself. In the letter she said that she would like to see him again and that she had spent a lot of time thinking about her future, but it was clear she had still not decided whether or not she was ready for a steady relationship, and it angered him. She told him that she had been transferred to a hospital in Maidstone and wondered whether he could come down to spend a weekend with her, but she didn't explain why she hadn't arranged to meet him on her return from leave. Danny puzzled over that. Maybe she had needed more time? He remembered that morning on the station when he had been left with so many questions unanswered. The feeling he carried around inside him since then had been a mixture of anger and rejection, a state of depression which was only just beginning to lift. He had resigned himself to believing that Alison would not bother to contact him again, and now here was a letter that threw everything into confusion – and just at the wrong time.

Kathy was back in his life, and with serious problems that had taken her to the edge of death. What had happened to her was terrible, and it had allowed a deep loyalty to become reawakened. Danny knew he needed time, but he wanted to see Kathy very soon. The future could now be very different. Did they have a future together? What would Mason do when Kathy came out of hospital? The questions twisted around in Danny's head and he found himself thinking again of Alison. Could he learn to cope with her demanding and unpredictable moods? Could the passion they had felt together ease the tension in their relationship? Why did he feel so uncertain?

Danny put the letter back in his pocket and stepped out into the morning air. He needed to be alone for a while to clear his head of his painful thoughts. The day was bright and he found himself strolling towards Tower Bridge, always his favourite place when he was in a pensive mood. The high white stone-work of the bridge and the massive sweep of the supporting girders towered above him as he reached the first span. On either side the wharves were busy as usual, and down below the river swirled around the curved bastions of the bridge and eddied in oily patches in midstream. On the far bank, the narrow strip of muddy sand was partly exposed and two young children were prodding at something by the water's edge. Above and behind them rose the indestructible Tower of London. Danny recalled his halcyon days, when he had bathed in the muddy river and scoured the empty barges for coconut husks and kernels of nuts and fruit. He remembered those walks down dark, scary lanes that led to the water's edge. It had been pure adventure, uncomplicated and exciting. Now those idyllic days were gone. He had been on a slowly rotating carousel which had gone faster and faster and suddenly he had been pitched off into adulthood. It was now a different place; life had become complex and twisted, and the bones of everything were laid bare. Danny grinned to himself when he realised how serious he had become. This walk always seems to have that effect on me, he thought as he turned for home.

The large, shapely woman lying on the bed raised herself on one elbow and chuckled at the antics of her companion. The pale, nude figure hobbled about the bedroom, frantically gathering up his clothes. He tripped over the carpet and cursed loudly. 'Look at the bleedin' time, Cora. If 'e finds me 'ere 'e'll spifflicate me!'

Cora lit a cigarette and watched as the young man dressed hurriedly. 'Don't get yerself in a panic,' she said, ''E won't be 'ere yet. Jack won't leave the pub till closin' time. Come an' give us a kiss,' her painted lips pouted.

'Bloody 'ell, Cora, ain't yer never satisfied? Mason's out fer me blood. I can't take a chance of 'im findin' me wiv yer.'

'Are yer gonna come back an' see me soon, Johnny?'

'Course I am, darlin', but I can't 'ang around 'ere now. The pubs'll be turnin' out soon. There's too many of 'is mates know me. If they clock my dial they'll punch 'oles in me. I'll look like an ole clockin'-in card.'

Cora chuckled and drew on her cigarette. 'Jus' one little teeny kiss?'

Johnny Ross finished tying up his shoe-laces and gave her a quick peck on her lips. 'I gotta go, it's ten ter ten now.'

Cora watched him make for the door and then called him back. 'Don't ferget yer cigarette case.'

'Christ, Cora!' he said, putting the case in his pocket. 'Well, I'm orf. Keep it warm fer me, won't yer?'

The long daylight hours were fading and dusk was deepening in the backstreets of Dockhead. The sounds of music and laughter came out from behind the heavy curtains at The Ferryman as three figures walked briskly up to the saloon bar door. Inside the air was stale, with cigarette smoke hanging like a cloud. A fat man with shirtsleeves rolled back over his wrists was tinkling on the stained piano keys, while behind the counter a huge man with pugilistic features and a shaven head was sharing a joke with one of his customers. The bar was full, and it took some time before the trio were served. They stood in one corner and studied the customers. Presently Tony Arpino nudged his companions. 'Don't look now, but 'e's over there near the pianer talkin' ter that brassy bird. See 'er? The one wiv the bunch o' grapes stuck on 'er 'at. Don't let 'im see yer lookin' over, fer Gawd's sake.'

The taller and heavier of Tony's two companions nodded. 'I've clocked 'im. 'E don't look all that tough ter me. What d'yer reckon, Mario?'

The other smiled and showed a gold tooth. 'Don't yer worry, Tony. 'E'll be no problem.'

Tony Arpino grinned nervously. 'Don't underestimate 'im. 'E ain't gonna be no pushover.'

The big Italian gripped Tony's arm. 'When yer ready give us the okay. We'll be waitin' fer 'im.'

The Ferryman was a dockside pub with a dubious reputation. The local criminal fraternity drank there, safe in the knowledge that they were on friendly territory. The pub was owned by an ex-fighter who was very careful to handpick his staff; the barman matched him for size, and everyone agreed that the features of the diminutive potman were enough to frighten babies in their prams. He had been a handy flyweight in his time and knew how to get rid of the dallying customers at closing time. If anyone did try it on with him, they could be sure that he was backed up by the ex-heavyweight champion of the Grenadier Guards.

The place was busy from Friday onwards. The local bookies, villains, and other mysterious characters met there regularly. The local police were well aware of the pub's reputation for harbouring and succouring the less law-abiding, but their attempts to infiltrate the premises had come to nothing. On one occasion, a covert attempt to put an 'ear' inside the pub had ended in disaster. The plant spent the last hour before closing time with a funny-tasting pint in his hand, and a notice pinned to his back that said: 'Beware the bluebottle'. The strange-tasting pint gave him a bad attack of diarrhoea and vomiting which necessitated a trip to the doctor. The landlord of the pub calmed the outrage quickly. He listened intently to what the visiting police inspector had to say and then informed him that the person responsible for the atrocious behaviour, so alien to the respectable character of The Ferryman, was a stranger who had been barred for life that same evening. A five pound note donated to the Police Orphans Fund and an afternoon drinking session with the inspector put everything right, and the pub was left in peace.

On this particular Friday night the beer was flowing and the customers stood shoulder to shoulder. Tony had moved away from his two companions as planned. He had visited the pub on a few occasions with Danny Sutton and Johnny Ross, and he did not want to draw any attention to the two Italians who stood in one corner keeping their eyes on Mason. When Tony Arpino eased his way towards the piano, the bigger of the two nudged his pal. 'C'mon, time ter go.'

Tony had reached Jack Mason, who gave him a strange

glance. 'What you doin' 'ere? Bit out of your way, ain't it?' he said in a malevolent tone.

'I got a message fer yer, Mr Mason. It's from Johnny Ross.'

Jack Mason's eyes glinted. 'Where is that little rat? I've bin lookin' fer 'im.'

Tony gulped and prayed that his ploy would work. ''E's outside by the oil shop. It's urgent. Can yer meet 'im there right away?'

'Why don't 'e come in 'ere? What's the matter wiv 'im?'

Tony took a breath. ''E's got some money fer yer. 'E said 'e don't want anybody ter see it change 'ands.'

'All right, I'll be out in a minute.'

Tony nodded casually but felt his heart pounding. If Mason brought anyone with him it would ruin the plan. He walked out of the pub and blinked as the darkness enveloped him. When he moved along to the oil shop Tony could see his two companions standing in the recess of the doorway. ''Old tight! 'E'll be out in a minute,' he said breathlessly. 'Mario, you stan' wiv me. 'E'll fink you're Rossy. Al, keep back fer Gawd's sake! If 'e sees yer 'e'll know it's a set-up.'

The saloon bar door opened and Tony bit on his bottom lip. An old gent emerged and walked unsteadily past the shop without noticing the three who were lying in wait. Tony took out his pocket watch. It showed ten minutes to ten.

Suddenly Mario nudged him. ''Ere 'e is!'

Mason had emerged from the pub and was walking towards them with his distinctive gait. His eyes opened in surprise as he saw the three men facing him.

Tony's features were set hard. 'We've got me ole man's pay-off, Mason!' he said, and he struck Mason full in the face.

Mason staggered back a pace and blood started to drip from his nose. Like an angry animal he charged at Tony, but Mario tripped him and stood back. Mason fell against the shop doorway and reeled back in a daze. Mario brought his foot up hard against the villain's jaw. Mason spat blood through his broken teeth and tried awkwardly to stagger to his feet, but Al stepped forward and grabbed Mason's coat collar. With a huge bellow he threw the man against the shop wall and pummelled him in the face. When Mason put his hands up to protect his head, Al kneed him hard in the stomach. The attack was too fast and too vicious for Mason to respond, and he sagged against the wall. The big Italian finally grabbed at Mason's coat-lapels and head-butted him across the bridge of his nose. The three looked down at the sprawled unlovely heap at their feet.

Tony leaned over the groaning figure. 'Keep away from Bermon'sey Lane, Mason. This is just a sample. There's money bin put up. Try it on again an' you'll be goin' fer a swim – wiv yer 'ands tied. Okay?'

As the three started away from the doorway Mason rolled over onto his side and swore at them through his swollen and bloody lips. Al stopped and turned back. Tony winced as he heard a thud. Al walked back casually. 'I fink 'e's got the message at last,' he grinned, and the three walked briskly out of the backstreet.

Jack Mason's beating had not gone unnoticed. A skulking figure had been standing in the shadows and watched the villain leave the pub. Cora was going to be the death of him, he rued. Five minutes later and he would have been caught with his trousers down. As he watched he noticed that Mason was not going to the buildings but towards some shadowy figures in the shop doorway. Johnny Ross held his breath as the assault took place. In the growing darkness he could recognise only one of the assailants. It was Tony Arpino. In seconds it was all over and he saw Jack Mason turn on his side and curse the three as they walked away. He saw the largest of the attackers turn back and bend over the sprawling figure. He heard the thump and saw Mason go limp. Only when the men had left the scene did he make his move. Slowly he walked over to the prone figure and looked down at him, an evil grin spreading over his pale face.

The last tram rumbled past, and the hands of the church clock were nearing the hour. Amy Wheelwright and her friend Carrie Horscroft had left the sewing circle meeting and were dissecting their fellow members' characters in a particularly brutal fashion.

'I wouldn't mind, Carrie, but she walks in the place like Lady Muck. She really upsets everybody wiv 'er fancy ways,' Amy said with an expression of disgust.

'You're right, Amy. I 'eard she's sweet on Billy Whybrow. You know Billy Whybrow, the one what does the books at the institute.'

'Oh, 'im. 'E's a dirty ole goat. Fair undresses yer wiv 'is eyes 'e does.'

Carrie touched her confidante's arm. 'I know you won't let this go any furver, Amy. I 'eard Liz Springett's 'avin' it orf wiv 'im from the greengrocer's in George Street.'

'Not 'im wiv the funny eye? What can she see in 'im?'

'Let's face it, Amy, she ain't no oil paintin' 'erself, is she?'

'Did yer see 'er the uvver night, Carrie? Proper madam she is, moanin' about the biscuits. Did you 'ear what she said? "I only like Peak Freans." She should fink 'erself lucky. She ain't backward in comin' forward, 'cept when it's time ter pay 'er subs.'

The two women reached the parting of the ways. Carrie stood with Amy on the street corner and was about to come to the juiciest tit-bit, which she had saved till last, when a hurrying figure pushed past them and disappeared into the night. 'Well I never!' Carrie gasped. 'The manners of some people. Not even a "sorry", "oops", or "by yer leave". 'Ere, while I fink of it, I mus' tell yer . . .'

*

Back in The Ferryman the merriment went on. The brassy blonde was feeling very put out. Her prey had somehow extricated himself and it seemed that all her efforts that evening had been in vain. She looked around the bar and realised she was going to have an early night after all. The usual crowd of drunks would no doubt be trying their luck at closing time, and the pawing would start in earnest. She finished her drink and decided it was home to bed and sod the lot of 'em. The cool air made her reel and she leaned against the wall of the pub until she recovered herself. Those drinks he had been plying her with must have been doubles. He needn't have bothered, she told herself, he could coax me into his bed any night of the week. She walked on from the pub and almost tripped against the bundle lying in the shop doorway. A stream of blood had formed a pool in the gutter and had stained the pavement dark red. Lillie Stannard fell against the shop-front and let out a piercing scream. Curtains were pulled back momentarily, and the less drunken customers emerged from the pub. Soon a crowd had gathered. They took the hysterical prostitute to one side while someone threw a coat over the body.

'It's Jack Mason! 'E's bin done in!' someone said.

'They've smashed 'is 'ead in!'

'Quick! Tell the guv'nor ter 'phone the law!'

'Gawd Almighty, what a sight! I was only talkin' to 'im only 'alf hour ago!' said an old man, shaking his head.

'Well 'e ain't talkin' now, Bert.'

Chapter Twenty-Three

The news of Jack Mason's murder made the Saturday morning papers. The story was on everyone's lips. There were very few sentiments of sympathy expressed, for most of those who knew him felt that he had had it coming. Mason had many enemies and someone had exacted vengeance. And there was concern for Kathy, who had still not heard the news, for Mrs Thompson was determined not to let her daughter know at least for a day or two. Her own feelings had frightened her when she had been told of the murder. It was as though a heavy burden had been lifted from her shoulders now that Kathy would not have to suffer any more at his hand. Mrs Thompson was a devout Christian who believed in the power of prayer and her pleas for Kathy's recovery had been answered. She had prayed that her daughter would be spared the ill treatment she herself had been forced to endure. But her hopes were fulfilled in a way that she had not foreseen, and Violet Thompson felt very humble.

When Danny walked into The Globe on that Saturday morning, the discussions raged around him. Eddie Kirkland was leaning over the counter talking to Biff Bowden. ''E didn't come in 'ere much. 'E only used this pub on the odd occasion. It was The Ferryman 'e used. That's where 'e was found, wasn't it?'

'That's right, Eddie. It ses 'ere that a young woman found 'im. 'E was layin' in a shop doorway. Accordin' ter what it ses 'ere, someone went an' smashed the back of 'is 'ead right in. Apparently 'e'd also bin done over, beaten about the face.'

Eddie leaned over the copy of the *Daily Mirror* that Biff had in his hands. 'What else does it say?'

Biff squinted his eyes up and moved the paper away to focus the wording. 'It ses a young man who was limpin' was seen leavin' the street in an' 'urry by two ladies who 'ave given the police a good description.'

'Bloody 'ell!' laughed Eddie. 'That could fit Johnny Ross!'

'It couldn't be 'im,' Biff snorted. 'Rossy couldn't punch 'is way out of a paper bag.'

Eddie pulled up a pint of ale for an old gent who was moaning about the quality of the beer. 'It's the 'ops, Fred, it's bin a bad year fer 'ops.'

When the old gent took his pint and moved away from the counter Eddie went back to talk to Biff. 'Silly ole sod. 'E's bin moanin' about the beer fer donkey's years. 'E still gets pissed on it though.'

Biff grinned. ''Ere, Eddie, talkin' about Johnny Ross, I ain't seen 'im around 'ere lately. 'Ave you?'

The landlord shook his head. 'It's funny, but Bonky come in 'ere last night. 'E told me Rossy's on the run from Mason. Over some money by all accounts.'

'Well Rossy ain't got ter run any more, that's fer sure,' Biff chuckled.

Danny sat at the bar with a pint of ale at his elbow. He recalled the conversation he had had with Tony Arpino, but he found it impossible to believe that Tony could have been responsible for Mason's murder. A good hiding was one thing but murder was another story. It couldn't be Tony, he decided. Poor Kathy, how would she take the news? Did she still have any feeling left for Mason? Whatever she felt, it was still going to be a terrible shock for her.

'Yer signed the pledge then, Danny?'

The young cockney looked up and saw Bonky Williams standing next to him.

''Ello, Bonky, I didn't see yer come in.'

Bonky grinned. 'I was watchin' yer starin' at that pint, an' I ses ter meself, Bonky, 'e's on the bleedin' wagon.'

Danny grinned. 'Wanna drink?'

'Ta, I'll 'ave a nice pint o' bitter, me ole mate.'

Danny ordered the drink. ''Eard the news?'

'Yeah. 'E's in the shite, ain't 'e?'

'Who?'

'Why, Rossy.'

''Ow d'yer mean?' Danny asked impatiently.

'They've got 'is description, ain't they?'

'Don't be stupid, Bonky. That description could fit anybody.'

Bonky glanced around the bar furtively and leaned forward until Danny smelt stale breath on his face. 'It was 'im.'

'What d'yer mean, it was 'im?'

'It was Johnny Ross, the one the paper said was runnin' out the street.'

''Ow d'yer know it was 'im?'

Bonky looked around the bar again, then his voice lowered to a whisper. 'Rossy was knockin' one o' Jack Mason's birds orf, wasn't 'e?'

'I dunno, was 'e?'

'Yeah, 'e told me 'imself. You know Rossy, 'e can't keep anyfink to 'imself. Anyway, this bird's called Cora. She lives in the buildin's opposite the boozer Mason used. I told Johnny ter be careful, 'e's in enough trouble as it is.'

Danny looked into Bonky's good eye. 'You ain't tryin' ter tell me Rossy done 'im in, are yer?'

''Course I ain't. What I am sayin' is, it's a pound to a pinch o' shit that it was Johnny comin' out o' the turnin' last night.'

'Christ Almighty!' Danny gasped. 'They should lock Rossy up fer 'is own good. 'E's a livin', breavin' disaster!'

'They prob'ly will,' Bonky said, picking up his drink.

'Do yer know where Rossy is?' Danny asked.

'I ain't seen 'im around. If 'e's got any sense 'e's scarpered. If 'e stays round 'ere they're bound ter pull 'im in.'

Danny finished his drink. 'Well, I've gotta be orf. If yer see Rossy about tell 'im ter get in touch. Okay?'

'Right. See yer, Danny.'

Danny left the pub and hurried to the Arpinos' shop. When he arrived Sofia and her husband Lou were serving some customers and he could see that they were trying to hide their anxiety. Lou waved Danny through to the back of the shop and followed him into the small room.

'Danny, ma Tony's in a lotta trouble,' he said. ''E's a gone away. 'E say the police they're a gonna come for 'im. What's ma Tony done, Danny?'

'Ain't yer seen the papers, Pop?'

'I donna read so good. What's a dis in da papers?'

Danny took the old man by his shoulders. 'Look, Pop,' he said, 'you've 'eard Tony talk about Jack Mason, ain't yer?'

'Yeah, I know dis Jack Mason. 'E's da gangster what break up a ma shop.'

''E's bin killed, Lou.'

The old Italian bit on his knuckles and his face drained of colour. 'Not ma Tony. 'E don't kill nobody. No ma Tony.'

'Where is 'e, Lou? Can I talk to 'im?'

''E's a jus' gone away. I swear I donna know where 'e's a gone. Maybe ter ma family in Clerkenwell. Ma family dey look after ma boy.'

'Whereabouts in Clerkenwell? 'Ave yer got an address?'

Lou Arpino raised his hands to the ceiling. 'I gotta no

address. Ma family all over da place. Dey gotta shops in Clerkenwell. It's all I know, Danny.'

'Don't worry, Pop, Tony's clean. 'E didn't kill Mason.'

As he left the shop Danny thought about going straight to Clerkenwell, but he realised that he might be followed. It was evident that the police had not called on the Arpinos yet, but someone might have spotted Tony and given the police a description. He himself might have been pointed out as a friend of Tony and there might be a tail on him. But the more he thought about it the less likely it seemed. Surely the police would call on the shop first. If they were unsuccessful in finding Tony there then they might tail him, or even pull him in for questioning. Danny was getting nervous and it was becoming difficult for him to think straight. Still, he knew it would be better not to go near Clerkenwell until he could work out a plan. He hurried along to Ginny's and found a few punters standing around waiting for him.

'Where yer bin, Danny boy?' one old gent said. 'I've got a fistful o' bets 'ere. 'Alf the street's left 'em wiv me.'

When it was a little quieter Ginny poked her head out from the parlour. 'Danny, when yer finished can yer pop over ter see Vi Thompson? She wants a word wiv yer.'

Detective Constable Stanley Stockbridge walked quickly towards Tony Allen's offices situated off Jamaica Road. He was a worried man. Jack Mason's murder had thrown his plans completely. The boys from the Yard were involved and the Station Inspector had made it plain that they were to get full co-operation. Stockbridge knew the identity of the man seen running from the scene of the crime. He had had his eye on Ross for some time, and his snout had informed him of the strained relations between Ross and Mason. The detective was certain Johnny Ross was his man, but before he named his suspect he thought he should have a word with Allen the bookie. As he walked up towards the offices in Wilson Street Fat Stan saw Tony Allen standing at the door.

'I've bin expectin' you, Stan. Let's go over the road fer a drink,' Tony said.

The Jamaica was almost empty at that time of the morning. There were only one or two regulars sitting around the small bar.

'Give us a Scotch an' soda an' a gin an' tonic, luv,' Tony Allen said to the barmaid. 'Oh, an' can we use yer snug bar? We've got a bit o' business ter take care of.'

Doreen flashed Tony a smile. 'I'll unlock it,' she said. 'You'll be okay in there.'

When they had seated themselves and the drinks were in front of them Fat Stan looked hard at Tony. 'Look, I can't afford ter mess around, Tony. Murder's way out of my league. The Yard are involved. You gonna put a name my way?'

Tony Allen smiled. 'I'd like ter 'elp yer, Stan. Jack Mason had 'is own little fings goin' fer 'im. I 'ad nuffink ter do wiv 'is killin'. I know we 'ad our differences, but 'e was straight wiv me. 'E wasn't turnin' me over, if that's what yer fink.'

The detective toyed with his glass. 'You've read the papers? Yer know we've got a description of a man seen runnin', or rather, limpin' out of the turnin'?'

The bookie nodded. ''Ave yer got a name?'

Fat Stan looked at the bookie. 'Me an' you go back a long way, Tony. Don't let's play games. Yer know who that man was as well as I do.'

Tony Allen smiled. 'Yer don't honestly fink Johnny Ross is capable of murder, do yer?'

'Maybe not. 'E's gotta be brought in though. If 'e's in the clear 'e ain't got nuffink ter worry about, but it looks suspicious all the same.'

The bookie downed his drink and called out to Doreen. 'Fill 'em up, luv.'

When the barmaid had replaced their drinks Tony leaned back in his seat. 'What else yer got ter go on, Stan?'

The fat detective emptied the remainder of the tonic into his gin. 'There was a conversation in the pub between Mason an' a stranger. Nobody knew 'is face, or they're not tellin'. Anyway, Mason followed this geezer out an' 'e didn't come back. The prosser who was chattin' Mason up before was the one who found 'is body. She can't tell us much. She was too pissed ter remember what the geezer who was talkin' ter Mason looked like. There's anuvver fing worryin' me, Tony. The squeeze that's goin' on in Bermon'sey Lane, was Mason involved in that?'

Tony Allen nodded. 'That was nuffink ter do wiv me, Stan, that was Mason's little perk. Yer know I don't work against the local traders. I employed Mason ter look after me interests at the race tracks. Yer know what it's like. It's a bleedin' 'ard business, an' we need 'ard men ter back us up. I tell yer one fing, when I found out about the Bermon'sey Lane affair I 'ad a set-to wiv Mason. Those mugs 'e brought in were bad news.'

Fat Stan showed a ghost of a smile. 'Yer didn't take an iron bar ter back up yer argument, did yer?'

The bookie's eyes narrowed. 'If it 'ad bin my intention ter do away wiv 'im, I'd 'ave made a tidier job of it, believe me.'

'I'm only jokin', Tony, but I've got a problem. There's a new gaffer at the station as yer know. 'E's a different kettle o' fish ter the uvver lecherous ole bastard. This one wants results. Take it from me, 'e's no mug, 'e's out ter cripple the likes o' you. So far I've kept yer name out o' the frame, but the gaffer ain't left me alone since the ware'ouse job in Shad Thames. If I can nail Ross, bring 'im in as a murder suspect I mean, it'll take the pressure orf, if yer know what I'm gettin' at?'

'Well yer won't find 'im at 'is own address, Stan.'

'Where's 'e 'oled up?'

Tony Allen studied his glass for a second or two. 'Try 'is

married sister's place. She runs a pub in Deptford, The Galleon just off Tanners 'Ill. Yer'll find 'im there I reckon.'

The detective finished his drink. 'I'm orf. Keep yer nose clean, Tone.'

The bookie reached into his coat pocket and pulled out a sealed envelope. 'There's a little appreciation of yer support, Stanley. I only like ter see 'orses' names goin' in the frame, if yer get me drift.'

Danny Sutton walked along St Thomas's Street and stopped at the gates of Guy's Hospital. A large, ruddy-faced woman in a man's cap, wearing a blue apron tied around her waist, smiled at him and stood with her hands on her hips while he inspected the colourful array of flowers. 'What's yer fancy, luvvy?' she asked. 'There's roses, carnations, an' there's some luvverly . . .'

'Jus' do us up a bundle, will yer?' Danny said quickly.

The flower-seller gathered a selection from the vases and wrapped them up in a large sheet of paper. 'There we are. 'Old 'em up, they won't bite yer,' she said, smiling wickedly.

Danny climbed the stairs and joined the waiting visitors outside the ward. He held the bundle of flowers down at his side and looked around self-consciously. Mrs Thompson had told him that Kathy wanted to see him, and that on no account must he talk about Jack Mason. She had also told him that Kathy was very depressed over the loss of the baby and she hoped his visit might help to cheer her up. Danny felt uncomfortable as he followed the Saturday afternoon visitors into the long ward. He spotted Kathy and walked over to the foot of her bed where she lay propped up against the pillows with her hands folded outside the bedclothes. He was shocked by her appearance; she looked white and drawn, and her dark hair spread out across the pillow made her pallor seem worse.

But Kathy smiled at him, and for an instant he saw a glimmer of welcome in her large dark eyes. He moved around the bed and bent down. His lips brushed her pale cheek and he could smell the scent of Lifebuoy soap. He sat down and leaned forward, covering her hands in his, and grinned. 'D'yer like the flowers?' he asked.

She nodded, her eyes fixing him solemnly. 'Fanks fer comin' in, Danny. I 'oped yer would.'

'Yer couldn't keep me away. 'Ow yer feelin'?'

'I'm okay. Yer know about the baby?'

Danny nodded. 'I'm sorry. Yer mum told me.'

'Did she tell yer not ter mention about Jack?'

'Yer know then?'

Kathy nodded slowly. 'They tried ter keep it from me, but I 'eard two of the patients talkin' an' I've seen the paper.'

Danny winced. 'It must 'ave bin an 'orrible shock, gettin' it that way,' he said.

Kathy turned her head towards him. 'There's nuffink inside me, Danny. I feel no pain, no sadness, nuffink. It's scary.'

Danny squeezed her hands in his and saw the tear slip down her cheek onto the pillow. 'Don't be scared,' he said, 'there's nuffink ter be scared about.'

'I'm scared 'cos I'm empty, Danny. I should feel somefink, shouldn't I?'

Danny took out a handkerchief and dabbed her cheek. 'Yer need time, Kath. It's shock. I know what me ole mum would say if she was 'ere. 'You 'ave a good cry dear, an' yer'll feel better.'

'I want ter cry, Danny. I want ter cry buckets, but I can't, I'm empty.'

Danny drew a line along the white counterpane with his finger, then he looked into her dark eyes. 'Listen ter me. I'm not very good at this sort o' fing but I tell yer, Kath, when I was in Dunkirk I saw grown men cryin'. They was soldiers who 'ad gone frew 'ell. I see 'em sittin' at the roadside cryin', an' you know what? I wished I could 'ave done the same. We'd all bin

275

frew a bad time an' some of us didn't know 'ow ter cry. I wished I could 'ave cried. Nobody was laughin' at 'em, we all felt the same. Some of us bottled it up, an' uvvers jus' cried. There's no shame in tears. Yer know, I saw me dad cry once.'

Kathy's eyes travelled over his face and he looked down at his clenched fists. 'We was at The Trocette. It was a real sad film. People was blowin' their noses an' I could 'eard the ole girls sobbin'. Me, I was tryin' 'ard not ter laugh. Anyway, I looked up at me dad, an' 'e was brushin' a tear away from 'is eye. 'E caught me clockin' 'im an' 'e said 'e 'ad a bit o' dirt in 'is eye. I knew 'e was cryin', an' 'e knew I knew, but 'e wouldn't admit it. I wouldn't 'ave minded though. I wouldn't mind if yer cried, Kath. Yer can cry all over me if yer like.'

Kathy's eyes filled with tears and she bit on her bottom lip. Danny reached out to her and her arms came up to him. He held her close and felt her sobs as she buried her head in his chest. 'Oh, Danny, why did I go to 'im? Why didn't I wait? I never stopped finkin' about yer. Every day I wondered if yer was gettin' wounded. I always wanted yer, but yer was never around. Yer never seemed ter be there when I wanted yer. Why didn't I wait, Danny?'

The young man gulped and patted her back gently. He could feel the tears falling onto his neck. 'I'm 'ere, Kathy, I'm 'ere,' he said softly.

The ward sister stopped at the foot of Kathy's bed and gave Danny a concerned look. Danny winked and eased Kathy back onto the pillow. 'There. Yer'll feel better soon. Dry yer eyes,' he said, handing her his handkerchief.

Kathy dabbed at her face and gave him a sheepish smile. 'I'm okay. Fanks.'

He pocketed his handkerchief. 'I've gotta be orf,' he said. 'Close yer eyes fer a while. Yer mum's comin' in soon.'

Kathy gripped his hand. 'I'm goin' ter me aunt's fer a couple o' weeks, Danny. I need some time ter meself. Will I see yer around when I get back?'

'I'll be around, Kath. I'm not goin' anywhere.'

Danny left the hospital and walked slowly back to Dawson Street. He felt a tightness in his chest and a heaviness weighing down on him. In his coat pocket he still had Alison's letter, and even while he had sat with Kathy the letter had flashed into his mind. He felt that he had betrayed Kathy. He had encouraged her to show her emotions, and then she had asked to see him and he had led her to believe that he would be around when she needed him. Danny realised he had promised too much. She might dwell on what he had told her and expect more of him that he was sure he could give. He might be around, but he could not guarantee his feelings. His need for Alison pulled hard on him; the thought of her sent his pulse racing – and he knew in his heart that he would answer her letter, very soon.

Danny battled with guilt as he walked home. He had not made any actual commitment to Kathy, he had only said that he would be around. She couldn't expect him to be forever ready to drop everything and rush to her when she called. He had his own life to lead. Then he suddenly realised how selfish his thoughts were. Was it love that made him want to dash to Alison, or was it purely lust? Was it love that made him go to Kathy or was it pity? What was that word 'love' Alison had said rolled easily from his tongue? Was it many different things appearing as one? He needed desperately to discover a real answer, but instead a hollowness had opened up inside him. As he turned into Dawson Street he was aware of nothing but pain tightening like a steel band around his head.

Right on closing time that Saturday two men walked into The Galleon in Deptford.

'Sorry, gents, it's after three o'clock,' the barman said, stiffening.

A warrant was flashed, and soon after Johnny Ross was led out between two large detectives. A bundle containing his personal belongings was collected and he sat quietly as he was driven to Deptford Police Station. When he arrived he was taken to a room where there was nothing but two chairs and a small table. He was left alone for over an hour, with only his thoughts for company, and he saw the whole picture opening up before him: the trial would be held at the Bailey of course; the many witnesses would naturally testify that Jack Mason was a law-abiding citizen, who had been cruelly murdered for the small amount of money on his person; the number one exhibit, an iron bar, would cause the jury to shake their heads in horror as it was passed among them. There was only one verdict he could expect, and the twelve good men and true would not even retire to consider. The formality over, the judge, who, in his mind's eye, looked remarkably like Bonky Williams, would put on the black cap and pronounce sentence. Johnny heard the words echoing around the court. '. . . and you will hang by the neck until you are dead.' He would try to stay calm and learn how to play chess. The warders would be okay, they would look pityingly at him as the footsteps in the corridor sounded and the mumbling priest read from the good book.

The door opened and Johnny jumped like a scared rabbit. 'Come on, Ross, you're goin' ter Dock'ead nick.'

Johnny Ross tried to control his shaking knees as he stared into the ugly face of Stanley Stockbridge. A huge hand took his arm in a tight grip and steered him out to the waiting car. 'I've seen you 'round the manor, Ross, ain't I?' Fat Stan leered.

Johnny could only nod as he was bundled into the police car.

Chapter Twenty-Four

On Monday the 5th of August Johnny Ross was hauled from the police station cell and the questions began once more. At first he had insisted that he did not go near the body, and he established through Cora a reason for being in the locality on that particular night. But the police were confident that a charge could be brought within a matter of hours. A distinctive footprint in the blood matched up to the suspect's shoes, and traces of blood were found in the tread. Johnny then changed his story and said that he had seen three men attack Jack Mason and he had gone over to find out if there was anything he could do to help the victim. When he had realised the man was past help, he had panicked and run away. The police interrogated Johnny for hours but he stuck to his story. A thorough search of the area around the scene of the crime was in operation and the police felt sure that as soon as the murder weapon was found their suspect would crack.

As he sat alone during a brief lull in the grilling, Johnny Ross could almost feel the hangman's noose tightening around his neck. They had even established a motive for the killing: they knew of the bad blood between him and Mason and they had supporting statements, or so they said. The lack of sleep and the futility of it all overcame him and he lowered his head onto the hard table top. He fell into a troubled doze and when he awoke he felt stiff all over. It seemed to Johnny as though he had been asleep for hours. Then he heard the gruff voices outside the locked door, and the key in the lock. Two stern-faced detectives came into the room and one of them sat down opposite him. A sheet of paper was thrust in front of him and a pen slapped onto the table.

Early on that Monday morning the pale, drawn figure of Violet Thompson walked wearily along Tooley Street. Her shopping bag seemed extra heavy and her legs felt as though they were going to give out on her. Alice Sutton had just left the greengrocer's and almost bumped into her.

''Ello, luv,' Alice said. 'Yer look done in. 'Ow's young Kathy?'

Violet put her bag down at her feet and pressed her hand against the small of her back. 'She's doin' well, Alice,' she said slowly, wincing visibly. 'Yer Danny's visit perked 'er up no end.'

Alice looked at Violet with concern and noticed a discolouring around her left eye and a swelling in the corner of her mouth. She put her hand on Violet's forearm. 'Yer all right, luv?' she asked gently. 'Yer don't look at all well.'

Kathy's mother drew in her breath and tears welled up in her eyes. 'Alice, I've gotta talk ter somebody,' she said in a shaky voice. 'I'm worried out o' me life.'

Alice picked up Violet's shopping bag and nodded her head towards Dawson Street. 'C'mon, let's 'ave a nice cuppa roun' my place. We'll 'ave a chat.'

A horse-cart trundled through the turning and the sound of its iron-rimmed wheels on the cobbles carried into the tidy parlour. The two women sat facing each other and Alice watched as Violet sipped her tea. When she had finished Alice took the cup out of her trembling hands and laid it down on the table. 'Are yer feelin' any better, luv?' she asked.

Violet nodded and dabbed at her eyes. 'I'm worried, sick, Alice.'

'Kathy'll be all right now, Vi. She's over the worst,' Alice said quietly.

'It's not Kathy, it's me ole man,' Violet replied, looking down at her clasped hands. 'We 'ad a terrible row last night. Over Mason.'

'Go on, Vi,' Alice prompted.

Violet took a deep breath. 'Charlie come in late last night, pissed as usual, an' 'e started on me.'

'I can see that,' Alice said quickly. 'Did 'e give yer that eye?'

Violet stared down at her hands. Alice began to feel uncomfortable and she decided to change the subject. She leaned forward in her chair. 'My Danny told me they've got young Johnny Ross fer the murder,' she said. 'Allen the bookie told 'im last night.'

Violet's hand came up to her mouth and she closed her eyes tightly. 'Oh my Gawd! What am I gonna do, Alice?' she groaned.

'What d'yer mean, Vi? There's nuffink yer can do.'

'But yer don't understan', Alice. Johnny Ross never killed Mason. Charlie done it,' she blurted out, and she began sobbing loudly.

Alice was shocked. 'Gawd Almighty Gawd! 'E can't 'ave!'

Violet's eyes opened wide and bored into Alice's. ''E told me 'imself.'

Alice shook her head slowly. 'It don't make any sense at all. Yer Charlie won't 'ave 'is own daughter back in the 'ouse.'

Violet laughed bitterly through her tears. ''E didn't do Jack Mason in fer Kathy. It was somefink else.'

Alice looked bewildered. 'Kathy ain't Charlie's daughter, Alice,' Violet said in a tired voice. 'I met 'im after I fell fer Kathy. 'E's never let me forget it neivver.'

Alice nodded. 'So that's why 'e knocks yer about, an' won't 'ave the poor little cow back in the 'ouse. But why did 'e kill Mason?'

'It's a long story, Alice,' Mrs Thompson began.

Alice stopped her. 'Let's fill yer cup, luv,' she said.

The two women faced each other in the small parlour and sipped their tea in silence. Violet studied the flower pattern on her cup. 'Yer see, Alice,' she began, 'I've never spoke ter Jack Mason, but my Charlie knows 'im well. Charlie comes from Dock'ead same as Mason. A long time ago there was some fiddlin' goin' on where Charlie used ter work. I fink it was one o' the wharves in Dock'ead. They was gettin' stuff out an' Mason was floggin' it. Charlie got done out o' some money an' 'e went after one o' Mason's mates. My Charlie was an' 'andful then, 'e give this bloke a goin' over, an' the police got involved. Charlie got six months fer assault. Then a few months ago there was an argument in the pub between Charlie an' Mason. Charlie was pissed an' 'e told Jack Mason ter leave Kathy alone. Mason must 'ave 'eard the talk about Kathy not bein' Charlie's an' 'e frew it up in 'is face. The pair of 'em nearly got at it but they was stopped. Charlie told me the same night 'e would end up doin' Mason in, but he didn't kill Mason fer Kathy, it was fer 'is own pride. When 'e come 'ome on Friday night wiv blood on 'is coat-sleeve 'e wouldn't stop goin' on about it. Now you've told me that Johnny Ross is bein' blamed fer it, I feel so guilty. What can I do, Alice?'

Alice pinched her bottom lip. ''E'll 'ave ter give 'imself up, Vi. Yer'll 'ave ter tell 'im.'

Violet laughed mirthlessly. 'I can't, Alice. 'E's gorn. 'E pissed orf on Sunday night after 'e'd finished knockin' me all over the 'ouse.'

'Where's 'e gorn to, Vi?'

''E's got a bruvver in Liverpool. 'E might 'ave gone there. 'E told me 'e was gettin' out o' London.'

Alice gripped her friend's arm. 'But yer can't leave it, Vi,' she said. 'That poor lad'll swing fer somefink 'e never done. Go ter the police, tell 'em. Yer don't 'ave ter say anyfink about yer ole man bein' in Liverpool. It's their job ter catch 'im. Yer'll only be gettin' poor Johnny Ross out o' trouble.'

Violet Thompson frowned. 'Ain't there somefink about a wife not bein' able ter give evidence against 'er 'usband?'

'I've 'eard it said, Vi, but yer gotta go ter the police. Tell 'em everyfing. It's up ter them ter get the evidence tergevver. At least yer'll be able ter sleep at night.'

Violet stood up suddenly. 'Do me one more favour, Alice,' she said with an imploring look. 'Come wiv me.'

In mid-August the battle of Britain was raging over the English Channel and Southern England. Every day the blue sky was slashed with vapour trails as planes dived and soared in deadly combat. Stricken machines fell into the sea around the coast and dived into the rolling green countryside. Each day the newspapers carried the tally of planes downed as though they were reporting county cricket scores. The battle for survival had begun, and everyone knew that if the battle was lost the invasion would be a certainty. As the news improved a heady feeling of hope prevailed. People were relieved that at last the months of uncertainty and anxiety were over. In dockland as in other parts of the country folk crowded around wireless sets listening to the news broadcasts, and German losses brought forth cheers. Corner shops stuck up posters with the latest scores in large lettering; pubs filled with merry-makers every evening, and patriotic songs rang out. It was a time of great excitement, and everyone's spirits were lifted.

In the middle of August, Danny Sutton boarded a train to Maidstone. He had mixed feelings as he watched the houses and factories give way to green fields from his carriage window, his sense of unease mingling with high excitement at the prospect of being with Alison. She had filled his thoughts constantly since her letter to him, and for all his misgivings Danny knew he had to make the journey. He had not been able to force her from his mind. There were times when he thought of Kathy and looked forward to her return, but the picture of Alison stayed with him and tortured his emotions; the strong physical urge to make love with her again sent his pulse racing.

The train pulled into Maidstone Station and Danny joined the Saturday lunchtime passengers as they walked from the platform. Alison was there at the barrier, and he was thrilled by her radiance. He held her closely and kissed her, tasting her warm lips. Together they walked from the station and out into the sunshine. They found a restaurant and chatted happily over their meal about day to day things, and Alison told him about her new post at the hospital. And the tension between them had gone. They had been lovers, and they had the night to know each other once more.

In the early afternoon they strolled in the park and found shade beneath a leafy tree. The grass felt cool and the whisper of a breeze fanned their hot faces. Alison lay propped on one elbow and looked down at Danny as he lay on his back and chewed on a blade of grass.

'I've missed you,' she said suddenly.

'Me too.'

'Tell me, Danny, that night we spent together. Has it stayed with you?'

Danny turned onto his side and looked into Alison's dark, brooding eyes. 'If yer mean do I still fink about that night, the answer's yes. I fink about it twenty times a day. Night times I lay finkin' about yer an' I wish I could turn over an' feel yer there beside me.'

'I feel lonely at night too, Danny. There have been nights when I've wanted you so badly. I imagine you're on your way to me, you're my secret lover and I'm waiting for you. Can we be secret lovers, Danny?'

Danny reached up and pulled her down to him. Their lips met and he felt her teeth close on his bottom lip.

As the sun dipped over the horizon and the evening sky took on a pinkish hue the lovers strolled hand in hand through the town, idling away the time until dusk. They found a pub with a garden and sat sipping their drinks at a log table. Blossoms overhung the stone courtyard and a grotesque vine scaled the ancient walls. The song of a bird split the silence, and up above grey-blue clouds rolled across a dark velvet sky and revealed diamonds of light. Time seemed to have stopped still for Danny and the war was a world away, the promise in Alison's eyes tantalising him. But deep down he felt misgivings stirring his conscience.

'You're shivering, Danny.'

Alison's words of concern jolted him back to reality. 'I was jus' dreamin',' he replied, taking her hand in his. 'This is like anuvver world. Who'd fink there was a war on?'

'This is magical,' Alison said, looking up at the night sky. 'Just you and me, and nothing else. We're lovers. Lovers who meet on nights like this and who carry the memory with us till we meet again. That's the magic for me, Danny. It doesn't spoil and get ordinary. I don't want it to be just ordinary. I want it to be magic always.'

Danny looked at her with sad eyes. 'Trouble is, it's an ordinary world, Alison. It's a real world. Yer can't live in fairyland. Fairyland is fer kids.'

Alison looked up again at the twinkling stars. 'That's fairyland out there,' she said.

Danny grinned. 'Them stars are a million miles away. It's a long way ter fairyland.'

They left the pub and walked slowly through a maze of little streets. Alison had her arm in his and he could feel her soft breast against him. She steered him down a narrow lane and stopped at a low-fronted house.

'Here we are,' she said. 'I share this place with three other nurses. We've all got our own rooms.'

Alison found her key and turned it in the lock. Inside the air smelt of lavender, and in the hall a rosewood chest and a grandfather clock stood against the white walls. Alison opened a door to their left and held Danny's hand as they entered. She closed the door behind them and switched on the light.

The room was cosy, with patchwork rugs covering the wooden floor, a large settee occupying the centre of the room and wicker chairs arranged around the sides. Close to the settee was a small coffee table scattered with magazines, and pictures of country scenes in ebony frames were hung around the walls. At the far end there was a doorway through to another room, and Danny caught a glimpse of a bed. Alison took off her coat and waited while Danny did the same. She hung up their coats behind the door and came to him slowly. 'Well, how do you like my little den?'

'It's real nice,' Danny said, looking around.

She was standing close to him and he pulled her nearer. Her arms went around his neck and they kissed long and urgently, and when they parted Danny lifted her into his arms and carried her to the bedroom. Alison rested her head on his shoulder and she could feel the muscles moving beneath his shirt. Her breath came quickly as he laid her gently down on the bed and fumbled with the buttons of her dress. He kissed her soft neck and smooth shoulders and caressed her hard nipples and silky thighs. Alison's quick breathing became faster and, moaning with pleasure, she pulled him to her. When the first light of dawn shone into the room Alison awoke and curled her sleepy body closer to Danny's. Her hands awoke him with gentle caresses, and a delicious giving of pleasure united their sleepy bodies and brought them to a dreamy climax. When they stirred once more it was late morning.

The day was warm, and after a leisurely breakfast they strolled through the town and visited the pub where they had spent the last evening. In the afternoon the lovers went into the park again and walked through the scented flower gardens and along shaded pathways. They rested in the sweet-smelling grass of a lush green field, Danny thinking of their imminent parting, while Alison made fun of his serious expression.

'Why so sad?' she asked.

'Goodbyes do that ter me,' Danny said, stroking her smooth arm.

'You shouldn't be sad, Danny. We can see each other again soon. If there were no goodbyes there'd be no hellos, would there?'

'We could get married,' Danny said suddenly.

Alison's face became serious and she picked at the grass. 'Don't let's spoil it all, Danny. We've got happiness, you and I. Marriage is not for me. I need you, I don't need a marriage.'

'I do, Alison, I need a marriage. I want ter wake up wiv yer every mornin', and not jus' now an' then, when yer can get time orf. I want yer, an' I want kids, an' a place fer us ter live in.'

Alison's eyes clouded and she looked away. 'There's no magic in a home and children, Danny. Not for me. I'm sorry if it hurts you when I say that. You may think I'm strange, but it's how I feel. I can't alter, any more than you can. You remember the last time we were together? I told you then that I needed an understanding. We can be lovers, there's nothing wrong in that. We can be happy, I know we can, Danny. We don't need a marriage to seal our love for each other. There's just no magic in a marriage for me. Can't you understand that?'

Danny looked at her, and knew that nothing he could say would make her change her mind. If he wanted her, it must be like this; fleeting and unsure.

The sun was slipping down as they walked slowly to the hospital gates. Alison looked at her watch and gave Danny a brief smile. 'We'd better say goodbye here, Danny. I've got to be on duty at seven.'

He pulled her to him and they kissed. She clung to him. 'Write to me soon, Danny. Maybe we can meet again soon. We can be happy this way, I know we can.'

Danny released his clasp and stood back from her, silent.

Alison touched his arm and walked away up the long gravel path to the entrance of the hospital. At the front steps she waved to him and then disappeared from his sight, and he walked wearily back to the station. It was cooler now and dark clouds were beginning to close out the sky. 'There'll be no fairyland up there ternight,' he said aloud.

288

Epilogue

August passed by and cool September breezes heralded the autumn. In the little backstreets of dockland life went on. A chastened and wiser Johnny Ross was welcomed back into The Globe. When he left the police station after signing for his belongings, he felt the dark shadow of the noose lifting from around his neck. On that Friday night when he had looked down on the battered face of Jack Mason he had been mistaken in thinking the villain was dead. Al Vincetti had merely rendered him unconscious with his parting blow, and if Johnny had delayed leaving Cora's for another few minutes he would have seen the grotesque murder.

Charlie Thompson had visited a few riverside pubs and was staggering along the turning that led out opposite The Ferryman. Even in his drunken state he decided that he would give that particular pub a miss as he knew that Jack Mason and his cronies used The Ferryman. The longstanding feud between the two had never been resolved, and Charlie Thompson's hatred for the villain was never more intense than when he was drunk. The docker crossed the street unsteadily and staggered up the kerb. He had left the pub behind him and was feeling his way along when he suddenly tripped over something hard and landed on all fours on the pavement. His eyes rolled and he saw the unconscious figure of Jack Mason lying only inches away from him. Looking down into the battered face he blinked in disbelief. Slowly he staggered to his feet and fought to keep his footing, then he snarled and kicked out hard with his heavy boots. Three times his boot thumped into Jack Mason's skull, then the docker lost his footing and fell into the gutter. He got up and stumbled awkwardly from the turning unseen. The ladies from the sewing circle had left the street corner only minutes before.

Soon after Johnny Ross was released from custody, Tony Arpino left his hideout in Clerkenwell and made his way apprehensively to his parents' shop in Bermondsey Lane. He had heard that the police had started looking for Charlie Thompson in connection with the murder of Mason after Violet Thompson made a statement at Dockhead police station. Tony was worried in case anything should emerge about how he and his pals had been involved in the Mason affair. The few words in the daily papers seemed to suggest that whoever killed Mason had done so in a very brutal fashion, but there was nothing he read that led him to believe he and his friends were likely to be implicated. The Bermondsey Lane shopkeepers were visibly relieved by the disappearance of the protection mob, relations between the Arpinos and the rest of the shopowners began to improve, and Lou and Sofia were welcoming a few of their old customers back to their store.

Tony was cheered by the letter that was waiting for him when he got home. It was from Melissa. She wrote that her family had been interned on the Isle of Man, conditions there were not too bad, and everyone seemed to be settling down in the camp. Melissa said in her letter that she loved him and missed him terribly, and Tony smiled. For the first time in what seemed to be ages, his future looked rosy.

The Globe carried on with business as usual. Customers

moaned over the quality of the beer but continued to drink there. Biff Bowden was drunk for a whole week when his dog won the coveted Blue Cross Stakes, and Shady Lady was then retired on her favourite diet of Guinness and arrowroot. At least once every week Bonky Williams sidled over to Biff and bought him a drink. Then he would look closely at Biff with an earnest glint in his one good eye and ask him, ''Ow's yer dog, Biff? She puppin' yet?'

Bonky's obsession with Shady Lady's sex life puzzled Biff. 'I reckon it's those bleedin' magazines 'e's readin',' he remarked to Eddie, rolling his eyes in an exaggerated gesture of shock.

The landlord of The Globe was reticent. 'I fink our friend Bonky's turnin' over a new leaf. D'yer know, 'e ain't took 'is eye out fer ages.' Eddie ran a 'sweet' pub as he called it, and he was hoping it was going to stay that way.

Down along the Tower Bridge Road the sounds of the mission organ rang out every Sunday morning. 'Dear old Mister Craddock', the elderly ladies would say to each other at every meeting, gazing at the frail figure bent over the organ keys with fervour. Mr Craddock the organist had given up his part-time job of letter writing – things were getting hot at the tribunal hearings, and his continued presence there seemed to be drawing suspicious glances from the court usher. But he had found another channel for his patriotic endeavours: when the weather was nice he wandered over to Speaker's Corner and heckled the pacifists. 'We had enough of you lot in the last war,' he would shout out to the orator.

'Go on, Pop, tell the bloody traitor about the trenches and the mustard gas,' others would call out.

Mr Craddock ignored the remarks of the audience and walked away. He could still see those soldiers in 1914, marching like heroes away to war.

Ben Morrison had received his call-up papers and he was

soon to be drafted into the Royal Army Medical Corps. Lucy's pregnancy was confirmed, and she and Ben were married rather hurriedly at a registry office. Lucy told her family that she had not wanted to wait, and being married would give Ben some extra responsibility and would help him to cope with army life that much better. Alice and her children exchanged knowing winks as she mentioned to her Frank that she had a feeling they would soon become grandparents. Frank, in his usual argumentative way, rejected the idea as nonsense. 'Lucy won't start a family yet, Muvver,' he said, 'she's got more sense.'

'All right, Mister Know-All, we'll jus' 'ave ter wait an' see won't we?' Alice said with a ghost of a grin on her lined face.

Danny's eldest sister Maggie and her husband Joe were very much relieved when a letter arrived from a farmer and his wife saying that their two children were enjoying their stay in the Cotswolds. The kids had taken to life on the farm and were both enrolled at the village school. There was a short letter enclosed from the children, saying how much they liked their new home, and Maggie and Joe were also given an invitation to go and meet the farmer and his wife and to stay for a long weekend when they could manage it. Maggie was enthusiastic about the trip, but Joe had reservations.

'It'll be nice ter see the kids, but the farm might be miles from anywhere,' Joe said. 'I bet there ain't a pub in the village.'

'Course there will be,' Maggie countered. 'I bet the locals won't be as bad as that scatty crowd you get wiv in The Globe every Saturday night.'

Joe was doubtful, although he had to admit to himself that the beer could not be any worse than the rubbish Eddie had been serving lately.

Connie Sutton was looking forward to the end of September with excitement. Jimmy was now back home in England and would be given leave soon. Connie had been to see the parish priest and their wedding was planned for the first week in October. Jimmy had been transferred to the Home Fleet and Connie was hoping to find a flat in Portsmouth as soon as the wedding was over.

'That'll be the girls all married off,' Alice remarked to Frank. 'That only leaves that wayward son of ours. I wish 'e'd get 'imself a nice girl.'

Frank Sutton grinned. 'Danny's got more sense. 'E ain't in too much of an' 'urry. I mean, there's all that naggin' and moanin'. A man's better off lovin' 'em an' leavin' 'em.'

Alice gave her husband an icy stare. 'Yer ain't done so bad. You know where yer arse 'angs.'

'On the bleedin' floor, what wiv all these weddin's in the family,' Frank quipped.

The Thompsons had moved away from Clink Lane. Violet and Kathy had gone to live in Rotherhithe. The little backwater off Tooley Street held too many bad memories, and being in Rotherhithe suited them. They were not too far away from their friends, and from their front door they could still smell the river and hear familiar sounds carrying into the quiet street. Kathy returned to her old job. On her first day back she had by chance bumped into Connie Sutton, who told her that Danny had stopped working for Tony Allen and was now going into the greengrocery business with his pal Johnny Ross. The mention of Danny's name had sent a familiar dull ache running around inside her, and Kathy knew that there would always be a special place for him in her heart. She had remembered him saying that he would be around, and that he wasn't going anywhere, but she realised he had only said that in an effort to cheer her up. A lot of water had gone under the bridge and she figured it wasn't realistic to imagine that she and Danny could get together once more. It was time now to pick up the pieces and start again. Maybe one day she would be able to meet Danny in the street without feeling ashamed and confused.

*

The young cockney felt a heaviness weighing down on him from which he could not escape. His surroundings, and the people he had known for years, could do nothing to lift his spirits. He tried to fill up the days by throwing himself into the new venture with Johnny Ross. Sometimes it worked. They were a good team. Their greengrocery shop was attracting customers and the trade was improving. Most of the time however, the nagging emptiness was still there, beneath all the activity and hard work. Danny felt his life was leading him nowhere. His love for the two women had left him feeling lost and inadequate. As much as he thought of those brief sojourns with Alison he realised that it could not go on in that way. The excitement of their meetings would dull in time and there would be nothing left. And yet she insisted on there being no more. It could have been different with Kathy. She was desperately unhappy and he could have said the right words when he held her close in the hospital; she was in love with him and wanted him to say he loved her, but the letter in his pocket had prevented him from grabbing happiness for both of them. In the beginning, the war had parted them just when he was becoming aware of how much she could mean to him, and so much had happened in the few months since his return. Now there was a ghastly shadow in Kathy's past, and he wondered whether she would ever be able to rid herself of the dark ghost of Jack Mason.

Danny realised with a sinking feeling that he had played such a small part in the events around him, and he felt suddenly sad and older. Deep down he had made a decision, and he knew there was only one thing he could do, and there would be no going back.

His pulse beat faster as he reached the little back lane and knocked on the front door. He heard light footsteps and the door opened. The pale, dark-eyed girl stood there looking at him for a few seconds without saying anything. Her eyes widened and two blotches of colour came to her face. Danny grinned, his thumbs hooked into his trouser pockets and his shoulders hunched. ''Ello, Kath,' he said.

Kathy Thompson stepped back a pace. ''Ello, Danny, it's nice ter see yer. Won't yer come in?'

Danny followed her into the small parlour. It was cool and shadowy, and he could smell the flowers that were arranged in a blue glass vase on the table.

It was a bright day outside. The Saturday afternoon sky was cloudless and sunlight danced on the Thames, making the water sparkle like a river of grey glass. The docks and wharves were quiet and deserted, ships and barges lay at anchor, rocking gently on the turning tide. Seagulls cried out as they glided through the air, diving suddenly down low around the deserted quays, and mooring hawsers strained against the wash from a slowly patrolling police launch. The cobbled riverside lanes were quiet. The street hawkers had come and gone, and inside the open windows the fresh lace curtains hung limp in the still air.

In the tiny parlour the two young people sat facing each other beside the black-leaded grate and gleaming brass fender. The girl looked down at her tightly clasped hands as the young man talked softly.

'What's past is past, Kathy. All the wishin' in the world won't make it any different. I'm talkin' about now. I should 'ave made it clear when I came ter see yer in the 'ospital. I couldn't say it then, Kath, but I can now. I luv yer, an' I want yer. Are yer listenin'?'

Kathy looked up with tears in her eyes. The lump in her throat prevented her from answering. She nodded and his hands reached out and took hers in a firm grip.

'Don't torture yerself, Kath,' he said, his voice sounding

loud in the quietness of the room. 'I told yer once we were good fer each uvver. I meant it, an' I'm sayin' it again. I used ter dream about you an' me gettin' married an' 'avin' kids. They don't 'ave ter be dreams any more, Kathy. We can bury the ghosts an' be 'appy tergevver. We can, can't we?'

Kathy's eyes blinked against the tears and she swallowed hard. 'I've never stopped lovin' yer, Danny, but I was never sure about you. You always seemed ter put a wall between us. I dunno what it was, but I was always aware of it. It seemed as though you was frightened ter say the fings I wanted to 'ear. When yer came back 'ome an' I first saw yer that night in the pub I wanted ter die. After we made love I knew that my feelin's fer yer were stronger than ever. That's what made it so bad. It 'appened too late, it should 'ave 'appened before yer left, Danny.'

The drone was far too distant for them to hear as Danny held her hands in his and looked deep into her eyes. 'Listen, Kath,' he said. 'I don't pretend ter understand the reasons fer what's 'appened. I dunno about this fate business, but I've asked meself, 'ow comes I got back 'ome an' the feller next ter me ended up dead on the beach? 'Ow comes Jack Mason gets killed an' you lose 'is baby? I don't know the answers. What I do know, is that yer an' me are sittin' 'ere tergevver. Will yer walk out wiv me?'

The drone was still some way off as Kathy smiled through her tears. 'If yer really want me to, Danny.'

He reached out and took her in his arms. His lips touched hers and he could taste her tears as they kissed softly and gently and her arms held him tightly. Their lips parted and Kathy buried her head into his shoulder.

'Yer know, I was glad ter leave Clink Lane,' she said. 'The only fing I regretted was that I wouldn't see yer around.'

Along the river estuary the formations of aircraft were darkening the summer sky. As the planes followed the bank of silver water the drone became nearer. Danny smiled. 'Anybody would fink yer moved ter the uvver side o' London.'

They could both hear the drone now, as he said, 'After all, it's only tuppence ter Tooley Street . . .'

Just for You

Find out . . .
All about Harry

Remember . . .
Popular wartime tunes

Discover . . .
Cockney Rhyming Slang

Harry Bowling

'I suppose most people would see the ability to tell a story as a talent to entertain, but where I was born and raised, being able to spin a yarn was considered an asset of survival and, at times, it became a necessity . . .'

Harry was born in 1931 in Leroy Street, a back street off the Tower Bridge Road close to Tooley Street. Harry was the second child of Annie and Henry Bowling and sadly his older sister Gladys died of meningitis before her second birthday. Harry's grandfather worked at a transport yard as a cartman-horsekeeper and he used to take Harry there to watch him and to pat the horses. Before he could walk, Harry was put on the back of a little horse named Titch and he was heartbroken when

Titch died. He spent his youth hanging around the Tower Bridge Road market or hunting through Borough Market, a wholesale fruit and veg market near London Bridge, exploring the docklands and wharves, and swimming in the Thames.

Harry's first contact with books began at the local library, encouraged by his father, who was permanently disabled after being wounded during the First World War. Henry Bowling was often unemployed and struggled to support the family. Harry was only ten when the Second World War broke out and he could vividly remember the day when Surrey Docks was bombed. His father helped him with his early education and he and his younger brother passed scholarships to Bermondsey Central School. He left the school at the age of fourteen to help the family income by working at a riverside provision merchant as an office boy. Harry grew up in a community that was drawn together, in laughter and in tears, in the never-ending battle against poverty, rationing and bombs. And he also saw, first-hand, the struggle the close-knit community underwent to get back on its feet after the war finally came to an end. It's these extraordinarily vivid memories that pervade Harry's writing and which bring this London, a London now disappeared, alive for his readers.

It was only when his own children began to ask questions about the war that Harry realised how many stories he had to tell. He started gathering scribbles and notes and then wrote his first book. It was a factual account of the war and Harry realised that it would probably have only a limited readership. He became aware that historical fiction was very popular and that there was no one writing about the East End of London and the war, at that time. In his fifties, he was given early retirement from his job as a brewery driver-drayman, and was at last able to devote his time to writing.

Harry became known as 'the King of Cockney sagas', and wrote eighteen bestselling novels about London life. Sadly

Harry died in 1999 and the Harry Bowling prize was set up in his memory. Harry's advice to aspiring authors was:

'Refuse defeat, copy no style, never be satisfied with anything that is not your very best and, above all, write from the heart.'

Popular wartime tunes

What morale-boosting songs were we listening to during World War Two?

'Run Rabbit Run'
'There Will Always Be An England'
'When the Lights Go On Again All Over the World'
'We'll Meet Again'
'The White Cliffs of Dover'

Perhaps the most famous British singer during World War Two was Vera Lynn, now a Dame of the British Empire. As one of the major entertainers during the war she earned the nickname 'The Forces' Sweetheart'. Do you remember 'We'll Meet Again' and 'The White Cliffs of Dover'?

'Get that cup of rosie down your gregory!': All about Cockney rhyming slang

A true Cockney is said to be someone who is born within the sound of Bow Bells – and these 'Bow Bells' refer to the Church of St Mary-le-Bow, in Cheapside, London.

Although Cockney slang originated in the East End, some slang phrases are used throughout the whole of Britain.

The rhyming slang phrases are derived from an expression which rhymes with the word in question – and then that expression, or a shortened version of it, is used instead of the word.

Here are some popular examples. How many have you used without realising their origin?

Barnet = Barnet Fair = Hair
Boat = Boat Race = Face
Loaf = Loaf of Bread = Head
Mincies = Mince Pies = Eyes
Gregory = Gregory Peck = Neck
Hampsteads = Hampstead Heath = Teeth
Plates = Plates of Meat = Feet

North and South = Mouth
Chalk Farms = Arms
Scotches = Scotch Eggs = Legs

Bread = Bread and Honey = Money
Dog and Bone = Phone
Frog and Toad = Road
Apples and Pears = Stairs
Jam = Jam Jar = Car

Bull and Cow = Row (argument)
(Have a) Butcher's = Butcher's Hook = Look
Donkey's = Donkey's Ears = Years
Rabbit = Rabbit and Pork = Talk
Sexton = Sexton Blake = Fake
Pen and Ink = Stink

Mutton = Mutt and Jeff = Deaf
Crackered (or Creamed) = Cream Crackered = Knackered (tired)
On your Jack (Jones) = Jack Jones = Alone
Taters = Potatoes in the Mould = Cold
Brown Bread = Dead
Elephant's = Elephant's Trunk = Drunk

Rosie = Rosie Lee = Tea
Ruby = Ruby Murray = Curry

(My old) China = China Plate = Mate
Trouble and Strife = Wife
Tea Leaf = Thief

Weasel = Weasel and Stoat = Coat
Titfer = Tit for Tat = Hat
Syrup = Syrup of Figs = Wig
Daisy Roots = Boots

Just for You

We hope you have enjoyed discovering more about Harry Bowling, as well as reading his heartwarming novel, *Tuppence to Tooley Street*. Don't miss Harry's other unforgettable novels about life in the East End.

As Time Goes By is a vivid portrayal of the East End struggling to survive the horror of the Blitz. Heartbreaking and compelling, this is the story of a community in its darkest and yet finest hour, one which has all but disappeared.

That Summer on Eagle Street vividly describes what post-war life in London was like for so many – a tight-knit community that laughed, cried and fought together. A poignant, nostalgic and funny portrayal of a London that has all but vanished.

The Glory and the Shame offers a rare and unforgettable glimpse of a hard-working community struggling to rebuild life after the destruction of World War Two. Both moving and compelling, it is the story of the East End during a terrible, but also hopeful, time.

The Girl from Cotton Lane vividly captures what life was like in Dockland Bermondsey after the devastation of the Great War – a heart-rending tale of a community pulling together despite terrible grief for all those that were lost.

Conner Street's War shows us a forgotten way of life behind the grimy wharves of London's docklands – a world where women stand gossiping in doorways, small boys play marbles on the cobbles and dockers pop down to the 'Eagle' for a quick pint.

Paragon Place is a touching depiction of the devastating toll World War Two took on London and the way in which a close-knit community pulled together to build a brighter future for themselves – and their children.

And you might also enjoy: *Waggoner's Way, Gaslight in Page Street, Backstreet Child, Ironmonger's Daughter* and *Pedlar's Row*.

As Time Goes By

Harry Bowling

Carter Lane is an ordinary backstreet in Bermondsey and, for Dolly and Mick Flynn, it is home. They've raised their family with not much money but lots of love. When World War Two breaks out they know that nothing will be quite the same again.

As the Blitz takes its toll and the close-knit community in Carter Lane endures the sorrows and partings which they had dreaded above all else, they find comfort in one another and solace in the knowledge that their wounds will eventually heal – as time goes by.

As Time Goes By is a vivid portrayal of an East End community struggling to survive the horror of the Blitz. Heartbreaking and compelling, this is the story of a community in its darkest and yet finest hour, a community which has all but disappeared.

Warm praise for Harry Bowling's novels:

'What makes Harry's novels work is their warmth and authenticity. Their spirit comes from the author himself and his abiding memories of family life as it was once lived in the slums of south-east London' *Today*

'The king of Cockney sagas packs close-knit community good-heartedness into East End epics' *Daily Mail*

978 0 7553 4030 9

headline

That Summer in Eagle Street

Harry Bowling

Linda Weston has always lived in Eagle Street, a backwater off the Tower Bridge Road market. Life in the street isn't easy: money is tight, the house is overcrowded and everyone knows your business – whether you like it or not. But it's a solid, tight-knit community that laughs, cries and fights together – and helps one another out in difficult times.

Linda fell in love with Charlie Bradley just before the outbreak of World War Two and now the war is over, they hope to build a bright new future together. But Linda and Charlie are to find themselves caught in the middle of two rival gangs fighting for a stranglehold over south-east London. The consequences could be devastating.

Poignant, nostalgic and funny, *That Summer in Eagle Street* is a vivid and atmospheric portrayal of a south-east London that has all but vanished.

Warm praise for Harry Bowling's novels:

'What makes Harry's novels work is their warmth and authenticity. Their spirit comes from the author himself and his abiding memories of family life as it was once lived in the slums of south-east London' *Today*

'The king of Cockney sagas packs a close-knit community good-heartedness into East End epics' *Daily Mail*

978 0 7553 4031 6

headline

The Glory and the Shame

Harry Bowling

On the night of Saturday 10th May 1941, amidst the horror of the devastation caused by enemy bombers, Joe Carey and Charlie Duggan risked their lives to save people trapped in an air-raid shelter. Despite their efforts, six men and women died.

It's now 1947 and the inhabitants of Totterdown Street are trying to rebuild their lives. The post-war years are proving to be difficult and, already faced with a violent factory strike, the close-knit inhabitants of the street must also cope with news which not only exposes the glory of the past but the shame as well.

The Glory and the Shame is a vivid portrayal of a hard-working community struggling to rebuild their lives in the post-war era. Heartwarming and compelling, this is the story of the East End in its finest and yet darkest hour, a community in which most, but not all, behaved heroically.

Warm praise for Harry Bowling's novels:

'What makes Harry's novels work is their warmth and authenticity. Their spirit comes from the author himself and his abiding memories of family life as it was once lived in the slums of south-east London' *Today*

'The king of Cockney sagas packs a close-knit community good-heartedness into East End epics' *Daily Mail*

978 0 7553 4032 3

headline

Paragon Place

Harry Bowling

Paragon Place, an ordinary square of two-up, two-down houses in Bermondsey, has pretty well survived the Blitz. But the war has taken its toll on a hard-working and tight-knit community – even the old sycamore tree in the middle of the square has been scarred by shrapnel.

Despite going through the very worst of times – the never-ending fight against poverty, rationing and bombs – the residents of Paragon Place have been drawn even closer together by laughter and tears in the face of despair. And now that the war is finally over, they can look forward to a brighter future.

Paragon Place is a powerful and compelling portrayal of the East End during its finest hour, and a way of life that has vanished forever.

Warm praise for Harry Bowling's novels:

'What makes Harry's novels work is their warmth and authenticity. Their spirit comes from the author himself and his abiding memories of family life as it was once lived in the slums of south-east London' *Today*

'The king of Cockney sagas packs a close-knit community good-heartedness into East End epics' *Daily Mail*

978 0 7553 4033 0

headline

Now you can buy any of these bestselling
Harry Bowling books from your bookshop
or *direct from the publisher*.

FREE P&P AND UK DELIVERY
(Overseas and Ireland £3.50 per book)

As Time Goes By	£6.99
That Summer in Eagle Street	£6.99
The Glory and the Shame	£6.99
Paragon Place	£6.99
Tuppence to Tooley Street	£6.99

TO ORDER SIMPLY CALL THIS NUMBER

01235 400 414

or visit our website: www.headline.co.uk

Prices and availability subject to change without notice.